'Bell's strength lies in fusing fairytale and psychological suspense in compelling modern narrative, combined with efective character-isation. Bell charts original territory with considerable charm'
Guardian

'Occasionally heart-wrenching, occasionally creepy but altogether deeply personal character study. Bell's characterisation and prose is infectious, expressed on he page with an oddly compulsive pace. All in all, this is a fine piece of literature'　　　*SciFiNow*

'*Jasmyn* is Alex Bell's second novel and quite a stunning one. Bell's skill is in introducing unsettling elements gradually so you abso-lutely believe even the most fantastical prts of her novel. The story is both terrifying and beautiful, as all good fairytales are'
Fortean Times

'There is beautiful descriptiveness as well as classical fantasy addi-tions within these pages'　　　*Falcata Times*

'*Jasmyn* is a mix of fairytale, fantasy and character-driven thriller, and it is a potent brew. I loved *Jasmyn*. I laughed, I cried, I felt that desperate heart-twisting sensation that only great stories can inspire. This is a fantastic, deceptively emotional novel, and one that I highly recommend'　　　*Book Smugglers*

'A magical novel which is highly, highly recommended, a fairy-tale for adults that will enchant and cheer you up in the end. Also in its expandd descriptive range and very smoothly flowing prose, the book shows Ms Bell's growth as an author and any new book by her is a read asap for me'　　　*Fantasy Book Critic*

Also by Alex Bell from Gollancz:

The Ninth Circle

JASMYN

Alex Bell

This edition first published in Great Britain in 2018 by Gollancz

First published in Great Britain in 2009 by Gollancz
an imprint of the Orion Publishing Group Ltd
Carmelite House, 50 Victoria Embankment
London EC4Y 0DZ

An Hachette UK Company

1 3 5 7 9 10 8 6 4 2

A CIP catalogue record for this book is
available from the British Library.

ISBN (Paperback) 978 1 473 22445 2
ISBN (eBook) 978 0 575 08817 7

Printed and bound by CPI Group (UK) Ltd, Croydon, CR0 4YY

www.alex-bell.co.uk
www.gollancz.co.uk

For Shirley Bell –
my Mum, my best friend, my role model,
my Wizard of Oz – the lady who has inspired me
more than any other person on this earth.

You have never heard a story quite like this one. I can hear you protesting already but, the fact is, it doesn't matter how old you are, how many books you've read, how many things you've seen ... this story will be new to you. Maybe it will even haunt you a little. Because what happened to me ... well, I don't think it's ever happened before ...

Have you ever read a dark fairy tale that, for some reason, niggled at you afterwards? A story that was quite clearly made up but which, nonetheless, contained some tiny grain of truth that prickled at you uncomfortably like the pea beneath the princess's mattress? Fairy tales are fluid things, changing and adapting all the time, but they're also based upon events that really did, at some point – in some form – actually happen.

This story is like that. It has the ribbons and the glitter and the magic. But it also has the blood and the sacrifice and the twisting evil – for this is a real fairy tale, not the sugar-coated imitation. It is a story of love, loss, illusion, castles, hatred, seduction, ice palaces, adventure and knights.

Don't start this book unless you mean to finish it.

I

Dead Swans

Things started to happen after Liam died ... strange things that I could not explain and did not understand. As if trying to work out how to live without him wasn't difficult enough on its own. The incident at the funeral was only the start, which is ironic when you consider that I stood there thinking it was the end. I thought it was the last difficult thing I had to do before I could concentrate on nothing but grieving and hurting and coping.

When the time came, I couldn't imagine Liam inside the coffin. The very idea that he was sealed inside that wooden box seemed laughable to me and, indeed, for some moments I was afraid that I really was going to burst into shrill, hysterical laughter. It bubbled up in my chest, but I thrust it back down and in another moment the urge to laugh was completely gone as a fresh wave of sadness swept over me. This was so unfair. I shouldn't be here doing this right now. I shouldn't have to do this for years and years.

For the first time in my life, I longed for old age. In fact I *yearned* for it. I wanted to put as much time as possible between myself and this present moment of raw, undiluted pain. No one I'd loved had ever died before. I'd only known two of my grandparents and they were both still alive so I'd never even seen a funeral before, except on TV.

I met Liam's parents outside the church. At first I thought Ben wasn't there and anger flared inside me. Liam had fallen out with his older brother about ten months ago, just before we were married, and they hadn't seen much of each other since then. They were complete opposites in personality. Where Liam had been outgoing,

Ben was introverted; where Liam had been popular and well-liked, Ben was solitary and antisocial; where Liam had always been a chatterbox, Ben used words sparingly if he used them at all.

His parents had told me earlier in the week that Ben was abroad, working in Germany, and they weren't sure if he was going to come back for the funeral or not. I could hardly believe it. I knew the two of them had not been on the best of terms recently but the idea that Ben wouldn't bother to attend his brother's funeral disgusted me.

But then I saw him standing a little apart from his parents outside the church and an overwhelming flood of emotion swept over me. For whilst he may have been Liam's opposite in character, he was remarkably similar to him in looks. Just two years older, he was of a similar height and build with the same chestnut-brown hair. The only obvious difference between them was that Ben's hair was cut slightly shorter and he had brown eyes instead of green. I hadn't seen him for ten months or so and I'd forgotten just how similar they looked. Even some of their mannerisms were the same. It could almost have been Liam standing there and a lump rose in my throat at the sight of him.

He looked more angry than sad – grinding his jaw as if he was going to file right through his teeth, his eyes dark and bitter. He saw me then and walked over to us. 'Hello, Jasmyn,' he said quietly, holding out his hand to shake mine.

A half-sob rose in my throat and I flung my arms around his neck. He looked so much like Liam that I just wanted to cling to him and never let him go. He recoiled a little at my touch and I felt him stiffen. If he'd tried to push me away I think I would have redoubled my grip like some kind of limpet, holding on for dear life because he made me feel closer to my husband than I had done since the evening he died. But in the end, Ben did the sensible thing and patted my back awkwardly until I released him, horribly aware that I'd made a mess of his black jacket.

We walked into the church and took our places on the front pew reserved for close family. Being an albino, I looked awful in black – it made my white hair and skin look even whiter and my pale-blue eyes even stranger, especially as I was only twenty-seven years old.

The vicar had asked me if I wanted to speak during the service but the very idea had horrified me for I knew I couldn't do it. I wanted to. I just couldn't. So in a fit of madness, I'd said I would play something instead. We'd been asked to pick out one of Liam's favourite songs for the service and that, at least, was easy for I knew he had always loved 'Bridge over Troubled Water'. But rather than bringing a CD, I was going to play the song myself on my violin. I wanted to contribute to the service even if I couldn't speak and – this will sound odd if you're not a musician – but I needed an excuse to bring my violin with me. I felt somehow that the whole thing would be easier to bear with the reassuring feel of the familiar instrument on my lap.

I kept myself under control in the church until the first hymn but after that it was quite hopeless. Music has a way of amplifying my emotions. It makes me happier when I'm happy but it unravels me altogether when I'm sad. Throughout the service I desperately willed my hands to stop shaking and the tears to stop pouring down my cheeks. I couldn't play the violin like this and I had to play it – otherwise I would regret my weakness for the rest of my life.

My lovely electric violin lay on my lap and as I stared down at it I couldn't help remembering how I had got it. I'd wanted one for some time but they were all too expensive. And then, one October, Liam had gone out and bought me one. It was meant to be a Christmas present but he was so excited about it that he couldn't wait to give it to me. So one Saturday afternoon I was surprised by his particular insistence that I play 'Bridge over Troubled Water' for him.

'I'm in the middle of an exciting bit,' I said, keeping my eyes on the novel I was reading on the couch. 'I'll play it for you later.'

'Play it for me now, Jaz,' Liam insisted, pulling the book out of my hands.

'Hey!' I said, sitting up and trying to snatch it back. But Liam held it above his head out of my reach.

'I'm your fiancé,' he said with a grin, 'and I'm commanding you to play for me now, not later.'

I sighed and rolled my eyes as I got off the couch but really I liked the fact that he enjoyed my music. I liked him taking pride in my one talent and that he was interested enough in it to have special requests whenever I played for him.

'All right,' I grumbled, walking over to my violin case, lying against the wall. 'But I'm just playing it once and then I'm going back to my book. I'm in the middle of a really good bit.'

But I soon forgot all about the book. I knelt on the carpet and unzipped the violin case, and as I flipped it open I turned around to grab a piece of sheet music from the coffee table. When I turned back to the case I jumped with a cry of alarm. For where my gleaming golden violin had been nestled in the red interior there was now a silver and blue skeletal-looking thing in its place. It was a beautiful new electric violin.

I let out a sort of strangled yelp of delight. 'That's ... that's a *Violectra*!' I gasped.

'It's the right one, isn't it?' Liam asked, looking anxious for a moment. 'That was the one you wanted?'

I stared around at him incredulously. 'Are you kidding? Are you *kidding*? I was going to spend a few hundred pounds and buy a Yamaha Silent Violin. I just ... God, I just never *dreamed* I'd be able to get a Violectra! Are you sure we can afford it?'

'Oh yes,' he said with an airy wave of his hand and the boyish grin I knew so well. 'It's an investment. So you won't forget all about me when you're a world-famous violinist ...'

'Jasmyn,' my mother whispered in my ear. 'It's time for you to play.'

Her voice brought me sharply back to the funeral. I clenched and unclenched my hands but they were still trembling.

'You don't have to,' she said, noticing at once. 'It doesn't matter. I gave the priest a CD of the song before the service. He can play that instead if you want.'

I shook my head, my throat too frozen up with the numbness of trying not to cry to be able to talk. I had to play. I owed him

6

that. I got up from my seat and walked to the front of the church on legs that felt as if they were going to betray me at any second. Of course the whole thing was a farce, really. I wasn't doing this for Liam. Liam was dead – it hardly mattered to him what I did any more. I was doing it for myself, trying to wring some small measure of comfort from anything that I possibly could. I plugged the violin into the amplifier and tucked it under my chin, hoping its familiar feel might relax me a little. But as my fingertips pressed down on the strings and I gazed down its neck, hesitating, I clearly heard Liam's voice from two years ago when he'd first given it to me and I was still staring at it in its case – love at first sight:

'Are you going to play that thing or just look at it?'

His voice seemed to echo round the church, even though it had only been in my head. I kept my eyes firmly turned away from the coffin and the man I knew to be inside it, so close to me and yet at the same time so very far away. He was in there. Liam was right there in that box and I was afraid that if I dwelt on that I'd throw down the violin, run to the coffin, pull open the lid and cling to him to stop them from taking him away, not letting go until my fingers were forcibly prised off and I was dragged out of the church like some kind of a lunatic.

I took a deep breath and raised the bow, but for all that I had played this instrument hundreds of times before, my arm was shaking so much that I didn't put the right amount of pressure on the strings and the note came out faint. I tried again, but this time I overcompensated and the bow scraped off the strings altogether with a horribly discordant sound quite unlike the beautiful music the violin usually made for me. It was almost as if the Violectra itself was refusing to play funeral music because it would be too awful, too heartbreaking, too utterly devastating ... I took another deep breath, desperately trying to steady myself but starting to feel light-headed by now.

I saw my mother half-rise from her chair as if about to come and take me back to my seat. I think it was this that panicked me into pulling it together at last. I raised the bow again and this time the note came out clear and perfect. I had played this song for

Liam many times before and now – playing it for the last time – I meant to play it well. But I couldn't stop the tears from running down my face. I could feel them collecting in the hollow of the chin rest so that the violin would have slipped from my grip had it not been for the shoulder rest holding it firmly in place.

When I was halfway through the piece, I noticed Ben stand up and leave the church. I knew how he felt. I wished I could walk out too. Even as I played it, the music seemed to almost rip my heart out. But I carried on and finally it was over and – half-blinded with tears – I was able to go back to my seat amongst my family.

By the end of the service the tissue clutched in my hand was little more than a grotty bit of sodden rag – I was making a mess of myself and fumbled blindly through my pockets for a clean one. I knew I'd brought a whole handful from home, but I couldn't find a single tissue. Then I realised my mother was holding a handkerchief out to me and I took it from her gratefully.

The coffin was being carried outside. It was time to go. I realised for the first time as we followed on behind that the pall-bearers were all men from the undertaker's. That wasn't right. That wasn't right at all. They hadn't known Liam and his death meant nothing to them. I should have asked his father and Ben and his friends … I shouldn't have allowed him to be carried away by strangers like this. I knew the undertakers must have asked me about the pall-bearers when we were making the arrangements but I couldn't remember. In fact I could remember practically nothing of any of my conversations with them. At some point it had all become a blur. I had stopped caring and just agreed to whatever they or my family suggested. For what did it matter? What did *any* of it matter? The type of wood for the coffin, the hymns, the pall-bearers, the food served at the reception … it all seemed so pointless.

But now that it was actually happening it suddenly did seem important – ridiculously so, even. I silently apologised to Liam for not getting his funeral right and gritted my teeth to stop myself from wailing into my handkerchief. Before the ceremony I had

8

been so determined not to cry but now I simply couldn't stop. I hated that other people were seeing my tears – they should have been saved for a more private place. I didn't want them to see my pain, and I didn't want their sympathy, for it only intensified my sense of loss to see myself through their eyes:

That poor widow … And she's so young … As was her husband, of course … An aneurysm, apparently. Tragic, simply tragic …

A juicy tragedy – something to be relished and gossiped about over the coffee cups before going on with their day as if nothing was different and things weren't horribly, horribly, *horribly* wrong and would never be right ever again …

When we stepped out of the church I was surprised to discover that the sky had darkened whilst we'd been inside: the sullen clouds of a summer thunderstorm covered the sky and it was raining. A yellow flash forked overhead, followed moments later by a dull rumble of thunder. I was aware of other people putting up umbrellas behind me. I hadn't brought one and I pushed aside the one my mother tried to give me. I wanted to be cold and wet. I wanted to be soaked through and chilled to the bone. It couldn't make me feel any worse than I already did and at least it would match my mood. Ben had been waiting by the front doors and fell into step beside us as we walked across the wet grass to the graveside.

The vicar was talking but, hard as I tried, I just couldn't focus on what he was saying. My attention was fixed instead on the drumming sound the raindrops made as they hit the coffin and the little splashes they created across its smooth, clean surface. This was it, then. I really was burying Liam today. God help me, this was not a dream. And as I stood there I wondered hopelessly how I could ever possibly recover from the agonising pain of it. Nothing could ever be good after this, nothing.

The coffin had just been lowered into the ground when something large and black fell from the sky to land right on top of it with a heavy, wet thud. The vicar broke off mid-sentence as everyone peered down into the grave, shocked, frowning, muttering …

'Oh my God,' I heard my mother exclaim quietly at my side.

It was a dead swan – each feather raven black, its beak red and its eyes pink – right there on top of the coffin. I tilted my head back, blinking against the rain that fell into my eyes as I peered up into the dark clouds above. There was another blurred shape and a thump just a few feet to my left as a second black swan fell to the ground, its long neck twisted at a horrible angle on the sodden grass. Several people shrieked this time and automatically shied away from the bird. I found myself staring down at it blankly, cool raindrops running to the ends of my eyelashes and falling to the ground.

A third dead swan thumped down on my right. The ceremony over, people started to scatter, heading back through the rain to their cars and the reception that was to be held at the Town Hall. I found myself grinning manically. So it wasn't real after all, then. This had to be a dream. Thank God. Thunder rumbled again, much louder than before – a great tearing crack as if the sky were being rent apart above us.

'I think we should get inside,' my mother said, raising her voice above the rain.

'I can't wait to wake up from this,' I said softly, not really intending to speak aloud although I doubt she could hear me over the rain anyway. 'I'm going to hold on to him so tightly. I'll never take him for granted ever again.'

'Come on, Jasmyn,' Ben said, appearing at my side and gripping my elbow.

Without an umbrella my white hair was soaked through and sticking to my face. I brushed it back out of my eyes in time to see two more black swans fall from the sky at the edge of my vision. Ben took my arms and twisted me round to face him. He had no umbrella either and his dark hair was plastered to his head, raindrops dripping from the end of his long nose. It was only because he bent his head so close to mine that I heard what he said over the noise of the storm.

'Don't look at the swans. Don't look at them. Look at me.'

I gazed blankly up into his face and for a second saw Liam there instead. Their features were so heartbreakingly similar that in that moment, when I looked into Ben's eyes, I felt I was looking into the eyes of the man I loved. I felt numb – with cold, with grief, with shock – and all I wanted was to curl up in a ball on the wet grass and never move again. But Ben tightened his grip, denying me the sweet relief of giving up. Instead he turned and pulled me along beside him like a sleepwalker, away from the coffin and the black swans and the sodden graveyard ... and Liam, left behind on his own in the cold, wet earth.

2

Black Knight

I dreamt about the day of Liam's death for weeks. But always, in my dreams, it would turn out to be a mistake, a joke, a ridiculous misunderstanding ... Liam had always been a joker, so, for a few moments, I could almost believe it when I dreamt that the hospital worker dropped me off at home and, instead of going into an empty house, I would go in to find him there, laughing, saying he couldn't believe I'd fallen for it. Or I would dream that the telephone rang and it was the hospital saying that they'd made a mistake, Liam wasn't dead, and I should come back and pick him up right away. How I hated those dreams.

Overwhelming relief, joy and gladness would rush through me and I would vow never to argue with him again, never to say another harsh word or waste another precious moment. But then I'd dimly realise I was dreaming and sickening disappointment would almost crush me. And then the dream would start all over again – this time I really *was* awake and the hospital really *were* calling to tell me Liam wasn't dead ... Each time my mind would struggle with it, so desperately wanting to believe it, and yet I kept asking myself over and over again – *Am I dreaming right now? Am I?*

When the phone rang for real the day after the funeral, I opened my bloodshot eyes and my hand fumbled desperately around the bedside table. I grabbed the phone, quite sure in my mind that it was the hospital, and raised it to my ear, half-propped up on my elbows to say a breathless, rather hoarse, 'Hello?'

'Oh, did I wake you, dear?' my mother's voice said.

I closed my eyes for a moment, taking a deep breath and trying to thrust down the anger I unfairly felt towards her for waking me up like this, making me believe for a moment that it was the hospital calling to tell me Liam wasn't dead.

'That's all right,' I managed.

'It's one o'clock in the afternoon,' she said, a little reproachfully.

'Is it?'

'Do you want me to come over?'

'No!' I said hurriedly. 'No. Look, I just want to be on my own today. Please.'

'All right,' she said reluctantly. 'The swans have been burnt. Did you know?'

'What?'

'The five swans that fell into the graveyard yesterday. They've been cremated. You know – in case they were carrying a contagious disease. The vicar tried to phone to let you know but he said you didn't answer so he called me. He thinks they probably died of fright because of the thunderstorm, that's all.'

'Okay,' I replied. 'Mum, I have to go. I'll speak to you later.'

I couldn't have cared less about the dead swans right then and barely spared a thought for them as the next couple of months crawled slowly by. Suddenly I realised that it was getting dark in the evenings and cold during the day. It was now November. Autumn had gone. I'd missed it. Liam had been dead for two months and still it took an extreme amount of willpower just to get out of bed in the morning. The school where I'd worked as a violin teacher had allowed me to take the autumn term off but they would be expecting me back in January, which suddenly seemed much closer than it had before. I would certainly have to go back to work next year, for the bereavement benefit payment I had received would have run out by that time and – as everyone kept telling me – life moved on.

Mine didn't seem to, though. I found myself dwelling on the arguments I'd had with Liam, bitterly regretting every angry word or spiteful comment – words that I hadn't even meant at the time and so cursed myself for saying. I hoped he'd known I hadn't meant it. I hoped he'd dismissed my words for the complete nonsense that they were.

Once, after a particularly heated argument just after we got engaged, Liam brought me flowers and suggested a truce. But I was still angry and not ready to make up. When he held the lilies out to me I threw them back in his face. Even as I did it I felt awful – disgusted with myself. But my guilt only made me angrier and when Liam stormed off, trampling the crushed flowers, I didn't go after him. I just let him walk away – a petty act of nastiness that now I could never take back.

One of the things I found most difficult to cope with was that friends and family kept phoning me or turning up at the door, trying to help, trying to do things for me. I knew they had good intentions but I just wanted to be left alone and no one seemed to be able to understand that. In another month I was supposed to be going to California for a week in early December to stay with Laura, a friend who had emigrated to America last year. Liam and I had bought plane tickets to visit her months ago. When she phoned after the funeral I burst into tears and told her I couldn't possibly still go, but she begged me to wait and see how I felt nearer the time. It was too late to get my money back on the plane tickets so I agreed, just to keep her happy, even though I had no intention whatsoever of going. The only time I really went out of the house was to buy food and even that was torturous – not the actual *leaving* so much as the coming back to an empty house afterwards. When I was away I longed to be back at home and when I was at home I longed to be away. I was trapped in a state of constant restlessness that never seemed to get any easier no matter where I was or what I was doing.

Friends and family members would turn up, trying to persuade me to go out for the day with them, saying that it wasn't good for me to be all alone in the house. But I always refused to leave. The house was my haven. I couldn't bear to see anyone who'd known Liam for they might try to talk to me about him, they might bring up old memories, they might drive the knife in and twist it even

14

further. So I cut myself off from everyone as much as I could, and if I was having a really bad day then I unplugged the phone and stayed out of sight of the windows if the doorbell rang until whoever was out there gave up and went away.

Unfortunately, this didn't work with my mother because she had her own key. There was no point in hiding from her when she would only barge in by herself if I did. One day, after two months of watching me wallow in misery, she came by to lecture me about all the things that still had to be done.

'Done?' I repeated stupidly. 'What do you mean? I've done everything already.'

I had done the funeral and after that I had done all the tedious legal practicalities – gone to my bank and my solicitor, obtained all the necessary documentation to secure my bereavement payment, broken down into stupid laugher when I collected the death certificate, for it seemed such a silly thing to be given a certificate *for* … I had arranged to have time off from the school I worked at, I had ensured that the mortgage continued to be paid every month along with the loan we had taken out to pay for the widescreen TV that had been a joint Christmas present. I had forced myself to do all those things before finally coming back to shut myself away in the house, like a wounded animal returning to its den to heal. What more could there possibly be still to do after all that?

'You haven't even started on the house yet,' my mother said patiently.

'I sorted out the mortgage—' I began, but she cut me off.

'That's not what I mean.' She hesitated for a moment before going on, 'There's his study and his clothes and all of his things still lying around. You should start clearing some of them away. See if his parents want anything. Turn the study into something else. Make a fresh start—'

'*Stop it!*' I snapped, desperate to prevent her from saying even one more word. Deep down I knew she was right but I had already had to do so much and I couldn't face doing any more. Just the thought of it made me feel hot and clammy and panicky – trapped, helpless and unable to breathe. I forced myself to hold it together.

I knew that if I lost it in front of my mother now, there would be no stopping her from coming over ten times a day to check on me. I refused, as calmly as I could, to pack away any of Liam's things, for I feared it would be like losing him all over again.

But, a few days later, I began to think that perhaps she was right. At first I had been comforted by Liam's clothes, had worn his shirts and felt close to him. But his smell had faded from them now and seeing them hanging in the wardrobe every day was a constant reminder that he was not coming home. When I realised I had worn my pyjamas all day just to avoid opening the wardrobe door I decided to grit my teeth and set to work clearing it out. It had never really been big enough for both of us anyway, so at least my clothes would no longer be creased and it would keep my mother off my back for a little while.

The first time I tried, I only managed to take one shirt out of the cupboard and drop it into one of the empty boxes standing nearby before I lost my resolve and walked away, unable to bear it for it just seemed so final. Instead I went into his study, so carefully preserved, and curled up in the large chair behind his desk, sobbing cowardly tears into the tissue clutched in my hand.

I had always loved the room. There were as many bookcases crammed in as would fit – all filled with books about myth, legend, history, superstition, folklore and fairy tales. Even the calendar on the wall still said it was September, as if the room were some kind of timeless bubble. Whenever Liam was home he would always be in here working on his laptop. He'd been away several times over the ten months we'd been married for he insisted on doing relevant research abroad where he could. I'd missed him when he'd been gone but at least then I'd always known that he was coming back. It had not been anything at all like this …

A book lay before me on the desk, still open on the last page Liam had been looking at. It was one of those huge, ancient volumes, bound in leather and smelling of age and dry paper. He had been in the middle of a chapter detailing how to identify the devil's familiars when they disguised themselves as animals.

It seemed that any black animal could be linked with the devil – black cats, black dogs, black swans ...

A horrible shudder went through me at the mention of black swans and the memory it summoned of them falling from the sky on the day of the funeral. Before that I hadn't even known that there was such a thing as a black swan. The book went on to say that in ancient times villagers had killed black animals on sight for fear that the devil's servants walked amongst them. The words sent a chill through me, although I tried to dismiss the idea for the superstition that it was.

I ran my finger over the page, feeling closer to Liam as I did so. He loved reading. And he loved folklore. The words on this page were probably the last thing he ever read. In fact, he was probably reading this right up until he got up to go and fetch me from work ... I closed the book and pushed it away. This was it. I had to get used to the idea that Liam wouldn't be sitting here waiting for me any more when I got home. He was gone and that was that – no amount of crying was ever going to bring him back.

I picked the book up and found a gap on the shelves to slot it into alongside a book Liam had written himself about magical creatures. I took it out and opened it to the contents page to see if there was anything in there about black swans. There wasn't, but there was a small section about magic swans so I flicked to the page and read it. Of course, I had read all of Liam's books before, but I particularly liked this one for the fact that it was full of his colourful, whimsical illustrations of mermaids, yetis and faeries.

I flicked to the page about magic swans and reacquainted myself with the myth immortalised by *Swan Lake* of beings who were swans by day and beautiful women by night. Liam had also noted that, like mermaids, these swan princesses were said to possess magical voices with which they could enchant any human they chose – especially in swan form, when their song was said to be the most potent of all enchantments. But where mermaids and harpies used their silvery voices to lure sailors to a watery grave, it seemed that the swan princesses sang so that their true love would be able to find them however far apart they might be from one another. The book reassured me with its sweet interpretation of the myth, distinctly devoid of anything sinister or demonic.

The next day I tried again with the wardrobe and, this time, I made myself finish it, although it took me the entire day and was almost as difficult as the funeral itself. I could picture him in every piece of clothing that I packed away – every jumper, jacket and pair of trousers ... One of his shirts was stained with red wine where I had spilt my drink on him at a friend's birthday party we had gone to just the night before he died. And his lucky jeans were ripped and still stained from the two parachute jumps he'd done since our wedding. He'd come to love speed and adrenalin rushes and had been planning on doing a skydive next. In the last year he had developed something of a daredevil nature where his hobbies were concerned and it seemed ironic now that I had worried a little about him dying doing something dangerous.

Finally I came to the bag of things I'd been given by the undertakers containing everything Liam had had on him when he'd died. The grass stains on the T-shirt and jeans made me feel sick as I remembered how he'd crumpled to the ground, half-dragging me with him. We'd been at the lake near the house, tossing stale bread into the water for the ducks and swans clustered by the bank. The water was painted golden by the low sun and there was a balmy warmth even though we were now coming towards the end of summer. Children ran about behind us, playing and eating ice creams from the omnipresent ice cream van, or else feeding the ducks like we were.

I can't remember what Liam and I talked about as we stood there on that warm summer evening. I spent a lot of time afterwards trying to recall our conversation but found I couldn't. It was eclipsed by the thing that happened next. He had been complaining of a headache all day but had taken some painkillers that morning and I had thought nothing more of it. He got headaches sometimes, but they were never severe and didn't usually last very long.

When the birds had eaten all the bread we brushed off our hands and started strolling towards one of the benches. We were about halfway there when Liam stopped.

'What's the matter?' I asked, stopping too.

'It's this headache,' Liam replied in a strange voice, both hands massaging his temples.

'Take some more aspirin,' I suggested.

'I've been taking aspirin all day,' he said. 'It's not … helping.'

I started to say something else – I can't remember what. Even then I wasn't really concerned. After all, it was only a headache. But then he staggered, clutching at my shoulders to support himself.

'Hey, are you okay?' I asked sharply, suddenly very concerned indeed.

I'll always remember the look he gave me. It was one of those funny, crooked half-smiles I knew so well – warm and reassuring despite the strange puzzlement in his eyes. But then he collapsed – folding up on the green grass and dragging me with him. By the time my mobile phone was in my hand, Liam was unconscious. He was still alive when the ambulance arrived but he died before we reached the hospital. I didn't even get to do the hours of anxious waiting in the waiting room. The doctor explained to me that he had suffered a cerebral aneurysm. I stared at him blankly, waiting for more. That couldn't just be it. It had all happened so fast. We had been feeding the ducks together less than half an hour ago. This was ridiculous beyond belief. Somebody must have made a most dreadful mistake …

'I don't understand how this can happen,' I said flatly, vaguely aware that my voice sounded completely and utterly emotionless. The doctor started rattling off causes – high blood pressure, head trauma or even just a matter of a pre-existing congenital disorder – they couldn't be sure and sometimes these things just happened and that was all there was to it …

There was an itemised list inside the bag and I ran my eye down it to distract myself: T-shirt, jeans, trainers, watch, wallet, knight, wedding ring, loose change … I frowned and my eyes moved back up the list. Knight? I emptied the bag out onto the floor, moved the clothes and shoes to one side and then found four small clear plastic bags. One held Liam's wallet, the second about two pounds in loose change, the third held his watch and in the fourth bag was a small black knight just a little taller than my thumb. A large, rusty nail had been shoved though his visored helmet.

I gazed at the little figure in surprise. According to the list it had been found in Liam's jacket pocket. I had never seen it before and could only assume a child had lost it, Liam had found it and, for some odd reason, picked it up. I put it to one side with the other things. Then I picked up the grass-stained clothes and put them in the box with the others, profoundly glad to be rid of that particular outfit. I never, ever wanted to see it again.

I drove the boxes to a clothes bank that afternoon. And that was when I first began to feel it – that prickly sensation of being watched. As I carried the boxes out I kept turning around to look behind me, sure that someone must be staring at me intently to make the sensation so strong and insistent. But there was nobody around apart from a few people waiting at a bus stop who didn't seem to be paying me any attention. In another moment the feeling had passed so I shrugged it off, put the empty boxes back in the car and drove home.

Ever since Liam's funeral I had occasionally had strange, surreal dreams involving swans and that night I dreamt I stood on the deck of a large, majestic old ship. The deck was deserted but for me. It was quiet. And icy cold. I strained my eyes out across the black ocean but it was too dark to see anything. I wondered absently if it was going to snow. Even as the thought flew through my mind the sky filled with falling black feathers. They brushed against my bare arms, falling over the side of the boat to float in the water and landing at my feet to cover the deck in a sleek black carpet. I stretched out my arms, twirling on the spot, enjoying the silky touch of the feathers as they brushed against my skin. It was like being inside a large, rather surreal snow globe.

The odd thing about these dreams was that I quite enjoyed them at the time. I felt ... a sort of contentment. There was no grief pressing down on me any more. But when I woke up I would be swamped with an intense sense of loss ... only it wasn't for

Liam. It was for something else. Almost as if I'd lost something I hadn't even known I'd had …

3

Wedding Photos

It was another couple of weeks – right at the end of November – before something else happened. Ever since that day when I'd cleared out Liam's clothes I had experienced those strange moments when I was convinced I was being watched. The back of my neck would prickle and the fine hairs along my arms would stand up. I mentioned it to my mother one day, who promptly prattled off some sentimental rubbish about Liam watching over me from wherever he was now. But it wasn't Liam.

It never lasted very long – only ever a moment or two – so it was hard to know if I was really imagining it or not. I never saw anyone and it did, after all, seem a ridiculous notion that there was some unseen observer lurking about all the time.

But then, one day, I decided to look at my wedding album. Since Liam had died I hadn't been able to look at any of the photos, but that evening I took the album out of the cupboard, sat down in the middle of the bed with it and opened the front cover. My eyes automatically went to Liam on the first page of photographs of the two of us in front of the church. It had been a sunny day and the golden light gleamed off his chestnut hair. In every photo he had that boyish grin I knew so well and triumphant happiness shone in his eyes as if he truly believed that every man there must envy him the freakish white bride on his arm.

Then my gaze flicked to myself in my pale-blue wedding dress and I jumped in horror. There was something wrong – dreadfully wrong – with my face. I had spent my entire wedding day grinning like an idiot but in this photo ... it was hideous ... my face was screwed up in pain. I looked like I was in physical agony. There I was, in that lovely dress, holding the arm of the man I loved most in the whole world on the happiest day of my life and yet I looked as if I was dying.

I gripped the wedding album and hurriedly flicked all the way through the photos. It was the same in every single one. My posture was as it should have been but my face ... On the last page my mouth gaped open almost unnaturally wide as if I were screaming with the full force of my lungs. Liam stood beside me grinning, oblivious to whatever was wrong with me. I knew I hadn't looked like that on my wedding day. I knew I hadn't looked like that in these photos before. When Liam and I had gone through this album together we had both looked as happy in the photos as we had felt at the time. I snapped the album shut as if some awful *thing* might escape from those dreadful pictures and devour me.

The deep sadness I had felt moments ago was now eclipsed by a terrible, cold fear that chilled me to the bone. I wondered if I could be missing Liam so much that the grief of it was actually starting to turn me a little mad. The thought terrified me ... I tried to tell myself that I was just tired. I would go to sleep and, in the morning, the photos would be back to normal. I hurriedly put the album back in the wardrobe and then went to bed.

But I couldn't sleep. I felt unsafe and uneasy being alone in the house. The photos weighed on my mind, filling me with a horrible sense of strangeness which made everything feel odd. Even the familiar bed seemed different. I lay there for a while, listening to the sound of the heavy rain that had started half an hour ago splattering against the glass. In the end I gave up and got out of bed. I had no need to turn on the light as I'd left the curtains tied back and the street lamp on the quiet road outside shed a soft glow into the room. I went over to the wardrobe and took the wedding album out. It was illogical, but I felt I would rest easier if it wasn't in the same room with me, so I carried it out of the bedroom, treading softly even though there was no one else there for me to disturb any more. After dumping it on the coffee table in the lounge, I went back to the bedroom.

And that was when I saw the man outside.

He stood beneath the street lamp on the other side of the road and appeared to be watching the house. I froze with my hand still gripping the edge of the quilt where I had been about to get back into the bed, wondering if he could see me. It was almost two in the morning and chucking it down with rain. What on earth was he doing out there?

I couldn't see him properly because he wore a dark waterproof coat with the hood drawn up over his head. The light from the street lamp above him cast a slick, shiny sheen across that hood, reflecting rainbow colours as if drops of oil rolled down it rather than water. The effect was frightening and out of place and un-natural. His face was lost in shadows and his hands were thrust into his pockets. The sudden and completely unexpected sight of him sent a horrible chill right through me and I felt my heart speed up fearfully in my chest.

If he had been a drunk, stumbling home from the nearby pub, singing tunelessly, I would not have felt so threatened for I could have explained his presence. But he was just standing there motion-less, staring directly towards my house, getting soaked by the rain and I was suddenly painfully aware that without Liam I was alone and vulnerable here.

I decided to call the police, but as soon as my hand began to move towards the phone on the nearby table, the man outside turned abruptly, his hooded head bowed against the force of the rain as he slowly walked away. I moved closer to the window and watched until he turned a corner at the end of the road and disap-peared from sight.

How long had he been there and what did he want? I didn't think he would have been able to see me from that distance, for when I got up I hadn't turned on the light, but it was possible he had caught some hint of movement and that that was why he had left … Perhaps he was a thief who'd been checking out the properties in the area. Perhaps he was the reason I had had that occasional feeling of being watched. Perhaps I had not been imagining it after all …

After a brief hesitation, I phoned the police. Of course I could tell them next to nothing about the man – I couldn't even describe him – and so there wasn't very much they could do, but the officer I spoke to seemed to take what I had to say seriously and just the act of reporting it made me feel a little better. But I did not sleep that night. And as the dark hours dragged by I felt Liam's absence in the house even more keenly than usual.

4

Jaxon Thorpe

It was only when the sun started shining through the windows the next morning that I at last felt safe enough to fall asleep. About four hours later I was woken up by the sound of the doorbell and scrambled out of bed thinking it was probably the postman. But when I opened the front door I found a man I didn't recognise standing on the doorstep, his car parked in the drive behind my own.

He was thirty years old or so, quite tall, with strawberry-blond hair and laughing blue eyes. A grin of delight spread across his pleasant face at the sight of me.

'You must be Jasmyn,' he said.

I was suddenly self-consciously aware of my appearance. I was wearing long pyjama bottoms but only a strapped top. I didn't often wear clothes like that in public for they showed too much of my white skin, emphasising the fact that I was different rather than disguising it. My self-confidence had taken a plunge since Liam died. When he'd been around I'd felt good whatever I was wearing. Now I was horribly aware of my white arms and shoulders and my long white hair, still tousled from sleep. It was painfully obvious that I had only just got out of bed, even though it was practically midday, but, to my relief, the stranger tactfully pretended not to notice.

'I'm sorry,' I said, running my hand self-consciously through my hair, trying to neaten it. 'Do I know you?'

His smile broadened. 'Not yet, my dear. But I feel like I know you already, Liam always talked about you so much. My name's

Jaxon Thorpe. I expect your husband's told you all about me. Is he here? I've come a long way to see him.'

My mind was in a whirl. I'd never heard the name Jaxon Thorpe before and yet this man seemed to expect me to know him. Worse still, he obviously had no idea that Liam was dead. 'How ... how do you know Liam?' I stammered foolishly.

'We worked together a year or so ago,' Jaxon replied. 'You don't mean he didn't tell you all about me? It's lucky I'm not the sensitive type or I might be quite upset by that.'

'Jaxon,' I said and then swallowed. 'I'm sorry but Liam ... he died. Almost three months ago now.'

I expected the colour to drain from the man's face, for him to gasp and for the smile to disappear altogether. I expected the usual shocked, horrified reaction, especially in light of what he had just been saying.

Instead he laughed humourlessly. 'So he *did* tell you about me!' he exclaimed, a gleam in his eye. 'That won't work, you know. Come on, tell me where he is.'

I stared at him. 'I don't know what you're talking about,' I said coldly.

I made to close the door but Jaxon thrust his foot into the crack before I could do so and forced it open.

'What are you doing?' I exclaimed in alarm as he barged inside.

'Where is he?' he snapped, his blue eyes no longer at all friendly.

'I already told you!' Suddenly a horrible thought occurred to me and I said, 'Did you ... did you come to the house last night?'

'I only arrived in the country this morning. Now, tell me where he is!'

'Get out!' I snapped, not knowing whether to believe him or not, appalled by his rudeness and frightened by the way he had turned nasty so quickly. 'What the hell is wrong with you?'

He didn't answer but instead walked straight past me, opening the first door he came across, which happened to be the bed-room.

'If the bastard's dead,' he snarled, walking over to the cupboard, 'then why are all his clothes in—' He broke off in surprise when he flung the doors open to see only my clothes hanging up inside.

His head snapped around and his gaze swept the room, searching in vain for some sign that a man shared it with me. When he found none he looked again at my face and for the first time it seemed to occur to him that I might be telling the truth.

'Who did it?' he growled, pale with anger. 'Was it Lukas? Adrian? Was it Ben?'

'Ben?' I repeated stupidly.

'His brother.'

'I know who Ben is! Liam died from natural causes. Nobody killed him! Ben certainly would never—'

'I ... I want to see his death certificate,' Jaxon said hoarsely.

I took a deep breath. 'If you don't leave my house right now,' I said, 'I'm calling the police.'

He hesitated for a moment before walking past me to the front door. He didn't go through it but stood beside it, hands held up placatingly as he said, 'Are you sure – are you *sure* – that he's dead? Did you see his body? Did you—'

'I saw the body!' I snapped. 'Trust me, he's dead!'

Scowling, he turned away without another word, but I found myself grabbing his arm to stop him from leaving, suddenly feeling more angry than scared as I said, 'How the hell did you even know Liam? I can't imagine him having much time for someone like you!'

'Someone like me?' Jaxon repeated quietly, gazing into my face with an expression I found impossible to read. 'Oh dear, he really didn't tell you anything at all, did he?' He leaned closer to whisper in my ear, the warmth of his breath on my neck making me cringe. 'Brace yourself, darling. Liam was far blacker than I could ever be.'

He stepped back with a smile, clearly pleased with himself as he shook off my hand and stalked out of the house to his car. I glared after him, trying to think of some insult to shout at his back but I was too slow and in another moment he was inside the

28

car. The image of that smug smile remained in my mind and I ran out to pick up one of the loose stones on the drive. I just couldn't bear the thought of that arrogant bastard driving away thinking I would doubt Liam – even for a second – based on what he had just said to me. I hadn't had the wit to tell him to his face that I didn't believe him so I did the only thing I could think of, and that was to draw back my arm and throw the stone at his car as he pulled out of the drive, sending it straight through the back window with a profoundly satisfying breaking of glass.

I half-expected him to stop the car, storm back to the house and demand money to pay for it but he just pulled into the road and drove away, leaving me standing there in the drive shaking a little. I regretted throwing the stone almost at once for now he might come back. I glanced at the houses on either side of mine, hoping none of my neighbours had seen what I'd just done.

I hurried back inside and automatically reached for the phone, but hesitated before dialling 999. What exactly could I say to the police? That a man who didn't like my late husband very much had come to my house and been very angry to learn of his death? That he assumed instantly that it had been premeditated murder? I'd never heard the other two names – Adrian and Lukas – that he'd mentioned. As for Ben … well, the idea of him killing anyone, let alone his own brother, was quite absurd. So I picked up the phone and called him. Jaxon obviously knew him and I thought that he might be able to explain this lunatic and the madness he'd babbled at me.

I hadn't seen him since the funeral. After taking me back to the car from the graveyard, he had left, not even coming to the reception afterwards. When I asked his mother about it a few days later she said that he'd gone back to Germany.

'You understand, of course, how difficult all this is for Ben,' she said when I expressed surprise.

'Difficult for *Ben*?' I spluttered before I could stop myself.

It had been difficult for *me*, but I had still made all the funeral arrangements, I had sat there enduring the service, I had cleared out his clothes and possessions. I sympathised with Ben for the horrible situation he found himself in, having parted from his brother on bad terms before his death, but he only had himself to blame. I didn't know what they had fallen out about for Liam had refused to tell me. That in itself had worried me at the time as he usually told me everything. Liam did not bear grudges and so I knew Ben must have done something very unpleasant indeed to cause such a long rift between them.

The last time I ever saw them together was just a couple of weeks before the wedding when Liam and I had walked into our house one afternoon to find Ben sitting at our kitchen table with a glass and a bottle of Jameson's in front of him.

'Christ, Ben, you scared me half to death!' Liam exclaimed when we walked in and found him sitting there. 'How did you get in?'

'Spare key under the doormat,' Ben replied sourly. 'Still. You should find a more imaginative place to hide it.'

He disguised it well but I could tell from the slight slur in his voice that he was drunk – the first time I'd ever seen him so in all the years I had known him. I felt uneasy at once and thought that something must have happened to make him come to our house like this.

'Would you like some coffee, Ben?' I said, aware of him watching me from heavily lidded eyes as I walked over to the machine.

'No thanks.' He turned his gaze back to Liam and said, 'I've just come from Mum's. I understand congratulations are in order.'

Liam glanced at me, then said with a smile, 'That's right. Jaz and I are engaged. I wish Mum hadn't told you, though. I wanted to do it myself.'

'Huh,' Ben grunted and I could tell he'd already lost interest in the topic. He stood up and you would never have known from his movements that he was drunk as he picked up the bottle and replaced it neatly where he'd found it in the cupboard before glancing at me and saying, 'This is where it goes, isn't it, Jasmyn?'

'Yes,' I replied.

'It's in the right place?'

'Yes,' I said again.

'Good, I'm glad about that,' he said, sounding a little churlish

30

as he turned back around to Liam. 'I need to talk to you,' he said, 'about a business proposition.'

'Business proposition?' Liam repeated, instantly sounding wary. 'Ben, I don't have a lot of money. You know that.'

'You'll hear me out, though.' It sounded more like an order than a request. 'Besides, I need you to give me a ride home. I got a lift over here. My car's in the garage.'

He wouldn't be able to drive in his state anyway, I thought, a little resentfully. Who did he think he was, turning up like this and ordering Liam about in his own house? I even wondered if he was in some kind of trouble. After all, I had known Ben for a long time and I had never seen him like this before.

But Liam took him home and was gone for several hours. And when he got back he seemed to be in a cheerful enough mood and tried to brush over Ben's drunkenness, saying he was only a little put out because he couldn't find anyone to invest in a certain German business with him. Although that was the last time I ever saw the two of them in the same room together, I found it hard to believe that was what they'd fallen out about so irrevocably. Liam had seemed in a perfectly good mood when he got home and had told me that Ben wasn't overly upset about his refusal to get involved in the business venture, for he hadn't really expected anything else anyway. I thought that their argument must have occurred shortly afterwards but I couldn't be sure. The only time Liam had spoken to me about it was when I'd tried to talk him into inviting Ben to the family Christmas party last year.

'Can't you even tell me what the argument was about?' I'd asked. 'I can't believe it was really as bad as all that. I know he's quiet but he never seemed the malicious type to me and he is your brother—'

'Don't let him fool you!' Liam interrupted in an uncharacteristically sharp voice. 'He's clever, I'll give him that, but Ben's problem is that he's never cared about anyone but Ben!'

'What did he do?' I asked again.

But Liam just shrugged and said, 'Do me a favour, Jaz, and stop all this Ben talk. You know what he's like at parties, he'd only stand in the corner by himself looking miserable anyway.'

I giggled despite myself as Liam did a very accurate impression of the aloof, rather superior expression that Ben always seemed to wear whenever there were large numbers of people around. I dropped the subject, intending to work on him again later. I hadn't known then that my time with Liam was almost over.

I didn't have any contact details for Ben so I had to phone his parents to get his mobile number. His mother sounded surprised and asked why I wanted to get in touch with him, so I simply told her that I had been clearing out Liam's things and thought Ben might like to have some of them. She seemed oddly reluctant to give me his number but I got it from her in the end.

Throughout the day I left five messages asking him to call me back. On the sixth message I said I needed to talk to him about a man named Jaxon Thorpe.

He called me back within five minutes.

'Where did you hear that name?' Ben snapped without preamble as soon as I answered the phone.

'He came to my house this morning,' I replied, instantly feeling irritated by his tone.

'I beg your pardon?' he asked in a dangerously low voice, as if I had just said something disgusting.

'He came to the house,' I repeated. 'He wanted to see Liam. When I told him he was dead he assumed he'd been murdered. He even asked me if *you* were the one who'd done it! So can you please tell me what the hell is going on? How do you know that man?'

'He's ... he's an old friend of Liam's.'

'Old friend?' I repeated, somewhat shrilly. 'Old *friend*? Liam would never have been friends with someone like that. What about Adrian and Lukas?'

I heard Ben take a deep breath on the other end of the line. 'I have no idea,' he said. 'I've never heard those names before. Liam didn't seek my approval for every one of his many acquaintances.

He was a popular man. I don't know why you expect me to know who all his friends were.'

'But why did Jaxon Thorpe think that *you* might have—?' The words stuck in my throat and I found I was unable to finish the sentence.

'I'm sure he wasn't being serious when he said that,' Ben said impatiently. 'He was just referring to the argument we had. What else did he say?'

'When I told him Liam was dead he didn't believe me and forced his way into the house!' I said.

There was silence for a moment, but if I was expecting Ben to be loudly indignant and furious on my behalf I was sadly disappointed.

'And?' he prompted impatiently. 'What then?'

I sighed. 'He realised I was telling the truth and left. If you don't tell me what's going on I'm going to call the police.'

'And tell them what?'

I hesitated for, of course, this was the problem. What *could* I say?

'Do what you want, Jasmyn, but Jaxon doesn't even live in England. He's probably on his way back to America by now already.'

'How did he know Liam?'

'They met whilst Liam was in Munich researching the Swan King.'

'*Munich?* But what—'

'I have to go. I'm extremely busy. Don't worry about Jaxon Thorpe. The man's an idiot. I'm sure he won't bother you again.'

And then he hung up on me. I stared at the receiver still clutched in my hand, scarcely able to believe his rudeness. Ben had never been particularly chatty but at least he had always been polite to me before. I shook my head and replaced the receiver, Ben's words still echoing loudly in my mind ...

'*They met whilst Liam was in Munich researching the Swan King ...*'

It was true that just over a year ago Liam had toyed with the idea of writing a book about the legends and myths surrounding the Bavarian King Ludwig II – also known as the Swan King, the Fairy Tale King or the Mad King depending on which stories you chose to believe. But after some preliminary research he gave the idea up as he didn't feel there was enough material to write an entire book on it. But he had done all this research from home over the Internet. Liam and I had gone to Munich for a long weekend two years ago. We had loved the city and talked about going back one day. But as far as I knew Liam had not been back to Germany at all since then.

I picked up the phone and rang Ben straight back but all I got was the machine. So I turned on the computer in the living room and looked for Jaxon Thorpe. After a little searching, I found an American website for a photographer by that name and – after a brief hesitation – I called the mobile number that was listed, but it just rang out. I hung up feeling frustrated by the dead end but at the same time relieved that I hadn't had to talk to him again.

I made one last attempt to phone Ben about an hour later. This time the phone was answered straight away, but by a German woman whose voice I didn't recognise.

'Oh,' I said, wondering if I could have got the wrong number. 'Do you speak English?'

'Yes.'

'I'm looking for Ben Gracey?'

'May I ask who is calling?'

I could tell that she was young, and she spoke with only a very slight accent.

'It's Jasmyn. Jasmyn Gracey.'

'Wait a moment, please,' she said. 'I will go and find him.'

'Okay. Thanks.'

She was obviously on a wireless phone for I heard her go into another room and say, 'There's a woman called Jasmyn on the phone for you.'

Ben's muffled response made my blood boil. 'Tell her I'm not in.'

He spoke carelessly, as if it didn't matter at all to him whether I heard him speak or not.

'But, Ben—'

'I don't want to speak to her, Heidi!'

When the German woman came back onto the phone she at least had the grace to sound a little embarrassed as she said, 'I'm sorry but he is very busy right now. Shall I ask him to call you back?'

'Yes. Could you tell him it's important, please?' I said, trying not to sound too irritated for it was hardly her fault.

I hung up the phone feeling frustrated. I couldn't get hold of Ben, I couldn't get hold of Jaxon and they both lived far away in different countries. There was nothing for it – if turning up on his doorstep was what it would take to make Ben talk to me then so be it. I had no address for him so I phoned his mother once again to ask her for it.

'Why do you want it?' she demanded.

I started to make up some excuse about wanting to stay in contact but she cut me off dead. 'Look, Jasmyn,' she said coldly, 'I hate to say anything but … I really don't want you staying in touch with Ben. In fact I'd rather you didn't speak to him at all.'

'Why?' I asked in surprise. 'Has something happened?'

There was silence for a moment before she said with an air of only barely concealed impatience, 'Surely you must realise that things have changed now. None of us can go back to how things were. I want you to leave Ben alone. He's been through enough already.'

I gripped the phone numbly, hardly able to believe what I was hearing. I would have expected to slowly drift away a little from Liam's family now, but I had thought it would happen gradually over time. Liam had often told me that I was just imagining that his family disapproved of our marriage and I had tried desperately to believe him, but now it seemed that I had been right all along. I had never dreamed that they would cut me out in this way though. It was like being kicked in the stomach and new hurt blossomed painfully all the way through me.

'I'm ... I'm sorry I bothered you,' I stammered and then hung up before she had the chance to reply.

My hand shook a little on the phone and I cursed myself for being so meek. I should have said something – I should not have made it so easy for her. The hurt was suddenly replaced with anger and I seized the phone again, intending to call back and have a really vicious go at her. It would feel good to have an argument with someone, to vent some of the hurt and frustration ... But I paused in the act of dialling. I longed to shout at the woman for being so cruel but ... after all, she was Liam's mother. She had just lost one of her sons, so I supposed I couldn't blame her for lashing out at me. I did it myself all the time – lashing out blindly at my own family when all they were trying to do was help. I took a deep breath and forced myself to put down the phone. Screaming at her wouldn't do any good anyway.

I turned away from the desk and my eye fell on the wedding album I had moved to the coffee table last night. With everything else that had happened that morning I had forgotten all about it. I walked over, knelt down by the table and flipped the front cover open – doing it quickly, like pulling off a plaster, hoping against hope that last night had been ... last night ... and that everything was now back to normal.

But my heart sank as soon as I looked at the first photo for it was exactly the same, and when I flipped through the rest of the album I found that all the others were as well. Something had clearly been done to them. Someone had changed them, ruined them. In the light of day I could be calmer about it and see clearly that this was a trick. Suddenly I thought of Jaxon. He was a professional photographer and it occurred to me that he must be the one responsible. It was the only possible explanation. He had doctored these photos for some ungodly reason. He must have picked the lock, or found the spare key, and got into the house when I had been out food shopping, found the album, taken it away and then brought it back. It would have been difficult, of course, for he would have had a very small window of opportunity seeing as I rarely left the house and even then not for very long. But he must have waited patiently for his chance and that had to explain why I had had that sense of being watched in the months since Liam died. It had been Jaxon. He had probably been the man in the rain I had seen last night as well.

I reconsidered phoning the police but quickly abandoned the idea for I had no proof that Jaxon was the one responsible. I put my head in my hands and tried to think about what to do. I felt sure Jaxon must have been in the house whilst I'd been out, even though I didn't know how he'd done it or why. I hated the thought of a stranger rummaging around in my bedroom, going through my personal things. And if he'd done it before, who was to say that he might not do it again? I should never have thrown that stone at his car ...

I would have to get some sort of security system installed. But, in the meantime, I no longer felt safe and the thought of being in the house alone again at night frightened me. It was a horrible feeling because I wanted to be at home, in familiar surroundings, with all my own things ... but I was too scared to stay by myself and knew I wouldn't be able to sleep that night if I did.

Then I thought of Laura and her offer for me to go and stay with her in California and suddenly it was appealing. I could go far away from here and arrange for a new security system to be put in place whilst I was gone. My mother could oversee it and, by the time I got back, the house would be properly secured. I hadn't bothered to cancel the non-refundable plane ticket and Laura had made it quite clear that I could still come if I changed my mind. So I picked up the phone and called her.

5

Luke

As there was still a week to go until the California trip, I called my grandparents as soon as I got off the phone with Laura and asked if I could come and stay with them for a few days. I knew they would welcome me and I found I was suddenly desperate to get out of the house.

This was partly because of Jaxon and the fact that I no longer felt safe but it wasn't the only reason. I had simply had enough. It was too painful being at home without Liam – sitting on the couch where we had sat, eating alone in the dining room where we had eaten, sleeping in our double bed by myself, constantly reminded of him in every single room that we had decorated together.

What had at first seemed like a haven now felt like a terrible prison. I couldn't even begin to think what I would do with the room that had been his study. How could I possibly turn it into anything else now? I thought seriously about selling the house – buying something new, something smaller, and making a fresh start. In some ways the idea appealed to me but ... at the same time I revolted at the very thought. Partly because – although they tormented me – I couldn't bear to lose all the memories inside the house. To simply sell it to strangers and know other people were now living there, filling those rooms with their own things. To know that I couldn't go back even if I wanted to. Besides which, moving just seemed like too much effort. When I remembered how difficult it had been packing away Liam's clothes, the thought of having to go through every other item in the house, even the things still left in the attic – and then unpack them at the other end – was just too hard.

The post was a particular torment to me too for, of course, so many letters still came for him, even if most of them were nothing more than junk mail. I realised that I'd been opening my own letters and leaving Liam's on the table in the hall as I always used to do when he was away on one of his trips. Once I realised what I'd been doing I hated sorting through the post and would regularly leave it to pile up in an untidy heap on the doormat, too disheartened to go through it all.

The junk mail I threw away unopened, but when a letter arrived from a travel agency I opened it, thinking that it must be something to do with the California trip we had booked. But, to my surprise, the envelope contained one plane ticket to Munich for Liam on a flight leaving Gatwick at the end of December. And when I looked more closely at the letterhead, I realised that this was not even our usual travel agency but a different one. I phoned the number listed, thinking there must be some mistake, but the agent I spoke to was quite adamant. A plane ticket to Munich had been booked and paid for by Mr Liam Gracey just a week before his death. If there had been two tickets I would have assumed that Liam must have booked a surprise trip for us. But there was only one ticket and he had said nothing at all to me about booking it, said nothing about the fact that he would be away over New Year. And it was to Munich ... the city Ben had mentioned on the phone earlier ... Not booked through our normal travel agency ... The whole thing was extremely odd and made me feel a little uneasy. But I would never know, now, why Liam had bought the plane ticket, so I put it to one side and tried to forget about it as I drove to my grandparents'.

They lived in the country in a beautiful, large house and they had stables on their land. Although they were too old to do much riding themselves now, my grandfather adored horses and still showed them on occasion. I had gone there often whilst growing up and he had taught me to ride. He'd taught Liam too when we'd come here as children in the school holidays. Liam had been just as enthusiastic about riding as I was and would spend several hours a day on horseback – but without my grandfather he would never have been able to learn for it was simply too expensive and his family had never had much money.

I arrived mid-afternoon with my luggage and my violin case, feeling a little nervous. I'd been avoiding people for so long that I wasn't sure if I could handle being around them again even though – at the same time – I was sick of being alone. My grandmother tried to persuade me to have coffee and cake in the living room but, thankfully, my grandfather intervened and said that I must go down and get reacquainted with the horses first.

'Do you still have Mr Ed?' I asked, biting my lip in anxiety. If he told me they'd sold my favourite horse I was afraid I might start weeping like a child, but he just smiled and nodded.

'And Hemp too,' he said. 'We sold Ambrosia and Demmy but we still have Mr Ed, Hemp, Rumba and Polo. Enough to keep you busy, eh?'

I nodded, suddenly feeling I couldn't wait to get into the saddle. 'Do you think Gran will mind if I take Ed out for a ride now?' I asked.

'Of course not,' my grandfather replied. 'Take him out for a good long run and we'll have dinner waiting when you get back.'

I pulled riding boots on and went down to the stables, too impatient to change first. When I opened the door of the barn I was overwhelmed at once by the familiar smells – the sweet scent of hay mixed in with saddle soap and that distinctive horsey smell that instantly made me feel like I was eight years old again. Even after all those years it was still an ingrained habit of mine to move as quietly as possible around the stables in case I should see a faery again. I'd been no more than five years old but I still remembered it so clearly, like it was yesterday. I was not allowed in unsupervised at that age so was with my grandfather, standing on one of the mounting blocks and helping to groom the horses. After a while he picked me up off the block and sent me around to Bessie's stall next door to fetch the brush he'd left there. I went in, keeping to the walls to avoid the horse's back legs as I'd been taught.

And that was when I saw her. She was sitting on Bessie's shoulder, apparently making a tiny plait in the horse's mane. My mouth dropped open and I stood there staring, completely motionless. She was not quite like the faeries I had seen in books for her hair was ice blue in colour, falling loose about her perfect, elfin features; her wings were transparent and delicate, like woven strands of a spider's web; and her cyan blue dress was raggedy about the hem where it fell down to her tiny bare feet.

I didn't move, hardly even daring to breathe in case I scared her away. But she had seen me and leapt up into the air at once. I couldn't help it – a squeal of pure delight burst from my lips and when my grandfather rushed around into the stall to see if I'd hurt myself I pointed up at the faery fluttering about in the rafters.

She was up there for at least a minute and seemed to shine with a sort of white glow that made her easily visible, so I remember being frustrated with my grandfather who stared up stupidly in the wrong direction saying, 'Where? I can't see anything.'

'*There!*' I cried, tugging at his sleeve and pointing. 'There! She's right there!'

Then she flew out through the door and was gone. I showed my grandfather the tiny plait in Bessie's mane and for weeks afterwards I talked of nothing but the faery until my parents must have been sick of hearing about it. Of course, I told Liam all about her too and when he came to stay during the school holidays we would spend hours at a time sitting silently in the stable with the shuffling horses, hoping to catch a glimpse of another one. I had more patience for this game than Liam and if he spoke I would promptly shut him up with a sharp poke to the ribs lest his voice should frighten a faery away.

My grandfather encouraged my belief that faeries came to the stable sometimes and told me he'd seen the faery too but, years later, during one of my visits with Liam just before we got engaged, he admitted that he'd never seen a thing, for all that she had been right there, flying about in plain sight.

'I saw her,' I insisted. 'She was there.'

'Maybe she was,' he replied with an indulgent smile.

'He doesn't believe me,' I said to Liam when we were alone later on in the stable, saddling up to go out for a ride. 'No one does.'

'I believe you, Jaz,' he said with a smile, taking my hand and kissing the palm softly. 'If anyone could see faeries it would be you.'

There would certainly be no faeries in the stable today, however, for Ed was making far too much noise kicking his treat ball around in his box. They'd been bought for all the horses but Ed seemed to have been the only one smart, or greedy, enough to work out that if he kicked the ball, a treat would eventually fall out of one of the holes. The problem was that he didn't seem to understand the concept of the ball being empty and once the treats were all gone he would continue kicking the ball around for hours, getting more and more bad-tempered when no treat emerged to reward him. As I stopped at his box, a particularly savage kick sent the ball into the door hard enough to shake it on its hinges and Ed snorted irritably.

'Temper, temper,' I said with a smile.

The beautiful chestnut horse looked up at once, ears pricked forwards alertly and eyes as bright as I remembered them. Somehow I had almost expected him to be an old horse now – so much had happened since the day my grandfather had bought him and Liam and I had gone out riding him and Hemp. It felt like a hundred years ago to me. How odd that the rest of the world had stayed the same – it was only me who had changed.

I unlatched the door and stepped into the box and straight away Ed was pushing his velvety muzzle into my palm, looking for Polos.

'You greedy boy,' I smiled, running my hand down his nose. 'We haven't even got reacquainted yet.'

I took a mint from my pocket and held my hand out flat for him to take the sweet and crunch it between his large, yellow teeth.

'Liam died,' I said quietly. 'So he won't be coming out with us this time. But I'm going to ride you as often as I can whilst I'm here and we can still have fun even if it's just you and me, can't we, Ed? Although I suppose you won't talk to me.'

Mr Ed only talked to Liam. In fact, that was how he got his new name. It had originally been something else when my grandfather had bought him three years ago but then Liam and I had come to stay and minutes after our arrival we'd been taken into the stable to be introduced to him. And as soon as Liam began to talk, Ed started flapping his lips back from his teeth in that strange, comical way that horses sometimes do. We didn't realise at first that Ed was doing it in response to Liam's voice.

But then the two of us went riding along one of the bridle paths and, after a little while when we'd slowed down to a walk, we started to talk, and I noticed Ed moving his lips again. We stopped and Liam dismounted to adjust the bridle in case the bit was making him uncomfortable, and that was when I finally realised that the horse was reacting directly to Liam's voice and would only stop moving his mouth when Liam stopped talking. And the sight of it was so ridiculous that I had laughed until tears ran down my cheeks and my sides ached. It was lucky that Hemp automatically followed Ed when Liam got back in the saddle for I certainly wasn't telling him where to go. In fact I was so limp with laughter that I was only just holding on to the reins, which would have been unfortunate if something had spooked Hemp and he'd bolted. And every time Liam tried to speak to me he just made it worse, for then Ed would curl his lips back from his teeth, twitching and flapping them until Liam stopped talking.

Finally I stopped laughing – it was either that or suffocate – but the horse was Mr Ed from that day. It made my heart ache to think that I would never see that comical sight again. My grandfather had told me that Ed never spoke for anyone but my husband. For some reason the horse had taken a shine to him straight away, and Liam always rode Ed when we came here.

I wished we could have got back here just one more time before he died. The last visit had been before we were engaged. After our marriage we had moved house and I had been settling into my new job at the school and we had both been so busy. And every time I mentioned going to visit my grandparents Liam always seemed to have some reason he couldn't go. I had even wondered

43

briefly whether he was avoiding it deliberately but I couldn't really believe that was the case for we had always had so much fun there and Liam had loved my grandfather for teaching him to ride.

I fetched Ed's tack and as I was putting it on an idea occurred to me. I got out my mobile, rang my home number and put it on speakerphone so that Liam's voice on our answering machine came out. I hadn't been able to bring myself to change the message although I knew it made people uncomfortable to hear him when they rang, as if he was speaking from beyond the grave: '*You've reached Liam and Jasmyn. Sorry we can't come to the phone right now. Leave a message and we'll get back to you as soon as we can.*'

I just couldn't stomach the idea of recording it anew: '*You've reached Jasmyn ... Sorry I can't come to the phone right now ... Leave a message and I'll get back to you as soon as I can ...*'

I, I, I ... Who would have thought that a simple pronoun was capable of causing so much pain? The message started to play from my mobile but Liam's voice didn't sound the same coming out of such a small speaker and Ed did not react other than to gaze at me patiently until I flipped the mobile shut.

'I know. A voice on a machine isn't enough, is it?' I said, patting the horse's neck before grasping the reins and leading him outside where I pulled myself up into the saddle and we set off down one of the familiar bridle paths.

Ed was one of those horses who didn't like having to go at a sedate walk and I had to keep him on a tight rein until we reached open ground and I could finally give him his head. It had been a long time since I'd been on a horse and bitter experience had taught me that I should therefore keep this ride down to about half an hour, but I was enjoying myself too much to turn back.

My grandfather's land joined directly onto common forest, so we kept straight on when we reached the boundary. There were no people around, possibly because of the frosty weather, which was perfect for riding. Ed and I passed forest ponies and a couple of pigs rooting for truffles but there wasn't a car or a person insight – just rolling green countryside beneath a slate-grey sky.

After an hour and a half we reluctantly turned back. I would have gladly continued the ride. I felt almost content for the first time in ages. But the sky was starting to darken and I knew my grandmother would be getting dinner ready. It seemed terrible that I would rather be with Ed than with my grandparents, but the fact was that I didn't have to struggle to appear cheerful with him. And the horse acted exactly the same way around me as he always had with none of that all too familiar awkwardness or embarrassment that seemed to be all I'd seen in other people for months.

We had just turned back onto my grandfather's land when we rounded a corner in the path to find that it was blocked by a magnificent black horse. It was huge, even bigger than Ed. It wore no saddle or bridle but it was quite clearly a thoroughbred and – from the look of its glossy coat and beautiful physique – it must have been worth an absolute fortune. It stood completely motionless, the only movement coming from its dark mane and tail where they were tugged a little by the breeze. It stood in the very centre of the path looking straight in our direction as if it had been waiting for us.

But I only had a couple of seconds to take him in because, for some reason, this black horse spooked Ed, who reared up. Not expecting it – for Ed was usually so dependable – I almost fell off, but tightened my grip and tensed my stomach muscles just in time, leaning forwards and keeping hold of the reins so that when Ed bolted past the other horse and down the path, I just about managed to stay on his back.

I expected this sort of thing from Rumba, who would shy nervously if a twig snapped or a car horn went off in the distance, but I had never known Ed to be rattled before. The bridle path was a dangerous place to gallop because it was narrow and lined with trees that sometimes had low branches cutting across the path. I had to lean down close to Ed's neck and cling on as best I could to avoid a branch smacking into me and knocking me off altogether. Despite myself, I couldn't help enjoying it just a little. Although nowhere near Liam's level when it came to daredevilry, I had found it quite exciting being on a bolting horse on the two occasions that it had happened before, for all that it was dangerous ... But then perhaps that was simply because I had fallen prey to that common human delusion that nothing bad could ever possibly happen to *me* – that I was invincible and could not ever really be hurt, not seriously ... I couldn't have known it then but, before the year was out, I would learn just how untrue that belief actually was ...

When we finally broke out of the trees onto the three acres of lawn surrounding my grandparents' house, Ed finally allowed himself to be slowed down to a trot before coming to a stop outside the familiar stable, still snorting and stamping his hooves nervously. I eased myself upright and stroked his neck, talking softly and reassuringly to him until I could be sure he wasn't going to bolt again. Then I pulled my boots out of the stirrups to dismount, but when I slid off, my legs were so stiff from the long ride that I had to cling to the saddle to stop myself from crumpling to the ground as pain shot up my inner thighs, and I couldn't help but groan.

'Out of practice?' a voice behind me said.

I whipped my head around to see a man standing in the lit doorway of the stable, smiling at me. He was unusually tall – at least six foot eight – with brown hair and eyes. It was strangely difficult to judge his age. He could have been anything between twenty-five and thirty-five.

'It's been a while,' I admitted.

'You must be Jasmyn. I heard you were coming to stay.'

'Who are you?' I asked.

'I'm Luke – one of the stable-hands. I'll rub Ed down for you if you want to go up to the house?'

'Thanks,' I said, passing him the reins. 'There was a black horse–' I gestured vaguely back towards the bridle path '–wandering about loose—'

'That was probably Kini,' Luke interrupted. 'Don't worry, he knows his way back.'

I stared at him in confusion for a moment, then shook my head, 'What do you mean, he knows his way back? Who does that horse belong to?'

'He's mine. Your grandfather lets me stable him here. It's just that he doesn't much like being inside, you see.'

'But what the hell are you thinking, letting him wander around loose like that? The garden isn't secure – he could get out onto the road or he could be stolen or anything!'

Luke frowned faintly for a moment before saying, 'You're right. I suppose I'd better go and find him. I'll do it as soon as I've finished with Ed.'

'Good luck,' I said, aware that I sounded frosty. 'There's a huge amount of ground to cover and it's starting to get dark.'

'Oh, I can always find Kini when I want him,' Luke replied with a smile. And then he turned away and led Ed into the stable.

He hadn't seemed particularly offended but privately he probably resented me for telling him how to look after his own horse. I knew how I must appear – the hoity-toity granddaughter of the rich old man. It was just that Kini had been the most beautiful animal and I hated the thought that something might happen to him. If anyone who knew anything about horses saw him they would recognise what a fine beast he was and might be tempted to steal him, and I knew that my grandfather would have a fit if he knew.

I walked back to the house with just enough time before dinner for a hot bath to ease my aching muscles. At least now I knew where the horse had come from. The way we had come across him so suddenly and the strange way Ed had reacted to him might have made me feel a little uneasy otherwise …

I hesitated to say anything to my grandparents that evening about what had happened for I didn't want to get Luke into trouble or, even worse, to lose him his job. So I didn't mention him or his horse, deciding instead to check whether Kini was safe the next morning myself.

The meal was a pleasant one and making conversation was much easier than I had expected. It was nice to be looked after just like when I'd been a child – to be in a safe, familiar place that had always seemed somewhat detached from the real world, out in the peace of the countryside. The only thing about the evening that upset me was that I noticed my grandfather seemed to have aged since I'd last seen him. He was starting to forget things and sometimes he got names mixed up as well. It shouldn't have been a galloping shock – after all, he was almost eighty now, although he didn't look it. But after everything that had happened recently, I didn't think I could cope with losing anybody else any time soon.

When he asked if I wanted a drink early in the evening but then forgot to bring me one, I didn't think too much of it. Then, a little later, when we were all sitting around the table, he asked how Harry was. It took me a moment to realise who he was talking about, for Harry was the dog I'd had at home who'd died five years ago now. Then when we started talking about the horses, he said something about the funny way Ed always used to talk for Ben. I didn't have the heart to correct him and neither, it seemed, did my grandmother, who hurriedly changed the subject. When I mentioned it to her later on when we were alone in the kitchen she sighed and said, 'It's not too bad. It's just the odd thing he forgets or mixes up. These things happen as you get older.'

I nodded dumbly, feeling fresh fear squeeze round my heart – as well as guilt over not coming to visit them for so long. From now on I would make an effort to come and see them more regularly, for who knew how much time together we might have left? And I didn't want to waste a single moment of it.

When I went down to the stables early the next morning, I found that Luke had done a beautiful job of rubbing down Ed and had left him with plenty of fresh hay. But there was no sign of Kini. I checked the paddock, remembering what Luke had said about his horse not liking it inside. But the field was empty. So when I went back to the house for breakfast, I reluctantly brought the subject up. 'I think you need to talk to Luke about his horse.'

My grandfather looked at me as if I was talking in a foreign language. 'Luke?' he said blankly.

At first I thought he was having one of his forgetful moments, so I swallowed and tried again, 'You know – one of the men who looks after the horses. He said his stallion doesn't like being kept inside so he's been letting him roam around the garden loose.'

'Jasmyn, I have no idea what you're talking about,' my grandfather replied. 'Larry and Calum look after the horses. I've never heard of anyone called Luke.'

'But he was there in the stable,' I said. 'He has this beautiful black horse called Kini. You must have seen him.'

I could believe that my grandfather might have forgotten Luke but it seemed very odd that he would forget such a remarkable horse. Then my grandmother came in carrying a plate piled high with toast. I asked her, but she, too, was quite adamant on the point – there was no stable-hand called Luke and there never had been.

6

Mischief-Maker

My grandparents were very upset about the incident and my grandfather rushed straight down to the stables to check on the horses himself whilst my grandmother called the police. Everyone seemed to assume Luke must have been a thief and that he had simply been caught off guard by my timely return with Ed.

But I knew that couldn't be true. It didn't make sense given our conversation. Luke had addressed me by name. And he had rubbed Ed down and looked after him as he'd said he was going to. If he'd been a horse thief, he would have simply taken Ed. I had handed him over fully tacked up and it would have been painfully easy to just lead him away.

I had to give a description of Luke to the police and everyone seemed pleased by his unusual height, for that would make him stand out in a crowd and it wasn't as if it were a feature he could do much to disguise. I also had to describe Kini in case he was a horse Luke had already stolen. But there turned out to be no reported thefts of a horse matching Kini's description. Besides which, if Luke really had gone to all the trouble of stealing him from someone else, he would have to be an exceptionally incompetent thief to then allow the horse to escape whilst attempting to steal another.

None of it added up but I didn't point this out to my grandparents for they were already very upset about it all. My grandfather lost no time in increasing the security in the stable and putting surveillance cameras around the boundary of his land. At the end of my week with them there had been no further sign of Luke, and things had settled down a little by the time I left. As I drove home, I worried about whether I should have told them – or the police – my belief that Luke hadn't been there to steal the horses at all but that he had been there watching me – just as Jaxon Thorpe had been watching me at home. Of course, Jaxon had denied being the man standing in the rain outside my house that night and now the thought occurred to me that perhaps it had been Luke beneath that hood … And now that my thoughts returned to Jaxon, I remembered one of the names he had thrown at me in my bedroom – Lukas – and the similarity seemed too big a coincidence to ignore. Surely they must know each other, they had both known Liam and now they were both watching me. And I couldn't even begin to imagine why.

I hesitated to phone the police because it all sounded so hazy and melodramatic and I was worried that they might believe it was all in my head – that I was making too much of a big deal over a couple of chance meetings with strangers. During the drive home I managed to convince myself to leave things as they were for now. I was only stopping at the house to pack anyway and then I was going to an airport hotel ready for my flight to California the next morning. I had arranged for a new security system to be fitted in a couple of days and my mother had agreed to come round to oversee it.

But everything changed when I arrived home. Its appearance was deceptive from the outside for there were no broken windows and the door was not open. But it was unlocked and that was the first thing that alerted me to the fact that something was wrong. And as soon as I walked in, dragging my case behind me, I saw that somebody had ransacked my house from top to bottom.

Every drawer, cupboard, desk and bookcase had been emptied, the contents strewn about the floor. The mattress had been cut open and the stuffing pulled out. The same thing had happened to the couch and the armchairs in the living room. Every single carpet had been ripped out, rolled up and shoved into a corner; the chimney had been unblocked and the desk in Liam's study had been completely taken apart, piece by piece.

At first I simply couldn't believe what I was seeing. I picked my way through the wreckage, numbly checking every room. The sense of violation I had felt at the idea of Jaxon sneaking into my house to do something to my wedding photos had been nothing compared to this. Finally I went outside and called my mother and when she arrived I burst into tears, feeling desperately sorry for myself.

'I just wish that something good would happen!' I sobbed. Recently it seemed to have been one relentless blow after another and I didn't think I could face any more of it. My mother called the police and, this time, I told them everything I knew about Jaxon Thorpe and Luke and my sense of being watched, no longer caring if I sounded paranoid or hysterical.

I spent the rest of the day with my mother, wearily making a start on the huge mess in the house. We spent hours on it but still weren't even halfway through by the end of the day. As far as I could tell, nothing had been stolen. Certainly nothing valuable had been taken. We found all the jewellery Liam had given me scattered about in the bedroom. The plasma TV was still there, as was the CD player and the computer and my laptop and all the other expensive things that would usually go in a robbery.

The police said either the perpetrator had been looking for something or they had simply been trying to make mischief. As it seemed highly unlikely that either Liam or I had ever owned anything that warranted that sort of desperate searching, the police said it was probably the latter explanation. Someone had picked my house at random. I had just been unlucky. None of the neighbours had seen or heard anything, so the vandalism must have been carried out during the day when everyone was at work.

The police asked if I could cancel or postpone my trip to California until all of this was sorted out but I wailed pathetically into my tissue that I couldn't get a refund on the plane ticket; that my husband was dead; that all I wanted to do was go to America and see my friend. I must have been a dreadful sight but I didn't care how I looked at that moment and the embarrassed policemen said hurriedly that if the trip was that important to me then it was best I should go. After all, nothing had been taken, there were no obvious leads to follow and my new security system was to be put in next week. They were clearly profoundly relieved to get away and leave me to the care of my mother, with promises to be in contact if they should find whoever was responsible.

I emptied the suitcase I'd taken to my grandparents and then filled it with clean clothes, which I seized at random from the floor. I hated the thought that someone I didn't know had touched them and, if I'd had the money, I would have thrown them away and bought new ones. Anyone could have broken into my house but, somehow, I couldn't help thinking that it must have been Jaxon. After all, I was almost sure he was responsible for the doctored wedding photos. Perhaps he'd just wanted to get his own back for the stone through his car window.

I spent the night at my parents' house and my father drove me to the airport the next morning.

'I know it's hard, Jaz,' he said when he dropped me off, 'but just try to enjoy yourself, okay? And by the time you get back your house will be as good as new.'

'Don't let Mum spend too much money,' I said.

The day before, my mother had hinted at finding some new furniture for me. I knew it was hard on her, seeing me go through all this. I knew that she wanted to put everything right and so was likely to go out and spend more money than she should. But my father dismissed my concern with a wave of his hand. 'You'd better go,' he said with a smile.

I hugged him, waved as he drove away and then went into the airport. It didn't occur to me until then that I had never travelled abroad on my own before. Not once. There had been holidays with my parents and friends and then there had been holidays with Liam. I checked in and then went through to departures where I hesitated. I was hungry. But when my eyes fell on Garfunkel's I cringed at the thought of going inside. Whenever Liam and I had been at the airport about to go on holiday we had always started with a fried breakfast at Garfunkel's. The thought made me lose my appetite, so I bought a coffee to drink instead whilst I waited for my gate number to appear on the screens.

I was being stared at. It was not my hair that was the problem so much as my white skin and pale eyes. People found them creepy, especially children who didn't know what albinism was. My appearance had always set me apart from everyone else. I held my violin closer – feeling a little less lonely because it was there – its presence warm and familiar like an old friend. It hadn't occurred to me not to bring it. Leaving it at home would have been like leaving a child behind. I was only glad that it had been with me at my grandparents' when the house had been broken into for I would have been beside myself if something had happened to it. It was precious to me and there could be no replacing it.

As I hunched self-consciously over the paper cup of coffee, one arm draped round the violin case, I wondered if I should get my hair cut so it wouldn't be quite so obvious. I had only kept it long because Liam liked it that way. When we lay in bed at night he would run his fingers through it, splaying it out on the pillow in the silver moonlight as he told me how beautiful I was. I could always believe it when Liam said it. When my mother had said it, or my father, in a desperate attempt to make me feel less like an alienated freak, I would cringe at words that seemed to bite mockingly into me.

With Liam, not only did he find me attractive himself, but it simply didn't seem to occur to him that other people might not see me that way – that they might find my white skin ghostly and my blue eyes cold. When he touched me, when his hands ran over my body, I found that I didn't cringe within my own skin any more. I loved my white hair because he did. To Liam my appearance made me special, made me unique, made me beautiful in a way that other women could never be.

I should have known as I lay there warm and safe in his arms that it was all too good to be true. With Liam gone I found it almost impossible to see myself that way any more. It was like a dream I could only barely remember. Now I was just a freak to be pointed at.

A great wave of aching longing rose up in me once again and this time I had to fight hard to thrust it back down. The bustling airport around me was filled with families and couples about to go on holiday. It seemed that I was the only person in the whole building who was there on my own. Liam should be here with me ... we should be sitting together in Garfunkel's having a fried breakfast as we always did, talking, laughing ... I should not be here alone preparing to go and visit Laura by myself, leaving his unused plane ticket tucked away in an envelope on the mantelpiece at home. And once again I was swept with this desperate yearning for things to be other than the way they were.

The flight seemed to drag on so much longer without anyone to talk to. I couldn't even sleep for I was used to leaning my head against Liam's shoulder when I got tired on planes. On my own, the hours crawled by excruciatingly, torturously slowly.

After the eleven-hour flight I was glad to be off the plane, stretching my legs and breathing normal air. I collected my luggage and then went through to arrivals where Laura was waiting for me. We were complete opposites physically. Laura had gorgeous chocolate-coloured skin in contrast to my own ghostly white complexion. Her eyes were a warm brown where mine were a cold blue. And she was so petite that the top of her head only just came up to my chin when she hugged me.

'Sweetie, I'm so glad you came,' she said, squeezing me tight.

To my relief she didn't say anything about my being alone. She didn't ask me how I was or whether I was coping. She didn't say she was sorry about Liam or any of the other things people usually said to me. It wasn't their fault. Those were the things you said to someone who had suffered a bereavement. It was polite and it was good manners. You didn't just pass over the fact that someone had died. But Laura had been friends with both of us and so she didn't need to say all the things I knew she felt.

Instead she tucked her arm through mine and led me out to her parked car. I had decided not to mention the break-in to her because if she knew about all the misfortunes I had suffered recently, it would make it harder for me to put up a cheerful facade. But now that I'd seen her it didn't feel quite so much like a facade and, for the first time since I'd got up that morning, I felt like I was on holiday.

It was almost 10 o'clock at night local time and Laura insisted on stopping at a diner on the way back to her house for coffee and doughnuts.

'You've lost weight, haven't you?' she said in the first reference she'd made to Liam's death since I arrived.

I shrugged it off and, to my relief, she dropped it, for I was already fed up with being pestered about this by the rest of my family. We sat on red and white striped vinyl seats in one of the booths, ate doughnuts and talked as if we'd never been apart. I hadn't realised quite how much I'd missed Laura until that moment and it felt wonderful to be with her again. Her house was only a few minutes' drive from the diner. When we got there she gave me a tour – it was small but beautifully decorated. There was one spare bedroom with a large, comfortable double bed covered in crisp, white sheets that smelled of freshly done laundry.

When Laura said goodnight and left me in the room alone, I tried not to dwell on the bed and the fact that I was going to be the only one in it. Instead I took out the framed photo of Liam I had brought from home to put on the dressing table and then went into the bathroom to brush my teeth. When I came back and pulled my pyjamas out of the case, something metal and black fell out with them and I bent down to pick it up, realising that it was the little knight I had found with Liam's things. It must have got caught up with the clothes on the floor in my bedroom. I set it down on the bedside table beside the framed photo. The fact that it had been in Liam's pocket when he died made me feel oddly attached to it despite the nail some kid had shoved through its helmet.

As I got into bed I promised myself that I was going to make the most of this trip and not dwell on what had happened at home. For now, at least, I was far away from it all – far enough away from both Jaxon and Luke that for the first time in a long while I actually felt safe.

7

Bones and Roses

Over the next week Laura and I went shopping and sightseeing and out to coffee houses and wine bars. She had taken the time off from work to be with me and at the end of the week, Laura said she had arranged for us to go and eat on the *Queen Mary* with Charlie, the new boyfriend she wanted me to meet. I did not feel at all comfortable about doing this. Being with Laura was one thing, but this man was a stranger to me and the last thing I felt like doing was making conversation with someone I hardly knew. Besides which it was bound to be awkward. Liam's death was still so recent that this man wouldn't know what to say to me either. In fact he was probably dreading it as much as I was.

But it was clearly important to Laura that I meet him and so I really didn't have any choice – I couldn't voice my recent insecurities and antisocial feelings without sounding childish. I hadn't brought any posh clothes with me so, as there was a dress code for dinner aboard the ship, Laura said that this gave us an excuse to shop for something to wear and, somehow, she managed to talk me into buying a long, dark-blue velvet dress. Usually I tried to avoid dark colours because they clashed so horribly with my freakish skin but Laura insisted I try it on.

'I can't wear this,' I said, staring at myself in the mirror in the changing rooms. 'It makes me look even whiter than I am.'

'Rubbish. It's stunning on you.'

'People will stare.'

'You look beautiful in it,' Laura said, 'so of course they'll stare.'

I glanced at my reflection again and failed to suppress the cringe. 'I look ghastly,' I mumbled, already fumbling to undo the zip.

But Laura reached out her hand to stop me.

'How can you not see how lovely you look in that? You'd have worn it if you'd been going out with Liam,' she said quietly. 'Wouldn't you?'

'He made me forget I was ugly,' I said.

'No, he made you see that you're beautiful,' she replied sharply. 'That dress is striking on you. It's more striking on you than it would be on anyone else. You know how you look in it, don't you?'

I bit back the obvious range of sarcastic responses that rose in my throat and said nothing.

'You look like a snow princess,' Laura said, echoing what she knew to be the first compliment anyone had ever paid my albinism.

As an only child who had spent most of the time with her doting parents, I was unprepared for the cold shock of the other children's reactions to me when I first started school and was horrified to see them pointing and asking their mothers:

'*Is that girl a ghost, Mummy? Is she?*'

Being an albino did not do anything for first impressions. At lunchtime everyone ran outside to play noisy, energetic games but I stayed in the arch of the doorway, sitting against the wall with my knees drawn up to my chin trying to be invisible. A couple of children ran past yelling, '*Ghost!*' at one point but soon forgot me and went back to playing with the others. I was utterly miserable. I missed my home, I missed my mother and I missed my dog. I hated this school place and all the people in it.

And then a ball rolled into the archway, stopping right next to my feet. I picked it up hurriedly with the intention of throwing it back out to the playground before anyone could come looking for it, but it was too late. Running feet skidded to a halt before the entrance right in front of me. They were boy's shoes, scuffed on the toes and with the laces half-undone. Without looking up I held the ball in the air, hoping he would just take it without

58

laughing at my appearance or making some cruel joke or asking me if I was a ghost.

'Thanks,' he said, taking the ball from my hand.

I expected him to leave now that he had his ball back but instead he stayed in front of me, bouncing it on the tarmac beside him. After a few moments I glanced up but he was looking right at me so I ducked my head again hurriedly.

'What's your name?' he asked at last.

'Jasmyn,' I said, the word coming out as barely more than a whisper.

He was silent for a moment before saying, 'Are you a snow princess?'

I looked up at him in surprise, forgetting to be ashamed of my appearance for a moment. 'Snow princess?' I repeated. 'I ... don't know.'

'I think you are,' he decided. He then promptly sat down cross-legged and rolled the ball towards me. It didn't seem to occur to him that I would do anything other than roll it back so I tentatively did so, half-thinking that this might be some new trick to make me feel small and worthless. We rolled the ball back and forth to each other across the tarmac until the bell rang to signal the end of break. Then we both stood up and I handed the ball back to him.

'Thanks,' he said, thrusting it into the pocket of his shorts. Then he said, 'Do you want to play again at lunchtime?'

I nodded shyly, a tiny glow of happiness – and relief – fluttering in my stomach at the thought of having someone to spend the lunch break with. He grinned at me and said, 'I'll bring the ball.' As he turned towards the doors, he added over his shoulder, 'My name's Liam.'

Right from the beginning, he saw me differently from everyone else. I was never a freak to him. I swallowed the lump that rose in my throat and looked in the mirror once again. Something shifted and suddenly – for a brief moment – I didn't see a white, freakish misfit standing in the glass before me. Instead I saw a tall, slender woman with flawless pale skin – smooth and perfect, like alabaster; straight white hair cascading down her shoulders and cool blue eyes set in a face with high cheekbones. The dark-blue velvet dress complimented her white skin dramatically, as if blue blood coursed through her veins and she really was a princess from some mythical winter wonderland who lived in a palace made of ice and snow ...

Then the image was gone – like an optical illusion I had clutched at just for a moment – and all I saw was myself in the mirror. But I knew that Laura was right, and the image I'd seen for a moment was exactly how Liam would have seen me in this dress. So I bought it, feeling like I was doing it for him as much as for me.

As I was getting changed into it in Laura's guest room that evening, my mobile went. I could see from the caller ID that it was Ben.

'Where are you?' he asked abruptly as soon as I answered.

'I'm in California,' I replied.

'Yes, I know. But where *exactly* are you?'

'In Anaheim staying with a friend.' Then I remembered that Ben knew her too, for I had met her through the Gracey family, and added, 'I'm with Laura. How do you know I'm in California?'

'I ... your mother told me when she rang.'

'Why did she ring you?' I asked, my eyes narrowing suspiciously.

'Have you found Jaxon yet?' he said, ignoring my question.

I frowned and said nothing, trying to work out what on earth he was talking about.

'That's why you're in California, isn't it?' Ben demanded. 'To talk to him?'

I opened my mouth to say that this holiday with Laura had been booked long before Liam's death but then I hesitated, remembering what Ben had said about Jaxon living in America, and I wondered if he was anywhere near California. It occurred to me then that if Ben thought I was talking to Jaxon, he might unwittingly tell me why the photographer had acted the way he had when he'd come to my house.

'You didn't return my calls,' I said evasively. 'And your mother wouldn't give me your address. I had no way of getting hold of you.'

Ben took a deep breath and I heard the irritation in his voice when he spoke. 'I don't know why the hell she didn't give you my address. She's very upset right now – I don't think she knows what she's doing half the time. Why haven't you had your phone on? I've been trying to get hold of you all week.'

'I didn't feel like talking to anyone,' I said rather coldly, for I was starting to feel quite irritated by his tone.

'All right, well, at least I've got hold of you now. Jasmyn, I forbid you to try and contact Jaxon.'

My breath came out in an incredulous snort. 'Piss off!' I snapped. 'You can't forbid me to do anything whatsoever! I haven't spoken to Jaxon yet but if you refuse to tell me what he meant when he came to my house then I don't see that I've got much choice but to look him up myself whilst I'm here.' I had no intention of doing anything of the sort. I didn't know if Jaxon had been the one who broke into my house when I was away or not but he had frightened me before. I'd given his name to the police and had no wish ever to see him again. But Ben wasn't to know that.

'Listen to me, Jasmyn, and listen very carefully. Jaxon Thorpe is a dangerous man. The photography thing is just a front. He's a career criminal. A thief and a blackmailer. The police arrested him a few years ago for beating a man almost to death behind a pub but he wasn't prosecuted because of lack of evidence. The sole witness suddenly changed his mind, for no apparent reason, and was not prepared to testify. I wouldn't have told you any of this if I didn't have to. I didn't want to scare you but you've given me no choice.'

For a moment I was silent, filled with horror at what Ben was telling me for I had never dreamt that Jaxon was as dangerous as that. And to think he'd been in my *house* ...

'Jasmyn?' Ben said. 'Are you still there?'

'Yes. Look, Ben, the only reason I came out here was to have a holiday with Laura. I never had any intention of trying to find

Jaxon. But before I left home, someone ... someone broke into my house—'

'I know. Your mother told me. It must have been him.'

'But I've got nothing that valuable to steal,' I said. 'Besides, nothing was taken, the place was just ransacked.'

'That's because he was looking for—' Ben broke off, then said, 'Look, we really need to talk face to face.'

'Face to face?' I repeated. 'Are you going to be in England again soon, then?'

'No, but I'm in California right now. I came as soon as I heard you were here.'

'*What?*' I gasped, hardly able to believe that he really was so close when a moment ago I'd thought he was half the world away in Germany. 'Why?'

'To keep you away from Jaxon Thorpe, of course,' he said irritably. 'Up until now I haven't been able to get you on the phone. I didn't know what else to do other than come out here and put you on the next flight home myself.'

His patronising tone aside, I couldn't help feeling just a little touched that he had spent the time and money to drop everything and come all the way to America to warn me and I felt a little burst of warmth towards Ben in that moment ... but he deftly ruined all that with what he said next.

'Meet me tonight,' he ordered brusquely.

'Tonight? Why? I've already told you I'm not going to look for Jaxon.'

'This isn't just about Jaxon,' Ben replied impatiently. 'I need to ... there's something I have to ask you.'

'Can't you just ask me now? On the phone? I can't meet you later, Ben, I'm just about to go to the *Queen Mary* for dinner.'

'This is about Liam,' Ben said stonily. 'And it's important. Your dinner plans aside, I would have thought you might have taken an interest in the matter.'

My hand gripped tighter around the phone as anger rose up in my chest and I silently cursed him and his heartless tongue. The truth was that every time I came close to enjoying myself I felt guilty, as if I was being grossly disrespectful to Liam somehow – as if I shouldn't be able to be cheerful, or even to fake cheerfulness, when such a horrible thing had happened. Then I would become miserable and no doubt depress everyone who was around me as well. But the way Ben spoke was as if he believed I'd been out living the high life every night since Liam died. Like I didn't miss him or even notice that he wasn't there any more. Like I didn't have to struggle desperately to appear normal every second of every minute that I was around other people. In Ben's eyes I was sure all he saw was me swanning off to America for shopping and expensive meals and sightseeing, with Liam not yet cold in his grave, but the truth of it was that any pleasure I'd got from the trip I already felt guilty over – even without Ben condemning me for it.

'Of course I'm interested,' I said through gritted teeth, trying to keep my voice level and determined not to give him the satisfaction of knowing that he'd touched a nerve. 'But I can't just cancel on Laura when we're minutes away from leaving the house. I've been her guest all week and she really wants me to meet her boyfriend, so I have to—'

'All right, all right, I'll meet you at the *Queen Mary*, then,' Ben replied. 'At midnight up on deck at the prow. You can manage that, can't you?' he said in the tone of voice usually reserved for dealing with impossible people.

'Yes.' I sighed. Dinner would be over by then and we would likely have moved on to the bar for an after-dinner drink. I would just have to excuse myself halfway through to go and talk with my brother-in-law.

'Good. I'll see you then,' Ben said. And before I could say another word, the rude bastard hung up on me and I felt all the earlier warmth melting away. He hadn't travelled to America to look out for me. He'd come because he wanted something and I could no more say no to him than I could stop missing Liam, for if this was anything to do with my husband then I had to know about it. I had to prod the bruise and pick the scab and pour more salt into the open wound by meeting Ben and listening to what he had to say ...

I told Laura about the phone call as we drove to pick her boyfriend up, explaining that I would have to go and talk to Ben once we had finished dinner. I was sketchy with the details as I was reluctant even to mention Jaxon Thorpe to her. I hadn't said anything about the swans or the wedding photos or my nightmares or the break-in. I wanted her to think that everything was normal. *I* wanted to think that everything was normal and if Laura started exclaiming in surprise about Jaxon and the other things, it would only make me feel even worse than I already did.

As it happened, she made me feel worse anyway when she said, 'I always did like Ben. I imagine all this must be terribly difficult for him.'

'Why the hell does everybody keep saying that?' I exclaimed in frustration. 'It's no more difficult for Ben than it is for anybody else! This isn't easy for anyone!'

'Of course it isn't, hun, but ... well, the circumstances are different for him, aren't they? I mean, there was all that upset last year and he wasn't on good terms with Liam when he died ... '

She trailed off into silence, no doubt because of the look on my face. I bit my tongue and said nothing. I didn't want to take my worry and anxiety out on Laura and I could sense how easily I might start an argument with somebody in my current mood. But the fact was that if Ben had wanted to make up with Liam then he had had nearly a whole year to do so.

The *Queen Mary* was beautiful – over seventy years old, yet inside she was all gleaming brass and polished wood and the Sir Winston restaurant was stylish, sophisticated and elegant, reeking of 1930s glamour with men dining in suits and women in long dresses. I was too distracted to feel self-conscious in my own dress even though I was aware of turning peoples' heads. Laura's boyfriend, Charlie, was surprisingly easy to talk to and I'm sure that, had the circumstances been different, I would have enjoyed myself immensely. As it was I had to resist the urge to look at my watch every five minutes for I felt so on edge with anticipation about my upcoming meeting with Ben that I could barely eat. He would hardly have come all the way to California to find me if it wasn't important. Whilst forcing the food into my mouth, I tried to comfort myself with the thought that nothing Ben could say would make Liam any more dead than he already was.

We finished the meal and moved on to the bar. Finally it was quarter to twelve and I was able to excuse myself and go up on deck. Ben hadn't arrived yet and there was no one else around either. It was icy cold and there was a bitter wind blowing in from the sea. It seemed that everyone had been driven below deck into the warmth and the light and the noise. But I hardly felt the cold as I stood at the railing looking out across the dark ocean. Perhaps there was a bit of snow princess in me after all. Up there it was silent. And in that silence Jaxon's voice filled my mind once again … *'If the bastard's dead then why are all his clothes in—'* … and then stopping short at the realisation that none of Liam's clothes were in the wardrobe any more.

'Are you sure *he's dead?'* Jaxon had croaked in a voice that was strained with anger rather than grief.

Yes. I'm quite sure. Can't you see the huge gaping hole where my heart used to be?

I turned away from the railing and started to walk back across the deck towards the wooden bench I had seen, my heels echoing in the brittle silence and my velvet dress tugged back by the arctic breeze. When I was about halfway across the wooden boards, a single black feather fluttered down from the dark sky to land on the ground before me. I stopped and picked it up, only now realising, as I held it, the stark similarity between the deck of this majestic old ship and the one in my nightmare where I'd twirled about as hundreds of swan feathers fell from the sky like dark snow around me.

I tried to tell myself that it was my mind filling in the blanks of the dream with the *Queen Mary*'s appearance. And anyway, only one feather had fallen down now, not hundreds. It probably wasn't even a swan feather at all, I thought as I ran my fingers over it. It was silky smooth and seemed very large and blacker than night itself against my white hands. My mother had told me when I was a child that any stray feathers I found were from angels' wings, not from birds'. But those feathers had been white, not devilish black things like this. I felt a great surge of dread and let the wind tug the feather from my fingers, fluttering across the deck and over the railing to land in the cold sea so many feet below. Then I turned towards the bench.

But as I did so, a sound from the prow of the ship caught my attention and I turned back. The deck was only softly lit but I could see a huge shape moving out of the darkness towards me, far too big to be a man. I recognised the distinctive clip-clop of hooves and then a black stallion came out into the light. It was huge and beautiful, snorting in the frosty air and stamping at the wooden deck agitatedly with its shiny black hooves. There was a scattering of snowflakes across its back and shoulders and clinging to its glossy mane and tail. In every way it looked identical to Kini – the horse I had seen back on my grandparents' estate.

I couldn't think how it had come to be there on the deck of the *Queen Mary* and for a moment I stood transfixed, wondering if I should go downstairs and tell someone or if I should try to approach it myself to calm it down. But the next moment I heard the door open behind me, startling the horse into taking a few frisky steps back. I looked around and saw Ben on the deck, staring at the stallion.

'There's a—' I began, but Ben cut me off.

'Don't move,' he ordered, in a low, quiet voice.

He walked very slowly towards me, keeping his eyes on the horse, which had now broken into a trot, going round the deck in agitated circles.

'Where did it come from?' I whispered as Ben stopped at my side.

'The same place the black swans came from, I expect,' he muttered.

Snorting clouds of mist into the freezing air, the handsome stallion broke into a canter, large hooves thundering on the wooden deck. Its mane and tail streaming out behind it as Ben and I pressed ourselves back against the wall. Then, to my horror, it headed straight towards the sea-facing side of the ship and cleared the railing in one jump. I ran to the side as fast as my high heels would allow, appalled at the idea of the black horse falling down into the ocean below. But the expected splash never came. I gripped the icy railing and leaned out over the water, my eyes searching the darkness for any sign of a horse struggling in the water below.

'I can't see it, can you?' I asked Ben who was also at the railing, gazing down.

'No,' he muttered. 'It's gone.'

'Gone *where*?' I asked, turning from the rails to stare at him.

He hesitated, then said flatly, 'I think Liam may have … been involved in some dark things before he died.'

'Like what? If you know something, then for God's sake tell me!'

'I *know* very little,' Ben replied. 'Mostly I just suspect.'

'Well, I know nothing,' I said – and that one word went right through me like a knife. I was his wife and I knew *nothing*. 'So tell me what you *suspect*.'

Ben sighed. 'All right. Let's go inside.'

We turned away from the railing and both stopped short simultaneously. The deck that had been clean mere moments ago was now scattered with human bones. It would have been easier to pretend they were animal if it hadn't been for the five or six obviously human skulls all staring right at us.

'Oh my God,' I muttered. 'How did they get here?'

'Let's just get inside,' Ben said.

Without waiting for me, he started picking his way across the deck. I hurried after him, through the grinning skulls. When I caught up with him at the door I grabbed his arm to stop him walking through it and said, 'Are we just going to *leave* these bones here?'

'They've already gone,' Ben replied.

I looked back over my shoulder and was startled to see that he was right. The deck was completely clear but for a chalky film of dust across the wooden planks where the bones had been just seconds earlier. And one dark flower – looking rather lost and forlorn in the middle of the huge deck.

'What is that?' I said.

'What?' Ben replied.

I released his arm and walked towards it, quite sure that it had not been there before. When I picked it up I saw that it was a black rose – long-stemmed and beautiful … but I couldn't help seeing it as sinister when it had been left behind by a pile of bones. I knew there was no such thing as a black rose and yet I could tell this flower wasn't fake because of its scent – sweet, rich and seductive. In the light of the lamps on deck, the edges of the petals looked almost dark gold, striking, captivating and enchanting …

'What is it?' Ben said, coming up behind me.

I jumped and pricked myself with one of the rose's thorns, spots of blood vividly red against my white skin.

'It's a black rose—' I began, but then broke off with a gasp of alarm for – as I spoke – the flower fell apart in my hands and all the petals tumbled loose to be scattered across the deck by the breeze and carried away by the wind, along with the chalky powder left by the bones. I was left holding only a thorny stem and – in another moment – it too turned to dust between my fingers.

'Come on,' Ben said grimly. 'Let's go inside and talk.'

It was a little awkward for, of course, I had left Laura and Charlie downstairs in the bar. It was already quite late and they would probably be going back home soon. If I didn't leave with them then I would have to take a taxi as I had no other way of getting back, but then Laura would have to wait up for me and I realised now that, whatever Ben had to say to me, it wasn't going to be said within the space of a half hour.

'Stay on the boat tonight,' Ben said. 'That's what I'm doing. You can go back to Laura's tomorrow.'

I hesitated, worried that this would seem rude and she might take offence. But I simply couldn't sit and make small talk with them now so I didn't have much choice.

'I need to think of some excuse to tell Laura,' I muttered. I was speaking to myself really for I didn't expect Ben to care if I appeared rude or to offer to help me with my predicament. So I was surprised when he said, 'Where is she? I'll get rid of her.'

'No, you won't. She's my friend and I won't have you being rude to her!'

'Calm down,' Ben replied, not bothering to hide his dislike as he scowled at me. 'She's my friend too. I won't be rude. Surely you must realise that I'm quite capable of being civil when I want to.'

'You could have fooled me!'

He shrugged and said, 'Like it or not, this whole situation is Liam's doing, not mine. If you're going to blame anyone then blame him. Now where is Laura? Is she in the bar?'

'Yes,' I snapped. 'She is.'

'Come on then.' He opened the door and we stepped off the deck and went downstairs.

And as soon as we stepped into the bar, Ben became a different person. It was as if a switch had been flipped. I watched in amazement as he greeted Laura warmly – even hugging her – before shaking hands with Charlie like it was a genuine pleasure to meet him. Laura tried to persuade him to join us all for a drink but Ben glanced briefly at me before saying, 'Actually, I'm terribly sorry but I was hoping to have a talk with Jasmyn. There are ... some things we need to discuss and—'

'Of course. I understand. Take as long as you need and I'll wait here.'

'Oh no,' I said at once. 'Laura, we could be a while. I'd rather you just went home and—'

'I've booked Jasmyn a room on the ship,' Ben interrupted. 'We thought it would be easier if she stayed here for the night and went back to your house in the morning. That's okay, isn't it?'

'But ... but you don't have any night things,' Laura protested.

'There's toothpaste and stuff in the rooms,' Ben said.

Laura turned to me and I nodded, trying to look as if I'd heard of the plan myself before that moment.

'Well, all right, if you're sure that's what you want.'

At long last, Laura and Charlie had gathered up their coats and were gone.

'Do you want something to drink?' Ben asked, glancing over at the bar.

'No, I don't want anything to drink!' I said impatiently. 'I want to talk about what happened outside!'

'Fine,' Ben said with a shrug.

We went to a small table at the back of the room. The ambient noise of piano music and people chatting meant that we could talk softly without being overheard by nearby tables as Ben started to talk in a quiet, level voice. 'I don't know how to explain the horse or the bones or the swans, but I think they must all be something to do with what Liam got himself involved in. About eighteen months ago he came to my flat in the early hours of the morning, babbling like a lunatic with this wild story of how he'd just come from Neuschwanstein Castle. He told me that he walked a little way along the mountain path that King Ludwig used to take to Linderhof when he heard horses' hooves and sleigh bells and a moment later a huge sleigh came out of the tree line towards him pulled by six white horses. He'd read stories of how Ludwig used to travel between the two castles in this way, so in the first moment he thought it must be some kind of historic recreation. But then he realised that he was the only person around for miles.'

Ben stopped, chewing at his lower lip, and I said impatiently, 'So it was some eccentric rich man imitating Ludwig or something?'

Ben shrugged. 'That's what I said. But Liam swore that as the sleigh went past he saw King Ludwig himself inside it.'

My face was already twisting into an expression of incredulous disbelief as Ben went on in a flat voice, 'But that wasn't even the craziest part of it. Liam admitted that the sleigh was going very fast and whoever was inside was wearing a thick fur coat and hat, that he couldn't see him properly or for very long and that he may have only borne a passing resemblance to Ludwig. But he saw something else as well and this he was adamant about.' Ben drew a breath and I could tell that he did not particularly want to continue the story. 'He said that the horses turned from white to

70

black and that at the same time he practically had to duck to avoid all the black swans – hundreds of them – that came swooping out of the forest chasing the sleigh, flying low over his head.

'He said the whole thing disappeared around a corner in the mountain path and when he followed it, the sleigh, the horses and the swans were gone. There were tracks in the snow but they just stopped as if they had all disappeared into thin air. I didn't think of the story again until recently ... after what happened at Liam's funeral. And now what we just saw up on deck. It's made me think that maybe Liam was telling the truth about what he thought he saw after all.'

'If he really saw all that in the mountains,' I said, 'then there's no way he wouldn't have written a book on King Ludwig and his castles. He told me he gave up because there wasn't enough material. Besides, if he saw something that extraordinary he would have told me about it.'

Ben was silent for a moment before saying, 'He said something fell out of the sleigh.'

'What do you mean?'

'An object, although I don't know exactly what because he refused to tell me. But he said that something fell out – something that was going to make us all rich. He said the horses were galloping so fast that the sleigh almost tipped over altogether when it rounded the corner and that was when this thing fell out onto the snow. And at first I thought that, whatever it was, he'd stolen it and spun the ridiculous sleigh story just to avoid telling me where he'd got it. Now – what with the black swans and the horse and the skulls and roses ... I'm not so sure myself.'

I stared at him for a moment, my lip curling with contempt. 'Liam would never steal something!' I snapped at last.

'That,' Ben replied calmly, 'would depend upon how much he wanted it. But it doesn't matter. How Liam came across this object is irrelevant. What matters is where he hid it.'

'If this thing was really as valuable as you say, then why would Liam hide it at all? Why not simply sell it?'

'If it was a stolen object then it might not have been very easy to sell.'

'You don't know what the hell you're talking about, Ben! Liam was not a thief!'

Ben practically sneered as he said, 'I think you're going to have to accept that there was a lot about him you didn't know. I realise you were only married ten months but you knew him for many years before that and surely you must have noticed his thrill-seeking personality? Surely you haven't forgotten the parachute jumps or the racing cars or the black-slope skiing? Whenever he had any spare money, what did he spend it on? Getting high on adrenalin! Liam got bored easily. Surely you must have noticed this.'

For a moment I said nothing, suddenly feeling uncomfortable. For what Ben had said was true. Liam had been a thrill-seeker and I had noticed a certain ... restlessness in him at times after we were married that had bothered me a little ...

'That doesn't mean he was a criminal!' I said sharply.

'He was careful never to say anything to me directly, as I'm sure he was to you. But there was the odd hint he dropped, the occasional thinly veiled comment that led me to think he might sometimes have bent the law even if he didn't actually break it. Anyway, it's up to you, you can believe what you like – the sleigh story or the criminal idea or perhaps you can create a third theory all of your own. In the end it really doesn't matter much now. What does matter is that, soon after coming by this object, Liam became frightened.'

'Of what?'

'I don't know,' Ben said and for the first time that night he avoided my eyes. 'It was around the time that we fell out. He turned up at my flat again – said he wanted to talk about the Swan King. But I told him to leave.'

He looked at me, a challenging, sullen expression on his face as if daring me to reprimand him. I wanted to. If a member of your family comes to you for help you don't send them away. But I bit my tongue. Still, my voice came out rather coldly as I said, 'So you don't know anything at all about what he was going to tell you?'

'No. Soon after that he was married to you and I never heard anything more about it. He never tried to contact me again.'

'What did you two fall out about anyway?' I asked, hoping that perhaps Ben would tell me what Liam had been unwilling to.

'Don't you know?' Ben asked, looking startled.

I shook my head. 'Liam wouldn't tell me.'

He looked at me, a strange expression on his face as he said, 'You have absolutely no idea what the argument was about?'

'No!' I replied sharply, unnerved by his expression. 'What *was* it about?'

'If Liam didn't tell you then I don't think I should.'

Avid curiosity burnt like a flame inside me and I cursed myself for giving away the fact that I didn't know already.

'Tell me what it was about!' I insisted – giving it one more try. 'I have a right to know.'

'You have no right,' Ben replied calmly. 'And I'm not going to talk to you about it so just drop it.'

I suppressed a sigh and tried to suppress my curiosity as well. There was nothing I could do to force him to tell me if he didn't want to. And, after all, it didn't really matter now what they had fallen out about anyway. So I promised myself that I would pursue it later and then said, 'Well, how does Jaxon Thorpe come into this anyway? You haven't even mentioned him yet.'

Ben shrugged. 'Jaxon was there at Neuschwanstein that night. Apparently he ran out of the trees a few minutes later, followed the tracks in the snow and asked Liam if he'd seen the sleigh. I don't know what he was doing up there in the first place. He told me he had his cameras and was trying to get a good shot of Neuschwanstein at night when the sleigh went past him. I think it more likely he was up there trying to work out how best to break into the castle, but he does have to do some genuine photography to keep up appearances and he certainly had a camera of some kind with him that night, for he got a photo of the sleigh.'

'Have you seen it?' I asked eagerly.

'Yes, I've seen it. There's a sleigh in the photo, being pulled by horses, and Neuschwanstein's there in the distance. But the whole thing is indistinct and blurred. It certainly isn't enough to prove anything. Besides, Jaxon is a professional photographer – if he wanted to he could easily create a very startling photo out of thin air just using all the computer programmes he has access to.'

I couldn't help but think back to my wedding photos.

'The photo proves nothing,' Ben went on. 'Jaxon contacted me shortly after he turned up at your house. From what I understand, it seems he and Liam reached an agreement to share the proceeds of selling the object to a buyer Jaxon found through his black market contacts. The sale was all ready to go through when – for some reason – Liam changed his mind and told Jaxon that he wanted to keep it for a year before selling it.'

'Jaxon turned up at the house just after what would have been our one-year anniversary,' I said.

'Yes,' Ben replied. 'Apparently Liam told Jaxon about this change of plan just two weeks before your wedding. He hid the object somewhere Jaxon couldn't find it, with promises to retrieve it when a year was up and sell it as they'd agreed. Unfortunately, he died before he could do so. That's why Jaxon must have come back and trashed your house looking for it, the idiot. Like Liam would ever be stupid enough to hide it at home.'

'How many other people know about this thing Liam supposedly took?' I asked, thinking back to the way I had felt watched back in England – Jaxon Thorpe's appearance, the man in the rain and Luke posing as a stable-worker at my grandparents' home.

'I can't be sure,' Ben said. 'I have no way of knowing who Liam told, but I doubt he told very many because he wouldn't want them coming after it themselves. I don't suppose you know where it is, do you?' he asked, not sounding particularly hopeful.

'Why? Are you searching for this mystery object too?'

'I am, actually.'

'But what's the point if you don't even know what it is?'

'I have my reasons,' Ben said in a tone that made it quite clear he was not about to explain those reasons to me. 'Look, I think you know where it is,' he said, leaning slightly across the table towards me. 'That's why I wanted to see you tonight.'

For a moment I was taken aback but then I glared at him, anger flaring inside me at being accused so bluntly of lying. 'What's the matter with you?' I snapped. 'I've just told you I have no idea. Tonight's the first time I've heard of any of this—'

'No, no,' Ben interrupted impatiently. 'Obviously you don't *consciously* know. But I think you can help me find out.'

'How?'

'By telling me exactly where you think Liam went over the last year or so and when.'

'What's the point?' I asked, aware of a sullen note creeping into my voice. 'If Liam lied to me about going to Munich, then how do I know he didn't lie to me about his other trips? I can't prove where he was – he could have been anywhere.'

'You misunderstand me,' Ben said with a kind of grim satisfaction. 'I don't need you to tell me where Liam actually *was*. I just need you to tell me where you *think* he was.'

'What good will that do?'

'I already know exactly which other countries Liam visited over the last year.'

'How can you when you weren't speaking to him during that time?'

'Just because we weren't speaking doesn't mean that I didn't keep an eye on him. I hired an investigator to inform me whenever Liam left the country and what his destination was.'

'You spied on him,' I said flatly.

'What choice did I have?' Ben said sourly. 'We weren't talking any more. I had to have some way of keeping track of him. I was ... concerned about what he might be doing.'

'Well, if you already know where he was then why the hell do you need me to tell you?'

'I've no doubt some of Liam's trips were genuine – that he really was doing research for other books. But some of the trips were to do with this German business. If I compare where Liam really was with where he told you he was going, then every time the two don't add up and he lied to you about his trip I'll know that he went away for some other purpose.'

I said nothing. It made sense, but the suggestion put a profoundly bad taste in my mouth. I disliked the idea that Liam had lied to me about one visit to Munich, but the thought that he had lied to me consistently about where he was going for almost a year was ... devastating. The idea that there was an aspect of Liam's life he had deliberately kept hidden from me was extremely hurtful and I struggled to believe it for I thought we had been so close. I'd never dreamed, never even *considered* that Liam was keeping such a huge secret. If this was all true then it meant I was stupid and incredibly naïve – so happy to be in love that I had been blind to what was really going on.

'Well?' Ben said curtly.

'Fine,' I replied with equal sharpness. 'We can go through it tomorrow.'

During our conversation I had been unsure whether I should mention the black horse I had seen in England or not. Ed had been spooked by it, but otherwise I had no particular reason to believe the horse was anything other than ordinary. But, finally, I decided to say something just to see whether Ben would react.

'Do you know a man called Luke?'

After a moment Ben slowly shook his head, 'Why do you ask?'

'There was a man hanging around my grandparents' estate. He claimed to work at the stable but that wasn't true. He had a black horse that looked just like the one we saw on deck.'

'What did he say to you?'

'Nothing much. He just offered to rub Ed down for me. But he knew who I was.'

Ben shrugged. 'Well, I don't know any Luke but I suppose it's possible that there's another person out there who knows about this object.'

'I found a knight in Liam's things,' I blurted out suddenly.

'What?'

I frowned. I wasn't really sure why I'd spoken, for the little metal knight could hardly be the object Ben had spoken of as it certainly wasn't valuable in any way. But still I felt the pressing

76

need to mention it, perhaps because it seemed such an incongruous find – something in Liam's pockets the day he died that should not have been there. Ben would no doubt scorn me for bringing up something so trivial but I had started now, so I might as well continue.

'When the undertakers gave me his effects,' I said, 'I found a little metal knight with a nail shoved through its head.'

'And?' Ben prompted when I didn't go on.

I shrugged. 'That's it. I just thought it was odd.' Even though it seemed highly doubtful, I couldn't help going on, 'Perhaps that's the object you're looking for.'

'It's not,' Ben replied at once.

'How do you know?' I replied, rather annoyed by his instant dismissal. 'You haven't even seen it.'

'You said it was in Liam's pocket the day he died?'

'Yes.'

'Then it's not the object from Neuschwanstein. Liam would never have been stupid enough to carry it around with him. He would have hidden it very carefully. I doubt it's even in England.'

I sighed. 'Well, what are we going to do once we've worked out where Liam's been over the last year?'

'I'll retrace his footsteps.'

'You mean *we'll* retrace his footsteps, don't you?'

'We?' Ben repeated, looking startled. 'Oh no, you've got to go back home.'

'Ha, ha,' I said flatly. 'Very funny. Don't look so horrified, Ben. You drop this bombshell on me and then expect me to quietly catch the next flight home? Come on! He was my husband and I loved him and if there was something going on that he kept secret then I want to know what it was and why he didn't tell me. There's no way I can possibly get on with my life with all this hanging over my head unanswered.'

'I'll share any information I get with you,' Ben offered stiffly.

'Nice try. But not good enough. I can't sit around at home waiting, not knowing what's going on, worried that black horses or swans or murderous photographers might turn up at my house at any moment. If you want my help then you'll have to accept that I'm involved in this now, and I'm coming with you.'

'Highly inadvisable,' Ben said coldly. 'But if you can't be dissuaded then I suppose I have no choice.'

'Good, I'm glad we're agreed,' I said, standing up and pointedly ignoring his sullen look. 'I'd better go and book a cabin for the night. When and where do you want to meet in the morning?'

Ben shrugged. 'We might as well meet in the restaurant for breakfast. But like I told Laura, I've already booked you a cabin.'

'You have? I thought you made that up to reassure her.'

'No, I booked you a room before I met you on deck.'

'That was a little presumptuous, wasn't it?' I asked, irritated, for some reason, by his action.

Ben shrugged as he drew the room key out of his pocket and dropped it on the table. 'There's the key,' he said. 'You can use the room or not as you like. It hardly matters to me.'

I ignored his words and narrowed my eyes suspiciously at his right hand, still resting on the table, as I noticed for the first time that it was a mess. There were fresh cuts on his knuckles, only recently scabbed over, with ugly bruises mottling the skin there and around the plain black ring he wore on his index finger.

'What happened to your hand?' I said.

He looked down and then quickly stood up, burying his hand in his pocket. 'Nothing,' he said shortly.

'You've been fighting with someone,' I said accusingly.

He gave me a withering stare. 'Do I look like I've been fighting with anyone?' he asked.

I had to admit that, apart from the scarred knuckles, he didn't. There wasn't so much as a scratch on his face and he didn't move with any hint of stiffness. I shrugged it off. What did it matter to me what he'd been doing anyway? I snatched up the key and said irritably, 'How much is this going to cost?'

'I'll tell you tomorrow after we've checked out.'

After everything Ben had told me that night I could hardly bear to look at him, so was glad to disappear into my cabin when we

78

reached it and leave Ben to go into his next door, relieved to be alone at last.

It was lovely inside – decorated in 1930s style in keeping with the rest of the ship and a porthole looked out at the lights of the nearby shoreline. I sat down on the bed and ran my hands through my hair. I wished that I could just *ask* Liam about all this. That I could just go home and into his study to find him sitting behind his desk as usual, and then I would ask him about what had happened at Neuschwanstein and why he had lied to me about going there. He would have had a reasonable explanation for me. I was quite, quite certain of that. He might have been a thrill-seeker, but he was *not* a criminal. He was not a bad man. If I could only *ask* him then he would be able to clear this whole thing up at once. But I couldn't. I would never be able to speak to Liam about any of this and that squeezed at my heart far more than the fact that he had lied. Liam was gone and the only person I could look for answers with now was cold, aloof Ben who looked so similar, but was so unlike Liam in every other way.

I had seen him be perfectly pleasant with Laura and her boyfriend so I knew that he wasn't acting this way with me merely because he was Ben – he was acting like this because he simply didn't like me, just as his parents and the rest of his family had disliked me from the moment I married Liam. The reason for this dislike was a total mystery to me for, as far as I knew, I had never done a single one of them any wrong and before our engagement was announced we had all got on well. But then several of them – including Liam's mother and Ben himself – had promptly come up with excuses as to why they could not attend the wedding just two weeks before it was about to take place. It was my albinism, it had to be …

Liam continued to laugh it off when I voiced my insecurities to him, saying, 'They're a strange lot, Jaz. I don't pretend to understand them. I expect they're just jealous because you're so pretty …'

Before I went to sleep I sat on the bed for some time, hugging the pillow to my chest in the soft glow of the bedside lamp, trying to digest all that I had learned that evening and the extraordinary spectacle I had witnessed with Ben on deck. How I wished that Liam was here with me instead.

8

Adrian Halsbach

I was woken up the next day by someone banging on my cabin door. I staggered out of the bed, dragging the sheet off to wrap around myself before answering it to find Ben on the other side.

'I'm going down for breakfast,' he said. 'Are you coming?'

Everything that had happened last night came flooding back into my mind, making me wish I could crawl back under the sheets and stay there.

'Yes,' I sighed, rubbing sleep from my eyes. 'Just give me a moment to get changed – oh—' I broke off as I remembered that I had no clothes and that was why I was currently wearing nothing but a sheet. 'I haven't got anything to wear,' I said.

'Can't you just wear the dress you wore last night?' Ben asked, his eyes flicking to where I had carefully hung it up on the wardrobe door.

'I can't wear a long evening dress into breakfast!' I exclaimed.

'Why not?' Ben asked stonily.

'I just can't,' I replied, resisting the urge to roll my eyes.

I glanced round the cabin as if expecting to see something respectable I could put on and caught a glimpse of myself in the mirror, causing me to cringe and the blood to rush to my face. My bare arms and shoulders were terrible. They were so *white*! And quite a lot of leg was on display too. Only Liam saw me this way, not other men. I practically closed the door in Ben's face, leaving it open a mere crack as I peered through it at him and said, 'Can you go and buy me a tracksuit from the shops, please? I saw them there in the window last night. Get me a pair of flip-flops too.'

He started to protest but I grabbed my purse from the table beside the door and thrust some money at him. 'For God's sake, I'm not asking you to drive to a mall. Just go upstairs and get me something. I'm not leaving until I have some clothes.'

And I shut the door, aware that I was being a little short with him but finding it too early in the morning to care. I only realised after Ben had left that I hadn't told him my size, but he returned a few minutes later with a tracksuit that fit.

'I didn't know what colour you wanted,' he mumbled, holding the bag out to me awkwardly. I took it from him and looked inside. He had chosen the pink one. Not my favourite colour but at least it didn't clash horribly with my white skin and hair. Liam had always liked it when I wore pink ...

'Thanks, this is fine,' I said. 'I'll just be a second.'

I closed the door and put on the tracksuit. It was velour with a *Queen Mary* insignia on the shoulder and hip and felt velvety soft against my skin. I combed my hair back into a ponytail and then pulled on the flip-flops before walking upstairs in silence with Ben into the restaurant where a large buffet breakfast had been laid out. Despite the fact that the food looked very good I found I had no appetite and would have preferred to skip breakfast altogether and get straight down to business. But Ben clearly did not feel the same way. After we were seated at a table by the window, he went up to the buffet and returned with a plate piled high with food. I don't know why that made me feel resentful. I suppose I just felt that he should be as distressed by all this as I was. He shouldn't be able to eat.

He hardly looked at me all through breakfast, much less spoke to me, and I wondered if he was still angry about my refusal to return to England. As I didn't have the spirit or the inclination to try to make conversation, we just sat there in silence; him tucking into his fried breakfast and me drinking a cup of black coffee. It was good coffee. It was a nice restaurant and a lovely setting. Under any other circumstances I would have been enjoying myself immensely on the ship. When Ben at last finished eating we moved to one of the lounges, which was quiet at this time of day.

'All right,' he said, calmly taking a pen and piece of paper out of his pocket and sliding them across the table to me. 'There's a list of the places Liam visited over the last thirteen months. Read through them and mark the ones he lied to you about.'

I cringed at the blunt way he said it, wishing he could have phrased it a little more tactfully. Liam had gone away on short business trips seven times since we'd been married – once to Bermuda when he'd been researching the Bermuda Triangle, four times to Scotland to write about Scottish ghosts and the Loch Ness Monster and twice to Peru when he'd started work on the Nazca lines. Or so I'd thought … But, in fact, there was just one trip to Bermuda and one to Peru on the list before me – nothing at all to Scotland – and two entirely new places: Munich and Paris. As far as I knew, Liam had never been to Paris and had only been to Munich once with me before our wedding. But it seemed from Ben's list that he had visited Paris thirteen months ago, a couple of weeks before we were married, and had been to Munich a total of four times, not including the trip Ben had already told me about. These trips had been spread fairly evenly across the ten months of our marriage. Indeed, if Ben's information was accurate then Liam had returned to Munich just two weeks before he died. He'd told me to my face that he was going to Peru to look at the Nazca lines. He had even brought back photos of them.

I slid the piece of paper across the table to Ben and leaned back in my chair, eyeing him doubtfully. He was Liam's brother, but how well did I really know him? It seemed absurd that Liam had been in Munich rather than Peru. I simply couldn't imagine him lying to me like that. Think of the effort it would have involved: hiding his real travel documents from me, getting photos of the Nazca lines from somewhere, blithely telling me all about them, brazenly lying to my face. I couldn't imagine him doing it. Why on earth should I trust Ben's word over my husband's?

'This is ridiculous,' I said. 'I can't believe Liam went to Munich so often and didn't tell me, never mind Paris.'

'Fine.' Ben shrugged, running his eye down the list. 'I'm making it all up. Go back home to England.'

I scowled at him. 'Don't you have any proof you can show me?'

He glanced up with a scowl of his own. 'I have no intention of trying to prove all this to you. It would be impossible anyway. You can believe me or not as you like.'

I curled my hands into fists, my nails digging into my palms, resisting the urge to shake him. Couldn't he see what he was doing to me? Couldn't he see that he was making an unbearable situation even more intolerable? It was bad enough that I'd lost Liam without having to doubt him like this as well. It was bad enough that I was a twenty-seven-year-old widow, without having to always wonder if these things Ben had told me were true or not. If he wasn't prepared to prove it then he shouldn't have said anything to me in the first place. At least knowing for sure would be better than all this doubting.

'You're being such a bastard, Ben!' I said quietly. 'Can't you see how awful this is for me?'

He sighed and spread his hands on the table between us. 'What do you want from me, Jasmyn? I've told you what I know. I'm sorry if you don't like it or you can't accept it. I know you want to think that Liam was perfect but that's not true and that's all there is to it. For the most part I'm as much in the dark as you are.'

'But how do I know you're even telling me the truth?' I asked outright, abandoning politeness in my desperation.

Ben scowled. 'Don't you trust me?' he said bitterly.

He was Liam's brother and for that reason alone I wanted to trust him. Ben looked like Liam; he even sounded a little like him. And because of that I wanted to be near him even though he was not the man I had loved and married. But although he was my brother-in-law, we had never had much to do with each other. When I'd visited his house as a child it had been to play with Liam. Ben had always been closeted away in his own bedroom. And as adults I had seen very little of him even before his argument with his brother. It would therefore be stupid of me to blindly trust every word he said.

'Why would I lie to you about all this?' Ben asked coldly. 'What exactly is it that you think I'm hoping to achieve?'

'Look, I'm sorry if I offended you,' I said, 'but you say Liam went off all over the place without telling me. Either Liam lied to me when he was alive or you're lying to me now. You can't blame me for wanting to believe that my husband was the one telling the truth.'

'Fine,' Ben replied. 'Believe what you want. But I can show you the report I have from the private investigators I hired if that will make any difference to you.'

And he reached into the bag on the floor by his feet, rummaging around in it for a moment before dropping a brown file on the table between us. Inside it was a very official looking report containing the list of places Ben had already showed me, as well as flight numbers. There were even a couple of credit card statements, which had obviously been retrieved from a rubbish bin for they were creased and stained, but payments to a travel agency had been highlighted on each one and it was the same agency that had sent the plane ticket to Munich to my house shortly before I left.

It seemed that Ben had been telling the truth after all. Liam had gone to Germany and France whilst we'd been married and yet he had never said so much as a word about it to me. He had lied about where he was going and he had done so consistently and convincingly. It was utterly devastating and even now with the evidence before me I struggled to believe it.

'Satisfied?' Ben asked calmly, holding out his hand for the file.

'What are we going to do now?' I asked as I handed it back, making an effort to keep my voice level.

'Go to Germany. That's where all this started.'

'You mean go back to Neuschwanstein?'

'No, not Neuschwanstein. Not yet, anyway. I want to go to Munich first.'

'Why?'

'To find Adrian Halsbach.'

'Is this the same Adrian that Jaxon mentioned to me?' I asked, narrowing my eyes as I remembered this was another name Jaxon had thrown out as a possible candidate for murdering my husband.

'Yes, Jaxon knows him. He told me where to find him. He's a scientist so I'm not sure how he's involved in all this, but they all seem to have spent a fair amount of time in Munich together, so perhaps he can tell us a little more about what Liam was doing there – and why he turned up at my flat the second time.'

Ben and I got a taxi to the airport, going via Laura's house so I could pick up my suitcase and violin and apologise for leaving earlier than planned. I was sketchy on the reason, just saying vaguely that Ben was going through some stuff and I would be staying with him for a while.

'Oh, Jasmyn,' Laura said quietly. 'Are you sure that's a good idea?'

I had expected her to be disappointed that I had to leave, but I was a little surprised by the undertone of disapproval in her voice.

'What do you mean?' I asked.

'Well ...' She hesitated, then said, 'It's none of my business, but I would have thought you'd want to stay away from Ben for a while.'

'I *do* want to stay away from him,' I replied. 'He's irritating the hell out of me. He's rude, arrogant, tactless and cruel. But he's Liam's brother and he needs my help so I haven't got any choice.'

Laura didn't say much else but she seemed distinctly withdrawn as she said goodbye and I wondered if I had offended her by cutting the trip short. I was sorry if that was the case but it was out of my hands. I couldn't stay. I had to go with Ben and that was all there was to it.

It was just over an eleven-hour flight from Los Angeles International Airport to Munich and I was not relishing the thought of being stuck with him for so long. For the most part we simply didn't talk to each other. Ben seemed completely unaffected by the awkward silence and made no attempt to fill it and I was too preoccupied with everything I had so recently learned to attempt to do so. As soon as we got onto the plane Ben put his

86

earphones in, leaned back in the chair and closed his eyes, putting an end to any further questions I might have thought of asking him.

The flight was a night-time one but I struggled to sleep. This was partly because Ben kept fidgeting in his seat beside me, clearly finding the cramped conditions uncomfortable. Being tall, there was barely enough room for him and his knees were wedged against the chair in front. I was cold, even with the thin aeroplane blanket clutched tightly around myself. But I didn't overly mind not being able to sleep. With the lights dimmed and the only sound the soft hum of the engines, I found the flight strangely relaxing. Until we got to Germany I didn't have to think about anything, I didn't have to do anything. I could just sit there and let my mind go blank.

Eventually I did drift off, but I had only been asleep for a little while before I dreamt that I woke up, looked out of the window and saw a black swan sitting on the wing outside. The image jerked me awake and at once I lifted the blind to look out of the window, but there was just the dark night sky out there and no sign of any black swan on the wing. Unfortunately, my movement also woke Ben.

'Can't you sleep?' he said quietly.

'No. I'm cold,' I said, not wanting to admit that it was the nightmare that had woken me.

'Take my blanket,' Ben said, picking it up off his knees and holding it out to me.

'Oh,' I said, taken aback. 'Thanks, but you'd better keep it or you'll be—'

'It's fine,' Ben interrupted quietly. 'Just take it.'

He sounded oddly weary, as if I was some kind of burden that he didn't want and hadn't asked for. So I took the blanket from him, mildly annoyed that he had somehow managed to make me feel guilty. With the second blanket over my knees I was instantly much warmer, which improved my mood slightly.

'Are you all right?' I asked, for now that I looked at him properly he didn't just look tired – he looked ill. I was scared of people

87

looking ill now. I couldn't brush it aside. Not when I knew that, sometimes, apparently healthy people simply died with no warning at all. He glanced at me and I hoped it was just the dim lighting in the cabin that made his eyes look so sunken in his face.

'You must realise how impossible this is for me,' he said.

'What? Don't you like flying?'

'No, I meant this situation.'

I stared at him, taken aback. '*Situation?* If you mean Liam's death and everything we've found out since, then of *course* I know how difficult it is for you because it's about ten times more difficult for me!'

'That's not true at all,' Ben replied evenly.

I knew he had parted from Liam on bad terms and that must be hard now, but it was his own fault for not making amends with him whilst he was alive. If his younger brother had meant that much to him then why did he never even try to repair the rift? Liam didn't bear grudges, so I was quite sure that whatever had happened between them had been Ben's fault.

'Jasmyn—' He began.

But I cut him off sharply: 'You had a whole year to make up with Liam and you never so much as sent him a Christmas card!'

To my surprise, Ben looked as though he'd been slapped and I silently cursed my loose tongue. What I'd said was perfectly true but there was no point in saying such things now when they could only hurt and not make any difference anyway.

For a moment I thought he was going to say something but then he just shrugged, leaned back in his chair and closed his eyes once again.

When we arrived in Munich we hired a car and booked two rooms in the Deutsche Eiche in the Old Town sector of the city. We were both tired from travelling and had eaten on the plane so we agreed to have an early night. The hotel was nice enough and reasonably priced but when I got to my room next door to Ben's, I found that I still couldn't sleep. So I took out my Violectra, plugged the earphones in and played for a while, sitting cross-legged on the bed. That was the beauty of an electric violin – you could play it anywhere and no one would be able to hear you. To anyone else it would look like I was playing a silent violin, for the music was only playing through my earphones. After half an hour I was much more relaxed but still didn't feel ready to sleep, so I unpacked my laptop and made use of the Internet access in the room by reading about King Ludwig online.

Liam, and now Ben, had both referred to him as the Swan King, but as I read more about him I realised that most people called him the Mad King, for he was proclaimed insane shortly before he died. I found a photo of him as a young man just come to the throne – he was very handsome, with intelligent, gentle eyes. He may have looked like a dreamer but he certainly did not look mad ... But then maybe one can't always see madness in a person's face ...

I found a quote from the Empress Elisabeth – who knew Ludwig perhaps as well as anyone – saying: '*The king was not mad; he was just an eccentric living in a world of dreams.*' I very much liked the phrasing she'd used.

Ludwig's death was the strangest thing I read about and it was easy to see why conspiracy theories abounded over it. He was declared insane on June 10th, 1886, arrested and taken to Castle Berg south of Munich. On the evening of June 13th he asked to take a walk with Professor Gudden – the doctor who had declared him insane three days earlier. The doctor agreed and told the guards not to follow them. Five hours later, at 11:30 that night, the two men were found dead floating in Lake Starnberg. The king's death was officially declared a suicide, despite the fact that he had been a strong swimmer and the water was only waist deep. And Gudden was found dead too – an inconvenient fact which seemed to have been quietly overlooked at the time.

But I found one website that said Ludwig hadn't truly died when he'd drowned in the lake that day – the Fairy Tale King had escaped, the website claimed, straight into faeryland itself where he still dwelt to this day, far better suited to ruling the faery court than a human one.

I looked again at the photograph of the handsome young king – '*an eccentric living in a world of dreams*' – and felt sorry that he should have come to such a violent end for, whether murder or suicide, forty-one years old was far too young to die.

The next morning, after a hasty early breakfast, Ben and I left the hotel to meet Adrian Halsbach. It seemed that he worked in a laboratory on the outskirts of Munich. I couldn't imagine what part he played in all this, but I disliked the smell of the multi-storey building as soon as Ben and I walked in through the front doors. It was too white and shiny and bright and the air was too stuffy. The whole place made my skin prickle and the warm air clogged in my throat.

'What kind of lab is this?' I muttered to Ben.

'Cosmetics,' he replied briefly.

We stopped at the reception desk and I was mildly irritated when the immaculately manicured woman behind it did a double take at the sight of me. The washed out, fluorescent lighting did nothing for my appearance whatsoever.

'*Kann ich Ihnen helfen?*' she asked, in a voice ringing with false cheerfulness – like nails on a blackboard.

'*Sprechen Sie Englisch?*' Ben replied.

'Of course,' she said smoothly.

'We'd like to see Adrian Halsbach.'

'Is he expecting you?'

'No.'

'I'll call down to the lab but he may be busy,' she said sweetly, her hand reaching for the phone. 'What's the name please?'

'Liam Gracey,' Ben replied.

I gave him a sharp look as the receptionist dialled a number but he gave an almost imperceptible shake of his head so I said nothing.

'He can spare you a few minutes, Mr Gracey,' she told us after hanging up the phone.

We were given visitors' badges and asked to wait until someone came to escort us.

'I had to lie about the name,' Ben said to me quietly whilst we were waiting to one side, 'otherwise he might not have agreed to see us.'

I nodded and, in another moment, a young man came to lead us down a corridor to some kind of observation room with large windows along one side of the wall that faced right into a laboratory. He left us there saying that Dr Halsbach would be with us shortly but I hardly heard him. I was too consumed with horror at what I could see going on in the lab. There were rows upon rows of cages containing rabbits, most of which had sections of their fur shaved away to reveal red, blistering skin where chemicals had been forcibly rubbed into them. As I stared in revulsion, I saw a man in a white lab coat drip dark liquid from a pipette into the pink eyes of a small albino rabbit that was being held in a vice with its eyelids clamped back, its paws and long ears twitching feebly in the iron grip.

'My God,' I said in disgust. 'And you said this was a *cosmetics* lab?'

'That's right,' Ben replied and I thought I heard disapproval in his voice. 'They test lipsticks and perfumes here. Make-up is very important, Jasmyn.' He caught my eye and gave me a small, tired smile. 'Probably best not to look.'

A moment later, the door opened and the man in the white lab coat I had just seen walked inside. About fifty years old, he was tall and thin with grey hair and small, hard eyes.

'I thought I made it quite clear, Liam, that I wanted nothing to—' he began in a rather high voice with a thick German accent, but then broke off when he looked at Ben properly. 'You are not Liam Gracey.'

'No,' Ben replied. 'I'm sorry, but we had to make sure you'd see us.'

'You're his brother?' Halsbach asked, obviously noting the physical similarities between them.

'Yes. My name is Ben.'

Halsbach stripped off the white rubber gloves he was wearing – still stained with blood from the rabbit he had just been handling.

He dropped them in the bin by the door and then walked over to us.

'Adrian Halsbach.'

He shook hands with Ben but when he held his hand out to me, I couldn't bring myself to take it.

'I'm not shaking your hand!' I snapped, practically cringing at his proximity. 'Not after what you've just been doing to that rabbit.'

Not helpful, I knew. After all, we wanted answers from him, so insulting him probably wasn't the best way to start. But these were *cosmetics* laboratories, for God's sake, and there were rabbits twitching and writhing in pain in the next room all for the sake of lipstick. It was outrageous.

'One of the animal lovers,' Halsbach said nonchalantly, but with an undertone of scorn. 'Is there something I can do for you or am I going to have to call security?'

'That won't be necessary,' Ben said, flashing me a warning look. 'We just want to talk to you about Liam.'

'I see,' Adrian said, wandering over to the sink in one corner and turning on the tap to wash his hands. 'And how is Liam?'

'He's dead,' Ben replied calmly.

Adrian glanced over his shoulder at us, one eyebrow slightly raised. 'Dead?' he repeated, turning off the tap and reaching for a towel. 'How did that happen?'

'An aneurysm.'

'Then what do you want to talk to me about?' Adrian asked, not even bothering to offer the usual commiserations.

'We want to know about what happened on the lake behind Neuschwanstein.'

'I'm not sure that I know what you mean,' Halsbach said evasively.

'I understand that the three of you crept down there late one night.'

I frowned at Ben, for this was the first I'd heard of it and it irritated me that he had not mentioned it earlier.

'Perhaps we did,' Halsbach replied. 'But it was a while ago now and my memory is not good.'

I realised he was fishing for a bribe as Ben drew a one hundred Euro note from his pocket and held it out to him. Halsbach grabbed it from his hand greedily.

'Why did the three of you go down to the lake that night?' Ben asked again.

Halsbach shrugged. 'To steal one of the swans, of course.'

'Why?'

Halsbach glanced through the window into his horrible lab and a small smile twitched at the corner of his mouth. 'Liam said they were going to make us all rich. That the swans at Neuschwanstein and Ludwig's other castles were actually magic swans.'

'*Magic* swans?' I said incredulously.

Halsbach gave me a cold look. 'Yes, Fräulein, I know how it sounds. But he said that they turned into beautiful women at night – like the legend of the *Swan Lake*, no?' He looked at Ben and said, 'He was not a stupid man, your brother. And he seemed so *convinced* that I couldn't help but be intrigued.'

'Intrigued?' Ben repeated, raising an eyebrow. 'Are you sure it wasn't greed that motivated you?'

'A little bit of both, I should say,' the scientist replied with a shrug. 'We were going to bring the swan back here, cut it open and find out how they managed to transform between the two forms, and then sell the information to the highest bidder.' An ugly gleam lit his small eyes. 'It would have made us three of the richest men in the world.'

'And yet here you are still toiling away with rabbits and cosmetics,' Ben said. 'So what happened?'

'Your brother – how do you say in English? – cocked it up, that's what happened!' Halsbach said bitterly. 'When the three of us got to the lake there were just ordinary swans sleeping on the banks. Liam insisted there had been beautiful women there before. So he and Jaxon decided to take one of the swans anyway. They grabbed one and tried to get it into a sack but somehow – in

93

the struggle – its neck broke.' Halsbach shrugged. 'So they tried to grab a second one …'

'Yes?' Ben prompted when he did not continue.

'It didn't work and we came home,' Halsbach said. 'That's it.'

'Please don't lie to me again,' Ben said quietly. 'I've already heard this story once from Jaxon so I know there's more to it than that.'

'Jaxon!' Halsbach sneered. 'You can't trust a word that man tells you. Unless you beat it from him, of course.'

He glanced down at Ben's hands and I saw the sneer falter on his face when he noticed his scarred knuckles.

'Just tell us what you saw,' Ben said calmly, his hands disappearing into his pockets. 'We can worry about which – if either of you – is telling the truth later.'

'You won't believe me,' Halsbach protested.

'Well, that's our problem, isn't it?' Ben said. He took another hundred Euro note from his pocket and held it out to the scientist, who took it – albeit a little less eagerly this time.

'Well, if Jaxon told you the truth then you'll already know that as soon as they killed the swan a black horse appeared on the surface of the lake. With a knight on its back, dressed all in silver armour. We … tried to escape into the trees but Jaxon was the only one who got away. Liam and I—' Halsbach folded his arms in front of his chest and avoided our gaze before continuing in an expressionless voice, 'The knight dragged us into the water. He was huge – almost seven feet tall. There was no resisting him. He held us under the surface and almost killed us. But he brought us up at the last moment and leaned down to say something in Liam's ear. Then he dropped us – half-drowned – in the shallow water, got back onto his horse and rode off into the forest.' Halsbach spread his hands. 'And that's the truth of it.'

'Assuming that you're not insane yourself, what did the knight say to Liam?' Ben asked.

'I have no idea. When I asked him later he said he didn't know. When I pushed him he got angry and said he'd been too pre-occupied with drowning to take it in. He was in a foul temper after what had happened, angry with everyone, and he said he was going to have his revenge although I don't know on whom. I don't know if they ever tried again but I refused to have any further part in it. If it wasn't for the knight I would have thought all this talk of magic swans was pure nonsense. And that's all I know. Now don't ever come to my place of work again.'

'What about the object that was taken from Neuschwanstein?' I asked. 'Do you know anything about that?'

Halsbach frowned for a moment before saying, 'If I remember it right, Liam found something in the mountains that tipped him off to the fact that the swans were magical. There were plans to sell it but I wasn't involved in them and I don't even know what this thing was.'

'Have you ever heard of anyone called Lukas?' I said.

He shook his head.

'What about Luke?'

'I'm afraid I can't help you, Fräulein,' he said, looking at me with a contemptuous expression in his narrow eyes as if I were one of the poor animals in his lab. 'What did you say your name was again?'

'Jasmyn Gracey,' I replied. 'I'm Liam's widow.'

'Now *that*,' he said, '*does* surprise me.'

'And why is that?' Ben asked stiffly.

'Because Liam was an arrogant prick who always wanted the very best of everything,' Halsbach replied with a nasty smile.

I flushed to the roots of my white hair at the insult. People might occasionally stare at me in the street but it had been a long time since I'd had to endure such playground-like gibes about my albinism. But my own shame was eclipsed by a hot, indignant anger on Liam's behalf. Somehow, the fact that he was dead meant I just couldn't bear to hear anyone say so much as a word against him. I was about to snarl an insult back at the scientist when Ben said steadily, 'Say that again.'

Halsbach turned his gaze towards him and began with a smirk, 'I said, Liam was an arrogant prick who—' He didn't get any further, however, because Ben hit him in the mouth. Either Halsbach had been utterly unprepared for it or Ben had put more force behind the punch than it seemed, for Halsbach went staggering back to crash into the table behind him, sprawling on the floor with one hand clamped to his bleeding mouth.

'Be that as it may,' Ben said calmly, without any hint of anger, 'try to have some respect for the dead.'

Halsbach flinched as Ben approached him but he merely leaned down and picked the hundred Euro notes up off the floor, pocketing them before saying politely, 'Thank you very much for your time, Herr Halsbach. We'll show ourselves out.'

He turned away from the cringing scientist and took me by the elbow, steering me out of the room and back out to the car park, which felt blissfully cool and fresh after the stuffy, warm air inside.

'You shouldn't have lost your temper like that,' I said reproachfully as we got back into the car. I couldn't deny that it had been immensely satisfying seeing Halsbach get punched in the face, but for all we knew he might be reporting us to the police right this minute ...

Ben glanced at me. 'I didn't lose my temper,' he said levelly. 'You were there, you saw what happened. I just wanted my money back, that's all.'

He started the car engine and I frowned, trying to work him out. Now that I thought about it, it was true that he hadn't appeared to lose control and he hadn't so much as raised his voice to Halsbach, not even once. So perhaps he hadn't been angry on Liam's behalf, as I was. Perhaps he really had simply wanted his bribe money back and that was it.

'What if he phones the police?' I asked.

'He won't,' Ben said. 'Trust me. He'll leave it be.'

As we pulled out of the car park, my eyes went to Ben's hands on the steering wheel and the fact that he'd knocked the scabs off his knuckles and they were bleeding again – although he didn't seem to be aware of it. I would almost have preferred it if he *had* lost his temper. At least that would have made him seem human, rather than cold and calculating ...

Ben must have noticed my expression for he said, 'Look – I'm sorry if what I did back there upset you. Just think of it as one for the rabbits – God knows the man deserved a punch in the face from them. Now what do you say we go and have some lunch courtesy of Herr Halsbach in a nice restaurant somewhere and get that horrible laboratory feeling off our skin?'

The weather in Munich was an unwelcome change from California, which, apart from that last night on the *Queen Mary*, had been pleasantly mild. In Munich it was bitterly cold but fortunately I still had the coat I had worn to the airport in England. We parked the car in the city centre and then walked towards Marienplatz – the main square in Munich – currently filled with the one-hundred-and-sixty-plus stalls of the *Christkindlmarkt*. I recognised it because I had been there with Liam two years ago when we had come for our long weekend.

The market was as atmospheric, lively, festive and colourful as I remembered. Liam and I had spent a whole morning looking at the stalls selling baked apples, roasted almonds, sparkly Christmas decorations, marzipan, toys, gingerbread, candles and handicrafts. Then we had stood before the impressive Neues Rathaus and eaten hot sausages and drunk mugs of spiced *Glühwein*.

The gingerbread stalls were my favourite. They had iced Lebkuchen hearts hanging from their covered roofs and beneath them stood traditional gingerbread witch houses from *Hansel and Gretel*, ranging in size, prettiness and price. The smell was warm and spicy and instantly brought another painful memory to the surface – Liam had bought me one of those Lebkuchen hearts when we came back to the Christmas markets one evening. The memory of that distinctively Germanic gingerbread was firmly linked in my mind with a sense of carefree happiness that made the sight of them now all the more melancholic. I had never dreamt then, as Liam and I wandered through the stalls together saying that we must come back again some day, that the next time I returned to Munich Liam would not be with me but would be in a coffin back home instead.

I pushed the memories aside and concentrated on keeping up with Ben who was striding through the throng, sparing no time for the gaily decorated stalls. Instead, he headed straight for the Café Glockenspiel on the fifth floor of a building directly opposite the Rathaus. By chance, we were seated at our table by the window just on the stroke of twelve o'clock and so had a good view of the mechanical figures of the Glockenspiel in the tower opposite coming out to perform their dance whilst a large crowd of tourists watched from the bustling square below. It was a welcome relief to be in a bright, lively, festive place after the awful laboratory and I felt a burst of warmth towards Ben for suggesting it – which was probably why I didn't have more of a go at him for not telling me about the lake story earlier.

'Did Jaxon tell the same version of it?' I asked.

'More or less,' Ben replied. 'Only he claimed it was Adrian and Liam between them who managed to kill the swan. I half-thought he might have been making the whole thing up, but now that Adrian's verified it independently ...'

A few months ago I would never have believed such a wild story, no matter how many people verified it. But since then I had seen black swans falling out of the air dead for no apparent reason and a black horse galloping around on the deck of the *Queen Mary* before disappearing into thin air before my eyes.

'It was probably Adrian and Jaxon who killed the swan,' I said.

Ben raised an eyebrow. 'I would have said it was probably Adrian and Liam – as they were the ones who were apparently dragged into the lake.'

'I can't imagine Liam killing a swan, even by accident.'

Ben stared at me for a moment before giving a harsh, humourless laugh. 'It's not the magic swans you find hard to accept but the idea that Liam could kill one!'

'Obviously I find the idea of a magic swan hard to accept,' I replied irritably. 'And the knight, too! But Liam loved animals – he would never have hurt one!'

'And yet Adrian Halsbach was most certainly there that night,' Ben replied calmly. 'How do you explain his presence if you don't believe the three of them were planning to dissect the swan in his laboratory later?'

I shook my head firmly. 'I don't know, but there must be another explanation. Liam would never have got involved in something like that.'

'Huh,' Ben grunted, sullenly. 'Well, perhaps you're right. Perhaps it's just a story they've made up between them and no such thing ever happened at the lake at all. But you're wrong about Liam liking animals. He never liked them. I caught him torturing insects in the garden many times when we were growing up. He used to set traps for them. He even caught a rabbit once. He seemed fascinated with their struggles.'

'Oh, don't be absurd!' I said abruptly, my skin prickling with distaste at such a blatant lie. I'd known Liam since he was four years old and I'd never seen him be anything other than gentle with every animal he'd handled. I couldn't understand why Ben would even tell me such a story in the first place. What could he possibly hope to gain from it? He must realise I'd never believe it.

'You never had any pets,' he remarked calmly.

'What?'

'After you were married. If Liam loved animals so much, then why didn't you ever have any pets?'

I frowned uncomfortably. We'd bought a dog just after moving into our new house but, oddly, it had taken an instant dislike to Liam. He couldn't even get near the animal without it growling at him and, in the end, we'd been forced to find another home for it. I also remembered the strange way Liam had suddenly become reluctant to go riding at my grandparents' stables when he had always enjoyed it so much before ... But Ben wasn't to know any of those things so I simply said, 'It wasn't the right time for us to have pets.'

Ben's mouth twitched in what might have been a small smile but he said nothing and, at that moment, our food arrived.

'Was Liam happy?' Ben said abruptly once the waitress had gone.

'What?'

'Over the last year – was he happy?'

'Yes,' I replied. 'We both were.'

While we ate, he went on to ask me several other questions about Liam and the life we'd had together and I realised how little he'd really known about us. I supposed it made sense, for they had stopped talking just before Liam and I were married.

'How did it happen?' he asked.

'What?'

'The engagement. I always thought the two of you were just friends.'

'We were at first. But he bought me a Violectra,' I said with a laugh. 'How could I not love him?'

'Liam bought you the Violectra?' Ben asked, raising an eyebrow.

'Yes,' I replied. 'He knew how much I wanted an electric violin and he surprised me with it one day.'

'It's a striking instrument,' Ben said, then added more quietly, 'You play beautifully.'

'Thank you,' I replied, warming to him for the kinder manner he had suddenly adopted.

'So have you ever been to Munich before yourself?' Ben asked casually.

'Just once,' I said. 'Liam and I came for a long weekend two years ago.'

'I see. Did you enjoy it?'

'Yes,' I said, looking out of the window at Marienplatz below and remembering how we had stood there in that very square.

'Jasmyn,' Ben said after a moment. I turned to look at him, wondering whether I was imagining that odd undertone in his voice. He seemed to be looking at me very intently too. 'After you got married,' he began slowly, 'did Liam seem at all different?'

'Different?' I repeated with a frown. 'What do you mean?'

Ben made an impatient gesture with one hand and then leaned slightly forwards over the table. 'You knew him for a long time,' he said. 'But after you were married, surely you must have noticed changes. They might have just been little things. Perhaps they only lasted a few months and then he went back to normal. Think! Surely there must have been something?'

I gazed at him, trying to keep my expression blank. I *had* noticed a few little changes but they had been small innocuous things that Ben couldn't possibly have known about. After all, Liam had looked the same, sounded the same … The first time I noticed him change a habit was when he started putting his used tea bags in the sink rather than the bin. And then he started leaving the toilet seat up. And dropping his clothes on the bedroom floor in a messy heap rather than putting them away in the cupboard or into the wash as he'd always done before. I thought he was just being lazy and, at any rate, when I mentioned it to him he stopped doing it at once.

But the other thing I noticed was that he started kissing me differently. It wasn't worse or better. It was just different. I thought at first that it was because of the split lip a drunken guest gave him on his way to the ice machine while we were on our honeymoon in the Caribbean. It's a strange quirk of human nature that such things seem worse when they've been done intentionally rather than when they're simply the result of an accident. The person who attacked Liam didn't do it for any good reason – it just seemed to be a drunken guest looking to make trouble who was quickly scared off by another group drawn·by the noise. But Liam came back to our room with a swollen eye and a split lip. They were not bad injuries – he didn't even need stitches – so I was surprised by how much the whole thing upset me. He'd had a bit to drink by that time and if he'd fallen down the stairs by accident and got the bruises that way I know I would not have been anywhere near as distressed – indeed, I probably would have teased him over it mercilessly. But the thought of someone hitting him turned my stomach. The next morning he could hardly open his eye, it was so swollen.

He told me the hotel had kicked the drunken guest out but I almost wished they hadn't so that if I saw him during the holiday I could hit him hard myself with something really heavy. At any rate, I had thought at first that his kisses felt different because of his split lip, but even after it healed they still weren't quite the same somehow. And now that I *really* thought about it, I was not convinced that the difference had started in the Caribbean anyway. Perhaps that punch in the face had had nothing at all to do with it ...

The daredevil stunts like parachute jumping definitely hadn't started until after our marriage. I remembered teasing him that if he were ten or twenty years older I would have worried that they were the manifestation of a midlife crisis. And he no longer wanted pets and didn't seem to want to go near horses any more ...

I didn't know if these could be the things Ben was referring to or not but it seemed unlikely for – apart from the sudden interest in extreme sports – they would only be noticeable to someone who actually *lived* with him.

'I don't know,' I said at last. 'Maybe the odd little thing but nothing major. Why do you ask?'

'I just thought you might have noticed something, that's all,' he said, looking irritable. 'After all, there was a lot going on with him at that time and you *were* his wife.'

He seemed determined to kick me where it hurt and I found myself wondering once again what I could possibly have done to make him dislike me so. There'd never been any argument between us as far as I was aware.

'That's true, but *my* door wasn't the one he knocked on one night asking for help,' I replied sharply. That fact didn't make me feel any better, but perhaps it might make Ben feel a little worse. I was pleased to see him look suitably pained at my remark. *That's right*, I thought, *there's plenty of blame to go around.*

'Tell me about what you've been doing,' I said to change the subject before it could turn into another nasty argument.

'You would be bored,' Ben said abruptly.

'Try me,' I insisted, through gritted teeth. He must think I had the attention span of a gnat.

'Well, I've been working,' he shrugged. 'That's it.'

'You can be an architect anywhere,' I said. 'Why did you move to Germany?'

Ben hesitated for just a moment before saying, 'I met someone.'

I suddenly remembered the woman who had answered the phone that time I had been trying to reach Ben and said, 'A lady friend?'

'Yes.'

'Is it serious?' I didn't know why I asked that question but Ben answered it by holding up his hand and, for the first time, I noticed the engagement ring on his finger. It was a simple band of white gold and I was struck by how beautiful it was.

'Wow,' I said, genuinely pleased for him. 'What's her name?'

'Heidi.'

'What does she do?'

To my surprise, Ben said with sudden iciness, 'I'd rather not talk about her with you!'

Then he raised his hand to call the waiter over with the bill before I could respond. I was shocked by the speed with which he had gone from pleasantly amicable to coldly rude once again. When he had said that he didn't want to talk about his fiancée there had been something almost ... *vicious* in his tone.

'Look, Ben,' I said quietly once the waiter had left, 'have I done something to piss you off or do you treat everybody this way?'

He looked right at me and the dislike he felt was almost palpable. 'No,' he said flatly. 'You haven't done anything to piss me off. I just don't want to discuss my private life with you, if that's all right.'

My fingers itched to throw something at him for being so cold but I managed to resist the temptation, and soon we were back outside in the chilly Marienplatz. The fact was that I needed Ben right now if I was to have any hope of finding out what had happened to Liam. After that I surely wouldn't need ever to see him or his parents again if I didn't want to. There was nothing tying me to them now.

Strangely, I found the thought of never seeing Ben again oddly distressing and this irritated me even more. The man looked like Liam, but really that was all he had going for him. Good luck to his poor fiancée – she had sounded a nice enough girl when I'd spoken to her on the phone and I wondered what the hell she was doing marrying Ben. It just seemed so flat and final – Liam was gone and with him my tenuous connection to his family, as we had never had any children. Liam had been desperate for them but I had wanted to wait until we had more money saved up … How bitterly I regretted my caution now … Liam's parents and I might send Christmas cards for a few years but after that … well, what reason did we have to stay in touch? The sight of me would probably dredge up painful memories for them and vice versa. And his mother had already made her feelings on the matter perfectly clear.

'So what now?' I asked, trying to sound neither annoyed nor intimidated.

'I want to go to Neuschwanstein and see it for myself,' Ben said. 'We'll go in the morning. I'll meet you at the hotel for breakfast at eight o'clock.'

'Fine,' I said. 'What are you going to do now?'

'I haven't decided yet.' He glanced at me. 'You might want to use the time to buy yourself some clothes. I don't know how long we'll be in Germany but I doubt your California wardrobe is going to work here.'

I did as Ben had suggested and found a Karstadt to buy a few things. He was right in that a lot of the clothes I had brought with me from California would not be suitable here in Europe's chillier climate. It was difficult for I didn't know how much longer it would be before I would be going home, but I tried to stick to the basics. I was already alarmed by the amount of money I was spending. I had not been rich when I'd been married but now that it was just me I certainly couldn't afford to be extravagant, especially since my bereavement payment had by now run out and I was having to dig into my savings. I wouldn't even have gone on the trip to California had the flight not already been paid for, and I knew there would be very little expense involved once I arrived because I was staying with a friend. This was different. It was becoming expensive and I could ill afford it. I knew my family would lend me money if I asked but I would have to tell them what it was for and I had no wish to start running up debts.

My feet hurt by the time I had finished shopping and I would have liked to have stopped by a *Konditorei* for a coffee on the way back to the hotel, but the money I had spent that afternoon was already weighing heavily on my mind, so when I came across one with beautifully dressed windows and a warm, welcoming smell wafting from the door, I steeled myself to walk right past it as if bitter coffee beans and rich marzipan gateau held no allure for me whatsoever.

My hotel room shared an interconnecting door with Ben's, so when I got back to my room I unlocked my side of it and tapped on his; but there was no answer, so I assumed he wasn't back yet. In an effort to further conserve my funds I had bought some food in the supermarket underneath Karstadt, and for dinner I made myself a sandwich in the hotel room rather than going out to find a restaurant. I turned the television on to the one English channel and stretched out across the bed, propped on my elbows, munching crisps and trying not to think about the things Adrian Halsbach had said that morning.

I was still out of synch with the nine-hour time difference between Germany and California so I went to bed early that evening. But, as so often seemed to be the case, I had nightmares instead of dreams. It felt as if I dreamt for hours about a huge, gleaming knight drowning Liam in a vast, silver lake. Ben, Jaxon and Adrian were all there watching on the shoreline but they were laughing – they thought the knight was joking, that he didn't really mean to kill Liam before their eyes. I knew better, but I was further away on a mountain path. I tried to run towards the lake but it was like moving through treacle and I could have screamed with frustration as I never seemed to get any nearer and I was acutely aware that every second was precious because – before my very eyes – the life was draining out of my husband.

Twice he managed to bring his head clear of the water, taking in gulping breaths to scream my name before the knight cruelly forced his head back under again. Even then I could hear his voice ringing in my mind. '*Jasmyn! Jasmyn!*'

'I'm coming!' I gasped, desperately trying to break into a sprint but quite unable to go beyond a creeping walk.

Then I saw Liam's hands – which had been clawing at the knight's arm – go limp and fall into the lake with a splash. At last the knight released his grip but it was already too late. Liam did not resurface and I knew that he was dead. Drowned at the bottom of the lake. Screaming through my tears I woke myself up with a start and fumbled clumsily for the light by my bed.

But then I yelled in fright to see Liam, motionless and dripping wet, standing with his back to me at the foot of the bed, staring straight at the wall. The clothes he wore were soaked through and water ran from his hair down the back of his head. Although I couldn't see his face I knew it was him. But instead of wanting to leap from the bed and throw my arms around him, I found myself shrinking back, not wanting him to turn around and look at me.

As soon as I became aware of this reluctance, Liam started to turn. I clutched the sheets up to my chin, paralysed by some vague sense of dread. When he faced me at last, I could see that his skin was pale and waxen. I was staring into the face of a dead man – a corpse. He had even started to rot a little. His green eyes were the only thing about him that looked the same but this brought me little comfort, for as they bored into me they were full of pain and fear – an anguished expression that I had never seen on his face when he'd been alive.

'Liam.' His name slipped from my lips almost subconsciously.

He opened his mouth and I flinched as a stream of water poured out to soak the carpet. I thought he was going to say my name, but when the torrent of water stopped and he spoke at last, the one word that came out in a hoarse whisper was: '*Lohengrin!*'

He took a lurching step towards me and I instinctively raised my arms to protect myself. But then, suddenly, it was not Liam standing before me dripping wet but Ben – his hair plastered to his face just as it had been at the funeral all those months ago. I thought this was part of the dream at first but then I realised that there was light slicing across the bed from the open interconnecting doors and that Ben was wearing a robe rather than clothes.

'What is it?' he asked, looking alarmed as he gazed at me from the foot of the bed. 'What's the matter?'

'Why are you wet?' I asked, still trying to untangle the dream from the reality.

'What? I've just had a shower.'

'Oh.'

'Are you all right?'

'Yes,' I said, then took a breath and said it more steadily. 'Yes. Sorry. I just ... had a nightmare. That's all.'

Ben hesitated and then said, 'About Liam?'

'Yes.' I tried to smile. 'I think it was just all those things Adrian said today ... about the knight almost drowning him.'

Ben simply nodded, then glanced around the room and took in the remnants of the dinner I'd made. 'Were you having a picnic?' he asked mildly.

'I bought some food in Karstadt so I wouldn't have to eat out.'

'Why?' he asked, frowning slightly.

'It's cheaper.'

'Oh. Are you all right now?'

'Yes. Sorry. I didn't mean to disturb you.'

'I'll see you in the morning, then,' Ben replied. His hand was on the door handle to draw it shut when he paused, staring at the table by my bed. 'That's the knight you mentioned,' he said.

'What?' I said, twisting my head to follow his gaze. 'Oh, yes. That's it.'

In the dim light I thought I saw the corner of Ben's mouth twitch. Then he looked at me with one eyebrow raised and said, 'Why did you keep it?'

'I don't know,' I replied. 'It got into my suitcase by mistake when I packed for California. I suppose I'm just used to seeing it by my bed now. Ben, if you don't know what the object that fell out of the sleigh looks like, then how will you know once you've found it?'

'I'll know it when I see it,' Ben replied quietly. 'I'm quite sure of that. Goodnight, Jasmyn.'

Before I could question him any further he disappeared back into his own room, drawing the door closed behind him and plunging my room into darkness once again.

9

Lohengrin

We left for Neuschwanstein the next morning but not before having breakfast at the hotel. Ben said something about getting a bite to eat on the road but I insisted on the hotel because breakfast was included in the price. If we stopped at motorway services en route then I would have to pay again. Ben was an architect earning good money and could no doubt easily afford all this, but Liam and I had never exactly been rich to begin with. So we went down to the little cellar restaurant where cold cheeses and salami had been laid out along with fresh bread, coffee and fruit juice.

Ben did not look good. There were dark rings beneath his eyes as if he hadn't slept all night and his skin was pale. I found myself watching him anxiously, feeling that new and unpleasant fear that he might just drop down dead as Liam had done.

'Are you okay?' I asked. 'You look a bit—'

'I'm fine. I just didn't sleep very well,' he replied, picking up the coffee pot and pouring black coffee into his cup and then into mine.

'Do you have bad dreams too?' I asked.

He seemed to hesitate a bare moment before saying, 'Yes. It's understandable given the circumstances.'

'What are yours about?' I asked.

'The same as yours, I expect. Swans and knights and human bones. Nonsensical nightmares.'

'In the one I had last night,' I said, 'Liam said the word *Lohengrin* to me. Do you know what that means?'

'It's the legend of the swan knights and the name of the

fairy-tale opera Richard Wagner wrote,' Ben replied. 'King Ludwig named his castle after it – Neuschwanstein translates as "New Swan Stone". You've probably heard of it at some point and dreamt about it last night because of all this talk about knights and swans.'

'Yes,' I said, trying hard to believe it. 'I expect that's it.'

After breakfast we packed up our things and went to the rented car we'd left parked in the hotel car park. It was a bright, fresh morning with a blue sky and cold, crisp air. Anyone looking at us would probably just assume we were a young couple holidaying together in the Bavarian Alps. I thrust down the familiar ache of longing and tried to ignore the bitter taste at the back of my throat as Ben took my suitcase from me to put in the boot of the car. Because we both had large cases, there was only just enough room for them and he had to struggle a little to get them both in.

I watched the back of his dark head as he leaned over the boot muttering bad-temperedly to himself as he tried to wedge the cases in, and the unwelcome, resentful thought flashed into my mind that it hardly seemed fair that Liam had died and Ben had lived. After all, Liam had surely been the one who'd enjoyed life more. He hadn't had any of those worry lines around his eyes. He had smiled more, laughed more. And he had been two years younger. So why was it that Ben got to live whilst Liam had died for no good reason at all?

'It's unlocked,' Ben said, glancing around at me. 'You can get in.'

I felt a sudden flush of hot guilt creep up my face as he looked at me. I hoped he hadn't been able to tell what I'd been thinking and felt suddenly terrible for allowing my thoughts to drift that way in the first place. Ben might not be my favourite person in the world but he was just as loved as Liam had been. It was no secret that he had always been his parents' favourite – I suppose because he had always been so responsible and sensible in contrast to Liam. And – of course – he also had a fiancée waiting for him at home.

'What does Heidi think about all this?' I blurted out before I remembered that he had snapped at me the last time I mentioned her.

'What?' he said as he slammed the boot shut at last.

It was too late to take the question back so I said, 'Your fiancée. What does she think about your going off around the world chasing after some mystery object with your dead brother's widow?'

'I don't think she's very happy about it.'

'Do you love her?' The question startled me, for I had asked it quite without meaning to and couldn't help but wince and wonder what had come over me.

'I wouldn't be marrying her if I didn't love her,' Ben replied before walking around to the driver's side and getting in.

He'd spoken calmly enough but I thought it was probably wise to drop the subject before it could turn into an argument and just count myself lucky that it hadn't done so already. It was a three-hour drive to Neuschwanstein and we spent the first two hours mostly in silence – we simply didn't have anything to say to each other. Although I rarely liked what he said, I did like it when Ben spoke because his voice reminded me of Liam's and made me feel closer to him.

After two hours we stopped at motorway services to fill up with petrol and, to my slight surprise, Ben suggested that we go inside and have a cup of coffee before carrying on. I was glad of the chance to stretch my legs, so we parked the car and walked into the building, which was bright and clean and smelled of hot soup. I got a seat by the window overlooking the motorway while Ben queued at the till for our drinks. After a few minutes, he walked over and put the tray down on the table.

'Thanks,' I said, as he handed me the paper cup and sat down.

'I got us one of these each too,' he said, opening his fist and dropping two miniature bottles of Jägermeister onto the table between us.

I felt a lump rise in my throat at the sight of the little green bottles with the familiar deer heads on their labels. When I had come to Germany with Liam we had had a miniature bottle each because the weather was so bitter and they helped with the cold, warming you up from the inside.

'I thought they might help with the cold,' Ben said.

I nodded and thanked him hurriedly as I put mine in my pocket, although I balked at the thought of so much as unscrewing the lid. I didn't want to remember that distinctive smell or that distinctive taste because they were associated with too many happy memories that were now more bitter than sweet to me, for the man I had shared them with was dead and incapable of remembering anything ever again. The pain of the fresh sense of loss squeezed around my heart and I turned my head to look out of the window, knowing that the wave would pass.

I was taken aback when, suddenly, Ben said quietly, 'I'm sorry I've been such a prat since all this began. Whatever I'm feeling, I know it must be even worse for you. So if I'm rude to you again just tell me to piss off. And I'll ... I'll try and do better.'

I tore my gaze from the window and looked at him to see if he'd meant what he'd said, half-expecting the usual thinly veiled contempt, but instead he really did look sincere – even anxious – as if I might rebuff his attempt to make things easier between us. Before I could say anything, he went on, 'Sometimes it seems impossible that things can ever go back to the way they were and I find that ... unbearable. That's why I snap – at you, at my parents, at everyone. I can't ... contain it. I can't be dignified about it. It's too difficult. And if I've made it even harder for you, Jasmyn, then I really am sorry.'

'Thanks, Ben,' I said. 'I suppose we've both done quite a good job of making this even more difficult for each other.'

He nodded, looking relieved. Eager to move on from the moment before one of us said something to spoil it, I changed the subject by saying, 'Tell me about the *Lohengrin* legend.'

'It's a German medieval romance,' Ben replied, looking more relaxed as he took the lid off his coffee. 'Wagner wasn't the first to tell it and there are different versions of the story, but the basic premise is that a knight appears in a boat pulled by a swan and comes to the rescue of a maiden falsely accused of killing her brother. He offers to help her on the one condition that she must never ask him his name. It turns out that her brother is alive but was turned into a swan by an evil magician. The maiden and the knight later fall in love and marry but in the end, of course, she asks the forbidden question. He tells her that his name is Lohengrin but now that she knows he has to leave and can never return. She dies of a broken heart as he sails away. It's a typical opera – lots of death and unnecessary angst.'

'Why isn't she allowed to know his name?' I asked.

'Because the swan knights are supposed to have mysterious powers that stem from the Holy Grail, but these will only work if their nature is unknown. So by telling her his name and revealing himself as a Knight of the Grail, he comes too close to revealing the source of his power.'

'And King Ludwig was fond of this story?'

'Not fond so much as obsessed. He seemed to be fascinated by it even before he heard Wagner's opera. He designed Neuschwanstein with *Lohengrin* in mind, decorating many of the walls with painted scenes from the legend and apparently the swan motif is everywhere – practically in every room. He wanted swans kept on the lake and he wanted them in his grotto at Hohenschwangau too.'

'Have you ever heard of there being black swans at any of his castles?'

'No,' Ben replied.

'Do you have any theories about why they fell out of the sky like that at Liam's funeral?'

'No,' he said again. 'I have no idea. I suppose it could just have been a freakish natural occurrence like everyone thinks. But it's hard to believe that when swans seem to be so relevant in all this.'

'Yes,' I replied. 'Have you been to Neuschwanstein before?'

'I've been to this area of Germany,' Ben replied, 'and I've seen the castle up in the mountains from outside but I've never … been inside—' He broke off to jerk his hand to his head with a grimace.

'What's the matter?'

'Nothing. I just have a headache.'

'Headache?' I repeated shrilly – the very word was enough to send tremors of sick fear coursing through me now.

'It's just a headache, Jasmyn,' Ben muttered. 'I've always had them. It's nothing to worry about. Come on, we'd better get back on the road.'

We left the services and went back to the car, driving on in a more comfortable silence than before. We didn't have to go much further before both the castles came into view and Ben pulled the car over into a lay-by at the side of the road so we could get out and look at them. Schloss Hohenschwangau was to our right – a squat, bulky fortress painted yellow, surrounded by green, snow-capped pines against the mountainous backdrop of the Alps. And Schloss Neuschwanstein stood to our left – tall, white spires and turrets reaching up into the blue sky – the definitive fairy-tale castle in every sense of the word, situated in the same Alpine beauty as its stockier counterpart. We could not see either of them in any great detail from that distance for they were too high above us, but they were a striking sight nonetheless.

'Neuschwanstein was used in the *Chitty Chitty Bang Bang* film,' Ben said, leaning on the car door as we gazed up into the mountains. 'And it's the real-life inspiration for all of Walt Disney's castles.'

That didn't surprise me, for it certainly looked like something from a Disney storybook.

'Where's the lake Liam went to?' I asked.

'It's behind Hohenschwangau. You can't see it from here.'

He got back in the car and I followed him, expecting him to drive on to one of the castles from where we could then go down to the lake. Instead he sat there in silence, gripping the steering wheel.

'So where are we heading for?' I prompted.

'We need to find somewhere to stay,' Ben said, suddenly sounding a little odd. 'Can you take over the driving?'

'Why?' I asked in alarm. I'd never driven in a foreign country before and although I was insured to drive the hire car, I wasn't hugely confident about doing so.

'Because I'm going to be sick,' Ben replied, abruptly undoing his seat belt, fumbling for the door and scrambling out of the car to throw up at the side of the road.

I undid my own belt and got out to walk around the front of the car to him. 'You're ill, aren't you?' I said sharply. 'You've looked rough all day. What's wrong with you?'

'Don't worry,' Ben muttered, not looking at me but keeping his head bent. 'I'm not contagious.'

'What is it then?' I asked, vaguely aware that fear was making my voice come out more angry than concerned because for a moment I was sure he was going to say he had some sort of serious, life-threatening illness – that he was dying too.

'It's food poisoning,' he said, dragging himself up to lean against the bonnet of the car.

'Food poisoning?' I repeated.

'Yes. I went to a sausage house last night and ... I noticed one of the bratwursts they brought was slightly undercooked but I ate it anyway.'

'Why the hell did you do that?'

He shrugged. 'I was hungry.'

'That was unbelievably stupid of you,' I said.

For some reason I felt unaccountably annoyed with him. Perhaps it was for making me worry, perhaps it was for losing us time or perhaps I couldn't help slightly resenting the fact that he had been out feasting in some sausage house last night whilst I'd been eating crisps in my hotel room. But that had been hours ago now ... I frowned and said, 'Surely you'd have felt the effects of food poisoning earlier than this?'

'Oh, I don't know!' he said irritably. 'Maybe it's a virus. I really don't care what caused it!'

'All right, all right! No need to bite my head off! Do you think you're okay to get back in the car without throwing up all over the place?'

'Yes,' he muttered, flashing me a dark look. 'But be ready to stop again if I ask you to.'

That hardly filled me with confidence and I kept my eyes peeled for a guest house as we drove on. Ben was no use at all, sitting hunched in the passenger seat with his elbow resting against the window and his head in his hand as if the sun was hurting his eyes. Fortunately, we soon came across a guest house with a painted exterior and immaculately tended flower boxes full of heather at the windows. We went inside, booked two rooms and then went upstairs. Before Ben could disappear into his room I said, 'I'm going to go and visit Hohenschwangau.'

I fully expected him to protest that I must wait until he was better so that we could go together but instead he just shrugged and said, 'All right.'

'Are you going to be okay here? Do you want me to bring you anything?'

'No thanks,' he replied.

Then he disappeared into his room, shutting the door firmly behind him. His reaction puzzled me. He had seemed very keen to get here – as if he expected to find something at one of the castles or at the lake behind them – but now he didn't seem bothered at all about me going on my own, almost as if he knew the visits would be pointless. But then, perhaps he simply felt too ill to care. Either way I wanted to see these castles – and the lake in particular – for myself. I wouldn't have time to visit both in what remained of the day but I could certainly take a look at one of them. I was about to turn away when I heard the sound of something being knocked over and breaking in Ben's room. I frowned and called through the door, 'Are you all right in there?'

For a moment there was silence, then Ben's muffled voice replied, 'I already told you I'm fine. Just leave me alone.'

'Fine,' I said, throwing up my hands and wondering why I even bothered as I walked away down the corridor.

10

Hohenshwangau

I parked the car in the car park and then walked up the hill towards the castle. From a distance, Hohenschwangau was very much outdone by Neuschwanstein, for its squat, yellow structure could hardly compete with the latter's tall, elegant white spires. But, up close, Hohenschwangau too was a lovely building, in an absolutely breathtaking setting.

The tour guide explained that Ludwig had lived here whilst Neuschwanstein was being built – watching it progress from the other side of the mountain and looking forward to the day when he could finally move in. People said he was bankrupting the country with these castles but the truth was that he paid for them out of his own pocket. And the irony of it was that they drew more tourist dollars between them now than any other attraction in Bavaria.

The building work started on Neuschwanstein when Ludwig was twenty-four, but it was fifteen years before he was able to move into his dream castle, although it was still unfinished even then. He was thirty-nine by that time and had very much withdrawn from politics and Munich, disenchanted with the sordidness of it, to spend most of his remaining two years in the mountains instead, staying inside his fairy-tale castles where the walls were covered with paintings of German myths and legends and things he considered to be noble and majestic. As his political problems increased, so did his shyness and he took to travelling only under cover of night in his sleigh across the mountains. It was eccentric behaviour like that which made it so easy for the Bavarian government to have him proclaimed insane when they decided to get rid of him. A medical commission was set up and they forced their way into Neuschwanstein one night and took him away to Schloss Berg. Ludwig never saw the castle again, for he was found dead in Lake Starnberg with his doctor the following evening.

The fortress was lavishly decorated inside although some of the rooms were smaller and more intimate than I had expected, with family photos of Ludwig as well as his parents and brother. The many wall paintings were full of myths, legends and Germanic fairy tales – especially in the Hall of the Swan Knight and the Hall of Heroes. Add to that the extraordinary scenery that could be glimpsed out of every window – snow-covered pines and white-capped mountains rising against a blue sky – and I could easily imagine living here to be a surreal, fairy-tale-like sort of existence in its own right.

Even the air felt different. It was the cleanest, freshest, sweetest air I'd ever breathed in my life. I had always preferred the country-side to cities and I could fully sympathise with Ludwig and his desire to stay here in this place of incredible, silent, peaceful beauty rather than remain in the Royal Court at Munich. As someone who had also craved solitude on occasions, I could appreciate why this lonely place would hold such appeal to a young king said to be a shy dreamer who intensely disliked the insincere fawning and petty political bickering that went on in the city. Indeed, I defy anyone to go to Bavaria, to look at Hohenschwangau and Neuschwanstein in all their Alpine finery, and not be moved by their beauty. It seems to me that it would have been madness for the king to wish to remain in Munich when he had these castles in the mountains, not the other way round.

By the time the tour of the castle was over it was getting dark, so I decided to leave the lake for another day. The path leading down to it was not very well lit and … I felt uneasy about going there at night without Ben. The place had been too built-up in my mind what with everything Adrian said had happened there. So I returned to the guest house.

I ate in the restaurant that evening on my own for Ben still wasn't feeling well and stayed put upstairs. It was relatively early when I got back to my room – only just gone ten o'clock – so I plugged the earphones into my Violectra and played for a couple of hours. I soon got hot doing this – playing fast music warms you up more than you might think – and had to keep opening the window to let some wintry air blow into the room. Really I would have liked to go and play outside but that would have looked very odd if someone were to happen to see me, so I reluctantly stayed in my room.

Finally I put the violin away in its case and went to bed. I hadn't agreed a time to meet Ben in the morning but I set the alarm for eight o'clock, assuming that if he got up any earlier he would knock on my door before going downstairs. I lay down at midnight and woke up about three hours later because I was cold. I liked to have fresh air whilst I slept but it was too icy outside to leave the window open, so I clambered out of bed to close it. The room looked out onto the car park and I noticed that it was snowing. It must have started some time ago for at least a couple of inches lay upon the bonnets and roofs of the cars below.

I turned away, eager to get back to the warmth of the comfortable bed, but then I froze – the image of the car park still fresh in my mind. I returned to the window and looked again, frowning down at the snow-covered scene. In the light from the lamp post I could see five cars. None of them was the car Ben and I had arrived in.

I distinctly remembered parking it next to the lamp post when I got back from Hohenschwangau that evening but now there was no trace of it. It was gone and must have been for some time for the snow completely covered the ground where it had stood. I stared down, hardly able to believe that our car had been stolen. I wracked my brain, wondering if I had locked it but I couldn't remember. I briefly considered waking Ben but then thought better of it. The car would be just as stolen in the morning so there seemed little point in disturbing him. He might as well be pissed off tomorrow rather than tonight. It was lucky that we had taken our luggage out otherwise we would have been in serious trouble, for our passports and money were in our bags.

I sighed and was about to turn away and try to get back to sleep when a car pulled up to the guest house. I was surprised to see it arriving so late – for it was now past three o'clock in the morning. Then I realised that it looked very much like the car we had rented and for a wild moment I thought the thief must be returning it. But then it parked under the lamp post, right where I had left it. The engine and lights were turned off, the door opened and the driver got out of the car. It was Ben.

I stared in astonishment as he walked back into the guest house. Of course I knew that he had a set of car keys as well but it had simply never occurred to me that Ben – who had been ill all day – would have gone off somewhere in the middle of the night like that.

I thought about going upstairs to his bedroom and asking him where he'd gone but then thought better of it. There was sure to be a rational explanation. Perhaps he had just gone to get some air … At any rate, it was dark and cold out in the corridor and I was tired. It was late and this newest mystery could wait until the morning.

I was up and dressed when there was a knock on my door at half-past eight the next day and Ben's voice called, 'Jasmyn, I'm going down for breakfast.'

I crossed to the door within moments and opened it but he was already striding off down the corridor and I had to hurry to catch up with him.

'What's the big rush?' I asked.

'I'm hungry,' he replied. 'I didn't get much to eat yesterday.'

'You look a lot better now,' I said.

In fact I was taken aback by how improved he looked in sharp contrast to his sickly appearance the day before. He did not look at all tired or worn out as I would have expected of a man who had been ill all day and apparently up half the night.

When we were sitting at a table with plates full of bread, salami and cheeses, I waited for Ben to say something about where he had gone. Instead he said, 'How was your visit to Hohenschwangau?'

I was taken aback by this and frowned at him for a moment before saying, 'Well, it was interesting but not particularly useful.'

He nodded absently, hardly seeming even to be listening to what I was saying as he stuffed slices of salami into a bread roll and then wolfed it down. After a few minutes he looked up and saw me staring at him.

'What?' he said.

'Nothing,' I said, picking up my own bread roll and spreading cream cheese on it to give myself a moment to think. 'So did you sleep okay?'

'Yes. The beds here are really comfortable, aren't they?'

'They are,' I replied, narrowing my eyes as I realised that he really wasn't going to say anything about where he'd been last night and that instantly made me twice as suspicious. 'It snowed during the night, didn't it?' I prompted, giving him one last chance to mention that he'd driven off somewhere in the early hours of the morning.

'Did it?' Ben replied, pouring out more coffee. 'I didn't notice.'

And then I knew that not only was he simply avoiding telling me the truth but that he was actually lying. He knew full well that it had snowed in the night for he had been out in it himself.

'All right,' I said, pushing away my plate. 'Where did you go?'

'What?' Ben said, not even looking up as he started making another sandwich out of the salami and bread on his plate.

'I woke up in the middle of the night and got up to close the window. Our car wasn't there.'

'What do you mean, it wasn't there?' Ben asked, wrinkling his brow in a frown.

'I mean it was gone. I thought it had been stolen.'

'You probably just dreamt it,' Ben replied dismissively. 'It's there now.'

'I know it's there now!' I said sharply. 'I saw you drive back in it!'

Ben slowly lowered the bread roll to his plate and for a moment I thought he was going to try to deny it outright. But then he shook his head and said, 'All right. I did go out for a drive last night.'

'Where did you go?' I demanded. The fact that he had lied about it so brazenly to me made me exceedingly nervous, for it could surely only mean that I wasn't going to like wherever it was he'd gone.

'I ... just went to Neuschwanstein,' Ben said reluctantly with a sullen shrug, like a naughty child caught misbehaving. 'In case the sleigh appeared. Is that all right with you?'

'Why did you sneak off in the middle of the night like that? Why didn't you tell me you were going?'

'I assumed you'd be in bed like any normal person. And I didn't *sneak* anywhere.'

'But why the hell did you lie about it this morning?' I persisted.

Ben was silent for a moment and I could practically see him wracking his brain for an explanation.

'Because I knew you'd get ratty like this!' he snapped at last.

I was aware of a horrible sinking feeling in my stomach. Yesterday I had thought Ben was warming towards me a little but now I could see – as clear as day – that Ben knew more, and yet was deliberately not telling me about it.

'I thought we had agreed to be honest with each other!' I said angrily. 'But you're *still* hiding things from me, aren't you, you bastard?'

The knowledge filled me with a sort of desperate anger, not to mention a keen dread. How much more bad news and unwelcome truths could there be? I found myself ridiculously envious of other widows for just being able to concentrate all their attention on mourning and grieving and healing. What a luxury that seemed now. And – for the first time – I felt angry with Liam rather than just with Ben, for he was the one who had caused this situation, he was the one who had kept secrets from me and hidden things from me and lied to me. Of course, he hadn't known that he was going to die and so couldn't possibly have foreseen me getting mixed up in it all, but that's what had happened nonetheless, and being entirely reliant on Ben of all people for information and answers about my husband – the person I had thought I'd known better than anyone else in the world – was intolerable.

Ben was clearly finding the situation equally unpleasant and obviously resented having been caught out in a lie for he said irritably, 'I'm in an impossible situation here, Jasmyn. You were his wife – there are things that I just can't say to you about him.'

'Like what?' I asked, startled. 'Why should me being his wife make any difference?'

'Because you saw him in a different way from everyone else! You loved him more than anybody else! And I don't want to say anything that will ... that will hurt you.'

'Don't be ridiculous! Nothing you can say will make him any more dead than he already is, so how bad can it possibly be? I want you to tell me anything and everything you've left out and I want you to tell me *right now!*'

I desperately wished that I had some bargaining chip of my own to use but the truth was that I was absolutely powerless to make Ben tell me anything and he knew it. If he didn't want to tell me, there was nothing I could do to force him.

'I don't even know if it's true,' he said sullenly, raising his right arm to massage his left shoulder as if it ached. 'It's just something Jaxon told me about Liam.'

'Well, tell me and maybe I'll know if it's true.'

Ben met my gaze reluctantly. 'I don't think you will.'

'Tell me anyway,' I said through gritted teeth.

'All right, fine,' he said, throwing up his hands. 'But don't say I didn't try to avoid this. Jaxon told me ... he told me that he thought Liam had another woman here somewhere around Neuschwanstein.'

I stared at Ben in silence for a moment before laughter bubbled up in my chest and burst from my lips. It was actually something of a relief to realise that Ben did not, after all, know more about my husband than I did. I shook my head. 'Liam didn't have a woman here in Germany or anywhere else.'

Ben sighed. 'How can you possibly be sure of that?' he asked in a quiet voice, fidgeting uncomfortably with the bread roll on his plate.

I smiled. 'Liam would never, ever have cheated on me and nothing you can tell me about him will ever shake my faith in that, not ever.'

'But the fact is that you can't know. You weren't even in the same country half the time.'

'Look,' I said, 'if someone told you that Heidi had been unfaithful to you, would you ever believe it?'

Ben glanced at me. 'Probably. She's been unfaithful before.'

That threw me and I felt an embarrassed flush creep up my cheeks. 'Oh. I'm sorry. But ... in that case ... why do you still want to marry her?'

Ben avoided my gaze and looked out of the window. 'I don't blame her for doing what she did,' he said flatly. 'Besides, I suppose I haven't been entirely faithful myself.'

I sighed and said, 'Well ... I'm sorry. But ... Liam and I weren't like that. I know that he loved me. And if he lied then he must have had a reason.'

'Perhaps you're right,' Ben said. 'But you must admit that a woman would explain some of this. It would explain why he kept sneaking off to Germany without telling you and why he lied about where he was going.'

'It wouldn't explain why he went to Paris though,' I pointed out. 'Unless you think he had a mistress there too?'

Ben shrugged. 'Perhaps he took his German woman there.'

'No. An affair doesn't explain anything at all. There's nothing supernatural about an affair. There's nothing that could explain why black swans fell out of the sky at his funeral or that horse we saw on the *Queen Mary* or the bones and roses that were left behind—' I broke off with a snort of amusement. 'It's typical of another man to jump to the conclusion of infidelity even when there is nothing to support it.'

Ben shrugged. 'I believe Liam had at least one mistress for the simple reason that that's the kind of person he was – always wanting what he couldn't have.'

I stared at him incredulously. 'He was your own brother,' I said. 'How is it possible that you hardly knew him at all?'

'If there is a woman,' Ben went on doggedly, 'then we need to find her. She might know more about what Liam was doing here. He might have confided in her. When he was in Alpau he stayed in a guest house not far from here, just a few minutes down the road. These places are small and usually family-run so they'll probably remember him, especially if he stayed at the same place every time. And they'll be able to tell us if he ever took a woman back to his room or—'

He broke off then, because I slapped him. Suggesting a mistress as a possibility was one thing but talking about it as if it were a certainty was another and I was too furious on Liam's behalf to listen to any more of it.

'Don't talk about him that way, as if ... as if he was no better than ... than—'

'No better than me?' Ben suggested, raising a hand to the angry red mark on his cheek.

'Yes!' I snapped. 'I'm sorry to say it so bluntly but it's true. He was a better man than you, Ben! Whatever problems you have with your fiancée are one thing but Liam and I were entirely faithful to each other from the very beginning.'

'Well, be that as it may,' Ben said calmly, 'now you see why I can't talk about these things with you. If anything else occurs to my suspicious mind, I'll just keep it to myself, shall I?'

I wanted Ben to tell me everything he knew or suspected, but if he was going to come out with things like that then there really didn't seem a lot of point in insisting he told me everything. The frustrating thing was that if he had known his younger brother as well as he should have done, then he would never have suspected him of infidelity to begin with. But for the entire ten months of our marriage, Ben hadn't seen Liam, hadn't even spoken to him.

So how could he possibly presume to judge our life together and what it had been built upon?

'You didn't know him,' I said in frustration.

Ben just shrugged. 'One of us didn't know him, anyway,' he replied calmly.

'So am I to presume that that's how you're going to spend your day?' I asked coldly. 'Wandering around looking for a mistress who doesn't exist?'

'That's right,' Ben replied shortly. 'And tonight I'm going back to Neuschwanstein after dark, so if you want to come with me then you'd better make sure you're here at the guest house by about eleven o'clock.'

Without waiting for me to reply, he pushed back his chair and stormed out of the restaurant. I returned to my own room, grabbed my bag and coat and then went upstairs, but paused when I arrived outside Ben's door. My intention had been to ask him what we were going to do about the car for, of course, we only had one between us and it appeared we would be heading in different directions that day. My hand was raised to knock when I hesitated. He was the architect, he was the one with money, he was the one wanting to chase after some dead end. Why should I give him the chance to tell me to take public transport when I had my own car key?

I dropped my hand and turned away from the door, deciding that it would be a question of first one to the car wins. I was dressed and ready to go, but Ben, from the sounds of it, was bad-temperedly throwing things around his room and swearing to himself.

So I went straight out to the car and drove away towards Neuschwanstein before Ben could beat me to it. He could find his own way of trawling around the nearby guest houses and good luck to him.

11

Lukas

The castle was only a ten-minute drive away. I parked at the car park halfway up the mountain and then had the choice of walking or getting a horse-drawn carriage to the top. I decided to walk as it was a cold morning and I wanted to warm up. Besides which I couldn't really afford the luxury of a carriage ride.

Neuschwanstein was no less striking up close than it was from a distance. It truly was the definitive fairy-tale castle with its tall spires and pale stones – crisp white snow upon its turrets and weighing down the branches of the mountain pines that surrounded it.

I joined the English tour that was just starting and we walked through the grandly decorated rooms listening to the guide tell us about Ludwig and his sad life. As Ben had said, the swan motif was everywhere in this castle. I noticed the bird in paintings, fabric coverings, sculptures and even on flower vases.

One of the other great mysteries of Ludwig's life was the question of why he had never married, remaining a solitary and reclusive bachelor instead. He had come close once, the guide told us as we stopped in Ludwig's neo-Gothic, sumptuously decorated bedroom full of rich oak, colourful paintings and golden chandeliers.

She directed the group's attention to a photograph of Ludwig with his cousin, Princess Sophie Charlotte of Bavaria, to whom he became engaged when he was twenty-one years old. The wedding date was set, a golden wedding coach was specially built and gold coins had been minted when Ludwig, suddenly and unexpectedly – without explanation – changed his mind and called the wedding off. He never considered marriage again and no one knew what had caused his change of heart. It obviously hadn't been Sophie's looks, for she had quite clearly been unusually beautiful and it was this that led to the rumours that Ludwig was gay, and that that was why he never married. One American tourist nearby me was self-importantly assuring the rest of his party that Ludwig had most certainly been gay and, suddenly, all this scandalous speculation seemed rather vulgar.

The guide did not in any way lessen my discomfort when she explained that it was right here, in this very room, that the king was declared insane and removed from the throne, despite the fact that the doctor had never even examined him. He had been loved by his subjects – who had even attempted to protect him and prevent his deposition until he told them they could stand down and that he was prepared to leave if the commission wanted him to. Even today, the guide told us, the king was still affectionately known in Bavaria as Kini ... I was startled by the name, for the last time I had heard it was at my grandparents', talking to Luke about a black horse ...

The guide went on to tell us that as Ludwig left Neuschwanstein for the last time, he said to one of his trusted servants: '*Please guard these rooms for me as a shrine. Don't let them be profaned by the curious, because I have had to endure the bitterest hours of my life here!*'

She then added with a smile that, of course, thousands of people now visited the castle every year. Everyone laughed, but I felt uncomfortable as we continued our tour through the lavish rooms – like a common intruder thoughtlessly trespassing in a home that had once been so dear to somebody's heart.

It seemed sad that Ludwig had lived at Neuschwanstein for such a short amount of time before being forcibly taken away and drowning in a lake many miles from his beloved home. The guide told us that, even as a teenager, Ludwig had taken his responsibilities as king very seriously, but had quickly come to realise that the ideals of monarchy he aspired to simply didn't exist in nineteenth-century Germany. That he was a figurehead and nothing more – certainly never intended to actually govern himself. And so he retreated to his lonely castles in the mountains where he could be left in peace.

When the tour was over I was glad to get back outside to the fresh mountain air, stand at the veranda and look out towards the skyline of the Tyrolean Mountains, beneath which lay the Alpsee Lake at the end of a short road set with pretty houses. Perhaps it was my own recent troubles that made me overly sensitive to such things, but I disliked hearing people gossip in such a way about the king and his loneliness. Perhaps the truth was that he had simply never met the right person, and that was why he had remained alone. I wondered what was worse – to have lived a completely solitary life like Ludwig or to have had someone really special who couldn't stay with you ...

When I couldn't put it off any longer, I took the path down to the lake. My feet crunched on the gravel and I breathed in the sweet mountain air, my breath misting before me. I don't know why I felt so uneasy, for it wasn't as if I expected to see anything out of the ordinary. I certainly didn't expect magical swans to appear before my eyes or black knights to walk across the water ... But still – there it was – that sense of dread ...

I forced myself not to slow my steps or drag my feet and, when I at last got down to the lake, I stood on the bank looking out across the perfectly still, flat water. Tall pines made white with snow stood all the way around it and stretched up the surrounding mountains, and I could see Hohenschwangau high above me to the right. There didn't seem to be any swans on the lake though and suddenly it seemed impossible that Liam had been to this place at all, let alone that events had played out as Adrian Halsbach had described them to us – sneaking here in the middle of the night, killing a swan and then being half-drowned by a black knight in these very waters. I didn't feel close to Liam here at all. I couldn't imagine him creeping around the banks looking for magic swans. I suddenly felt that if he could see me now and knew why I was here, he would laugh at the absurdity of the things Ben had told me and the fact that I had believed them ...

But then, perhaps he wouldn't laugh at all ... perhaps he would be angry with me for listening to Ben – the man who, for whatever reason, he had felt so bitterly towards during the last year of his life …

Suddenly I noticed white shapes on the water and realised that a couple of swans were now on the lake. Although they looked just as superior and majestic as every other swan I had ever seen, they did not look magical and the very suggestion that they were anything other than normal seemed suddenly absurd. I stepped to the edge of the water and crouched down to dip my fingers in. After a moment I straightened up, shaking my hand dry. As I looked at the swans, I realised that the last time I had seen white swans on water was when I had been feeding them with Liam, just minutes before he died. The recollection made me feel a little sick and I suddenly found I wanted to be gone from the lake.

I turned away, but then stopped, for there was a man standing at the end of the path, blocking the way. Once again, the first thing I noticed about Luke was his height. Liam had been tall and so was Ben, but Luke must have been almost seven foot. I didn't understand how I could have failed to hear him approach for there was surely no way he would have been able to step lightly enough not to make a sound on the gravel path. I was suddenly very aware of the fact that there was no one else at all around except for us.

'You really shouldn't touch the water,' he said, breaking the silence at last. 'You don't know what lies beneath it.'

'Who are you?' I demanded, finding my tongue and forcing myself not to take a step back and thereby give away the fact that I was scared.

'Don't you remember me?' he asked, one corner of his mouth quirking up in a smile. 'It wasn't that long ago that we met.'

'I know you're not a stable-hand!' I snapped. 'Is your name even Luke?'

'Near enough. It's Lukas. Sorry about that. I just wanted to meet you, that's all. I didn't mean to cause you or your grandparents any anxiety.'

'How did you find me?' I demanded, a chill creeping up my spine at the reminder that he knew where my grandparents lived.

'Kini told me where you were,' Lukas said cheerfully, putting his hands in his pockets. 'He's pretty good at finding people.'

'Why are you here?' I said, secretly rather horrified that he seemed to have followed me all the way to Germany.

'Don't be afraid,' he said quickly. 'I just came to tell you something about ... about Liam and the object he took.'

'You knew Liam?'

'Yes, I knew him,' Lukas replied. 'I can't say I had any great liking for him, but I'm sorry for your loss.'

'How did you know him?' I snapped. I didn't know or care why this stranger had disliked Liam and at any rate it seemed more a slur on his character than on my husband's.

'I met him here, of course,' Lukas said, vaguely waving his hand to encompass Neuschwanstein and the surrounding area. 'I'm afraid we had a ... disagreement. Got off on the wrong foot. But none of that matters now. All I care about is the object that was taken.'

'Are you looking for it too?' I asked.

'Not as such ... but I want you to find it. Before Jaxon does.'

'Why do you—' I began, but he cut me off.

'I'm sorry, but there really isn't time. I've got to tell you something.'

I expected him to say something about Liam, or Jaxon, or Ben, or the mysterious object that had been taken, so I was surprised when, instead, he said, 'Do you know why King Ludwig called off his wedding to Princess Sophie at the last hour?'

The question seemed so absurdly irrelevant that it took me a moment to get my mind around it and I gave an impatient shrug in response.

'He was in love with someone else,' Lukas said evenly, his eyes not leaving my face.

'Another man?' I asked, remembering what the tour guide had said about Ludwig possibly being gay.

'No. A swan. A magic one. You've seen *Swan Lake*, haven't you? Swan by day and woman by night. Ludwig would never have found out if he hadn't liked to come down to the lake in the middle of the night. But he did and that's when he saw them in their human form. The problem is that swans and humans aren't allowed to fall in love. It's one of the Old Rules and the knights still enforce it even now. They're sticklers for the rules, you see, whether or not they make any sense. So Ludwig wasn't allowed to be with his swan princess. He tried to marry a human woman, but he cancelled the wedding at the last moment because he had these romantic ideas about what marriage should be and he didn't want to marry someone he didn't love.

'The knights forbade them from seeing each other but she would sing to let him know where she was. So they took away her voice and left her mute. Swansong is one of the most powerful forms of enchantment there is. That's what fell out of the sleigh. That's what your husband found.'

'How can someone possibly *find* the voice of a swan?' I asked. 'It's not as if it's something you can touch.'

'But it is,' Lukas replied. 'It can be anything you want it to be. I've heard that it looked like a jewelled tiara when he found it, but Liam could have changed its appearance. It could look like anything now. Do you see why so many people want it? It's like having a witch's wand or a wizard's staff. Swansong can be used to enchant anyone. That's why it's dangerous. That's why it must never fall into the wrong hands.'

I turned my head to glance at the two swans on the lake but my mind simply couldn't accept the idea that at night they were anything other than ordinary birds.

'You don't believe me, do you?' Lukas said.

'I don't know you,' I replied. 'I don't know who you are or where you've come from or how you're mixed up in this. So I would be stupid to believe a word you say without proof.'

'Jaxon knows what it is – he's known for a long time and he's looking for it too. You have to find it before he does. And you should stay close to Ben. Jaxon will come back if it occurs to him that you might know where the swansong is – if he isn't here already.'

'I have absolutely no idea where this thing might be, whatever it is,' I said impatiently. 'I don't know why people keep suggesting that I would. Liam never told me any of this – I'm the very last person who could find it.'

'That's not true,' Lukas replied evenly. 'It's the complete opposite, in fact. You might well be the only person in the world who can possibly find it now that Liam's dead.'

'If he was going to hide something,' I said, 'he would have put it in a bank. Surely that's obvious to anyone?'

'It's not hidden in a bank,' Lukas replied.

'How do you know?'

'Well, for one thing, Liam wouldn't have wanted anyone else to see the swansong, whatever form it happened to be in. He'd have been too paranoid that they would be drawn to it and steal it. But, more importantly, it's got to be hidden somewhere that's certain to be deserted at night.'

'Why?'

'Because the swansong sings then. Not always, but sometimes. And if anyone heard it then they'd be able to find it.'

'Well, in that case it's probably hidden up in the mountains somewhere and I'll never find it!'

'Oh no. I'm sure he's hidden it somewhere central. In case he ever needed it in a hurry. He wouldn't have put it somewhere that would take days to reach. It may not be in England – in fact it probably isn't – but I don't think it will be very far away. And it won't be difficult to get to.'

'But if, at the same time, it's supposedly far enough away that no one will hear it if it sings at night then that's a contradiction,' I pointed out.

'Yes, you would think so,' Lukas said quietly, a gleam in his eye. 'But your husband was very clever that way. I've no doubt he found the perfect hiding place. If you want to get to the swansong before Jaxon does – and trust me, you *do* want that – then go back to Neuschwanstein after dark.' He gestured over his shoulder towards the white spires of the castle. 'I have a strong suspicion you'll find the trip very useful. Go tonight – don't put it off. You don't know how vital it is that you get to the swansong first. You don't have to believe what I told you about King Ludwig if you don't want to, but you must believe me when I say that if you don't find the swansong soon, you're going to lose someone else.'

'Who?' I said, startled.

'I don't know where it's been hidden but ... if you come back here at night then you'll get a better idea.'

'Who else will I lose?' I said again. I certainly didn't take what he'd said at face value but if he'd made it up to scare me then he'd succeeded. Death was much harder to deal with than I had ever imagined because it was so final and immovable and I hated having to be so *young* with so many years without him stretching out before me ... The only thing I could take comfort in was that the person I loved most was already gone and – having happened once, it could not happen again. But there were still plenty of other loved ones still left ...

I shook myself a little, getting a grip, thinking it through. What Lukas had said didn't make any sense. My family were all safely back home in England, I didn't think it was even possible to steal a swan's song and he was probably making the whole thing up to scare me anyway ...

'It's the truth,' Lukas said. He looked suddenly troubled and his expression – assuming it was genuine – unnerved me. He took a step forwards and, backed up against the lake, I couldn't step away without ending up in the water. 'Listen,' he said quietly, taking hold of my elbows to stop me from walking away. 'I don't want to say too much. You wouldn't believe me. But ... something truly ...' He trailed off as if searching for the right word, then shook his head impatiently and said, 'Something truly evil has happened here. Something more devastating than you can possibly realise. You think you're in pain right now as a widow but – trust me – you don't even know the half of it. It's worse, it's much worse than you think.'

I shook him off, for the intensity in his eyes, not to mention the things he was saying, sent a chill down my spine.

'You've obviously never lost the love of your life before,' I said acidly. 'Nothing's more painful than that.'

I moved past him towards the path leading back to the castle. I had been uneasy even before he had walked forwards and grabbed my arms but now I was even more conscious of the fact that I was here at the secluded lake completely alone with him – a man I knew had been stalking me in England and who had now followed me to Germany as well. It seemed prudent to get back to other people as soon as possible.

But then Lukas said something that stopped me in my tracks.

'You've already lost something else, something you didn't even know you had.'

My mind flew back to the times I had woken from dreams about swans to experience that strange, inexplicable sense of loss that was for something other than Liam. As if something was gone but I couldn't remember what ...

'You've felt it, haven't you?' Lukas said as I turned back around, obviously realising from the expression on my face.

'What else have I lost?' The question tumbled from my lips and even I could hear the fear in my voice. I was desperate to find out and be rid of the terrible sensation. It was like knowing you'd forgotten to do something really important but having no idea what it was. 'What is it?' I asked again when Lukas didn't reply, but merely stood there looking at me with a strange expression on his face. 'Do you know?'

'If you want to find out,' Lukas said at last, 'find the swansong. All I can say is that if you find it quickly enough, you just might be able to get back what's gone. But you haven't got much time left, Jasmyn. If you don't find it – or if Jaxon gets there first – things are going to get even worse than they already are.'

'How do you know all this?' I asked, but he sidestepped the question completely.

'Look at the time,' he said with a sudden smile. 'I'd better be going. Kini will be around though, keeping an eye on you. And there's no need to lecture me about his wandering around loose again. He's not an ordinary horse, you know.'

And, without another word, he turned and walked away down one of the tree-lined paths around the lake. After hesitating for a few seconds, I hurried after him. But when I got to the mouth of the path there was no sign of Lukas or anyone else. I stared down the dark, dappled walkway stretching away before me. He couldn't have disappeared that quickly – it wasn't possible. And that could only mean that he had concealed himself amongst the trees, perhaps hoping that I would follow him out of sight where he could ... do whatever he liked – after all, he was almost seven feet tall ... But although I instinctively wanted to chase after him and insist on more answers, more explanations, I had watched enough horror films to know that you never set off down a dark, secluded path like that by yourself. So I turned on my heel and headed back towards the car, aware all the while of the horrible, unsettling sensation of unseen eyes burning into the back of my neck.

12

Travel Chess

As soon as I got back to the car I phoned Ben to ask him to meet me at the guest house. Our conversation was brief and abrupt. He said he would get back as soon as he could but that – as he had to wait for a taxi – it might take a little while. His pointed tone clearly indicated that he wanted me to drive down and pick him up but I decided that if that was what he wanted then he was going to have to come out and ask – and politely too. And as he couldn't bring himself to do that I just said, 'Don't worry. There's no rush,' and hung up on him.

When I got back to the guest house he still hadn't arrived so I went back up to my room. Ben would know that I was back because he would see the car, so I assumed he would knock on my door when he turned up. In the meantime, I took off my coat and unzipped my violin case to check on my Violectra. I felt nervous about leaving it alone in the room when I went out in case the unthinkable should happen and someone should steal it. It was, of course, insured, but that was not the point. I loved it for the smooth quality of its sound and the breathtaking beauty of its appearance but – most of all – I loved it because of where it had come from. I loved it for the fact that Liam had scrimped and saved to buy it for me, I loved it for the fact that he had been the one to pick out its colour and design, I loved it for being there with me at the funeral and for being here with me now. I loved it like an old friend – a precious relic from my previous life when I had been happy and everything had been okay.

I took the skeletal thing out of its case and cradled it in my lap where I sat cross-legged on the floor – enjoying the familiar feel of it. Then I flipped open the compartment at the end of the case and took out the golden block of rosin, running my fingers over its smooth surface, breathing in the familiar scent – my favourite smell in the world, even more so than horses and saddle soap.

I reached for the bow still in the case with the intention of running the block of rosin down it a few times, but my hand froze halfway there – for there was something else in my violin case. Something that had not been there before.

Pinned between the bow and the soft interior was a thorny black rose. Slowly, I drew the bow out and laid it to one side, causing the rose to drop down into the main body of the case. I picked it up between thumb and forefinger, careful not to touch any of the thorns. It was identical to the one I had seen on the deck of the *Queen Mary* and when I lifted it to my face I could tell that it had the same sweet scent ...

'Where did you get that?' a sharp voice said from the doorway.

I jumped in alarm and almost dropped the rose. In my pre-occupation with it, I hadn't noticed the door opening behind me and when I turned around I saw Ben standing there, staring suspiciously at the flower in my hand.

'I found it in my violin case,' I said.

'The violin case?' he repeated, eyes narrowing even further.

'Yes, it was pinned behind my bow.'

'Let me see it,' he demanded, already striding into my room.

But before he could get to me, the rose disintegrated in my hand, just like the last time ... Well, not *quite* like the last time. On the *Queen Mary*, the petals had all dropped off and then been carried away by the wind before the stem turned to dust. This time, the petals fell into my lap and the thorny stem disintegrated as before, but when I looked down at the petals and gathered them up in my hand they were no longer petals, but small black feathers instead.

'Those roses seem to keep on finding you,' Ben said in an almost accusatory tone.

'Hmm.' I gazed down at the feathers in my hand, wondering what they meant.

'Was that why you phoned me?'

'No,' I said, dropping the feathers to put my violin back in its case. 'I wanted to talk to you about Lukas. I met him again at the castle. He's the one I saw back in England on my grandparents' estate – the one with the black horse.'

'He's here in Germany? What did he want?'

I told Ben what Lukas had said about Ludwig and the magic swans and the enchanted swansong. He listened in silence until I said, 'So? Have you heard any of that before?'

He shrugged. 'I've come across the myth that magical swans can enchant people with their song but I've never heard of their voices being taken away before. If it's true it fits with what Liam told me. He said this object was proof that the swans were magical.'

'Lukas said that if we didn't find the swansong soon, I'd lose someone else.'

'Did he now?' Ben said evenly, raising one eyebrow just slightly.

'Do you think he means someone will actually die?'

'I have no idea,' Ben replied. 'But whether he's telling the truth or not I think we're agreed that we need to find this swansong, or whatever it is, quickly. If nothing else, to ensure that we get to it before Jaxon can find it and sell it.'

I told Ben what Lukas had said about returning to Neuschwanstein after dark. In that moment I felt glad that he was with me for I would have been distinctly uneasy about going back to the castle at night on my own in case it was some kind of trap. Of course, I had no way of knowing that it *wasn't* a trap and Ben coming with me didn't mean it was necessarily safe. But still, the thought of returning was less frightening if he was going to be there as well. I remembered that he had talked about going to Neuschwanstein after dark himself that morning and said, 'Why did you suggest it anyway?'

He shrugged. 'It's the obvious thing to do,' he said quietly. Then added, 'Things change around Neuschwanstein at night, if the stories are anything to go by. With nothing else to go on, all we can do is retrace Liam's footsteps for now.'

After a brief hesitation, I decided to tell him about the other thing Lukas had said to me, about losing something I hadn't even known I'd had. I was right on the verge of confiding to him the strange, unsettling feeling I sometimes got when Ben said coolly, 'Aren't you going to ask what I've been doing this morning?'

'I know what you've been doing,' I replied sharply. 'Wasting your time.'

'You're not even a tiny bit curious about whether or not I found a mistress?'

'No. Because I know there isn't one.'

'It must be nice,' he grunted, 'to trust someone so completely.'

His tone didn't match his words, for he spoke as if I was some kind of idiot. So I ignored him and said calmly – as if he hadn't upset me at all, 'I'm going to get some lunch.'

It occurred to me as I walked past Ben and out through the door that, although he may not have found a mistress who could give us any information, he might have come across someone else – a receptionist or a waitress – who remembered Liam and could tell us something about what he'd done whilst he was staying here. I shouldn't have been so quick to dismiss what he'd been doing that morning for he might have discovered something of value. But now I didn't like to ask because ... I had just told him I wasn't interested ... and to ask now would make me look like a fool ...

I shook myself impatiently. This was about Liam – looking a fool shouldn't come into it. How could I possibly let something as petty as vanity have any influence over me now? I stopped in the corridor and turned around. Ben had followed me and was closing my door behind him.

'So *did* you learn anything this morning?' I asked.

He seemed to take an almost malicious delight in the question and replied, 'I thought you and Liam *trusted* each other from the very beginning!'

I scowled at him with a sudden surge of dislike. It seemed that every time he had the chance to make things harder for me he did so.

'You smug git!' I snapped, fervently wishing I didn't need him so that I could tell him to go to hell. 'I don't believe for a second that there was a mistress but you could still have found someone else who knew something. Besides, even if I didn't trust Liam, I would know you hadn't found another woman because if you had you would have rammed it down my throat the moment you saw me!'

'You're right about that!' Ben said and – in that moment – he didn't look like Liam one bit. He looked hard and cold and mean so that I could no longer see my husband in him at all. This was a stranger – a man I hardly knew ...

'*Be very careful around Ben ...*' Liam's voice seemed to echo inside my head. '*Sometimes he does things ... without meaning to ...*'

I had been letting myself feel safe with him but I mustn't forget that Liam hadn't trusted his brother, hadn't wanted him in our lives, hadn't even wanted him in the house. And there must have been a reason for that ...

'I think you'd better tell me why the two of you fell out,' I said sharply, suddenly desperate to clear this up once and for all. 'I need to know I can trust you!'

To my surprise, Ben started to laugh. It seemed to burst from him against his will, until his shoulders shook and tears streamed down his face. I stared at him in alarm. I had never seen him like that before. And if he didn't take a breath soon I thought he might suffocate. Death by laughing ...

Finally he took a great shuddering gasp of air, one hand on the wall to steady himself as he wiped away the tears and pulled himself together. Then his eyes met mine and I flinched at the look on his face – a horrible mixture of anger, contempt and bitterness.

'At least that makes us even!' he snapped. 'Because I don't trust you either! Not one bit!'

'What *possible* reason could you have not to trust me?' I shouted, not caring that we were in the corridor and people would hear us.

'You're—' But then he broke off abruptly and shook his head. 'Never mind,' he said. 'Forget it. I trust you. More or less. Let's go and get something to eat.'

And with that he strode past me towards the stairs as though the last few heated minutes had never happened. I thought about not following him but decided against it, for it would just make the situation worse. If we ate together – even in stilted silence – it might help clear the air and smooth things over between us. So I went down to the restaurant with him and – as I'd expected – Ben was in a dour, silent mood, picking grumpily at the food on his plate, looking out of the window rather than at me. When I asked him again if he'd learned anything useful that morning, he replied that the guest house down the road remembered Liam staying there but could tell him nothing useful. So I decided that he must be sulking because he'd wasted his morning and been proved wrong. Served him right for being so smug.

I just wished I knew what he and Liam had fallen out about last year. It was eating away at me – a great weight on my mind. When Liam had been alive it hadn't mattered much because we had never seen Ben anyway. But now I was here with him and I needed to know that I wasn't somehow betraying Liam. They could have fallen out over any number of things, but I knew it had to be something serious because it had lasted so long and neither one of them wanted to tell me what it was about. The more I thought about it now, the stranger it seemed that Liam himself had refused to tell me. I could understand Ben not wanting to, as I was sure whatever had happened was his fault. But if Liam had been blameless it seemed strange that he had not told me about it and I suddenly had the uncomfortable feeling that, perhaps, he hadn't been *completely* blameless after all ...

I looked out of the window to distract myself from such unwelcome thoughts and noticed a small group of horse riders passing the guest house in the light snowfall that had started – probably on their way back to the stable I had seen just down the road.

'You had a horse-drawn carriage at your wedding, didn't you?' Ben grunted suddenly.

'Yes,' I replied vaguely, my mind going back at once to that magical day. The two grey horses had had ribbons in their manes and flowers tied to their livery ...

'How did you manage to talk him into that?'

'What?' I said, confused.

'Liam,' Ben said, gazing at me sullenly. 'How did you talk him into the horses?'

'I didn't talk him into it. They were his idea.'

'But he didn't like horses.'

I stared at him. He had said a couple of other things about Liam that had been incorrect but I had assumed that was because he'd not seen him for a year and so there were things that he had missed or – possibly – things that he'd forgotten. But Liam had always loved horses, right from when he'd been a little boy coming to spend the summer holidays with me at my grandparents'. Surely Ben must remember that. It suddenly occurred to me that perhaps Ben was not quite as balanced – or as stable – as he appeared to be.

'He used to come and stay with me at my grandparents',' I said. 'My grandfather taught him to ride.'

'Oh, yes,' Ben said, shaking his head as if impatient with himself. 'I remember now.'

Well, it had been twenty-odd years ago. Perhaps it wasn't so very strange that Ben didn't remember where Liam had been during the holidays.

'Of course, if you'd been at the wedding you'd know he liked horses,' I said, unable to keep some frost from creeping into my voice. I knew Liam had been disappointed that his brother hadn't been there.

'Perhaps you can show me your wedding album some day,' Ben replied, in a tone of voice that suggested he'd rather see himself drowned at the bottom of a lake first.

'I asked my mother to send you some photos,' I said. 'She said she was going to.'

'They must have got lost in the post.'

'Well, if you ever find them I'd like them back,' I said. 'There's … something wrong with mine.'

'I've never seen any photos,' Ben said abruptly, massaging his left shoulder with his right hand. 'Your mother never sent—' He broke off suddenly, eyes narrowing. Slowly, he lowered his arm and said quietly, 'What did you just say?'

'I said … if you find the photos I'd like them back.'

'Because there's something wrong with your own?' he said, a strange eagerness in his voice.

'Yes,' I replied, now wishing I hadn't mentioned it.

'What's wrong with them?' He still spoke quietly but I was startled by the sudden eager, bright look in his eyes and the way he had gone utterly still as he watched me.

I thought about lying. I could say I spilt coffee on them or something … But I could tell by the way he was looking at me that, somehow, he already knew it was more than that.

'The woman in the photos,' I said reluctantly, 'isn't me.'

'What do you mean?'

'She's … not smiling. There's something wrong with her face. And I know I didn't stop smiling all day. I think Jaxon must have done something to them. It's the only explanation I can come up with.'

To my surprise, Ben gave a sort of disbelieving laugh and then smiled at me, his whole face transformed by it, his brown eyes suddenly genuinely warm for the first time since all this began.

'The same thing happened to my photos,' he beamed.

'Oh,' I replied stupidly, unable to think of anything sensible to say. His reaction puzzled me for it hardly felt like something to celebrate. If anything it was something to be worried about for it seemed unlikely that Jaxon could – or would – have broken into Ben's flat too. 'What do you think it means?'

He shrugged. 'I don't know. I don't think it was Jaxon. I think it's something else. But I'm glad I'm not the only one. Aren't you?'

'I suppose. I'd just like to know why it's happening at all.' I wished Ben hadn't told me the same thing had happened to his own photos, for then I could have gone on trying to believe that Jaxon was responsible. I turned my head to look out of the window and was taken aback by how heavily it was now snowing. 'It's really coming down out there.'

'Yes,' Ben replied. 'We'd better not go out while it's like this, we don't have any chains for the car. The roads will be too dangerous. Hopefully they'll be clearer by this evening so we can still go to Neuschwanstein. We'll wait until after dinner and then we'll go.'

'Okay,' I said, wondering what I was going to do with myself until then. If I'd been there with anyone other than Ben I would have suggested we go to the bar, have a drink, try to relax and talk of other things for a while. But that seemed pointless under the circumstances, so when we got up from the table I parted from Ben on the second-floor landing, leaving him to go up to his own room and I to mine, saying that we would meet again for dinner. Ben usually gave the impression that he found being with me a bother and was relieved to be on his own again whenever possible. I wasn't particularly offended by it for I knew he was solitary and antisocial and thought he'd probably be much the same whoever he happened to be with.

I automatically went straight to my violin when I got into my room. There was no black rose this time and, for a moment, I just looked at the beautiful instrument in its case. Of course I had a normal violin too but it just wasn't the same. I could never have played it in the middle of the night for fear of waking Liam up or disturbing the neighbours. I certainly couldn't have played it in a hotel. And the Violectra was so much more beautiful with its skeletal blue and silver frame and its haunting, mellow tone. Everything about it was perfect and – just like a normal violin – the quality of its sound only seemed to improve the more I played it.

I was probably being overly paranoid but I had packed two sets of spare strings because the thought of one breaking while I was abroad made me feel almost panic-stricken, like a smoker suddenly finding themselves without cigarettes. But that afternoon I didn't much feel like playing. I found I wanted company instead.

I was just thinking about taking a book and going down to the bar to while away the afternoon when there was a knock at my door. When I went to answer it, Ben was standing on the other side with a wooden box in his hands and a slightly uncertain look on his face.

'I ... wondered if you might like to play a game of chess while we're waiting,' he said. 'But ... if there's something else you'd rather do by yourself ...' His eyes flicked to my open violin case and he said, 'Never mind, it was a stupid idea. I expect you just want to play your violin.'

He was already walking away without even waiting for me to reply.

'Hang on,' I said. 'Do you have a chess set in there?'

'It's just a travel one,' Ben replied, turning back in the corridor.

'Are you any good?' I asked with a smile.

'Good enough to while away an hour or two,' he said.

'You're not going to get stroppy if I win, are you?'

Ben hesitated, then said, 'Heidi's told me that I'm a fair loser but a smug winner.'

I smiled, for that was just how Liam had been – laid back if he lost but insufferably smug if he won. Clearly it ran in the family.

'I'll try especially hard to beat you then,' I said.

We went back into my room and sat down on either side of the coffee table with the chessboard on the table between us.

'Is she clever?' I asked, making the most of Ben's apparent good mood to indulge my curiosity.

'She's extremely intelligent,' Ben replied as he set out the chessmen.

I found it hard to imagine someone who was called Heidi being intelligent but that was probably because I had been bullied mercilessly by a girl called Heidi at school and – even now – the name brought to my mind the image of a bimbo with a cruel tongue.

'White or black?' Ben said.

'What? Oh.' I realised he was talking about the chess pieces and I looked down at the board, wondering how good he really was.

'I'll take black,' I said, a surge of sudden competitiveness making me want to beat him without any advantages.

He twisted the board around so that the black pieces were on my side.

'Is she pretty?' I said.

'She's the most beautiful woman I've ever seen in my life,' Ben replied.

'Incredibly clever *and* beautiful,' I said with a smile. 'What does she see in you, I wonder?'

I half-thought he might take offence at the remark, for all that it had been spoken in jest, but he just looked up with warm amusement in his eyes and said solemnly, 'One of life's great mysteries, I suppose.'

'So are you going to invite me to the wedding?' I asked. Suddenly the thought of a wedding seemed incredibly appealing. It would be nice to overlay Liam's funeral with a happy church occasion.

'Sure,' Ben said. 'As long as you give my mother a wide berth. She hates you, you know.'

'Yes, I know!' I said, actually glad to hear someone admit it rather than try to convince me that it was all in my head. 'Do you know why?'

'I do.'

'Why?' I prompted impatiently when he didn't elaborate.

'She didn't want you to marry Liam.'

I knew he was right but there had to be a more specific reason. She had seemed very fond of me right up until a couple of weeks before the wedding when she had abruptly turned icy cold for no apparent reason.

'Is it because I'm an albino?' I asked, the question tumbling out of my mouth without my really meaning it to.

'What?' Ben said, frowning in what seemed to be genuine puzzlement.

'Did she resent me marrying Liam because of the way I look?'

He stared at me and I cursed myself for bringing up my appearance. Without glancing down I tried to remember what I was wearing and how I must appear to him ... Jeans and a pale-blue top – nothing too bad there – but my hair was down, streaming loose over my shoulders, and I wished that I'd tied it back, put on a hat, done *something* to try to disguise it a little.

My mind went back to an incident that had taken place during my last year at junior school. I couldn't remember how it began but, somehow, the gang of bullies – Heidi amongst them – who regularly used to torment me decided to find out whether or not I could bleed. It was as if – on some level – they really believed that I might not. It was during a PE lesson and a small group of us were standing to one side with our hockey sticks, waiting for our turn to play.

Of course there was a teacher there, but she was refereeing the hockey game and was not sparing any attention our way. Usually Liam was with me but as this was PE he was on the other half of the field playing football with the boys. He wasn't that far away but he wasn't close enough for me to get his attention by shouting. Besides which, I cringed at the idea of screaming for help like some sort of helpless victim. I should be able to stick up for myself. But there were five of them and I couldn't prevent them from wrestling me to the grass and holding me down so that Heidi could dig her long nails into the white skin of my upper arm and scratch me hard enough to draw blood.

I don't know how he realised what was happening for there was too much noise going on from the football and hockey games for Liam to have heard me but, suddenly, some muddy, dirty thing crashed into Heidi, knocking her over on the damp grass and pulling her blonde plaits until she squealed and the teacher came rushing over to drag him off. Liam got into a huge amount of trouble. He was put into detention for pulling Heidi's hair and then into another one for refusing to apologise to her afterwards.

It had always been that way – snow princess to Liam, freak to the rest of the world. Of course, my family loved me and accepted me because they saw past my looks. But with Liam it had been as if he really *liked* my white hair and white skin and pale-blue eyes. That he wouldn't change them even if he could …

Now I wished I'd never brought it up because I didn't like

the way Ben was looking at me. Finally, he said, 'I don't think my mother dislikes you because of the fact that you're an albino. You're not unattractive. Liam could have done worse.'

He looked back down at the chessboard and reached out to move his first pawn. I suppressed a sigh. '*Not unattractive.*' I supposed that was the best I could hope for now. I wished I didn't care. It seemed vain and stupid. But it mattered to me anyway and there was nothing I could do about it.

13

The White Lady

We spent most of the remaining afternoon playing chess. We played mainly in silence because we were both concentrating hard on beating the other. Ben won the first game and I won the second.

'You're almost as good as Liam was,' I said, as we packed the chessmen away.

'Liam?' Ben repeated, raising an eyebrow. 'I didn't realise he even knew how to play chess. I'd have thought he'd be more of a checkers man.'

His voice dripped with scorn and I scowled at him, irritated. 'Why do you do that?' I demanded.

He looked at me in surprise. 'Do what?' he asked.

'Take every opportunity to make some snide comment about him. We've spent a perfectly pleasant afternoon together – are you deliberately trying to spoil it?'

He was silent for a moment before saying, 'You're right. I apologise most sincerely.'

He didn't sound sincere. In fact he sounded blatantly ironic, but at least he was going through the motions so I let it drop. He closed the lid on the chess box and then lifted his arm to rub his left shoulder. I'd noticed him doing it a couple of times that day so I asked him if he'd hurt it. He dropped his hand at once, as if he hadn't realised what he was doing, and said that he had just got a little stiff being hunched over the coffee table for so long.

Shortly afterwards, we went downstairs for dinner and at about eleven o'clock we wrapped up warm before going out to the car to head back to Neuschwanstein. I found it strangely exciting ... driving to the castle in the middle of the night. There was a lot of snow around still but the roads had been salted by then and were safe to drive on. From a distance, Neuschwanstein looked blue and ghostly set against the dark mountains in the cold, crisp silence. Ben ignored the no entry signs and took the car as far up the mountain as he could before the road petered out and we had to get out and walk the last few steps.

'Do you think Lukas will turn up?' I asked, keeping my voice hushed even though it seemed unlikely that there was anyone around to hear us.

'Why should he?' Ben said. 'If he was telling you the truth then he won't want to get in the way.'

'I don't understand why he said we should go to the castle. You'd have thought he would have told us to go to the lake. Maybe we should go down there afterwards.'

'I don't think that's a good idea,' Ben said at once.

'Why?' I asked in surprise. 'You said you wanted to retrace Liam's footsteps – surely the lake is the most important location of them all. And if there really are swan princesses down there then I want to see them for myself. Don't you?'

Ben shrugged and said, 'I don't have anything against magical princesses frolicking about naked in the lake, but if they're real that means the swan knights are probably real too and we've already established that they're very territorial and protective. I think we should exercise a little more common sense and self-restraint than Liam did and have some sort of plan before we go down there rather than just blundering blindly in, don't you?'

I hated to admit it but Ben had a point. Still – it wasn't like *we* were going to try to steal a swan. We only wanted to look and we could take care to be quiet about it. I let it drop for the moment. We had now stopped beneath the shadow of the great castle looming above us. The floodlight turned its white bricks blue and made it appear phantasmal and ... lonely somehow ... all alone in the mountains when the man who had built and loved it was long since dead and lay far away. It was utterly magical being there in the middle of the night, with no one around for miles. And it was timeless. Surrounded only by snow and pines and mountains and stars, there was nothing whatsoever to distinguish the view from the way it would have looked a hundred years ago. Even the silence was complete and the mountain air was still.

We stood there for some moments, just looking up at the tall castle. It had been majestic during the day but at night – lit up with that pale-blue light and its turrets iced with snow – it would have put any fairy-tale castle to shame, and I remembered what Ben had said about Walt Disney basing his own castles on it. How strange to think that – on this occasion – the real thing had inspired the fairy tales rather than the other way around. It was almost difficult to believe that this was real in a real place – and we were not in storybook-land after all. Neuschwanstein was perfect – flawless in every detail. Remove one stone or alter the height of one spire a single foot and there would have been diminishment.

Suddenly, the idea of swan princesses and lonely kings and enchanted voices and aggressive knights did not seem *quite* as preposterous as they had by the light of day ... I tore my eyes from the castle and glanced around at the surrounding trees, picking them out in the darkness. When a branch rustled somewhere close I turned my head sharply, for a moment genuinely expecting to see a huge, ornate sleigh come around the corner, complete with black horses and swans ... But there was nothing there and, in another moment, everything was still.

Seeing it like that, I almost felt that I didn't want to ever leave Neuschwanstein – not when it was like this. Magic hung all about it like tinsel on a Christmas tree. It was beautiful and silent and lonely and I could see why Ludwig had loved it even more than his other castles. It had been stunning during the day too, of course, but then there had been other people traipsing about all over the place – something Ludwig had expressly not wanted – and now it was quiet and deserted and silent once again, a brief reprieve before the morning and the next batch of the seemingly endless supply of gossiping, gawking, garish tourists.

I thought it couldn't possibly be any more magical, but was

proved wrong a moment later when large snowflakes started to fall thickly from the sky, painted silver in the starlight but turning pale blue as they settled softly on the castle's floodlit spires, and all I wanted to do was stand there and stare at it. The lake could wait, answers could wait, the mysterious object could wait ... But then I remembered what Lukas had said and shook myself. If he'd been telling the truth then it couldn't wait. None of it could. If we didn't find the thing Liam had hidden then someone might die. And I might be left with that horrible sense of nameless loss for the rest of my life.

'We should go down to the lake,' I said reluctantly. 'There isn't anything here.'

'There's someone in the castle,' Ben replied evenly.

I looked at him sharply, and then followed his gaze to a lit window in one of the turrets – standing out sharply since all the other windows were cold and dark.

'Perhaps they leave it on at night—' I began, but then cut off abruptly as a woman appeared at the window. A woman with long white hair and ghostly pale skin.

It was me.

14

Swan Princess

In another moment, she was gone – slipped past the window like a ghost, leaving me with my heart hammering wildly in my chest as I stared up at the castle.

'Did you see that?' Ben said, in the same tone of voice as if he had just noticed a deer between the trees rather than a woman who appeared to be my double gazing down at us from the window of the castle.

'I saw her,' I gasped, feeling cold with horror and quite unable to look back towards the window. The lovely enchantment of the setting had been broken and now I felt nothing but dread. Suddenly I was stupidly afraid that Ben might walk away and leave me here so I grabbed his arm to stop him from going. 'What can it mean?' I croaked.

Ben frowned down at me as if disapproving of my fear. 'Calm down—' he began, but I cut him off.

'Don't tell me to calm down!' I hissed. 'I just saw myself up there in the turret window – I have every bloody right to be anything other than bloody calm!'

My fingers dug even harder into his arm as I glared at him but he just gazed back at me, looking puzzled. 'What,' he said, 'are you talking about?'

'You ... you did *see* her, didn't you?' My anger dropped away and I spoke almost pleadingly. I couldn't bear the thought that Ben might look at me like I was mad and declare that he hadn't seen a thing.

But, to my relief, he said, 'Of course I saw her. But she wasn't you, you daft woman!'

I still gripped his arm but said nothing as I tried to recall her image. She had only been at the window for a moment but she had most definitely had long white hair, just like mine, and pale, pale skin ...

'You think there's another albino woman here?' I said, desperately hoping that was the case but struggling with the gross improbability of it.

'I don't think she's an albino,' Ben replied. 'Go and knock on the door. I'll wait here.'

'*What?*' I looked at him to see if he was trying to make some sort of joke but he appeared to be quite serious. Suddenly I felt like a child creeping up to the castle to play some kind of truth-or-dare game. 'Why don't *you* go and knock on the door and *I'll* wait here?' I said. 'There's a white woman in there! Did the sight of her really not send a chill down your spine? What are you – made of iron or something?'

'Look, you told me so yourself,' Ben replied. 'Lukas said you were the one who had to come here. I don't think she'll answer the door to me. Of course, you don't have to try if you don't want to. We could just go back to the guest house if you like. If that means something bad happens later on – well – it can't be any worse than Liam's death, can it? Come on, you don't want to do it so let's just go back.'

He took a step towards the car, gripping my wrist to pull me along like a naughty child. I shook him off furiously, turned on my heel and marched up to the wooden door, so angry that I had no room left for fear as I banged on the door hard enough to send an echo back across the chilly mountains. Nothing happened and I glanced around at Ben who was standing back but watching the castle intently. He had clearly intended to provoke me into knocking on the door and it irritated the hell out of me that he had succeeded in pushing my buttons. The creak of a latch being lifted on the other side of the door brought my attention sharply back to it and, in another moment, it opened. I ducked with a yell as a large white swan came bursting out at me, knocking me over on my back in the snow. Something black fell from its beak and landed on the ground with a heavy thump, narrowly missing my head, before the swan swooped away into the darkness – a pale blur vanishing into the dark night.

I rolled over and pushed myself up to stare after it and then looked down at the thing it had dropped. It was a small black horse made of marble. I could even see a faint tracing of golden veins across its surface. It was perfect in every detail, as if someone had spent hours making it ... Its carved mane flowed about its shoulders and its thick, dark tail fell all the way down to brush against its shiny hooves ... A magical, enchanting thing, quite as captivating as any white unicorn ...

And almost as soon as I picked it up, I was aware of warmth emanating from it – some golden, beautiful warmth that seemed to creep into my hand and spread up through my arm and into my chest, lessening some of the pain I'd been carrying there and putting some bright, hopeful feeling in its place ...

In my preoccupation with it I had almost forgotten Ben for a moment, but suddenly his fingers were digging into my shoulder as he dropped down onto his knees and said, 'What did she give you?'

The warm feeling was gone so fast that it was almost as if I had imagined it. I held up the little black horse for him to see. He reached out to take it but I found myself drawing back my hand. I didn't want him to touch it. I didn't want anyone to touch it. It was mine and suddenly I was scared that ... somehow ... it was going to be taken from me. And I couldn't let that happen. Somehow I could sense how important it was – almost as if my whole life depended on not losing it ...

'I just want to look at it,' Ben said, sounding mildly hurt.

Reluctantly, I forced myself to hand it to him. He held it up so that the blue floodlight illuminating the castle glimmered off its smooth surface.

'What do you think?' I said eagerly, hoping that Ben would know what to do. 'What is it?'

'It appears to be a small ornamental horse,' he replied, sounding distinctly disgruntled and practically throwing it back at me. 'Perhaps she's gone insane, waiting alone for so long.'

'She?' I repeated, clutching the tiny horse and staring at him. 'Do you think that swan was a ... was Ludwig's ... ?' The question trailed off and I found I couldn't finish it, but Ben – for some reason – looked suddenly annoyed.

'How am I supposed to know?' he said shortly, still glaring at the horse in my hand. 'Your guess is as good as mine.'

'Could it be the swansong?' I asked, for it certainly seemed magical enough.

But Ben shook his head. 'No. We would know. Anyway, it's not singing. Let's get back to the guest house. Maybe, in better light, we'll be able to see ... I don't know ... writing on the horse or something. Something that makes it less meaningless than it appears to be right now.'

When I stood up my eyes went back to the door. It was closed, even though I hadn't seen or heard it move. Ben pushed his hand against it but it seemed to be locked once again, so we walked away from the castle and back towards the car.

We used the key to let ourselves into the guest house, taking care to tiptoe up the stairs as it was now past one o'clock and everyone else was in their rooms, the lights in the bar and restaurant had been turned off and everything was closed up for the night.

We headed for my bedroom as, being on the second floor, it was the closer of the two. I opened the door and stepped inside to turn on the light but, instantly, there was a horrible crunching underfoot and I could feel that I had trodden on – and broken – something. I hastily turned on the light and then Ben and I stared at the sight before us.

There were human bones all over the room. They were scattered about the carpet, on the bed and on the coffee table. Just like the ones on the *Queen Mary*, they were in very poor condition, chipped and yellowed with age. The skull on the pillow had a huge chunk missing between the eyes so that it was practically split in half right down the middle.

It seemed worse, somehow, than it had on the *Queen Mary*. Maybe it was because this was my bedroom – my personal space – not a public deck and it felt much more like an invasion, a violation … I had sat on those chairs and slept in that bed with my head upon the pillow in the exact spot where the gaping skull now lay. If they had just appeared out of thin air like they had before, then it was simply luck that I had not been in the bed at the time … I shuddered at the very thought of waking up with a skull tangled in my hair and dirty bones breaking beneath me …

Within seconds, the bones crumbled away into dust, just like on the *Queen Mary*. But because we weren't outside this time, the dust could not blow away. It lay there, coating the room with a horrible grimy film.

Next to me, Ben sighed. 'Well,' he said. 'Do you want to stay in my room?'

'What?'

'Or do you just want to try to clean all this up now?'

'Oh. No,' I said, my skin crawling at the thought of sleeping in that bed. We could shake the dust from the sheets but the idea of laying down my head where a grinning skull had been mere moments earlier made me cringe. 'I can't sleep here now.'

'All right. I'll take the couch.'

'No, I will,' I said. 'After all, it's your room.'

'I don't mind,' Ben said mildly. 'Why don't you just get what you need for the night?'

I rummaged around in my suitcase, which, fortunately, had been closed and so was free from bone dust, as was the bathroom. I took my violin too, without even thinking about it. It occurred to me as we left my room behind and walked up to the third floor that Ben's room could be in the exact same state. But, to my relief, when he opened the door and turned on the light, there wasn't a rib or a skull in sight.

His room was tidy and neat – much neater than mine, in fact. His bed was made, his suitcase was over in one corner of the room and the only personal possession I could see was the box containing his portable chess set on the coffee table.

We sat down on the couch; I then drew the tiny horse out of my pocket and held it up so we could examine it more closely. The better light illuminated even more clearly what an exquisite piece it was but, although we examined it from every possible angle, there did not appear to be any writing on it as Ben had suggested. No writing, no symbols, no clue or even the tiniest hint about what we were supposed to do with it or how it could possibly help us locate the swansong Liam had taken.

I was now finding it harder and harder to doubt that was what he had done. It fitted with everything else I had learned since coming to Neuschwanstein. If it really was as powerfully magical as everyone seemed to think then it explained why Jaxon and Lukas had an interest. But what I still couldn't work out was *why* Liam had taken it in the first place and what he had wanted it for. Ben was wrong – it couldn't have been to do with greed or money. We had not been rich, but we certainly hadn't been desperately poor either. And although Liam's parachute jumps and things cost quite a lot, there were no other expensive hobbies that we indulged in. We had been happy as we were. So he must have taken it for some other reason …

'It's not just an ornament,' I said at last.

'What makes you say that?' Ben asked.

'I don't know. But look at it. It feels,' I hesitated for a moment, but then forced myself to finish the sentence, 'magical. It seems magical. Like a unicorn or something.'

I half-expected Ben to ridicule me for that, but instead he said, 'Hmm. There *is* something about it.'

It was no ordinary ornament – I was quite certain of it. I felt like a child fascinated with a new toy. I wanted always to be touching it and looking at it.

'Well, we're just going to have to think again about what we do next tomorrow,' Ben said.

He sounded suddenly tired and I could practically feel his disappointment, which seemed a little odd for we could easily have gone to the castle that night and seen nothing. And I wondered whether, like Lukas, he had been expecting more to happen. I asked him about it as he stood up from the couch but he turned back and merely said evenly, 'No, of course I didn't expect anything to happen. Why should I?'

I shrugged, looked back at the horse and said, 'I'm sure it's important. I don't know why but, when I look at it, I feel sure it will lead us to something, somehow.'

'I hope you're right,' Ben replied.

It was late and there was nothing more to be done so we agreed to try and get some sleep. Whilst Ben was in the bathroom getting changed I rummaged through the bag of stuff I had brought from my room until I found the knight and the framed photo of Liam. Even though it was just for one night, I had grown used to having them by my bed and would have missed them if they hadn't been there.

I set them down on the coffee table to make it clear that I was settling in to sleep on the couch, for I genuinely didn't want Ben sleeping there. Chivalry was all very well but it was his room and it made sense for me to take the couch because I was a lot smaller than him. I had propped up the photo and was just setting down the knight when Ben came out of the bathroom.

We both noticed it at the same time. The knight and the horse matched each other. They looked like a pair – like they were meant to be together, despite the fact that they were made from different materials.

'Where did you say you found that knight again?' Ben asked.

'It was ... in Liam's pocket. The day he died.'

'But you'd never seen it before?'

'No. I assumed some children had lost it and that he found it and picked it up.'

'That could be it, I suppose.'

But I didn't think he really believed that and I found that I didn't either. Now that I looked at it more closely, it seemed hard to believe it was a toy. It was made of metal, not plastic, and felt heavy and expensive. And there was no '*Made in China*' stamp anywhere on the knight's form.

Finally I set it down by the black horse and went into the

bathroom to get changed and brush my teeth, for it was late and sleep was starting to beckon most temptingly, even if it meant being wedged on a couch rather than lying flat in a bed.

But when I went back into the bedroom, Ben had moved the knight, horse and photo onto the bedside table. He was already on the couch with a blanket and pillow and – although I tried – he could not be persuaded to shift. So, in the end, I was forced to take the bed, feeling distinctly guilty but more than a little bit warmer towards Ben.

Before getting in I sat down on the edge of the mattress and combed through my hair. It was so long that it easily became tangled if I didn't brush it through before sleeping. I found it an almost soothing ritual – the sweep of the comb gliding rhythmically through my hair ...

I abruptly stopped combing when I became aware, from the corner of my eye, that Ben was watching me from the couch. My white hair had been beautiful to Liam but I mustn't forget how freakish it was to everyone else. Hurriedly I put the comb down, my fingers fumbling with it so that it clattered noisily on the bedside table, making me cringe for I had given away the fact that I felt self-conscious.

What happened next was a pure quirk of fate. Usually I always left my comb on the bedside table so that it was the first thing I picked up the next morning. But, because I was feeling awkward and embarrassed, my hands searched for something else to do and I pulled open the little drawer in the table to put my comb inside. The ring would have been obvious at once even if I hadn't pulled the drawer open so hard that it hit the front with a loud, heavy clang.

The drawer was completely empty but for that one elegant band of white gold identical in every way to the one I had seen on Ben's finger. At first I thought it must be his and I glanced at him involuntarily where he sat frozen on the couch, staring towards the open drawer. His face had turned white. I could see from the book he was still holding that his own ring was on his finger. The one in the drawer belonged to somebody else.

'Ben—' I began, but broke off as he suddenly threw back the blanket and got up from the couch, the book falling disregarded from his hand to land on the floor as he strode across the room to the bed. He stopped by the table, reached in and grabbed the ring with a hand that seemed to shake slightly.

'I'm sorry.' The words burst from my mouth for he looked so upset that I felt I must have done something dreadfully wrong in opening the drawer. He hadn't told me not to but it suddenly felt like an invasion – as if I had been snooping and found something private and personal that I had no right to see ... 'I'm sorry, Ben,' I said again.

'I didn't lie to you,' he said quietly. 'I just couldn't bear to tell you the truth.'

'What happened?' I said tentatively.

He took a deep breath and said, 'She's ill.'

'Is it serious?' I said, my heart sinking.

His eyes closed briefly and his answer came out softly, 'Yes.'

'Oh, Ben, I'm so sorry,' I said.

He sat down next to me on the bed. 'I don't tell anyone who doesn't already know because it ... makes it more real,' he said.

I nodded. It was a sentiment I could fully understand. Every time I had to tell another person that Liam was dead I had to go through their horror and their grief, making the whole thing even more unbearable than it already was. I wondered if that was why Ben had hesitated before coming back for the funeral and felt suddenly guilty for my anger towards him when he had returned to Germany so quickly afterwards.

'What's ... what's wrong with her?'

'I don't want to go into it,' Ben replied wearily. 'What difference does it make? She's ill and if something doesn't change fairly soon then I'll lose her for good.'

I hesitated to say anything for it really was none of my business, but I couldn't shake the horrible image of Ben's poor, ill fiancée dying at home on her own and so I said, 'Why aren't you with her?'

'She doesn't want me.' He held up the engagement ring to

162

emphasise the point and said, 'She sent me away. We'll only be together again if she gets back to her usual self.'

'Is that why you're looking for the swansong?' I asked. 'Do you think if you sell it you could get enough money to help her?'

'Something like that,' Ben replied.

The strained voice he spoke in made me glance at him and I was horrified to see tears glimmering in his eyes and pain etched onto his face that he had always kept hidden from me before.

'Ben, I promise I'll do everything I can to help you,' I said.

'Thank you,' he replied, struggling a little with his voice. His hand tightened around the ring, his shoulders hunched even further forwards and he said, 'I don't know if it will even work. It might already be too late. It might have been hopeless from the start. We had something once but now ... what with everything ... maybe it's too late to ever get it back.'

'At least you have a chance,' I said. 'I'd give anything for that.'

He glanced at me with red-rimmed eyes, sunken in his face, and said, 'Would you?'

'Of course I would! If there were even the tiniest possibility of getting Liam back, I'd fight for it until I was dead! It's not over until it's over, Ben.'

I put a comforting hand on his arm, more than half-expecting him to pull away from my touch, but instead – after the briefest pause – he put his arms around me, crushing me to his chest in a rather suffocating hug. I was surprised but returned the hug dutifully; patting his back in what I hoped was a vaguely soothing way.

I wished he wouldn't hold me so tightly. I didn't like being touched. Justifiably or not, I always felt that people must recoil a little at my white skin. But I couldn't push him away and I tried not to express my discomfort by going tense in his arms.

His forehead rested on my shoulder so that when a single tear fell from his eye I felt it run slowly down my bare arm. He wasn't really crying but he was shaking slightly and I couldn't help but feel for him. Losing Liam had been horrific – but at least it had been quick. There had been no dreadful agonising over whether or not he was going to live.

I looked down at Ben's dark head and marvelled at how similar in colour his hair was to Liam's – almost black, but with a faint coppery tint if the light caught it just the right way ... I could see us in the mirror opposite the bed and because Ben's face was hidden, there was nothing to distinguish him from his younger brother. It was a flawless illusion and for some moments I gazed into the glass, captivated, seeing only my husband in Ben's place. I couldn't help giving in to the fairy tale, just for a moment – turning my head to rest my cheek against his hair and hold him tight ...

Then, without moving, Ben spoke, and his voice shattered the illusion, 'First ... Heidi and then all this with Liam ... I can't remember what happiness feels like any more.' He pulled back, looking at me with heavily lidded, bloodshot eyes and said, 'Can you? Do you think you ever will again?'

'Not right now,' I admitted. 'But ... maybe one day ...' I trailed off, for it suddenly seemed laughably naïve to ever hope to experience true happiness again with this dark cloud hanging over me – this awful thing I could never erase. It seemed impossible that the pain would ever fade and I felt sure that whenever I got anywhere near happiness in the future, I would surely think of Liam and what I'd lost and thus plunge myself into deep despair again. An ongoing, nightmarish, downward spiral that just went on and on ...

'I'm sorry,' Ben said quietly, trying to smile. 'I didn't mean to drag you down with me. I've depressed you, haven't I?'

'Only a little,' I replied, with an equally pathetic attempt at a smile. 'I wish we were looking for a magic wand rather than swansong. Then we could wave it and everything would go back to the way it was.'

'Sometimes there is no going back,' Ben said flatly. 'No matter how hard you try.' He glanced at his watch and said, 'It's really late and I've been keeping you up. We'd better go to sleep.'

When he leaned forwards to kiss me lightly on the cheek, my eyes were on the mirror and the false, bitter-sweet fantasy it por- trayed of a woman being kissed by the man she loved more than anyone else in the world.

In another moment, Ben stood up and was walking back to the couch. He said briefly over his shoulder, 'Goodnight, Jasmyn,' before lying down and turning off the nearby lamp. I got into bed and did the same, plunging the room into darkness.

15

Swan Tattoo

That night, I dreamt about the little black horse. It came to life and leapt from the bedside table onto the bed where it picked its way across the sheets towards me. One cold hoof stepped up onto my hand, followed by the others until it stood there in my palm. Then it lay down – front legs first, followed by back ones, rolling over onto its side and pressing its head against my skin as if listening for something.

And then there was another image – a faery forest beneath a dark sky full of twinkling stars. Human skulls and black roses lay everywhere in the snow and the tiny horse was there, picking its way through it all before finding itself back on my hand and stamping its hooves down hard upon my skin ...

I woke up in the bed with a start and the fingers of my left hand bunched into a fist, fully expecting to feel the cold horse in my palm. But there was nothing there and when I turned on the lamp, I saw that it was on the table by the knight, right where I had left it. I glanced around the room but everything seemed to be in order and the only sound came from Ben who was snoring on the couch. I turned off the lamp and lay back down, the strange dream still vivid in my mind.

It took me a while to get back to sleep because of Ben's snoring but it seemed a bit unreasonable to go over there and prod him when he had generously let me take the bed. Finally I fell asleep and didn't wake up until the sunlight was streaming through the windows. The couch was empty but I could hear the sound of the shower in the bathroom. I turned my head to look at the bedside table. The knight was there and so was the framed photograph. But the black horse was gone.

I flung back the covers to get out and check the floor in case it had fallen off. Then I looked under the bed – and in it – but I couldn't see the black horse anywhere. In my panic I was sure someone must have stolen it in the night and I practically ran to the other side of the room to hammer on the bathroom door, shouting for Ben.

In a matter of seconds I heard the water being turned off and Ben opened the door with a towel around his waist, dripping wet, looking alarmed.

'The horse is gone!' I said before he could speak. 'Do you have it in there?' I stood on tiptoe and craned my neck to look over his shoulder, hoping to see it lying on the sink next to our tooth-brushes.

'Of course it isn't in here!' Ben said with all of his old impatience – as if his opening up to me the night before had never happened. 'It's on the coffee table,' he said. 'I had another look at it when I woke up this morning.'

I spun around and saw at once that Ben was right – there the black horse was on the coffee table, quite safe.

'Sorry,' I said, turning back. 'I thought … someone must have taken it.'

'No one even knows we have it,' Ben replied.

He made to turn back into the bathroom but I grabbed the door handle to stop him from closing it.

'Wait!' I said sharply. 'What's that on your shoulder?'

As he'd turned I'd caught a glimpse of a dark shape there, suspiciously familiar …

'That? Oh, that's just a tattoo,' Ben said dismissively.

He was still trying to pull the door shut but I wedged my foot into the gap to stop him.

'Let me see it,' I insisted.

He turned reluctantly so that I could see the tattoo properly. It was a black swan – right there on his shoulder.

167

'Where did you get that?' I said quietly, prickles of horror creeping over my skin at the sight of it.

'I just ... woke up with it,' Ben replied, after a brief hesitation. 'About six months ago. I don't know how it got there.'

'You mean it ... just *appeared*?'

'Yes. It just appeared.'

'It hurts, doesn't it?' I said, remembering how I had noticed him massaging that shoulder on occasion.

'Sometimes,' Ben replied briefly.

'What does it mean?'

'I have absolutely no idea,' he said.

'Surely you can think of some reason? What were you doing the day you got it?'

'Nothing. Nothing special happened. I just woke up with it.'

'But, Ben—'

'Look, I've had the tattoo for months now and apart from making my shoulder ache every now and then it doesn't seem to have done me any harm, so can we just drop it?'

'All right,' I said, raising my hands at his aggressive tone. 'Fine.'

At the end of the day I had more important things to worry about than Ben's tattoo anyway. But, still, the fact that it had just appeared there all on its own like that made me feel distinctly ... uneasy.

'I'm going to get dressed,' Ben said – then he closed the door and was gone.

I walked over to the couch and sat down, automatically picking up the little marble horse from the coffee table.

And that was when it came alive in my hand.

The marble cracked and split – like an eggshell breaking apart – to reveal a tiny black horse inside, real in every sense but for the fact that it was a mere three inches tall. I yelled, my hands jerked and I dropped it without meaning to. It landed on the carpet with a thud and for a moment I was terrified that I might have hurt the tiny thing by dropping it so carelessly. But in another second it got back onto its feet and shook itself, quite unharmed, before trotting across the floor, past the couch.

It moved like a real horse, it *felt* like a real horse ... its coat had been soft to the touch and its glossy mane and tail swished about it as it pranced along the floor to my violin case, where it jumped up onto the lid and began walking up and down, its hooves clattering on the hard surface.

Ben, who'd heard me yell, opened the bathroom door only half dressed and said, 'What's wrong now?'

Wordlessly, I pointed at the tiny black horse walking around on my violin case. Ben gazed in the direction of my pointing finger and I saw him jump in alarm when his eyes found the horse. The two of us stared at it in silence. At first I thought it was just walking about randomly, tossing its head and snorting through its tiny nostrils as it went. But then I noticed the marks it was making in the thin layer of dust covering my violin case, left over from the bones the evening before. Incredible as it seemed, there were actually words forming beneath the horse's hooves – a name, in fact, that, once it was complete, read: *Henri Rol-Tanguy.*

Then the horse leapt off the case, trotted back to where I sat and nuzzled insistently at my ankle until I reached down and carefully picked it up to place it in the palm of my other hand, doing my best to keep it flat and steady.

Despite the circumstances, I couldn't help feeling a flutter of delight at the sight of the tiny horse walking about in my palm, stopping at the ends of my fingers to gaze over the edge before turning back around to look at me. In every way except its size it looked identical to Kini. Its beautiful lines, glossy coat and deep brown eyes were all the same – like a tiny, perfect faery horse. I was utterly captivated by it.

Ben, on the other hand, seemed more preoccupied with the writing on my violin case.

'Henri Rol-Tanguy,' I heard him mutter excitedly before turning his head to look at me. 'Do you know who that is?'

'No,' I said. 'Do you?'

He didn't reply for a moment but turned back to the violin

case, repeating the name under his breath as if willing himself to recognise it. But, finally, he shook his head and said, 'I don't remember ever hearing it before.'

His head snapped up, he looked around at the horse and said, 'Come on, let's take it outside.'

'Why?'

'Because there's snow out there,' he said, pulling on his shirt and fumbling hastily with the buttons. 'Perhaps it will spell out something else.'

I glanced at the violin case and saw that the name written in the dust did take up almost the entire surface so that if there was more the horse could spell out, it would not have had room.

'Give it to me,' Ben ordered, getting to his feet and holding out his hand.

'We can't just walk through the guest house with it like this,' I replied. 'Someone might see.'

Ben glanced around the room until his eye fell on the box containing the travel chess set. He picked it up, emptied out the chessmen and then held it out to me. 'Put him in here,' he said.

I carefully did so and then carried the box through the guest house and outside. There was no one else around, so we crouched down on the other side of the car, out of sight of the restaurant windows, and opened the box. The little horse did not seem particularly distressed by the journey and when Ben reached in, scooped it out and put it down on the snow, we both gazed down at it expectantly, almost holding our breath. It lifted its head and looked around, sniffing the air for a moment and flaring its nostrils, before kicking up the snow with its hooves and prancing about in what seemed to be pure delight. Soon it was rolling about on its back, hooves in the air, covering itself in a fine dusting of snowflakes. I couldn't help but smile at the sight of it enjoying itself so much, but it obviously wasn't going to be of any further help to us right now.

'I don't think it's going to write any more words,' Ben said resignedly, scooping it up and putting it back in the box. 'So let's concentrate on the ones we've already got.'

We skipped breakfast and went straight back to Ben's room to Google the name but without much success. There was a famous French communist called Henri Rol-Tanguy who kept cropping up but, although we spent some time reading about the man, he didn't appear to be connected to us or Liam or Neuschwanstein and, indeed, he had died several years ago anyway. It was most vexing and, as we waded through website after website, I began to notice Ben flashing distinctly disgruntled looks at the horse, which was happily trotting about the room, oblivious to any displeasure it had caused.

'Maybe we're wasting our time,' Ben said at last. 'For all we know that horse was just spelling out its own bloody name.'

The thought was so silly that I couldn't help laughing – although I quickly turned it into a cough at the look on Ben's face.

'I can't believe that's it,' I said, trying to sound grave.

'I'm going to go down and clean up your room,' Ben said. 'We don't want all that dust lying around when the maid goes in. Keep searching while I'm gone. The name has to be relevant somehow. Perhaps it refers to another man – one who's still alive – one who knows something about where Liam hid the swansong.'

'All right,' I said.

The tiny horse was no longer exploring the room but was standing by the couch at my feet. It didn't look likely to run away but I picked it up anyway as Ben walked towards the door. The last thing we needed was a three-inch-tall horse bolting out into the corridor where anyone might see it and start screaming.

As I stood up, my eyes were automatically drawn towards the window and the car park outside and I froze in alarm.

'Ben!' I said sharply.

'What?' he asked, glancing back.

'There's blood on the snow out there! It leads up to our car and then stops.'

We went quickly down to the parking lot, leaving the little horse upstairs behind us. There didn't seem to be anyone around but we were both painfully aware that anybody could appear at any moment. The trail of blood stretched from the entrance to the car park and – for all we knew – began some way down the road. The dark splatters were in disturbing, ugly contrast to the white snow they stained and sent cold shivers of fear running through me.

I suppose the most natural assumption was that an injured animal had created the blood trail but, somehow, that idea didn't really occur to me. I was therefore surprised when I got down on my knees beside Ben, icy dampness soaking through my jeans, to see a black swan underneath our car.

At first I thought it must be dead. Frost sparkled across its red beak; the blood on its wing had frozen, gluing its feathers together, and it seemed stiff and motionless in the snow. We were not far from the road; perhaps the bird had been hit by a car – just an ordinary, unfortunate, mundane accident … But still I couldn't help a shudder of unease, for the last time I had seen black swans had been when they'd fallen dead from the sky at Liam's funeral. Now, just seeing one – especially a dead one – elicited an almost Pavlovian response in me of sadness and a kind of squeamish horror. I couldn't help feeling that its appearance must *mean* something – and probably nothing good either. I tried to tell myself it was just a dead bird and nothing more …

But the next moment Ben was cursing under his breath and reaching under the car for the swan. As he lifted it up off the ground, some of its feathers were pulled out where they'd been frozen to the snow by blood. It seemed an incredibly big bird in Ben's arms, with its long neck dangling lifelessly over his elbow.

'Er … what are you doing?' I asked as Ben stood up.

'Give me your jacket,' he said urgently.

'Why?'

'To hide him. I can't risk someone seeing me carry him into the guest house like this.'

'The *guest house?*' I repeated. 'Ben, you can't take that dead bird into the guest house!'

'He isn't dead!' Ben said impatiently.

I looked at him sharply, startled by his tone as well as his use of the word 'he'. As if – ridiculous though it sounded – the swan was a personal acquaintance of his ...

Ben met my eyes, realising that he had given himself away. 'And he isn't just a swan,' he admitted reluctantly. 'Now give me your jacket.'

Still unsure whether Ben was telling the truth or not, I quickly stripped off my denim jacket. It was nowhere near big enough to cover the swan but I threw it on top of the bird anyway and then Ben and I rushed back into the guest house and up to my bedroom. Ben walked straight through to the bathroom and told me to turn on the taps over the bathtub.

'What are you going to do?' I asked as I did what he'd said.

'He's freezing, I've got to warm him up.'

'But it's a black swan!' I protested.

'A black swan near Neuschwanstein,' Ben grunted.

When the bath was half-full of hot water, Ben knelt down at the side, still holding the swan. Then he looked round at me. 'Stand back,' he ordered. 'Just in case. In fact, maybe you'd better leave the bathroom altogether.'

I took a step back so that I was standing in the narrow doorway, but I had no intention of leaving the room. I watched as Ben lifted his arms and dumped the bird into the water with a splash. It was hard to judge exactly what happened next for I did not have a particularly good view, standing well back as I was and with Ben in the way. But there was a lot of splashing and then I distinctly saw a human hand reach up to grip the edge of the bath, accompanied by a most un-swan-like sound of choking. In another second I was at Ben's shoulder where I could get a perfect view. The black swan had gone – the only sign that it had ever been there a few stray feathers floating on the surface of the water – and a man I recognised had appeared in its place. Tall, naked, dirty, bruised and bloody – it was Lukas.

16

Broken Violin

Someone swore, and it must have been me because Lukas was too busy half-drowning in the bath, drenching Ben at the same time. The water was tinged pink already from the gash down Lukas's upper arm. Judging from the colour of the water, he had obviously lost a fair amount of blood already and he was certainly going to need stitches. His wet coughing indicated that he had swallowed quite a lot of water when he'd been unceremoniously dumped into the bath. His lips were blue with cold and there were remnants of frost shards in his hair.

I had seen Lukas twice before – once at my grandparents' stables and then again at the Alpsee Lake. Ben, on the other hand, had always denied all knowledge of Lukas – claimed not to have recognised his name or my description of him. I was therefore astonished when, after brushing the wet hair out of his face, he said, 'I told you not to come back here, you idiot! Why won't you ever listen to me?'

'I didn't think ... they would find out—' Lukas began between chattering teeth, but Ben cut him off.

'Of course they were going to find out! You can't keep secrets from them – you of all people should know that!'

'You needed my help,' Lukas said stubbornly.

Ben sighed and said, 'I'm going to have to stitch up your arm. Sword, was it?'

'A mace,' Lukas replied, sounding almost proud about it. 'Only a scratch, though. I was so quick it barely touched me.'

'Huh,' Ben grunted. 'Any more of a scratch and it would have taken your whole arm off. Jasmyn, can you go and fetch—' He broke off mid-sentence as he turned his head and his eyes met my accusing stare. It was as if – even though he knew I was there – it hadn't really occurred to him what that meant until that moment. His mouth hung open stupidly for a second before he said weakly, 'Oh. Well. You know Lukas.'

He waved a hand vaguely in the direction of the man in the bath, who smiled at me and said, 'Hi, Jasmyn.'

'Hello,' I said – my voice sounding ludicrously stiff and formal given the circumstances.

Considering how pink the bathwater now was, I was surprised that Lukas did not seem worse than he did. It certainly appeared that he was not in any imminent danger but, until his wound was seen to, it seemed incredibly callous to give the third degree to a bleeding man naked in a bathtub. So I said to Ben, in the iciest voice I could muster, 'I'm going to go and fetch a first-aid kit. Whilst I'm doing that, perhaps you can come up with an explanation for the fact that you plainly know each other even though you told me to my face that you had no idea who Lukas was.'

I was so angry with Ben that I could have shaken him until his teeth rattled. Did the man have no sense of decency? He had spun me one lie after another. Liam had told me many a time that Ben was selfish and self-centred and suddenly I felt angry with myself for ever trusting him in the first place. I had been drawn to him simply because he was Liam's brother and he had been playing me like a fool all along. I only had myself to blame and that made it even worse.

'You stupid, stupid idiot,' I muttered to myself as I fumbled about in my suitcase with hands that shook slightly, searching for the first-aid kit. Why was my natural instinct still to trust people after all this? When Ben looked me in the eye and told me something – why, oh why did I believe him? I needed to make myself harder. I needed to put more armour on. I needed to learn from my mistakes. I was like the stupidest monkey in a scientific experiment – the one who didn't learn and just *kept on* pushing the button that would give it an electric shock until it killed itself.

'Jasmyn, it's not what you think,' Ben said, appearing at my elbow.

'Isn't it, Ben?' I said, pleased to hear how hard and unyielding my voice sounded. 'Because what I think is that you lied to me about Lukas. Just like you've lied about almost everything else.'

'It's ... No. I lied because ...' He trailed off, shook his head then said, 'I promise you there's a good reason for all of this!'

'Brilliant! Tell me what it is and if it's as good as you say then I won't be angry any more!'

Ben looked down at me, smudges of blood on his shirt from the black swan – from *Lukas* – and his hair damp with bathwater. The seconds dragged on and he remained maddeningly, infuriatingly silent.

'Just throw me the needle and thread,' Lukas called from the other room, 'and I'll do it myself.'

'What *is* he?' I hissed, jabbing my finger towards the bathroom.

'He's ... he's a knight,' Ben replied quietly. 'A swan knight. A rogue one. He's been exiled.'

'Why?'

'For breaking one of the rules. But he's on our side.'

'Are we on the same side then, Ben?' I retorted – aware of splashing sounds coming from the bathroom as I spoke.

For a moment he was silent, then his shoulders slumped and he just muttered wearily, 'I don't know any more, Jasmyn.'

He glanced around as Lukas appeared in the doorway, dripping wet and completely naked.

'Cover yourself up, can't you?' Ben snapped.

'Oh, right,' Lukas replied carelessly, grabbing a nearby towel. 'I forget that humans don't like nudity.'

'You and I are not the only ones here,' Ben said meaningfully as Lukas reappeared with a towel wrapped around his waist.

'Don't worry on my account,' I said coldly. 'It's nothing I haven't seen before. He can walk around starkers for all I care.' I handed Ben the first-aid box and narrowed my eyes at Lukas. 'You warmed up pretty quickly considering you were a half-frozen swan not that long ago.'

'We're difficult to kill,' Lukas acknowledged. He glanced over at Ben who was turning on the kettle and said, 'I'll have a cup if you're making tea.'

'I'm not making tea!' Ben scowled. 'I'm boiling the water to sterilise the needle.'

'Oh. Right,' Lukas said, sitting down on the edge of the bed. 'Don't be mad with Ben,' he said to me. 'I wasn't supposed to talk to you.'

'How do you two know each other?' I asked coldly.

'I met him here,' Ben said shortly. 'At Neuschwanstein.'

'So you've been here before,' I said, noting that this was yet another thing he had lied about.

'I've been here many, many times before!' Ben said impatiently. 'I haven't just been looking for the swansong since Liam's death. I've been looking for it ever since he hid it last year.'

'But … your mother told me you were working in Germany—'

Ben cut me off with an angry gesture. 'Well, I'm hardly going to tell her, am I?' he snapped. 'I'm hardly going to tell her that I haven't worked in over a year – that I've lost my reputation, my savings, my fiancée, that I've lost pretty near damn well everything – all because of your bloody husband!'

'Ben,' Lukas murmured in what sounded very much like a warning.

'So, yes, I know who he is,' Ben said, waving his hand in Lukas's direction. 'I know about the swan knights and King Ludwig and the swansong and I have done since the very beginning.'

'Then why didn't you just tell me?' I said, frustrated. 'Why did we waste time going to see Adrian Halsbach and the castles and the lake to find all this out if you knew it already?'

'Surely to God it's obvious, isn't it?' Ben said, glaring at me. 'If I'd taken you aside after the funeral and said, "Oh, by the way, Jasmyn, did you know that your husband stole the enchanted voice of a swan, that he hid it away somewhere and now all these people are trying to find it, and the swan knights are very angry and even more protective of the magic swans than they were before, so we shall have to go to Ludwig's mute and exiled swan princess to see if there's anything she can do to help or some unknown terrible thing will happen and we'll all be *even more* miserable than we already are ..." If I'd said all that, what do you think would have happened next? You'd have thought I was delusional. So I wanted you to hear some of it from other people and find it out piece by piece the way I did. I thought it would make it easier – or at least *possible* – for you to accept. But now it seems I've done the wrong thing yet again. I just can't do anything fucking right, can I?'

'You ... you ...' I stuttered, pale with anger. I didn't think I'd be able to express how furious I was with words and so I had to resist the urge to grab the nearest thing and throw it as hard as I could at his arrogant head. 'How *dare* you speak to me like that!' I said, finding my tongue at last. 'You unprincipled, cold, heartless, smug, selfish git! You've treated me like dirt ever since this whole thing began! You've lied to me, snapped at me and been unbelievably rude! You've been cruel and unfeeling and utterly without tact! You've made everything harder and *nothing* easier! Liam was right – all you bloody well care about is yourself!'

Ben raised a hand to his head and when he spoke it was in a horribly quiet voice. 'I don't know if I can keep doing this. It's too hard.'

'You *make* it hard, Ben! It doesn't have to be. We both want the same thing. We both loved the same man—'

'Love?' Ben interrupted, dropping his hand and staring at me with such a murderous expression on his face that I actually took a half-step back in alarm. '*Love?* I did *not* love Liam!'

Lukas stood up from the bed and I was vaguely aware of him saying something about calming down, but in another moment Ben had crossed the room and grabbed me by the arms, a bare few inches between us so that I could now clearly see the vein throbbing across his left temple and the horrible fury in his eyes. His fingers dug painfully into my white skin and he even shook me a little as he practically shouted in my face, 'I *hated* Liam, Jasmyn! I fucking *hated* him! I was *glad* to hear that he was dead! If it hadn't been for the lost swansong I would have cried tears of joy at the news! Do you understand what I'm saying? Do you? I loathed the man! I only wish to God that he'd died sooner!'

I could hardly believe what I was hearing. He seemed like a totally different person from the man who'd opened up to me a little last night. A mixture of fear and anger made me tremble and I think Ben must have felt it for he suddenly released me as if I had given him an electric shock. He stumbled back – the first uncontrolled action I had ever seen him take – and looked, if possible, even more horrified than I did myself.

'Jasmyn,' he said quietly – almost whispering. 'I'm sorry. I'm sorry. I can't stop myself any more. I'm losing my grip.'

For a moment there was no sound but for Ben's rather uneven breathing. Then I said in a stiff, strange voice that did not sound like my own, 'I'm going out.'

I turned on my heel and left, just wanting to be as far away from Ben as possible. I went up to his room where I'd left my bag, moving quickly for I was afraid that he might come after me and try to convince me not to go, and I really needed to be away from him at that moment.

When I opened the door, the movement must have frightened the tiny black horse under the coffee table, but it seemed to recognise me for when I walked into the room it ventured out from beneath the table, trotting happily up to me. I grabbed my bag then picked up Ben's chess box and put the little horse inside to take with me.

I managed to get out of the guest house and to the car without being followed and I couldn't start the engine up to drive away fast enough. I drove blindly in a random direction, taking as many turns as possible off the main road so that Ben would have no hope of being able to find me should he somehow get another car from somewhere.

When, at last, I felt safely hidden, I pulled up on a deserted stretch of silent mountain road and turned off the engine. I was shaking with disgust and angry tears filled my eyes. How I *hated* Ben for talking about Liam in that way! How *could* he? His own

179

brother! Up until then I had thought his bad-temperedness was because of the way he had parted from Liam. Now it seemed that he felt no remorse at all – not even a spark of grief over his brother's death. How was that even *possible*? How could you not mourn the loss of your own brother? I tried to tell myself that Ben hadn't meant what he'd said – that he was just angry with Liam for hiding the swansong or angry with him for dying ...

But deep down I knew. I knew that there was something very wrong with Ben. This was the side of him that Liam must have known about all along – the reason he hadn't wanted him in our home or our lives and the reason he hadn't tried to make peace with him after their argument. This was who Ben was underneath – nasty, cruel and almost inhuman in his coldness ...

I sat there in the car until an icy chill crept in and my breath smoked before me, trying to work out what to do. After his outburst I felt I didn't want to have anything more to do with him. I certainly didn't want to *help* him to find something he wanted ... But he needed the swansong for Heidi and I felt I should continue to try to find where Liam had hidden it for her sake if not for Ben's. It did occur to me that her mysterious illness might have been a sob story he had made up to trick me but I couldn't persuade myself that that was true. He had been so sincere, so convincing ... He might be a callous, cold-hearted bastard but I believed from the way he had spoken about her that there really was something wrong with Heidi and that Ben did love her. So what choice did I have but to try to help him?

Forcing my body into action, I got out of the car, took a few deep breaths of the chill mountain air, squared my shoulders and pulled myself together. The bottom line was that the sooner we found the swansong, the sooner I could be away from Ben and never ever see him again. Then the nightmare would be over and I could go back home – back to my safe haven, surrounded by my own familiar things, eating familiar, favourite food and sleeping in my warm, familiar bed ...

Thrusting down the sudden surge of homesickness, I got into the car and turned around to head back to the guest house, praying that I would be able to find my way without trouble, for I had just driven to that spot blindly without paying much attention to where I was going.

Fortunately, I managed to find my way back relatively easily. I parked up in the guest house parking lot and had to then force myself to get out of the car and go back inside. Ben and I had just started to get along and now he had completely ruined everything between us and I resented him most bitterly for it. I could only hope that he'd had the chance to cool down a bit by now, had pulled himself together and was capable of being civil once again. It certainly seemed that civility was going to be the very best I could hope for between us but even that seemed rather optimistic now.

I took the chess box inside and went up to my own bedroom, expecting Ben and Lukas to be there as that was where I had left them. Now that I knew who Lukas really was I was eager to talk to him again. The name Henri Rol-Tanguy might mean something to him but, more importantly than that, he might know more about what had truly happened at the lake the night Liam, Adrian and Jaxon had gone there. Indeed, Lukas may well have been there himself and at the very least I could see if his story matched what the others had said.

But when I opened the door to my bedroom it was deserted. And clean. There didn't seem to be a speck of bone dust anywhere. A bloody needle and spare end of thread lay on the bed where I presumed Ben had stitched Lukas's arm but the two of them were now gone. I remembered that Lukas had had nothing to wear and decided that they had probably gone up to Ben's room to try to find him something to make do with, although I wasn't sure how much success they would have, considering the fact that Lukas was several inches taller than Ben.

I left my room and went up to the third floor. I had one of Ben's room keys so I unlocked the door and walked in without knocking. Lukas was nowhere to be seen. But Ben was there. And he was holding my Violectra.

My heart flipped over at the sight of my beloved instrument in his hands and a surge of anger rose up inside me as I noticed my open case lying on the floor – newly appeared black roses scattered over the velvet interior. No one ever touched my violin but me. It was too precious and meant too much to let other people hold it. Besides which, non-violinists often failed to accord it due respect. They didn't understand how easily the pegs could be knocked out of tune if handled indelicately. And there Ben stood in the middle of the room with his horrible hands on my treasured violin – something that he had no right whatsoever to touch, especially when I wasn't even there.

'What the hell,' I said, in my iciest tone, 'are you doing?'

He glanced back around at me, an odd expression on his face. 'This is your most treasured possession, isn't it?' he said in a voice that seemed to be completely devoid of emotion.

'Yes,' I said warily, suddenly having a very bad feeling indeed. 'Why?'

Ben turned away from me to gaze at the beautiful blue and silver thing in his hands. I did not like the way he was looking at it one bit.

'Put it down!' I said sharply. 'Right now! You've got no right to be touching it!'

He glanced back at me with a flat expression in his eyes and, when he spoke, his words filled me with dread. 'I'm sorry, Jasmyn.'

Somehow I knew what he meant to do even though I didn't know why and I ran forwards, sick with fear, as he raised the instrument above his head. I crashed into him and he sprawled on the bed under my weight, the violin falling from his hands to bounce on the floor with a thump that made me cringe. Still lying on top of Ben, I twisted my neck around frantically to look down at it on the floor. The fall had surely knocked all the strings out of tune but, thankfully, it did not appear to be damaged.

'*What the hell is wrong with you?*' I shrieked in Ben's face.

But, without a word, he threw me off roughly to land on the other side of the bed. I lunged out a desperate hand to try to grab the back of his shirt and drag him back but my fingers missed him by a fraction, and although I scrambled off the bed I wasn't quick enough to stop him. The moment seemed to freeze in a tableau, etching itself forever into my mind: my skeletal, delicate Violectra lying on the floor, its blue and silver outline stark and elegant against the carpet; Ben's booted foot raised directly above it, the expression on his face even harder than usual so that although a wordless, desperate plea tore from my lips, I already knew that he was going to disregard it.

His foot came down with all his force behind it. I closed my eyes involuntarily but I heard the awful sound of wood breaking, plastic snapping and a sort of anguished squeal from the metal strings as Ben's boot scraped along them.

No violin could survive being stamped on like that but I couldn't accept that it was over and when I opened my eyes I flew at Ben, trying as hard as I possibly could to hit his face and scratch his skin. I managed to get one good blow in where my wedding ring tore at the skin on his cheek. But after that he quickly regained the upper hand, grabbing me roughly by the arms and shoving me back towards the bed so hard that I sprawled over it.

The only explanation for his behaviour seemed to be that he had gone completely mad. I scrambled to an upright position on the bed and called his name pleadingly, '*Ben!*'

To my surprise, he paused and looked back at me. I hadn't been expecting him to heed me and, now that I had his attention, I found that I didn't know what to say. What words could possibly be enough? How could I make him understand what that violin meant to me? I'd loved all the violins I'd ever had but this one – *this one* – there would never be another one like it. There could be no replacing it. Liam had chosen its colour and design; he had swapped it for the normal violin in my case that day; his money had paid for it and his hands had held it. He had listened to me play it many, many a time. I remembered him and felt close to him through that violin far more than through any photo or home video ...

Somehow I needed to make Ben understand all that before it was too late and something else indescribably precious to me was lost forever. He had stamped on it once already but perhaps it had sounded worse than it really was. Perhaps the violin could still be repaired ... Emotion clogged my throat, tears spilled from my eyes and my breath rasped horribly as I croaked in a voice that sounded childishly frightened, '*Please!* Please Ben. You ... you don't know what that violin means ... it ... it's so important to me ...' I trailed off into sobs, unable to say anything more for I could see in his eyes that it was no good. I had never seen anyone look so hard before. There wasn't a glimmer of warmth or sympathy in his face. Just an anger and bitterness that made him practically unrecognisable to me.

He turned his head away without a word and stamped down once again upon the remnants of my violin. This time I couldn't close my eyes. I couldn't even look away but stared transfixed as the wood splintered beneath his monstrous boot, the blue and silver paint chipped and flaked away, the pegs snapped and the strings tore out to curl uselessly and forlornly on top of the sad wreckage.

It was hardly recognisable as a violin any more – now it was just a pile of broken blue and silver bits mixed in with a few black pegs and loose strings. My heart aching as if it would burst right out of my chest, I dropped down onto the floor to gather the beloved pieces towards me – knowing full well that I couldn't save the instrument but wanting to touch it, to hold it in my hands anyway. In the meantime, Ben took the bow out of my case and broke it across his knee before throwing the two pieces onto the floor.

He stood there in silence for a moment, looking down at me before saying in that same cold voice, 'Did it work?'

My tears had frozen on my face and I felt numb – the same sort of numbness I had felt after the doctor told me that Liam was dead. *How could something like this have happened?* I looked up at Ben and could hardly focus on him. When I spoke it was with an effort, so the words came out a little slurred. 'Did ... what work?'

He didn't answer but turned his head sharply away and walked towards the door with long strides. Stirring myself into action, I jumped suddenly to my feet and said sharply and clearly, '*Ben!*'

He turned back with his hand on the doorknob and I swear for a moment he looked almost hopeful, as if I was going to say that his destroying my violin was no big deal and that he was forgiven. Instead, my voice came out so full of hatred and bitterness that I scarcely recognised it as my own, for I had never spoken to anybody like that before in my life. 'I don't know how or when,' I said quietly, 'but I swear to God that one day I'll find a way to pay you back for what you've just done. I *promise* I'll find a way to make you suffer horribly for this!'

He looked at me from heavily lidded eyes for a moment before muttering, 'I believe you.'

Then he opened the door and was gone. I dropped down to my knees as quickly as if someone had kicked my legs out from under me and gathered the broken pieces of the violin into my lap where I then sat and wept over them for what felt like hours. I cried until my eyes were so sore that I could hardly keep them open. I couldn't believe that my Violectra was really gone. And yet the pieces were all there in my lap. At that moment I felt that I would rather never play the violin again than play one that Liam hadn't given me.

Why? *Why?* What reason could Ben *possibly* have had for doing what he'd done? He must simply have been desperate to hurt me any way that he could. But none of it made any sense. It was the sort of thing that happened in nightmares. Yes, he had been withdrawn from me and rather cold and unsympathetic at times, but I had never, *never* in my wildest dreams believed him capable of this. I truly hadn't known him. Not at all. It was no wonder Liam had wanted nothing to do with him. *Why* hadn't I listened to him? Why had I ever trusted Ben in the first place?

I was filled with a sudden desperate longing to hear Liam's voice again and couldn't get my mobile out of my pocket fast enough. I phoned my home number and cried even harder when the answerphone message started to play: '*You've reached Liam and Jasmyn. Sorry we can't come to the phone right now. Leave us a message and we'll get back to you as soon as we can ...'*

I rang the number until I ran out of credit, then I threw the phone across the room and curled up in a sort of ball on the floor around my shattered violin, all my memories of Liam tearing through my mind – that first day in the playground when he had called me a snow princess; all those times at school when he had protected and defended me like my very own knight in shining armour; the day he gave me the Violectra; the time we came to Munich and ate Lebkuchen and drank spiced *Glühwein* outside in the snow; the day we got married and – finally – the afternoon he folded up and died by the lake, nothing more than an empty shell of a corpse by the time we reached the hospital. What was the point of it all? I almost hated him in that moment for dying and leaving me here to struggle like this on my own. How could he not be about to walk through that door at any moment to pick me up off the floor, hold me in his arms and tell me that everything was going to be okay?

I curled myself tighter around the broken violin, covered my head with my arms and was pulled down into a fitful, restless sleep that probably lasted no more than an hour. When I woke up and saw the carpet stretching out away from me I wished that I could escape back to sleep and nothingness. But it was midmorning and I was not tired, for all that I had been up late the night before. For a while I lay there wide awake, willing sleep to come but to no effect, just wanting never to move ever again.

But then an anger – a hot, horrible fury – crept in around the edges of my grief, gradually pushing all the sadness out and filling me with a cold, hard determination. What was I thinking of, lying pathetically here on the floor like this? I sat up abruptly, pushed my tangled hair out of my face and stood up. I was not going to be a helpless victim any longer. The violin was broken. And that was all there was to it. No amount of wishing would bring it back. I would just have to get on without it like I'd learned to get on without Liam.

I could hardly believe by this point that Ben really was looking for the swansong to save Heidi's life, for I suddenly found it impossible to imagine him capable of anything approaching love. She had probably left him and that was why he had her ring. Served him right, too. The story he told me had surely been an act, a ruse, a ploy, a cleverly calculated trick to ensure I would find the swansong and hand it straight over to him. Well, I meant to find it all right. But I would not be giving it to Ben.

17

Lost in the Mountains

The first thing I needed to do was get away from Ben. From this point on, our search for the swansong would be a separate one. He was quite clearly unhinged and, after the way he had behaved, I was afraid of him. Not enough to stop me from trying to beat him to the swansong, but certainly enough that I had no wish to be left alone with him. Indeed, I shuddered to think that we had been alone in his bedroom last night, sitting together on the bed while he clung to me like a child.

The thought occurred to me now that perhaps this was why his mother had been so abrupt with me when I'd said I wanted to stay in touch with him. Perhaps she had known these things about her son and had feared for my safety with him. Perhaps she simply hadn't wanted to come out and actually say *my son is mentally ill.* He'd wanted to hurt me – to cripple me even – so he had destroyed my violin as brutally as possible. But all he'd really achieved was that now I was mad as all hell. The thirst for revenge is an ugly feeling but at least it is a strengthening one. Somehow I would make him pay for it. I would hit him harder than he'd hit me.

I let myself into my bedroom on the second floor feeling slightly nervous in case he was there. But the room was empty, so I hurriedly packed my things – including every broken piece of my Violectra – and then went outside to the car. But it was gone. Ben had already taken it. And when I went back to his bedroom I found that all his things were gone as well. He must have had them packed and ready before I came back. He'd planned all along to leave after breaking my violin.

As he had not left so much as a toothbrush behind, it seemed unlikely that he would be coming back, so I paid the room bills before calling a taxi and going to another guest house. I didn't want to be where he knew I was. I needed to hide whilst I figured out what to do next. I had no idea where Ben had gone but could only assume that he was still pursuing the swansong alone, or perhaps with Lukas. For all I knew, Lukas had been able to tell him exactly who Henri Rol-Tanguy was and they had now gone off to find him together.

When I went into my room in the new guest house I put my luggage down by the door. The room was similar to the one I had just come from but for the fact that it was a little smaller. And darker. And generally more depressing, because this time I was here on my own with no idea what I should do next. I had already been to both castles and the lake. There was no obvious location left for me to visit – nowhere else I knew that Liam had been before me.

The lake. I had yet to visit it at night when it was supposed to change so dramatically. Ben had seemed curiously reluctant to go there but, really, it was the most important place of all. I couldn't help but shudder a little at the thought of going after nightfall by myself. The castle had been quite eerie enough, and Ben had been with me then, before I realised what a lunatic he was. Still, it had to be done, there was no one to go with me and that was all there was to it. I would wait until dark and then I would go alone, approaching through the trees and taking care not to be seen.

But, of course, I had no way of getting there because Ben had taken the car. I swore irritably to myself, realising now that I was going to have to get another taxi to the nearest car rental place, which could be miles away and would involve more time and expense. But perhaps, after all, it was better that Ben had taken the car, for I would have felt uncomfortable driving it now for fear that he would come across it and know who it belonged to.

So I went down to the reception and ordered yet another taxi. Fortunately, the nearby town of Füssen was not very far away and, as it was a popular tourist destination, there was a car rental agency there. I hired the cheapest car available and then drove back to the guest house, only going wrong a few times along the way.

Finally, I got back to my room feeling the tiniest glow of pride that I had managed to obtain a car, even if it had taken me an age to get back because of my poor sense of direction. It was almost four o'clock when I walked back into my room. I had missed lunch but still had some snacks left in my suitcase from the Karstadt in Munich, so I unpacked what was left along with my laptop. I didn't intend to sit around doing nothing while waiting for it to be dark enough and late enough to go to the lake. I had to do something useful to keep myself busy. So I spent the next few hours making use of the guest house's Wi-Fi access.

I continued to research the name Henri Rol-Tanguy, but without anything more to go on it was hopeless. After a while, fed up with looking through other Henri Rol-Tanguys who seemed to have nothing whatever to do with anything, I went back to the very beginning – the Germanic folklore that had drawn Liam to Neuschwanstein and Ludwig in the first place. He had told me before that Germany was a magical country and the birthplace of fairy tales, as documented by the Brothers Grimm in the stories they collected from people they met during their travels and then noted down so that they would not be forgotten – tales like 'Cinderella', 'Rapunzel', 'Hansel and Gretel' ... Full of magic, cruelty, wicked stepmothers, lost woodcutters and evil witches ...

I narrowed down my searches to look for anything to do with magical swans and their knights. The myths and legends were all slightly different, although the general consensus seemed to be that the swans were birds by day and women by night. And I came across one story that said the reason the swan knights had been deemed necessary in the first place was because swansong was so bewitching and powerful that the wicked witches who lived in the mountains kept on setting traps for the swans to steal their voices. That was why, in the end, all magical swans were bound to a lake – so that the knights would always know where they were and be better able to protect them.

As this seemed to be a largely Germanic myth, I had the

distinctly frustrating feeling that, had I been fluent in German and able to use German search terms, I would have been able to find out a lot more. As it was, I was limited to the sites written in English.

I'd let the little black horse out of the box whilst I was doing all this for it seemed unfair to keep it cooped up. For the most part it just wandered about the room exploring its new environment but, after a while, the sound of munching made me look down and I saw that it was nibbling at a crisp I'd dropped. I gazed at the little horse, frowning. It had simply never occurred to me that it might eat but now I felt bad for not thinking of it sooner. I put a few more crisps on the floor for it as well as a soap dish filled with water.

Then I turned back to my computer with a sudden thought. I had researched magic swans and Henri Rol-Tanguy, but the one thing I hadn't even tried to find out more about was the tiny horse. For a while I sat there, typing in various unsuccessful searches. Then I looked back down at it and remembered the idea that had occurred to me when I had first seen it – that it was like a little, perfect faery horse ... My thoughts went back to the blue faery I had seen in my grandparents' stable as a child. Unlike most adults, I fully believed in faeries for I had seen one all those years ago and knew that they were real. Who was to say that they did not have horses?

I spent the time I had left that afternoon reading of the faery-land that was said to exist beneath our own – in the hills and the mountains and the wild places. Some sources described the faeries themselves as mischievous and playful whilst others described them as fickle, cruel creatures who would trap any human who found their way into faeryland so that they could never leave ... And I read that the faeries were indeed said to have animals – tiny and delicate like themselves ... Just like the little horse wandering inquisitively about my room at that very moment ...

A little while later I had a hasty dinner downstairs. Although adequate, I found the food not quite as good as it had been at the previous guest house, nor were the staff as friendly. The rooms were all perfectly clean but not as bright or cosy as the last one and I couldn't help wishing that I could go back to it. Any kind of familiarity was a comfort to me, but I couldn't risk it. I had no wish to be found by Ben.

As the time crept slowly nearer I felt increasingly uneasy about going out to the mountains so late all by myself. But at half-past eleven I forced myself to put on my coat, put the tiny horse back into its box, pick up my bag and go to the car. Snow lay thickly on the branches of the surrounding pines along with many frozen waterfalls that clung solidly to the edges of the rock faces through which the weaving road was cut.

I was confident I knew the way, having driven to both castles and the surrounding lake before. Which was why it was so odd that I became lost so quickly. I came to a fork in the road that I had no memory of whatsoever. Indeed, if I hadn't known any better, I would have sworn that it hadn't been there before. I slowed almost to a halt, trying to work out which one to take. I knew I was going in vaguely the right direction because I could see Neuschwanstein up in the mountains, pale and ghostly in its blue floodlights. It seemed to me that the road to the left was going more that way so I turned down it. I couldn't know then that I had just made my first mistake of the evening ... But perhaps things would have worked out the way they did whatever I'd done. I did, after all, have one of their horses in the car with me.

I soon realised that I had made a wrong turning because the route was utterly unfamiliar to me. I considered turning back but thought that I must be going in the right direction because I could still see Neuschwanstein and Hohenschwangau above me, and so I hoped I had merely stumbled upon an alternate route. After all, there must have been several possible ways of getting to the castles and the lake. So I kept driving and soon turned onto a long, straight road I thought I recognised as the one that led to the Alpsee Lake. When I turned onto it I could clearly see both castles resting on their mountainous perches above me – like great eagles in their mountain nests.

But by the time I got to the end of the road both Neuschwanstein and Hohenschwangau had disappeared.

At first I thought that fog or low clouds must be hiding them from view for I could picture exactly where they should be and yet neither one of them was there. But it was a clear, starry night without a tendril of mist. My head whirling with incomprehension, I slowed the car to a stop and looked over my shoulder, out through the back window, wondering if I could have got turned around somehow so that they were now behind me. But all I could see back there was the long road I had just driven down, tall pines lining it on either side, the branches weighed down beneath the weight of so much snow.

This was madness. The castles had both been there less than five minutes ago. I pulled the car over to the side of the road and got out, just to get my bearings. I was sure that if I stood there, turning on the spot, I would see them again. But they were nowhere in sight – not even as little bright pinpricks in the distance. It was as if I had been driving for hours and left them far behind me. But I had only been driving for a matter of minutes and this was most definitely the same road I had started on. Indeed, it stood out for the fact that it was long and dead straight rather than twisty and turny like most of the other roads in the area.

I got back into the car. Dark mountains rose up all around me and a skyful of stars twinkled down softly upon the deserted road. I didn't understand how but there was no denying the fact that I was extremely lost. I rested my head briefly against the steering wheel. So much for taking charge of things myself. All I had managed to do was get in the car, drive straight into the maze of mountain roads and promptly lose myself. I was totally and completely bloody useless and my cheeks flushed pink at the thought. I had almost a full tank of petrol, so the only thing for it was to carry on driving until I either came to a road I recognised, caught sight of one of the castles again or got myself onto a main road that was signposted. One of those things was bound to happen soon enough – after all, the castles simply couldn't have disappeared. They had to be up there somewhere and close – I just couldn't see them, that was all. I sat back, buckled my seatbelt and turned the key in the ignition.

Nothing happened.

There was no reassuring *thrum* of the engine coming to life or even the choke and splutter of it trying to. There was just nothing – as if the car had no engine at all. I tried several times but it was useless and I felt panic rise up in my throat. I was on a deserted mountain road in the middle of the freezing night, completely alone with no one who even knew where I was ... But I forced myself to look at it calmly. Yes, it was a highly irritating inconvenience, but it was hardly anything more than that. I may have been lost but I was, at least, prepared. Before leaving I had packed a flashlight and the German guidebook I had bought in the Californian airport. I had also made sure that my phone was charged and had put more credit on it after using it all up that afternoon. With those things I should be able to call for help. There were emergency services numbers listed in the guidebook and there was sure to be a breakdown number amongst them. No doubt this would involve more time and money and I would have to give up on seeing the lake that night. It was extremely irritating, but how could I have known that the car would just inexplicably stop working like that?

I fumbled through my bag for the book and found the emergency numbers. But as I was getting my phone out of my pocket I hesitated. English was such an international language that I was sure someone would be able to understand me, but if anyone was going to come and pick me up I was going to have to tell them where I was first. I could not simply say that I was *in the mountains somewhere around Neuschwanstein*. They'd be looking for me all night, if they even agreed to come at all.

I sat there for a moment, trying not to wring my hands. Although my plan all along had been to venture outside on my own in the dark once I reached the lake, the prospect of going outside now seemed so much more unnerving, somehow, for the fact that I was lost and had become so in such a short space of time. But there was no getting away from the fact that if I wanted someone to come and tow my car then I was going to have to tell them where it was.

I couldn't risk wandering far in case I got even more lost but I decided that, at the very least, I could walk the remaining few yards of the road to the corner, in the hopes of seeing a sign or a road name or some identifiable landmark. So I took my flashlight which – thankfully – was a wind-up one rather than battery powered, meaning that the beam was weaker but at least was not going to suddenly run out on me, which seemed a good thing considering the way my luck was going that night.

As I walked down the utterly silent road, the snow compacting beneath my feet, I couldn't help turning back repeatedly to check that the car was still there. I carried on, trying hard not to think of knights or magical swans or hidden doors into faeryland. I jumped at every tiny noise or rustle of leaves and the breeze seemed to stir my hair in a most disconcerting way – as if long fingers were running themselves through its white strands ...

I forced myself to walk to the end of the road but, when I got there, there wasn't a sign in sight, just more empty road stretching away into the darkness. I turned back around, desperately trying to remain calm but rapidly becoming fearful at my predicament – as well as angry with myself for allowing this to happen in the first place. I walked back towards the car, my breath horribly loud in my ears. I felt watched. That horrible, all too familiar feeling that had plagued me on and off since Liam's death. When I glanced up at the trees they looked too tall and too thin – the dead branches at the top silhouetted against the full moon in a most disconcerting way so that they seemed alive and watchful ... I thought I heard the rustling of leaves even though all the trees were weighed down with snow. The wind stirred my hair unnaturally once again, threading through it like fingers. Then a lone wolf – or something like it – howled in the distance and I almost jumped out of my skin before breaking into a run. Not a good idea for I instantly became twice as scared, convinced that something was right behind me, about to latch on to me at any moment. I tripped and sprawled over in the snow. My heart in my mouth, I scrambled back to my feet, ran the last few paces to the car, jumped back into the driver's seat and then slammed the door behind me before reaching around to manually lock all the others.

The breakdown people would simply have to find me without a specific address. Perhaps they could trace the signal on my mobile phone or something ... I flipped the phone open but my heart instantly sank at the words *No Signal* clearly displayed on the screen.

I closed my eyes briefly. It was almost as if someone was testing me, relentlessly, and I honestly didn't know how much more bad luck I could take. I ran my hands through my hair in frustration and that was when I felt them. Physically jumping in alarm, as if I'd been electrocuted, I scrabbled to pull down the sunshield and look into the mirror. There were several plaits running down the left side of my head. They were loose and starting to come undone already but someone had most definitely plaited my hair. And it had not been me.

I can hardly do justice to the utter horror I felt as I stared at my reflection in the dark car. After all, they were only plaits. But my skin couldn't have crawled more if I had looked in the mirror to see a man sitting on the back seat behind me. As I'd walked down the road I had assumed it was the breeze that made it feel as if someone were touching my hair. Now I realised that someone – or some*thing* – really *had* been touching me. Something I had not so much as caught a glimpse of but that had been there just the same.

My hands tore through the plaits to undo them. I ran my hands through my hair, patted down my clothes and stared owlishly around the car, half-expecting to see someone in there with me. That was it. Nothing – *nothing* could possess me to take so much as one step out of the car again for the rest of that night. I would simply have to bear the cold and stay there until morning, hoping that I didn't freeze to death. Leaving was not an option. It simply was *not* an—

My mouth dropped open and my heart turned over in my chest

as I saw, by the silver light of the moon and stars, a tiny black horse standing in the middle of the road in front of my car, its head raised, sniffing the air. My head snapped around to the box on the passenger seat beside me and I saw at once that it had fallen over on its side, the lid was open and the horse was gone. Somehow, it must have slipped out of the car in the seconds it took me to jump in.

'No.' The word slipped softly from my lips as the little horse began to trot away down the road, leaving behind it a trail of tiny hoof prints. 'No, no, *no!*'

I lunged for the door, scrabbling to unlock it, hoping to catch up with the horse, grab it and run back to the safety of the car before it could go too far and disappear altogether. It was the one thing I had that Ben didn't. It was the one thing that might possibly lead me to the swansong before him. I could not allow something so precious and magical to simply trot away out of sight, lost to me forever. So I opened the car door and ran after it, torch in hand, my heart hammering in my chest and my heels kicking up an icy spray of snow behind me.

18

Faery Funeral

Of course, the horse could not possibly just run off down the long, straight road. It had to prance straight into the trees to the side, right into the thick of the forest. Instantly it was darker, with only a faint dappling of silver where the moonlight managed to push its way through the treetop roof. The air was still and slightly dank compared to the freshness of the road – as if last year's rotting leaves lay beneath the crisp blanket of snow, for all that the pines were evergreen.

With the weak beam of my torch I managed to keep the little horse in sight, stumbling after it desperately, horribly aware that I was moving steadily further and further from the car all the time. Every time my hair caught on a low hanging branch I whirled around in panic, thinking that unseen fingers were plaiting it again.

I couldn't afford to lose sight of the horse for more than a moment because then I would lose it for good. If it hadn't been for the snow it would have been quite impossible to keep it in sight at all but – fortunately – its black coat stood out against the white and I could see its little head bobbing along as it went. I tried calling out to it softly but the combination of running and fear had made me breathless and I was terrified that if I spoke someone might hear me – I was already making more noise than I was comfortable with, crashing through the trees after the horse.

The snow here was old, not soft and powdery but hard and jagged like glass so that when I tripped and sprawled over a tree root, I cut the palms of my hands on the sharp, unforgiving surface, leaving splatters of blood vivid against the white.

The torch flew away from me when I fell, the light went out and, for a moment, I lay there panting in what seemed like utter darkness. I had never been so scared before in my life and could almost have wept with fear. I should never have left the car. I should have simply let the horse go ... I felt blindly about for the torch but my fingers only came into contact with more snow, breaking through the crisp, brittle surface to the softer, slushier snow beneath.

Gradually, my eyes adjusted to the darkness and I saw my torch lying close by. Hurriedly I grabbed it and wound it up with trembling fingers, praying this would be all that was needed to set it going again. I gave a sigh of relief when, with a soft whirring sound, the beam of light shone out, softly illuminating my way and making me just a tiny bit less ridiculously helpless.

I brushed the snow off my knees and coat and looked around. There was nothing to distinguish this patch of wood from the rest that I had run through and the fall had disorientated me even further. But as I glanced down at the snow for any sign of the long-gone horse, I was relieved to realise that I was not lost after all. A clear trail of disturbed snow stretched back the way I had come where I had ploughed through it. If I wanted to get back to the car I only had to follow the trail of my own footprints. I could get back any time I wanted to.

The tracks ended where I stood but, when I looked closely, I saw that tiny hoof prints stretched on into the forest. I stood there for a moment, wracked with indecision. Should I summon up my courage and go after it? Or should I turn back right now? I longed to return to the car – to get into it, lock all the doors behind me and curl up in a terrified ball on the back seat to wait for morning.

Something was out here in the forest – something had plaited my hair out there on the road. Perhaps the sensible thing would be to turn back ... I very nearly did so. My desire to hurt Ben was not as strong as my desire to get out of the woods and I suddenly felt that maybe finding the swansong simply wasn't worth it. After all – what would I do with it if I found it? I certainly wouldn't sell it and, indeed, I would have no idea how to go about doing so at any rate ...

I shook my head and took a step back in the direction of the car. But then I stopped. A sense of terrible loss welled up inside me – the first time it had ever happened while I was fully awake. Usually I only experienced it in the first few seconds of waking from a dream – that overwhelming sense of having lost something irreplaceable – but it wasn't for Liam and I couldn't work out what else of importance it could possibly be. Lukas had mentioned it to me down at the Alpsee Lake. He had known somehow, and told me I might still be able to get it back if only I found the swansong quickly enough.

I had no reason whatsoever to trust Lukas. In fact, I distrusted him entirely for he seemed to be on friendly terms with Ben. But there was no denying that that sense of loss was there inside me, terrifying for the fact that I had no idea what it was for. And I suddenly felt – with a strange conviction – that if I walked away back to the car now, that would be it. I would never find whatever I was missing. It would be gone for good. So I took a deep breath and – as quietly as I could – carried on following the hoof prints in the snow, trying to reassure myself with the thought that I could turn around and follow my own tracks back to the car whenever I wanted to – like Hansel and Gretel following their trail of breadcrumbs home.

I walked on for a while, quickening my pace in an attempt to catch up with the horse, my feet crunching on the crisp snow. The tall trees around me seemed to be always reaching out their wet branches to tug at my clothes or entangle themselves in my hair. I struggled on for about five minutes in silence. If there were any animals nearby, I didn't hear them. It was as if I was the only living thing in the entire mountains. But after five minutes or so, the silence was broken by the sound of a swan singing somewhere close by. It was the most beautiful sound I had ever heard – as if I was listening to the voice of an angel – a clear, silvery song that echoed softly all around me, like falling snow. It seemed to be coming from the direction in which the tiny horse had disappeared and I blundered instinctively on, desperate to get nearer to that enchanting song, no longer caring about how much noise I made.

Moments later, I staggered into a little clearing that was surrounded by a circle of white candles and the singing stopped abruptly. There was a flurry of blurred movement around the edges of my vision as bright things flittered away into the trees. Even without the candles it would have been lighter in the clearing for thick beams of moonlight shone down, clearly illuminating the dozens of tiny little footprints that were all over the place. It was as if, by bursting out of the trees in such a way, I had disturbed something that had been taking place here. But I had caught up with the black horse at last. It stood in the middle of the clearing in one of the shafts of moonlight. I walked into the circle of candles to see what it was standing next to and then stopped in my tracks. It was a small, pearly white coffin no more than six inches long.

I had interrupted a faery funeral.

I stared for a moment, feeling faintly horrified. When something brushed against my arm I thought at first that it had started to snow again. But then I looked down and saw a black petal on the ground at my feet. Then there was another one beside it and, when I looked up, they were falling down all around me, velvety soft when they touched my skin, filling the air with that familiar sweet scent.

When the petal-fall stopped, the entire circle was covered in black, making the white coffin stand out starkly in contrast. Then a final object tumbled from the sky, heavier than the rest: a whole rose that landed right on the lid of the white coffin itself.

I had goosebumps, partly from where the petals had brushed against me on their way down but partly because this whole thing reminded me of the dreams I'd had of falling feathers. I brushed a few stray petals out of my hair, knocked them off my shoulders and then froze. The soft light I had at first taken to be one of the flickering candles was moving towards me and now that I looked straight at it I saw that, although it glowed softly, it was not a candle – but a faery – much like the one I had seen at my grandparents' all those years ago, except that this one was male.

He had the same cyan hair, elfin features and bare feet but much grander clothes – a long winter coat of royal blue with gleaming silver buttons. I wondered if I ought to get away from the circle in case he was angry with me for interrupting the funeral. But I couldn't move – in fact, I could hardly take my eyes off him. I felt quite as captivated as that first time when I'd been five years old and I couldn't help but watch as he picked the black rose up. The flower was much taller than him so he carried it horizontally, both hands carefully placed around non-thorny parts of the stem. Then he walked over to me and held the rose up, clearly intending that I take it.

Slowly, I knelt down onto the scented black carpet of rose petals before him, close enough to see that his eyes were silver and that he had long, pale lashes. I offered my hand palm upwards and he dropped the rose into it.

A sudden movement above caught my eye and I saw the glow of other indistinct faeries flitting between the treetops and sitting on the branches. I looked back down at the rose and it fell apart in my hand, the petals fluttering into my lap. And, at the exact same moment, the song I had heard before started again – seeming to burst right from within the rose as if it had been contained inside it. Now it rang out clear and perfect around the clearing.

The effect upon the faeries was instantaneous. They came dancing and tumbling down from the treetops. They all appeared to be wearing winter coats and dresses of the same royal blue as the first one; they all had cyan hair and the same silvery delicate wings. But I couldn't see them in any detail beyond that for they were moving too fast – leaping up into the air, flitting about the circle joyously in the starlight, apparently just as entranced by the song echoing around us as I was.

I can't be sure how long I sat there. In some ways it felt like an eternity. The song made me feel peaceful and content – happy simply to watch the faeries dancing about me forever, quite prepared never to leave this place ever again. When I glanced down into my lap I dimly noticed the petals that had fallen from the rose earlier. But five of them were different from the others: they each had a gold letter painted onto them.

I had just gathered them up into my hand when a great drowsiness swept over me. I looked at the soft bed of black petals and lying down in them to sleep suddenly seemed the most attractive prospect in the world. A small voice in the back of my mind kept on insisting that I mustn't go to sleep in this place and I was aware that the faeries had stopped dancing. They were perched up on the treetops, staring down at me with eager, bright eyes as if waiting for me to perform some sort of magic trick. I looked again at the bed of petals – fragrant, soft and alluring – and I couldn't help myself. I had to lie down in them ...

But just as I was about to lay my head on the scented carpet of flowers, there was the sound of something large crashing through the trees nearby. The faeries disappeared at once, the song faded away into silence and I was left in the clearing alone, clutching the petals and staring around in vain for somewhere to hide when a black horse broke out of the trees. This was not a faery horse but a full-size stallion, snorting and stamping in the frosty air. It was Kini – and he had a rider on his back. Lukas looked down at me with a frighteningly horrified expression on his face.

'So you *are* here!' he said, although he seemed to be speaking to himself more than to me. 'My God, what are you *doing*?'

'I—' I began, but that was as far as I got before he reached down, gripped my arm and dragged me bodily up onto the horse. No mean feat – especially as I tried to squirm out of his grip on principle. My arm felt like it had been half-yanked out of its socket, but as soon as I was sprawled across Kini's back he took off, thundering through the trees at a breakneck pace, leaving the faery ring with its carpet of petals far behind us. Riding a fast horse can be thrilling and exhilarating – when you're wearing a riding hat, holding on to the reins and have a strong grip, feet firmly in the stirrups. But when you have no protective clothing, the horse does not appear to be wearing tack of any kind and your seat is precarious, with both legs dangling over the same side, it ceases to be any fun whatsoever. It was no exaggeration to say that my life was entirely in Lukas's hands, for it was only his grip that stopped me from falling off. As it was I still bounced around painfully on the horse's back and every muscle in my stomach, arms and shoulders seemed to scream with the effort of staying upright and clinging to Lukas's arm.

Finally, we broke out of the trees onto a road and Kini slowed to a trot, then to a walk and then stopped. I shook off Lukas's hand and slid inelegantly off the horse, staggering on the tarmac before righting myself.

'You lunatic!' I gasped, still shaking from the fear of that awful ride. 'You might have killed us both!'

Lukas swung himself lightly off Kini's back, hardly seeming to have heard me. And, when he spoke, his words astonished me. 'Did you eat anything?' he demanded.

'What?' I frowned. 'When?'

'Just now! While you were in the forest!'

'No, of course I didn't eat anything!' I replied.

'The fey didn't offer you any food?'

'No,' I said. But my mind went back to how I had almost laid down and gone to sleep inside a faery ring – a fact that now both frightened and alarmed me. I would certainly have done it if Lukas hadn't turned up when he did.

'Thank God for that! Those damn faeries are a menace, Jasmyn, you have to be so careful around them! You mustn't ever wander about these mountains on your own after nightfall again. It's not safe! Looking the way you do, it's a miracle nothing happened to you this time!'

'What do you mean, *looking the way I do*?' I asked. 'What's that got to do with anything?'

'Your albinism makes you too similar to the swan princesses,' he said. 'That's what any random mountain witch will take you for and they'll try to steal your voice. But even for a normal person …' He shook his head, gestured back towards the forest and said, 'These mountains overlap with the faerylands below. People get lost out there for a few hours and then find their way out only to discover that – as far as everyone else is concerned

– they've been gone for years. Or they eat the food the faeries offer them and find themselves trapped there forever, unable to leave. Why the hell did you leave the road in the first place?'

'My car broke down,' I said vaguely, not wanting to say anything about the tiny horse. 'And then I heard the singing.'

'Singing?' Lukas said sharply. 'What singing?'

'It led me to that faery ring. I think it came from the black rose.'

'The swansong's trying to communicate with you,' Lukas said. 'You're linked to it.'

'How can *I* possibly be linked to it?'

He looked at me and said evasively, 'Well, you obviously have some degree of second sight otherwise you would not have been able to get into faeryland at all. The swansong itself comes from there, so it was probably able to communicate with you better whilst you were there too. It wants you to find it.' He paused, then said sharply, 'What are you holding in your hand?'

I looked down in surprise, for I had hardly been aware that my hand was still clenched. When I uncurled my fingers I saw the five petals I had picked up just before Lukas crashed into the clearing. They were a little crumpled but I could still clearly see that a different golden letter was printed on the surface of each.

I closed my fist back round them hurriedly, hoping that Lukas had not seen them properly. They didn't mean anything at all to me but if they were a clue or a message of some kind then I did not want it getting back to Ben somehow.

'I'll walk you back to your car,' Lukas said calmly.

I looked up sharply. 'How do you know where it is?'

'That's it just there, isn't it?' he said, pointing down the road.

I turned around and was taken aback at the sight of my car not far away, for I had thought we'd ridden from the faery ring in the opposite direction. We certainly hadn't gone back the way I had come … I tried to persuade myself that I had simply got turned around in the forest. That was all. But then I noticed the castles – both Neuschwanstein and Hohenschwangau – up there in the mountains glowing blue and orange respectively beneath their floodlights, right where they should have been all along.

'They ... they weren't there before,' I managed, staring in astonishment. 'I lost sight of them. That's how I got lost.'

I glanced around, wondering if someone had moved my car. But the road seemed to be the same one I had left – long and straight with tall tree sentries standing guard on either side. I expected Lukas to sneer at my preposterous suggestion that the castles had apparently ceased to exist for a few minutes or more but instead he said simply, 'This is what I'm talking about. Things change around here at night. Come on, let's get you back to the car.'

'It's no good, it's broken down.'

'Well, let's just see,' he replied.

I didn't trust Lukas and felt uncomfortable being out there alone with him but I didn't have much of a choice, my only other option being to run blindly back into the forest. So I walked down the road with him, Kini keeping step with us without any apparent command from Lukas. I found the clip-clop of hooves strangely reassuring – perhaps because I had long since associated anything to do with horses with feelings of happiness and contentment.

I sneaked a sideways glance at Lukas and saw that he was wearing a long, black winter coat that must have been his own, for it fitted him much better than any of Ben's clothes would have done.

'Your arm seems to be all better now,' I said, breaking the silence. In fact, from the way he had just been riding I would never have known his arm had ever been injured in the first place.

'We heal fast,' he said, with a brief glance at me.

I considered asking him if he knew where Ben had gone or why he had destroyed my Violectra so cruelly, but I found I hated the idea of even so much as saying his name aloud after what he had done. Besides, it didn't matter much where Ben was so long as he was nowhere near me. So instead I said, 'Were you at the lake the night Liam went there with the others?'

Lukas gave a brief nod. 'I was.'

'Did you see what happened?'

'You mean did I see Liam and Adrian kill the swan? Yes, I saw it. And I intervened, albeit belatedly.'

'Intervened?' I repeated. Then my eyes narrowed as I recalled Adrian's description of the knight he had seen that night – *almost seven feet tall* ... and Lukas's own statement that he had first met Liam at Lake Alpsee – that they had had a 'disagreement' ...

'You were the one who dragged Liam and Adrian into the lake and almost drowned them.' It wasn't a question so much as a flat statement. Suddenly I didn't see how I could have missed it before. I should have realised the truth as soon as I found out what Lukas truly was.

'That's right,' he said calmly, without any apparent hint of shame or regret.

'Did you mean for them to survive or was that a miscalculation on your part?' I asked in a voice of ice.

'No, it was deliberate,' he said calmly. 'Despite the fact that they were both bad men.'

Don't do anything rash, I said to myself as we stopped beside the car. *You're out here with him all alone. Don't do anything stupid.* I looked down at the snow to avoid looking at Lukas and my eyes focused on the little trail of tiny hoof prints alongside my own, both sets vanishing into the trees. This was definitely the place where I had left my car for all that the castles had not been there before.

'You obviously weren't exiled at that point,' I said, ignoring his previous remark and trying to keep my voice level.

'No. I was exiled after the incident with your husband.'

I looked up at him. 'They punished you for what you did?' I said, a gleam of satisfaction coming into my eye at the thought.

'No, they punished me for what I *didn't* do. It's supposed to be an eye for an eye, you see. Liam killed one of our swans so I should have killed him in return. That's the way it works. We're bound by strict rules.'

'So why didn't you?'

'Temporary lapse of judgement, I suppose,' he replied. 'But killing people isn't something I particularly want to be a part of. And

207

I'm not against humans the way most of the other knights are. I suppose I took pity on them, not that they deserved it. Looking back at it now it would have saved everyone a lot of trouble if I'd just drowned Liam in the lake that night. Especially as he was only going to die a year later anyway.'

Anger and hate welled up inside me so viciously that I drew my hand back to hit him, hardly caring that this might make him hit me back. But he caught my wrist easily, which infuriated me all the more, and so I jerked my knee upright in an attempt to kick him but he sidestepped deftly, then twisted my arm behind my back to pin me to the car. 'Calm *down*,' he said, almost beseechingly. 'I'm sorry for everything you've been through, Jasmyn. Ben is a good man, but the fact is that Liam was a cruel, selfish bastard.'

'He was my *husband*!' I shouted, my voice echoing back to us and disturbing a bird in a tree above, which hastily took flight. 'If he was as bad as all that, don't you think I would have *known*? You don't know what the hell you're talking about! Ben is the cruel one! He destroyed my Violectra a few hours ago out of spite! I knew Liam for years before we were married and in all that time I never knew him to be anything other than a kind, decent, honourable man! You've got no right to tell such awful lies about him and it doesn't matter how many people try to convince me, I will *never* believe a word of it! I know who Liam was! Whatever you think you know about him, you're wrong!'

I meant every word I said. They were the ones who must be wrong, not me. I would never doubt Liam for them. I *knew* him – I knew the little boy who'd sat in the stables with me watching for faeries and I knew him as the man I'd fallen in love with – the man who'd bought me a Violectra, who'd made me feel beautiful and safe and loved. Those feelings had been real and I would never doubt them – no matter what I might find out about Liam before all this was over. There wasn't anything iniquitous enough he could possibly have done that would ever make me stop loving him.

Lukas sighed and stepped back. 'You've got it all wrong, Jasmyn,' he said quietly – but surely – as though just as certain of his beliefs as I was. 'Why don't I drive back with you and direct you to the guest house? You might get lost again.'

'I won't be in the same car as you!' I spat venomously. 'I'd rather be lost forever than that!'

'There's a main road,' he said calmly, as if he hadn't heard me, 'about five minutes on from here. You should be able to find your way back if you follow the signposts.'

Loath to take so much as a word of advice from him, I pulled open the car door, intending to jump straight in and firmly lock all the doors behind me before trying to start it. But when I opened the door, something fell out onto the snow. It was the little metal knight. After noting how the marble horse and he had seemed to match, I had decided to carry him with me as Liam had done but he must have fallen from my pocket when I'd been in the car.

Lukas automatically bent to pick it up for me but no sooner had his fingers closed around it than there was a hiss, a cloud of steam and the pungent smell of burning flesh. Lukas dropped the figure and jumped back, smacking into Kini who was standing behind him.

'Damn!' he muttered, leaning down to grab a fistful of snow to soothe his burnt skin. Then he glanced at me and said, 'That's some powerful black magic you have there. I wonder if Liam found someone to curse it or if he learned to do it himself.'

He spoke in a light tone, but I noticed with a keen interest that he didn't take so much as a single step nearer, keeping his back firmly against his horse and his eyes on the little knight lying in the snow – as if he were a vampire and it was a crucifix.

'It's a curse that needs to be repeated regularly. So if a witch was doing it for him he would have needed to keep coming back to Germany with it,' Lukas went on. I thought back to Liam's repeated visits to the country but said nothing.

'Ben told me about the five dead swan knights that fell from the sky at the funeral,' Lukas said. 'Liam threatened that if anything were to happen to him, five of us would die on the day he was buried. That's the only reason they didn't go after him to get the swansong back. Sounds like the sort of thing a clever man might do, maybe, but hardly something a kind, decent, honourable man would consider, wouldn't you say?'

'I don't believe you,' I said stiffly, before scooping up the knight and getting into the car. The key was still in the ignition and when I turned it the engine sprang to life as if there had never been anything wrong with it. I pulled back onto the road and drove away, keeping my eyes on Lukas and his horse in the rear-view mirror until I turned a corner in the road and lost them from sight.

19

Separation of a Couple

I thought about trying to go on to the lake, but when I looked at the illuminated clock in the car I was shocked to see that it was gone five o'clock in the morning when it should have been more like only one o'clock. I checked my watch as well, but it showed the same hour. Here was firm proof indeed that time sometimes worked differently in the mountains, for I had surely been lost in the forest for no more than an hour and yet five had passed since my car broke down.

I did not want to get lost again, at any rate, and it was easier to head back towards Füssen and find the guest house than to try to find the lake. Thankfully the main road was where Lukas had said it would be and it was so easy finding my way back from there that it was as if I had never been lost to begin with.

It was a relief to finally let myself in and tiptoe up to my room. I was bone tired and my jeans were damp from kneeling in the snow. But I ignored the bed and sat at the desk instead where I spread the five petals out before me. The black roses had appeared several times and, on this last occasion, that beautiful song had seemed to burst right out of it. I remembered what Ben had said about being able to disguise the swansong as any everyday object and I was sure now that I knew what this object must be – it had to be a black rose. I felt a tiny surge of triumph for at least now I knew what I was looking for. And – as such – the letters on the petals had to mean something, if only I could arrange them into the right order.

I sat there arranging and rearranging the petals into countless different variations: IRSPA, SPARI, ARISP, SIRAP, PRISA, RAPIS, APSIR, SPIRA ... After half an hour I leaned back in the chair in frustration. None of these were even real words and for a horrible moment I wondered if I could be missing a petal, or even several of them. After all, I had only just gathered them up when Lukas came bursting out of the forest and dragged me onto his horse. I could easily have dropped one of them during the ride ...

But then I saw it – a single word that leapt up at me from those black petals. I leaned forwards eagerly to rearrange them and make sure, then gazed down as a slow smile spread across my face, convinced that I had suddenly managed to narrow down potential hiding places exponentially. The swansong itself was try-ing to communicate with me, Lukas had said. For some reason, it *wanted* me to find it. And the word spelled out in the petals before me read: PARIS.

I seriously thought about driving to Paris. I could have got in the car and set off that very minute rather than going through the bother and delay of air travel. But I had no idea how to get there, I hadn't slept all night and I was keen to avoid a drive like that if possible.

So I slept for an hour or so until the sun came up and I could call my travel agent to make arrangements. Then I packed up my things, returned the rental car and got a taxi to Munich Airport, no longer caring much about the expense but simply wanting to get to Paris as quickly as possible. I was sure that the swansong was there somewhere. I remembered that, according to Ben's list, the city had been the other place Liam had gone to secretly. And there was also the French name – Henri Rol-Tanguy, the significance of which I was still to discover. I was not overly concerned about the fact that the tiny horse had remained behind in the forest for that was where it appeared to belong and it had led me straight to the rose first. It had done what it was supposed to do.

I was annoyed with myself for looking at the petals in front of Lukas. They had only been visible in my hand for a moment but, for all I knew, he had still managed to pick the anagram out and might have communicated it to Ben by now, who could already be on his way to Paris. I didn't know exactly what I was going to do when I got there; my only thought was to start with Henri Rol-Tanguy and attempt to track him down. There surely couldn't be that many of them living in Paris.

Failing that, perhaps there was some sort of monument or statue of the famous communist himself and Liam had hidden the swansong around there somewhere ... But it seemed improbable. In fact, I thought it more likely that the black rose was in a safety deposit box in a bank somewhere, for all that Lukas had said he didn't think Liam would use a bank. After all – a bank would be the only feasible place to hide an object and keep it safe for any great length of time. If the rose were left out in the open then Liam couldn't have been sure that someone, at some point, wouldn't stumble across it, even accidentally.

And why should I trust anything Lukas had said anyway? For all I knew, everything he'd said about the swansong singing at night was a lie to throw me off course. I had already had quite enough of talking to bankers and lawyers about Liam's death, but I could lose nothing by checking if he'd had a safety deposit box of some kind in one of the banks in Paris.

Waiting for my gate number to come up in Munich Airport, I just about managed not to fall asleep on my suitcase, and when they finally loaded us onto the plane I was asleep before it even took off. Indeed it seemed I'd barely closed my eyes before we were landing in Charles de Gaulle. I collected my suitcase – thoroughly weary of airports by that point – and eventually managed to work out how to buy a train ticket and get myself into the city centre. It was, at least, a little easier for me to move around now that I only had a suitcase to worry about and not a bulky violin case as well. Although I had packed the broken pieces of my Violectra and brought them with me, I had decided to leave the case behind, unable to bear the heartbreak of carrying it around with nothing inside it.

I'd asked my travel agent to book me into whichever fairly

central hotel she could get the best deal for and she had reserved a single room for me at the Hotel Delambre in the Montparnasse district. I arrived in the afternoon and wanted nothing more than to curl up on the bed and sleep for the rest of the day. But I couldn't bear to do it knowing the ordeal that lay before me with the banks. So I dumped my stuff into yet another new room – wondering with a brief pang of homesickness when I would ever see my own bedroom again – and then went back out into the city with my Paris guidebook stowed in my shoulder bag.

To cut a long and boring story short, I spent the afternoon trailing from bank to bank. It was the same tedious, rather humiliating routine every time. A staff member would be fetched who spoke and understood English. I would explain that I had been recently widowed and wanted to check whether my late husband had held an account here. Some places were difficult and would insist on all the proper documentation being faxed over by my solicitor before they would even check for an account under the name of Liam Gracey, but a couple of the smaller banks saved us all a lot of trouble by looking straight away and telling me that there was no such account. They all looked at me like I was mad. After all, I clearly wasn't French and I could offer no sensible explanation whatsoever for why I thought my husband might have kept a secret account with their bank.

The afternoon was a total waste of time and – to make it an even more miserable experience – it had been raining constantly ever since I left the hotel. I'd had the foresight to take an umbrella with me but the rain blew under it and by the time my tour of Parisian banks was finished I was thoroughly soaked. With my white hair hanging down in damp tendrils and tiny droplets clinging to my pale skin, I looked like some sort of drowned Lady of the Lake and I was sure I saw several people in the street start at the sight of me.

By seven o'clock I found myself in the Invalides and Eiffel Tower quarter, as I realised when I saw the Eiffel Tower not too far away. The lights had been turned on and it shone golden against the dark sky. I stood looking at it for a moment, wondering what I should do now. It was no longer raining quite so hard but there was still a thin drizzle. I was starving. I had never been to Paris before but I knew that it was acclaimed for its cuisine ... I looked longingly at the restaurants and bistros lining the street – all with views of the Eiffel Tower and delicious smells wafting from the doors ...

But I knew I shouldn't spend the money. I cringed to think of what I had spent already between plane tickets and car rentals and train tickets and guest houses ... The responsible thing would be to look for a street stand and get a baguette to take back to the hotel with me. But it was raining, so it would probably be soggy and squashed by the time I got the Metro back. My feet ached from all the traipsing around I had done. Other than a sandwich at Munich Airport I hadn't had anything else to eat that day. I glanced again at the window of the nearest restaurant and saw warm, happy-looking people sitting at tables that were covered with crisp, white cloths, sharing bottles of wine and eating hot dishes bathed in rich, buttery sauces that I was sure I could practically *taste* when I looked at them ...

Ignoring the tiny voice still shouting about the expense in the back of my mind, I opened the door to the nearest restaurant and walked in. The smells made my mouth water and my stomach rumble. Because it was still early it was easy to get a table by the window looking back at the glittering outline of the Eiffel Tower.

I ordered the works. When I opened the menu I didn't even look at the prices. To start with I had a French onion soup with a baked cheese top served with crusty bread; *truffle feuillete* for the main course and then a cheese board to finish that included Tomme de Chèvre, Roquefort and Brie de Meaux. And to go with it all I ordered a bottle of Bordeaux.

I'm not ashamed to say I enjoyed it immensely. It was the first proper meal out I'd had since the dinner aboard the *Queen Mary*. It was hard to believe that had only been a week ago. When I'd finished eating I ordered coffee and lingered in the restaurant, for I could see that it had started to rain outside again and just the thought of the trek back to my hotel through the wet streets and damp, slippery Metro made me feel weary. So I turned my thoughts instead to where in Paris the swansong could possibly be, if it really wasn't in any of the banks.

My mind went to what Lukas had said back at the Alpsee Lake in Germany – that he thought Liam would have hidden it in a central, easy-to-reach place that, at the same time, was guaranteed to be deserted at night. Paris was central – it would only take a few hours to get there from home. But what hiding place was always going to be deserted at night in a city like Paris?

I was stirring cream into my second cup of coffee, watching it swirl about on the dark surface, when it hit me. Graveyards. On two of the occasions when a black rose had appeared – on the *Queen Mary* and in my first guest house room in Germany – it had either been accompanied, or followed, by old, yellowed human bones. Surely that must mean that it was hidden with bones somewhere. A graveyard seemed a perfect hiding place seeing as most people were uncomfortable being in them at night. And even if someone did happen to wander in after dark and hear a bird singing there they were unlikely to think anything much of it.

I dug into my bag and took out the Paris guidebook to look up cemeteries – praying that there would be one in the city. There were three. The largest one – Cimetière du Père Lachaise – was outside the city centre, the second was just a little way out in Montmartre but the third and smallest graveyard was right in the centre of the Montparnasse quarter, and from the looks of it, only about a street away from my hotel. I felt a momentary flicker of self-satisfaction, for a graveyard seemed to fit all the criteria. But then I realised what that meant and my heart sank. If the swansong really was hidden in a graveyard then I would have to go there. At night. By myself ...

Well, so what? I had done worse than that already. I'd take a little graveyard in the centre of Paris over wandering about the faery-and-knight-infested Bavarian Alps any day. They were only bones, after all.

I paid the bill and then, because I had only drunk half the

bottle of wine, I picked it up to take with me. But when I got to the door, one of the waiters stopped me, pointing at the bottle and saying something about not being licensed for guests to take it away.

'Oh, I'm sorry,' I began. I was already in the act of passing it over when I suddenly hesitated. Then I snatched the bottle back, clamped it to my chest and ran for it. It was my wine – I had paid for it and by God I was going to drink it.

Unsurprisingly, no one from the restaurant gave chase into the street to wrestle the bottle back from me and I made it to the Metro feeling highly pleased with myself for my petty victory. I was feeling so rebellious, I even drank some of the wine straight from the bottle as I walked back through the streets after getting off the Metro – probably the most unladylike thing I'd ever done in my cosy, sheltered, privileged life.

I had thought about just going straight back to my hotel, getting a good night's sleep and starting with the graveyards the next day but, as it happened, I saw the Montparnasse cemetery on the walk back. I must have passed it when I left the hotel earlier that day for it was only a few minutes away but, with my head down under an umbrella, I had not noticed it.

I paused outside the arch and looked in rather miserably. It was no longer raining but a chilly mist hung in the air and my clothes and hair were damp with it. I had been cold all afternoon and, more than anything, I wanted to return to my room so I could have a hot shower and warm up. But I was right here outside the gates. It would be so easy to just go in and have a quick walk around. If, by some glorious good luck, the swansong was there, then I might be able to find it, take it away with me and be back home in England by this time tomorrow with the whole traumatic experience behind me once and for all.

Of course, it did occur to me that if the black rose had been hidden there over a year ago then it would not simply be resting on top of a gravestone but would more likely actually be *inside* a grave, maybe even inside a coffin. So getting it out would involve digging and grave desecration. This was where I could really do with a large, strong man or two, armed with shovels. Even if I worked out which grave it was, it was sure to take me bloody ages to dig through that compact, damp earth on my own. And I would have to find a shovel from somewhere too ...

I squared my shoulders and walked into the cemetery. There was enough light from the surrounding street lamps for me to see by but I took out my torch anyway, in order to better read the names on the gravestones, for it occurred to me that perhaps the famous communist Colonel Henri Rol-Tanguy was buried there. Perhaps that was the significance of his name – perhaps his was the grave in which the swansong was hidden ... I was so taken with this idea, which seemed to me to be a very neat explanation, that I felt increasingly annoyed as I walked about the gravel paths, checking gravestone after gravestone but finding no Colonel Rol-Tanguy anywhere.

A few weeks ago I would have cringed to be walking around a graveyard alone at night. Now it hardly bothered me. There were buildings within sight and lamp-lit streets and roads with the odd car passing by. Although no one was walking with me I did not feel alone. And the graves seemed more peaceful than sinister anyway.

But then, as I turned a corner in the path, I came upon another person, standing before a white monument of some kind. He was wearing a long, waterproof coat and a closed umbrella dangled from his hand as he stood and glared at the monument. The soft light from the street lamps on the other side of the wall near the road illuminated his face enough for me to see the fading bruises around his left eye and the healing cut stretching from his upper lip down to his chin. He had strawberry-blond hair and blue eyes that I recognised from our meeting almost three weeks ago – it was Jaxon.

I stopped abruptly, touched by a cold fear at coming across him alone like this so suddenly. It was too late to hide for he had already seen me, but I tightened my hand around the neck of the wine bottle in case I needed it as a weapon. I already knew that he was ruthless and dangerous. I'm not sure what I expected him to do but his reaction stunned me. When his eyes fell on me they widened in a sort of horror, so that for a moment I was convinced that he must think I was a ghost – that being in a dark graveyard alone at night had made him nervous, and when I'd come suddenly around the corner he'd mistaken my pale skin and long white hair for a ghostly apparition. But then he scowled and said, 'This doesn't count. It's not my fault. Tell Ben I didn't know you were going to be here.'

I stared at him. He spoke quietly but I was sure I detected a note of fear concealed beneath his voice. Why should a career criminal – someone who had been arrested for beating a man almost to death – be afraid of *Ben*? For the first time it occurred to me that perhaps Jaxon wasn't all the things Ben had said he was. Still ... a deserted graveyard was not the ideal place to find out either way.

'Is he here?' Jaxon said, twisting his head to glance around the graveyard. 'I thought he was in the graveyard in Montmartre tonight.'

'He's right behind me,' I lied quickly, secretly rather horrified to find out that both Jaxon *and* Ben were in the city even if it did confirm that I was in the right place.

'He is, is he?' Jaxon said with a sudden smile. I wasn't sure what had given me away but he plainly did not believe me. 'You're nowhere near as good a liar as Liam was.'

The tilt of his head caused the lower half of his face to fall into the light of the nearby street lamp so that I could clearly see the ugly jagged cut that began at his upper lip and the fading mottled bruise surrounding it.

'Who have you been fighting with?' I said coldly.

'You mean who did all this?' Jaxon said, gesturing at his messed-up face. 'Well, it was Ben, naturally.'

'*Ben?*' I repeated. 'When?'

'Just over a week ago. Before he went to California.'

'I met up with Ben around that time and there wasn't a mark on him,' I said. As soon as I spoke, I realised that wasn't actually true – his knuckles had been in a terrible state ...

Jaxon scowled. 'That's because he waited until I was out of my head drunk, the coward! Ben only likes fighting defenceless men. You should know that.'

'*I* should know that?' I repeated, frowning in total non-comprehension.

'Ben knocked Liam around a bit while you were on your honey-moon, didn't he?'

'*Ben* did that?' I said. Or – at least – that was what I meant to say. The sound that came out was actually more like: '*Blerghh?*'

My mind went back to that occasion: waiting in our hotel room for Liam to return with the ice; thinking that he was taking a long time; feeling horrified when he walked through the door with a swollen eye and blood still dribbling from his lip and then burst-ing uselessly into tears once we'd cleaned him up.

'Ah, so Liam never told you it was Ben?' Jaxon said, correctly reading the expression on my face.

I didn't want to believe him. A few days ago I wouldn't even have considered it. But I had seen Ben smash my treasured Violectra into tiny broken bits and I had listened to him scream in my face that he hated Liam and always had. And I found myself believing Jaxon, for he hardly seemed likely to benefit from the statement whether it was true or not. Liam had told me it was just another guest looking to make trouble and that the hotel had thrown him out but ... I hadn't been there, I hadn't seen it. It was our honeymoon – perhaps Liam had lied to avoid upsetting me. In fact, considering the timing, perhaps that was the incident the two of them had fallen out about so irrevocably.

'Why is Ben so angry with you?' I asked, not wanting to think about Liam and the honeymoon right then.

'For coming to your house, of course,' Jaxon said sourly. 'Apparently it's a crime to knock on someone's door and ask a simple question.'

'I think forcing your way into someone's house is probably the crime part,' I said coldly.

'Ah well, it worked out all right in the end anyhow because we've agreed that if I reach the swansong first I'll simply sell it to Ben. He wants it more than I do. So that way everyone's happy.

As long as I stay away from you, of course.' He sighed. 'I was sure it would be hidden here somewhere but I haven't found it yet.'

'Why did you think it would be here?' I asked carefully, wondering if apparitions of bones and roses had appeared to Jaxon too.

But instead he said, 'Because of that.'

I turned around to follow his pointing finger and found myself looking right at the nearby white monument.

'What is that?' I asked.

'It's called the Separation of a Couple,' Jaxon said with a smirk.

I shone my torch right at it. It was a sad, beautiful, life-size work of art that portrayed a woman struggling to rise from her grave to comfort her lover who stood above her with his face in his hands. It made my heart ache just to look at it, so I lowered the torch and turned back to Jaxon.

'What's the statue got to do with anything?'

Jaxon said nothing for a long moment before finally saying, 'It's poetic. Liam would have liked that. It's the perfect hiding place. It *should* be here. When I first thought of it I was convinced that it would be. But I've come here four nights in a row now and haven't heard any singing.'

He was being evasive. I knew he had to have a better reason than that it was 'poetic' to be so convinced that Liam had hidden it there, but he obviously wasn't in a sharing mood ... But then it wasn't like I could really trust anything he said anyway. That being the case, I almost didn't say anything at all but one question forced itself from my lips. 'Is Ben's fiancée dying?'

Jaxon's face broke into a broad grin and he laughed loudly in what seemed to be genuine amusement. 'Is that what he told you?'

'It's not true, is it?'

He smiled even wider. 'Well, it is in a sense, my dear.' Then he added, 'I'd better go. I don't want to get another kicking from Ben over this little chat we've had so amiably.'

I didn't try to stop him from leaving the graveyard. After my recent experience with Ben it seemed better to work all this out on my own. But I felt my lip curl in contempt as I watched him go. Whether or not he was guilty of the crimes Ben had suggested, he certainly seemed a nasty, arrogant bastard from the two brief conversations I'd had with him, and I couldn't even imagine Liam being in the same room with him, let alone plotting and creeping about with him in Germany. I just couldn't see them together, not for a moment.

I dug into my handbag for my wallet and the photo of Liam that was inside. It was amazing how similar he looked to Ben – his height, his build, the shape of his nose and the colour of his hair ... Liam gazed out at me from the photo and I whispered softly to him, 'Don't worry, my darling. I know you would have disliked Jaxon intensely. And I know now why you didn't want Ben around us either. I should have trusted you about him from the start. I'm sorry.'

Up until that moment, the air in the graveyard had been cool and still with not the faintest hint of breeze. I was therefore unprepared when a wind suddenly blew up so unnaturally and so strongly that it whipped the photo straight from my fingers. Fortunately, because I was standing so close to the monument, the photo hit the side of it and stuck there, glued by the wind. I started forwards hastily and reached out for it but another hand got there first. It was a pale hand – as white as my own – for it belonged to the stone woman of the monument who was trying so hard to rise from her grave.

When her fingers closed around my photo, I jumped back with a cry of alarm and the half-full bottle I was still carrying slipped from my hand to shatter on the ground. I stared, paralysed to the spot, as the woman tightened her grip around the photograph for a moment, gave a choked sound of pain and anger and then dropped it to land in a screwed-up ball on the floor so that she had both hands free to reach up and grip the edge of the tomb where her lover stood, redoubling her efforts to try to pull herself out.

Whereas before she had only been half-visible, now she succeeded in pulling herself almost all the way out of the stone. But she wasn't quite able to escape to the ground above. It seemed to take all she had just to cling to the edge and keep herself from being sucked back into the tomb. Up until now, her lover above had remained set in stone, face in hands, unaware of her struggle. But then the fingers of one of her hands slipped from the edge. She flailed desperately to regain a grip but the next moment her other hand came off as well. In the split second before she started to fall, a hand from above clamped around her wrist and caught her. It was her lover, now kneeling at the edge, all the muscles in his shoulders and back straining to keep hold of her. The force that wanted her back down below was strong but – inch by slow inch – he managed to drag her up onto the surface. The wind dropped abruptly and, in the sudden silence, I heard the words the man said. He was on his knees, holding her to his chest as she clung to him, with his head bent to her shoulder. His voice was soft, as if I was hearing it from a great distance rather than a mere few feet away, but I was sure I was not mistaken in what I heard when he spoke:

'You're not supposed to be here!'

I clapped my hand over my mouth to muffle the cry that rose in my throat, for that had sounded – so very much – like Liam. I took another step back and my foot crunched on the broken glass of my fallen wine bottle ...

And then it was over. In the blink of an eye the monument was back to the way it had been before – she struggling beneath the ground and he standing above quite unaware of her and how close she was to him, for all that he had loved her with all his heart once and still did. My breath rasped in my throat and the graveyard suddenly seemed unnaturally silent and still. That had been Liam's voice – I was sure of it! If I had had more to drink that evening I would have worried that I might have just been seeing things, hearing things. But that wasn't the case and, despite myself, hope blossomed in my chest. I tried not to feel it, for I didn't dare to think that I might ever see Liam again. He was dead and gone forever. If I let myself believe – even for a moment – that he might come back, then it would be like having to lose him all over again and I was sure the pain of it would kill me.

The statue was enchanted somehow. That had to be the explanation. Perhaps Jaxon was right and the swansong was buried beneath it after all. Perhaps this was simply a new way for it to call out to me. Perhaps I should go and get a shovel right now ... I suppressed a groan, suddenly much more aware of how sore my feet were and how damp my clothes were and how tired I was ... I wished I hadn't dropped the wine bottle as finishing it off right there in the graveyard now seemed like a very good idea indeed.

I looked around for the photo of Liam but it had been blown away from the monument by the wind and, although I walked around for a while with my torch, I couldn't find it. I did not particularly relish the idea of having to dig holes all around the statue, for I was sure it would be harder than it looked and take a lot of time and effort to do. Besides which, I didn't have any firm proof that the swansong was even buried there and so was sorely tempted to go back to my hotel. But then I would have to wait until tomorrow night before I could return. Someone would be sure to notice me digging in the ground during broad daylight.

I stood there for a moment, wrestling with myself over what to do when I suddenly heard it. It was very faint and if the graveyard hadn't been so quiet I would never have heard it at all. But the notes of a lovely song drifted up to me through the ground I stood upon. I dropped down onto my hands and knees beside the monument and pressed my ear to the damp earth. Still I couldn't hear it properly but I could tell that it was the same song I had heard in the faery forest back in Germany the night before. The swansong was here – buried beneath the monument – but very far down from the sounds of it.

This time I groaned aloud and rested my head against the ground. I didn't have the faintest clue as to how to go about trying to find a shovel in Paris but it seemed most unlikely that I would be able to get one at this hour. And who knew how much digging I might have to do before I reached it? I sighed and straightened up. Well, at least now I knew where it was. In the morning I would get a shovel from somewhere and— I frowned and stared down at the ground, for the singing was suddenly moving, getting further away from me and even fainter.

Hurriedly, I walked forwards a few steps and found it again. But it continued to move until I had followed the sound of it right out of the cemetery. It was still underground but – somehow – it was moving, leaving me no choice but to follow the sound and see where it led.

For a while I walked on through the streets, glad that there was no one around to see me for I must have looked strangely erratic – or more likely drunk – first going in one direction, then another, and sometimes getting back down onto all fours when the song became particularly faint.

Finally, after almost ten minutes of going this way and that through a tangle of streets, I turned into another road and the song stopped dead, not leaving so much as a melancholy echo in its wake. I looked around in confusion. In every way it seemed a totally unremarkable street although it was busier than the others and cars passed by fairly regularly, heading towards the round-about at the end of the road that had a huge statue of a lion in the centre. Most of the nearby buildings seemed to be shops, although of course they were all closed up now.

I couldn't understand it. The graveyard had made sense but this road did not. I rubbed my eyes in weariness and a certain amount of annoyance. That was it. I had had enough for one day. I turned on my heel to walk straight back to my hotel. And that was when I saw the road sign: *l'avenue du Colonel Henri Rol-Tanguy*.

20

The Catacombs

At least I had been on the right track with graveyards. What lay beneath l'avenue du Colonel Henri Rol-Tanguy was similar in a way. After seeing the road sign I wandered up and down for some while trying to work out why it was relevant. I already knew there was no graveyard there. But there had to be something else – another monument or statue or some sort of X to mark the spot. After all, Liam had to have known how to find it again himself.

But the only statue I could see was the huge bronze lion in the very centre of the busy roundabout. I stood frowning at it from the other side of the road. It couldn't be that for, even now, late at night, there was a fairly regular stream of traffic passing round it. No one could ever get to it unnoticed. I wondered if the road may have been less busy a year ago … But it didn't seem likely and, at any rate, I couldn't imagine Liam being that stupid with his hiding place. If he knew he was leaving the swansong there for a significant amount of time, he would have chosen somewhere he was absolutely sure was not only safe but would remain so. He wouldn't have left it to chance.

But, excepting ultra-secure bank accounts, what hiding place could possibly offer that sort of guarantee? You could never be sure, especially with cities, what new planning developments might arise; what buildings may be pulled down and replaced; what streets might be dug up or where the next shopping mall might be built. If the swansong wasn't hidden in a bank then how could Liam possibly have been sure? Even graveyards themselves were sometimes cleared away to make room for new things. Nothing was that permanent.

Finally, fed up with peering into closed up shops and trying to work out if they had once been something else, I went back to my hotel room. It was dry and warm after the icy damp outside and it was a huge relief to get my shoes off and stretch out on the bed to rest my aching body. Before I could fall asleep where I lay, I forced myself to get up and reach for the guidebook tucked away in my bag.

I opened the page to the Montparnasse quarter and flicked through the section irritably, for all it seemed to have was art houses and cafés. If it hadn't been for the swansong stopping there so abruptly, I might have been tempted to think that the name of the avenue had been nothing more than a strange coincidence. But then I turned the page and froze. For grinning up at me were at least a dozen skulls arranged in the shape of a cross, surrounded on all sides by other, less readily identifiable human bones. The caption beneath it read: *The Catacombs of Paris* and, when I turned my eye to the text accompanying the photo, I saw that l'avenue du Colonel Henri Rol-Tanguy was listed as the address.

It seemed that, towards the end of the eighteenth century, the largest cemetery in Paris had been closed for health reasons and the bones and rotting corpses had been transported in carts across the city to Montparnasse over a period of fifteen months. Bones continued to be taken there until 1860, and today the catacombs were the final resting place of about six million people. They were sixty-five feet below the ground, far deeper than the sewage system or even the Metro, and consisted of a two and a half thousand foot quadrangle of galleries. People could visit the catacombs, but only until five p.m. after which they were securely locked up for the night.

They were perfect. Lying deep, deep underground, there was no way anyone would ever hear anything from them if the swansong were to sing – which did, of course, beg the question of how I had been able to hear it all the way from the cemetery, but I put that out of my mind for the time being. Liam could have guaranteed that the catacombs were not going to be moved or disrupted if the remains of six million people lay down there. It was in the centre of Paris but deep enough underground to be securely hidden away. And it explained why skulls and human bones had kept appearing with the black roses in California and Germany even better than my graveyard theory had. And, of course, it explained why the tiny faery horse had written Henri Rol-Tanguy in the dust. It had been an address, not a name.

I groaned and snapped the book shut, running my hands through my hair. I was sure the swansong must be down in the catacombs somewhere but finding it meant … It meant I was going to have to go down there with the other visitors, find a place to hide and then try to remain unnoticed when they were locked up for the night so that I could stay and hope to hear the swansong singing. It could be anywhere in that underground labyrinth and I would have no hope of finding it unless it called to me. Besides which, I couldn't hope to go burrowing through bones unnoticed if there were staff and other tourists down there. So it had to be at night. But once I'd found the swansong I would not be able to simply walk out with it. Even if I climbed the steps back to the surface, the exit would be locked. I would have to spend the entire night down there. On my own. By myself. In the dark. Waiting until ten a.m. the next day when visitors started being admitted once again and I could walk out with them as if I had only just arrived. An entire night in the catacombs, a full sixty-five feet underground with nothing but six million skeletons for company. The thought made me cringe.

There was no use dwelling on it. It had to be done and I would just have to try not to think about it too much between now and then. And get a good night's rest tonight, for I could pretty much guarantee not getting any sleep tomorrow. I needed to unwind before going to bed so I reached for my Violectra. For a moment, a brief spasm of panic rushed through me when I glanced around and couldn't see the violin case. Then I remembered why it wasn't there and despair settled on me so that I had to swallow hard to get rid of the lump in my throat. What on earth was I going to do? I needed the instrument. It helped me cope. After a difficult day – and every day on this trip had been damn difficult – the familiar music and the feel of the violin tucked beneath my chin had soothed me. I had to breathe deeply to slow the sudden anxious beating of my heart and wipe the cold sweat forming on my forehead away with the back of my hand.

My whole body ached for the Violectra. I think it must be similar to the way an alcoholic's body cramps for a drink. My right hand itched to hold the bow and my left hand longed to cradle the neck of the instrument. I wanted the music and the soothing sensation of the bow gliding over the strings, the smell of rosin in the air …

Out of sheer desperation I closed my eyes, raised my arms and drew a nonexistent bow over invisible strings, playing one of the many pieces I knew by heart, hearing the music inside my head. By the time the piece was finished, I could almost feel the Violectra tucked beneath my chin and the steel strings pressed against my fingertips. But when I opened my eyes my hands were empty and the illusion was broken. My real Violectra had been smashed to bits beneath Ben's boot back in Germany – the sad pieces tucked away in the suitcase at my feet.

I avoided looking at them as I dug out my pyjamas and toothbrush, and when I got into bed a few minutes later I pulled the covers up over my head and tried as hard as I could not to think about what I was going to have to do tomorrow.

I slept in the next day. I wanted to get as much rest as I could and to delay going down into the catacombs until the last possible moment. After all, once inside I was going to have to stay down there until the following morning and I wanted to minimise that time. The catacombs were open until five o'clock but the last visitors' entrance was at four.

So, at five minutes to four, I walked into the innocuous little building at the end of the road that I had dismissed the night before, and paid for my ticket. I had spent the morning buying everything I thought I might possibly need for that night as well as disguising myself as best I could. Once again I cursed my appearance for I knew that I could not blend anonymously with the rest of the visitors because of my albinism. With my long white hair, pale skin and light-blue eyes I would stick out to anyone who saw me. The staff might remember me and realise that I hadn't left the catacombs when they went to close up and I couldn't take any chances. So I was wearing a baseball cap pulled down low over my face with my long hair tucked into my jumper. I wore gloves to hide my hands and had pulled up the collar of my coat so that between it and my cap, my face was barely noticeable. This may have raised suspicion on a warmer day but, on this winter morning, most of the people around me were similarly bundled up.

I bought my ticket from the rather surly man behind the desk and then walked down the seemingly never-ending staircase. The deeper I went, the more the air changed – becoming older, cooler, stiller. Finally I reached the bottom, sixty-five feet below the surface, and found myself in a brightly lit room with photographs and tourist information on the walls.

It seemed sensible to learn all I could about the catacombs before rushing blindly into them so I stayed put and read every word there. It was mostly basic historical background I already knew from the guidebook and technical information about how a network of corridors so deep underground could be stabilised so as to remain safe.

I left the room and stepped out into the poorly lit passageway. It was long and narrow and seemed to go on forever. Small stones crunched beneath my feet and the walls on either side were damp. I expected the air to be stuffy but it was surprisingly cool, if a little dank.

There wasn't a bone in sight. Or any living people either, for that matter. If the corridor hadn't been the only way out of the first room, I might have thought that I had somehow gone wrong. The silence was a little oppressive and so was the shadowy darkness and the sense of being so far underground. I strained my eyes into the corners, constantly thinking that I'd seen something move there. Every now and then I passed gated doorways in the wall, through which I could see into smaller empty rooms, most of which seemed to be full of crumbling rock. I glanced up at the low ceiling carved out of the ground above me and tried not to think about what would happen if it were to collapse.

It seemed like I must have walked across half of Paris when I finally came to the entrance to the ossuary. There I was immensely relieved to come across other people for the first time. The fact that they obviously all saw the catacombs as nothing more than a strange and macabre tourist attraction instantly made me feel more relaxed. I tried not to think about what the place would be like later on that night when I had been down here for hours and all the tourists were gone, probably enjoying themselves in restaurants and bars whilst I scrabbled about alone down here amongst the bones. I felt another surge of anger towards Liam in that moment for putting me through all this and that almost made me feel slightly better. Anger was far, far easier to cope with than grief.

There was better lighting in this area, and I could clearly see the entrance to the ossuary, flanked by two stonework pillars. On the lintel above were inscribed the words:

'*Arrête! C'est ici l'empire de la mort*' – '*Halt, for this is the empire of death.*'

Even from outside, I could see beyond the entrance a solid wall of bones stacked from floor to ceiling. I walked in with the other tourists.

The air smelled of dust and damp and age. I was stunned by the sheer staggering number of bones. Chamber after chamber was full of them leaving only a path through the middle just wide enough to walk along. If I were to stretch out my hands, my fingers would brush two solid walls of yellow, flaking bones. The weirdest thing was the way they had been arranged. I had read in the first room that when they had originally been brought down here, the bones had simply been dumped but, around the year 1810, skulls and long bones had been rearranged into neat walls, behind which the remaining ones were left in a jumble. But someone had decided that neatening the bones was not enough – they must be arranged into patterns as well. The skulls had been put together, often in neat little rows and sometimes in the shape of a cross or even a barrel-shaped display.

I walked past hundreds and hundreds of skulls, aware that thousands – millions – more lay concealed in the darkness behind the ghoulishly artistic front layer. Most of them were missing their lower jaws, these having been broken off when they were originally moved or else had crumbled away since. There were so many of them that it was hard to believe that each and every one had once been a person like me – walking, talking, living – and now their remains were scattered around down here, mixed with the bones of millions of others.

Every time a chamber led into another I kept thinking that must be it – I must have seen all the bones by now – there surely couldn't be still more of them. But there would just be another room full of them and then another and another, stretching on into the dim, greenish light. I felt more and more disheartened with every passing step. How on earth was I ever going to find the swansong in all of this? The catacombs went on for miles. It was worse than looking for a needle in a haystack.

Finally, they came to an end and all that remained were a couple of bell-shaped subsidence cavities stretching high into the rock above to showcase the type of erosion that limestone quarries often suffer from. I lingered in these, for the high ceilings made me feel less claustrophobic than the low, bone-filled corridors I had come from. Plus, the fact that the staircase leading up to the exit was nearby meant that there was a greater supply of fresh air there.

I leaned against the cool rock and looked at the map contained in the pamphlet I had been given on admission to the catacombs. I could see from it that the entrance was a considerable distance from the exit as the tunnels stretched on for such a long way underground. I therefore needn't have worried about the same staff remembering me and realising I hadn't left.

I took off my cap, shook out my long hair and shoved the hat in my bag before looking at my watch. It was quarter to five – only fifteen minutes before the catacombs were due to be closed up. I turned my face in the direction of the staircase that would lead to the exit, feeling the fresh air on my skin. This was my last chance to think better of my plan to stay the night. I was sorely tempted. After barely an hour I had already had more than enough of the dark and the dank and the bones. The thought of staying down in the catacombs for another seventeen hours or more made me feel trapped and claustrophobic and a little panic-stricken ...

Hastily, I grabbed my backpack, turned away from the exit and walked back into the network of tunnels. I could feel myself weakening and I knew that if I allowed myself to dwell on it any further I would surely run up those stairs two at a time and never look back.

It was relatively easy to remain unnoticed at closing time. I simply slipped into the first gated area I came to. It was rusty and un-locked and seemed to be there more for the look of the thing than anything else. It was a small, empty room carved out of the rock that didn't lead anywhere. I made sure I was out of sight of the doorway and then sat against the wall and waited.

Guards came down with torches, doing a search that they had probably done every day for years without incident. It seemed to go on forever and the awful thought occurred to me that perhaps they knew I was down there. After all, I'd had to walk through a turnstile after buying my ticket and presumably there was also one at the exit to keep track of how many people had come out. But I felt sure that they must get little discrepancies all the time with mothers picking small children up and walking through with them or kids messing around with the turnstile.

I don't know if the guards were more vigilant than usual that night because the turnstile figures didn't add up or whether they always spent so long sweeping through the catacombs. Perhaps it just seemed to me as if they were down there a long time because my heart was hammering madly in my chest at the thought of being discovered there, crouched in the dark, having to explain what I was doing to angry French guards.

At one point the beam of torchlight came rather close to my foot and my heart leapt into my mouth at the thought that one of the guards might actually open the gate and come into the room. But in another moment he had walked by and, soon, all the lights had been turned out and the catacombs were plunged into such a complete and utter silent darkness that it made me realise I had never actually truly experienced either one before.

I sat there with my fist in my mouth to keep myself from whimpering. I couldn't see an inch in front of my face. The darkness was complete, pressing all around me in a most suffocating way with no moon or starlight to take the edge off. I had promised myself that I would wait half an hour before turning on my torch – just to be absolutely sure that all the staff had gone and I was alone. But it wasn't so easy to judge the time when I was sitting there in the dark, unable to look at my watch. My ears were straining for any kind of sound, but the only thing I could hear was the steady drip of water landing on rock somewhere to my right.

The minutes crawled by agonisingly and I tried desperately not to think about where I was, tried not to dwell on the fact that the bones of six million people lay behind me, though truth be told it wasn't actually the bones that bothered me so much as the fact that I was trapped sixty-five feet underground, unable to get out until the morning even if I wanted to. There could be no changing my mind at this point. It was far too late for that.

Finally I was sure that at least half an hour must have passed and my fumbling hand found the torch I had packed in my bag. I switched it on, blinking in the sudden light as I swept the beam around the room to ensure that all was as it should be. I then took one of the many candles I had packed out of my bag and lit it before securing it in a candlestick and setting it down on the floor. I did not want to use my torch all night for, even fully wound, it only provided a few minutes of light each time. And I didn't want to risk wearing it out and finding myself alone down there with no means of light whatsoever. I switched the torch off, glanced at my watch and was shocked to see that it was barely ten past five. What had seemed like half an hour had been a matter of mere minutes.

I sighed and leaned back against the cold wall, wishing the time away and promising myself that tomorrow night – wherever I happened to be – I would take a moment to relish the luxury of sleeping in a warm, comfortable bed.

The hours dragged by so unbelievably slowly that, more than once, I wondered whether my watch might actually have stopped and had to check to make sure it was still going. At six o'clock I ate the food I had packed and after that I whiled away the time by playing the violin in my head. I didn't move my arms because I didn't want to make the candle flame flicker but in my mind I could clearly feel the fingering and bowing as I steadily went through all the major and minor scales, the chromatics and the arpeggios. This gave me something to focus on and made the time pass much more quickly. After the scales I went on to some pieces and – with my favourite music filling my head – was almost able to forget where I was and what I was doing. The little rocky room I was in almost started to seem cosy to me. There was something comforting about the fact that everyone else was locked out and no one could bother or upset me while I was here. I put on the extra jacket I had brought, leaned back against the wall and nodded off for a little while.

I woke up just before nine o'clock. My whole body ached and I eased myself stiffly to my feet before bending down to pick up my bag and candle. It was now night-time rather than early evening. If the swansong was going to sing, it could start at any moment and so the sensible thing seemed to be to wander around the tunnels at regular intervals listening out for it. Besides which it would give me something to do and keep me from getting too cold and stiff.

So I took my things and left the little room to walk through the death-filled chambers once again, the light from my candle flickering over the endless walls of bones. They were creepier by candlelight, but not as much as I'd expected for – like the graves above – they seemed more peaceful than sinister. I was sure that the swansong must be hidden behind one of the neatly organised facades in the unseen jumble behind. It would have been an easy enough thing for Liam to wait until no one was around and then thrust the black rose into the stack, knowing it would not be disturbed even if it were left there for a hundred years. And even if visitors to the catacombs managed to steal bones on occasion, these would only be loose ones on top of the facade, not anything harder to reach from behind it. I lingered longer at the walls that had some sort of plaque to distinguish them from the others, for Liam would have had to have some way of remembering exactly where he had hidden it.

I had gone all the way around once and was about to sit down again for a while against a wall somewhere when I heard a noise – like the skittering of a bone being knocked from the top of a pile to land on the floor. I froze, paralysed to the spot, wondering if there could be anyone else down here in the catacombs with me. But I heard nothing more and so decided it had probably been a rat.

But still, as I continued to wander about, I couldn't shake the sudden sense that I was not alone. Although I walked back around all the chambers, I didn't see a single disturbed bone. I could believe that a rat might have knocked one off but it would hardly have been able to pick it up again and put it back. If someone else was down there, it was possible that we might never run into each other: even if we were both walking around the whole time, the catacombs were so large and branched off in so many different directions that there was no set route to follow, and so we could easily keep missing each other all night.

I was just trying to convince myself that the noise I had heard must have been a rat running over the bones when I heard voices. Panic-stricken, I blew out my candle and pressed my back against the wall, hoping smoke from the extinguished wick would go undetected. There were men – two of them – and the light from their torches cast a faint glow around me even though they were several chambers away. Their voices were muffled so I couldn't make out what they were saying. But they sounded horribly familiar nonetheless and for a moment I hesitated, wondering whether I should stay put or whether I should creep quietly closer and try to overhear them without being spotted myself. I knew the sensible thing would probably be to stay where I was and do nothing but I was consumed with the urge to know who they were and what they were doing down here. So, stepping as silently as possible, I crept into the next chamber, careful to move slowly in the dim light lest I should crash into something and give myself away. I passed through into the room beyond and crept as close to the doorway as possible, pressing my back against the stone. From the sounds of it, the two men were standing just around the corner and now I was left in no doubt whatsoever as to who they were.

'—need me to tell you where she went anyway?' Jaxon was saying. 'Isn't she keeping you informed herself? You *are* working together now, aren't you?'

'Not any more,' Ben replied shortly.

Dimly, I realised that Jaxon must have followed me when I'd left the cemetery the night before. I thought he'd already gone and had been too preoccupied with following the swansong to notice anyway. Trapped down here with them now, I could have kicked myself for being so stupid.

'Why's that?' Jaxon asked, a little too eagerly. 'What did you do to her?'

'I broke her violin,' Ben grunted.

'Oh, is that all?' Jaxon replied, sounding disappointed. 'That hardly seems like anything very much.'

'You don't know how much she loved it,' Ben said shortly.

Hot anger rose up in my chest and my hands bunched into fists, my nails digging into my palms as I remembered the sight of my Violectra shattering beneath Ben's boot. A monstrous act of petty spite and nastiness. How I hated him for it.

'I thought perhaps you'd told her the truth after all,' Jaxon said. Then, when Ben said nothing, he went on, 'Weren't you even tempted to? I know I would have been.'

'Of course I was tempted to!' Ben snapped. 'But she would never have believed me.'

'So you told her you had a sick fiancée instead.' Jaxon laughed,

237

the sound strangely out of place down here amongst the bones. 'Did she believe it, do you think?'

'She had no reason not to,' Ben replied calmly.

My hatred for him increased even further as I remembered how he had sat on the bed in the guest house in Germany, holding me in that tight embrace, a single crocodile tear trailing down my shoulder. Now I shuddered to think that he had laid so much as a finger on me, and anger tightened into a painful knot in my stomach when I thought back to how I had felt sorry for him and tried to comfort him. I should never have believed a word that bastard said.

'I don't think she knew you were the one who attacked Liam on their honeymoon,' Jaxon remarked cheerfully. I could plainly hear the goading intent in his voice.

'Did you tell her?' Ben demanded angrily.

'I'm afraid I did. I didn't realise it was a secret, you see.'

'What the hell's the matter with you?' Ben snapped.

'Well, it's true, isn't it?' Jaxon replied, mocking laughter in his voice. 'You would have beaten the crap out of your poor little brother – and on his honeymoon too – if you thought you could have found the swansong on your own.'

'I would have *killed* him on his honeymoon if I'd thought I could find the swansong on my own!' Ben said in a low, harsh voice.

I just about managed to suppress a gasp but my blood ran cold at his words. He meant it. I could hear it in his voice. My anger ebbed away to be replaced with fear. I'd hoped he hadn't meant what he'd said to me in Germany about hating Liam. I'd tried to believe it was something he'd blurted out in the heat of the argument. But now he was calm and composed and talking quite coldly of murder.

'I'm impressed by your self-restraint,' Jaxon said. 'I can't say I would have done the same.'

'It wouldn't have got me what I wanted,' Ben muttered.

'Brought you one step closer to it, though,' Jaxon replied. 'With Liam out of the way there'd be nothing to stop you from getting to

Jasmyn. If I were you I would have killed him on his honeymoon and had done with it.'

'Well, I'm not you!' Ben snarled. Then he added, in a quieter voice, 'But if I could do it over again I'm not sure that I'd let him go a second time. He was going to die anyway. Perhaps I just have … should have …' He stumbled over his words and trailed off, then I heard the clatter of a torch being dropped and there was a flicker as it went out.

'Hey, careful with that!' I heard Jaxon say. 'We haven't got an endless supply of those, you know, and I don't fancy being stuck down here in the dark.' The torch was picked up and switched back on. 'You didn't break it at least,' Jaxon said. Then he added, 'You don't look too good. Is there something—'

'I'm perfectly all right!' Ben snapped, and I heard him snatch the torch back. 'Why don't you just shut up for a while? If the swansong sings we need to make sure we can hear it.'

'Whatever you say, Ben,' Jaxon replied mildly.

To my horror, I realised that they had continued their walk and were heading right towards me. I stared around frantically but didn't have time to make a run for it into the next chamber. So I hurriedly crouched down and pressed my back even harder against the wall, utterly still, my heart beating painfully fast, the pulse of it ringing loudly in my ears as Jaxon and Ben passed through the arch of the doorway and right into the chamber mere paces away from me.

I kept utterly motionless, not even daring to breathe and wishing to God that I had black hair and skin rather than being so white and conspicuous. All either of them had to do was glance in my direction and they would see me. I had no idea what they would do but I was keenly aware that there were two of them and one of me, that I was deep underground where no one would hear me no matter how loudly I shouted and that I would not even be able to phone for help as there wasn't the remotest chance of getting any reception this far underground.

And one other thing I now knew for sure was that I had severely – *severely* – misjudged Ben. After so many years of knowing his family I had realised that he was quiet and antisocial, but it had never in my wildest dreams occurred to me that he was so cold, calculating and murderous. I cringed to think how many times I'd been alone with him since all this began. And now I was trapped down here in the catacombs with him and Jaxon and with no hope of escape until the morning.

Thankfully they walked past without looking in my direction. I kept my eyes glued to their backs as they walked through into the next chamber. My body was frozen and it required a great effort of will to make myself move. I had to find somewhere to hide and could only pray that I would remain undiscovered during the night. Moving as quickly as I could without making any noise, I turned the corner and slipped back into the room they had just come from, reaching out with both hands to gently guide myself along the wall of human bones. Ben and Jaxon had taken their torch with them and I didn't dare turn mine on or relight my candle in case they noticed. The only advantage I had was that I knew they were down here but they were unaware of me. For the moment.

I tried desperately not to panic, but the reality of it was that I had managed to trap myself down in the catacombs with two very dangerous men. What if I never got out? There were so many hours still to go before the morning when they'd be open once again. What if I was discovered by one of them first? Only a small portion of the catacombs were open to tourists – many of the underground passageways were shut off. It would be perfectly easy to hide a body down here that wouldn't be discovered for years and years, if ever …

I shook my head in an attempt to clear it. I mustn't think that way. I had to remain calm. Just because Ben obviously regretted not killing Liam before he died of natural causes didn't mean he would kill me. Surely if that had ever been his intention he would already have done it. After all, he had had opportunity enough. All he wanted was the swansong. I probably didn't matter much to him either way.

I wished to God that I'd never left the small room I'd been in earlier, for neither Ben nor Jaxon would have been likely to go in there and I would have been tucked out of the way then. But even if I were now able to find my way back to it, or somewhere like it, I couldn't risk the gate making any noise when I slipped through. At the same time, I didn't want to simply stay in the bone-filled chamber in case they should come back. But I didn't have much choice. It was pitch black once again and if I tried to move I was sure to knock something over and make a hideous racket. So I quietly sat down, far back from the door, beside the skeletons of the dead, and prayed that I would not be joining them any time soon.

As I sat there, my ears and eyes straining into the darkness, I told myself that it was okay. I had been lucky – they didn't know I was here. The catacombs branched off and doubled back on each other. I would always be alerted to Ben and Jaxon's return well in advance by the light of their torches. When they came back, I would simply have to dodge into another chamber, keeping one step ahead of them and staying just out of sight – like a petrified mouse fleeing from two fat, sleek, arrogant cats, I thought to myself angrily.

But the plan went wrong almost at once. For I was not expecting Jaxon and Ben to split up. When the glow of distant torchlight touched my chamber about half an hour later – just enough to take the edge off the darkness – and I could dimly make out the tread of footsteps, I assumed that it was Jaxon and Ben returning together. I got silently to my feet, shaking the stiffness out of my limbs, and then crept into the next chamber. I walked through it, keeping my fingers lightly in contact with the wall of bones to guide my way as I found the doorway and slipped into the next room.

And that was where it all went wrong.

As soon as I was inside, a voice I recognised spoke suddenly out of the blackness:

'*You're not supposed to be here!*'

I yelled in alarm, shocked to hear someone speaking to me when it was so dark that they should not have been able to even see me.

I had had no inkling whatsoever that there was anyone there until then and jumped back in fright, knocking straight into a wall of skulls, cringing as they landed noisily on the ground around me. The familiar words rang in my head and I remembered hearing them in the cemetery just the night before – spoken by the male statue with Liam's voice ...

Hope burst through me so savagely that it was physically painful. A torch was turned on and light was suddenly being shone in my face. I looked past it to the person standing before me and joy exploded in my chest – for the man holding the torch was Liam.

21

The Black Rose

It was Liam! He was right there before me – real and alive again! I reached a shaking hand out to touch him—

'I never thought you'd actually come down here,' he said, sounding horrified.

The voice froze me where I stood. For it wasn't Liam as I had first thought – of course it wasn't – it was Ben. The dim light and the fact that he'd spoken the words I had heard the statue speak in the graveyard had tricked me for a moment but, now that he spoke again, I knew that this certainly was not my husband and joy was replaced with terror as Ben lunged at me desperately.

Shocked into action, I lashed out at him viciously before he could touch me and, by pure luck, I managed to catch him on the chin with my fist. He staggered back and dropped the torch, which went rolling across the floor. I rushed towards the door but before I could get there he caught hold of the collar of my coat to drag me back, one arm clamping across my stomach and the other around my shoulders as he pinned me to him and hissed in my ear.

'*Hold still, Jasmyn!*'

His fingers dug into me painfully and I could hear the anger in his voice. I had never been so terrified in my life. Surely he was going to kill me. *Why* hadn't I listened to Liam when he'd said that Ben was not to be trusted? Why hadn't Liam made it clearer to me? Why hadn't he come out and told me frankly that his older brother was a dangerous lunatic?

I threw my head back hard, felt the crunch as I hit Ben's nose.

He didn't let go, but his grip loosened just enough for me to get one of my arms free and elbow him in the stomach. He doubled up and I took advantage of the moment by grabbing one of the long bones and bringing it down hard over his head. It was not as effective a weapon as I had hoped for it was so old that it shattered over him, crumbling into dusty bits. Still, it was enough to bring him to his knees. I didn't hang around waiting for him to get up again but grabbed his torch and fled.

I had barely passed into the next chamber when the swansong started. I needn't have worried about not hearing it for it seemed to echo all the way through the underground caves with a music so sweetly perfect that there could be no doubt that something magical had made it. It was coming from close by and I followed the sound even though I knew that Jaxon – and Ben when he got to his feet – would be doing the same thing. It seemed to me that finding the swansong was my only chance of getting out of there, for once I had it, I could enchant the pair of them to stay well away from me … Of course, I had no idea how to make it work and could only hope that it was as easy as waving a magic wand …

As I had predicted, the music was coming from one of the rooms marked with a distinguishing feature – there was a large plaque across one wall commemorating the *Battle of the Château des Tuileries*. In the right-hand corner was a semicircular display of long bones with four rows of skulls cutting across it at regular intervals. The music was coming from there.

There was no time to be discreet about it – Ben or Jaxon could be upon me at any moment. I dropped the torch and then grabbed great armfuls of bones from the top of the stack to scatter about me on the floor. I did not think the rose would be buried very deep, for Liam would most likely have hidden it there when the catacombs were open during the day and therefore would have had to be relatively quick about it. I was about a quarter of the way down, just removing the second layer of skulls, when I glimpsed a black petal nestled between two bones and caught the familiar seductive scent I had smelled before.

But the startling thing about it was that a word had been written on the petal in fine gold letters: *Jasmyn.* I frowned, reached out my hand towards it and was just about to pluck it from its bed of bones when Jaxon crashed into me from behind, knocking me right into the skulls, scattering them everywhere, clattering against each other noisily. He shoved me aside and grabbed the rather crushed black rose off the floor just as Ben ran into the room, blood smeared across his face from where I'd head-butted him.

'I found it first!' Jaxon shouted triumphantly. 'And I'm not handing it over until the money is wired to my account!'

Ben snorted a humourless laugh. 'The truth is, Jaxon, I can't pay you,' he said, throwing up his hands. 'Not a thing. I spent the lot on this search. I have nothing left whatsoever. I'm flat broke. In fact, I'm in debt. I'm on the verge of bankruptcy. Treasure hunting turned out to be a more expensive venture than I anticipated.'

Jaxon stared at him. 'You lying bastard!' he exclaimed. 'Well, you're not getting it until you fork over the money! Or perhaps I'll just venture out onto the black market with it after all.'

'No,' Ben said quietly. 'You won't do that.'

'Be reasonable! I've put a lot of money into this too!'

'Tough,' Ben said flatly. 'You can easily afford to lose some of your ill-gotten gains, I dare say. Hand it over.' And he held out his hand for it.

But Jaxon tightened his grip on the black rose and took a step back.

'All right,' he said. 'All right. I won't find another buyer. We'll come to some arrangement, Ben. You can pay me in instalments or—'

'You don't seem to understand,' Ben said and, for the first time, I heard impatience in his voice. 'I'm not paying you a thing, Jaxon. Not now, not ever. So hand it over. I've waited a long time for this.'

Jaxon twisted the rose agitatedly by its stem. The light of the dropped torches on the floor gleamed off the lettering that I now realised was on every single petal. They were all the same as the one I had caught a glimpse of before – every one had *Jasmyn* written across it in delicate gold letters.

'I could enchant you with it!' Jaxon said, suddenly struck with a brainwave. 'And force you to give me the money once you get it!'

Ben's teeth showed white in his face as his lips parted in a smile. 'That won't work on me,' he said. 'Here's what I want you to do – first you'll give me the rose, then you'll go back to the entrance to the catacombs and wait until morning, when you'll tell the security guards who find you that you stayed down here the night for a dare. Then you'll never breathe a word about this to anyone and you'll never come anywhere near me or Jasmyn ever again.'

He stopped talking and looked at Jaxon who was standing there hesitating, clearly wrestling with himself about what to do. When several seconds went by and he still didn't hand over the rose, Ben slowly bowed his head without another word. Jaxon glanced at me as if he thought I had any idea what was happening. I was half-standing, half-sprawled against the wall where the bones had been stacked until Jaxon knocked me into them. The light from the torches on the floor cast enough of a glow that when Ben lifted his head again just a moment later, I could clearly see the reason for Jaxon's whimper of fear.

Ben's eyes were entirely red. From the whites to the pupils, they were a vivid scarlet. Jaxon took one look, threw down the black rose with a frightened cry, grabbed one of the torches and fled, leaving me there alone. Ben bent down and picked up the rose. As he straightened up I considered making a bolt for it too. It would mean running blindly into the catacombs in the pitch dark, for I couldn't get to the torch behind Ben. But he was also blocking off the exit and would surely grab me if I made a run for it.

As he turned around I found myself pressing my shoulder blades into the damp wall behind me, as if hoping I might pass straight through it. His eyes were still that murderous shade of red – like a devil straight from hell – and the question slipped from my lips despite my fear: 'What *are* you?'

Ben blinked and – at once – his eyes returned to their normal, human shade of brown. He took a step towards me and I grabbed a bone from the floor by my feet, braced to defend myself, trying to judge the angle from which he would lunge at me. When he moved his arm I flinched and tightened my grip on the bone, preparing to strike him.

But he simply held the flower out to me.

'Take it,' he said quietly in a voice that was suddenly devoid of all the frightening coldness with which he'd spoken to Jaxon. 'Please, Jasmyn. Just take it.'

Perhaps he was mad. It certainly appeared that he was not completely human. My sweating hands clutched the long bone and for a moment I seriously considered smashing it over his head as hard as I could and then running after Jaxon. But something about his stance made me hesitate. He did not look like a dangerous attacker armed and ready for me to run or fight back. The way he held the rose out to me was as if it was the most beautiful bloom he had found in a field full of flowers that he had picked himself just so that he could give it to me. He was close enough that I could see the strange desperation in his bloodshot eyes.

I looked down at the black rose, with my name written on every one of its dark petals. He was holding the stem so tightly that I could see lines of blood trickling through the fingers of his shaking hand. But when I held out my own fingers and cupped them around the head of the flower, Ben let go of the stem at once and took a step back.

The petals were velvety smooth against my skin but I only had a bare second to notice before there was the sound of something breaking – like glass shattering. The rose fell apart in my grasp, all the petals fluttering loose to land at my feet before the stem turned to dust in my fingers. Then a memory rose so suddenly and unnaturally into my mind and with such vivid clarity that it was like it had happened only yesterday rather than more than twenty years ago.

I was hunched miserably in the doorway on my first day of school, cringing at the names the other children had been calling me all day and trying as hard as I could to be invisible by sitting there and not moving and therefore not giving anyone a reason to rip viciously into me. But then a ball rolled into the doorway and stopped beside me. Hastily, I grabbed it with the intention of flinging it back out before anyone could come looking for it.

But it was too late. A boy's shoes had already skidded around the corner and come to a stop in front of me. Miserably, I held the ball in the air, hoping he would just take it and go without saying anything horrible to me. The boy took the ball but stayed where he was, bouncing it on the spot. When I risked a glance at him, I saw that he was looking right at me and so I hurriedly lowered my head, trying not to do anything to provoke him, waiting for the dreaded question, '*Are you a ghost?*'

Instead, after a moment, he said, 'Are you a snow princess?'

'Snow princess?' I repeated – the words blurting out of my mouth before I remembered to be shy. 'I ... don't know.'

'I think you are,' he decided. He then promptly sat down cross-legged and rolled the ball towards me. We rolled it back and forth to each other across the tarmac until the bell rang to signal the end of break. Then we both stood up and I handed the ball back to him.

'Thanks,' he said, thrusting it into the pocket of his shorts. Then he said, 'Do you want to play again at lunchtime?'

I nodded shyly, a tiny glow of happiness – and relief – fluttering in my stomach at the thought of having someone to spend lunchtime with. He grinned at me and said, 'I'll bring the ball.' As he turned towards the doors, he added over his shoulder, 'My name's Ben.'

22

Bewitchment

The playground disappeared and another memory took its place. I was sitting hidden in the hay in my grandfather's stables as a six year old, watching eagerly for faeries.

'What did she look like again?' Ben whispered.

'Sshh,' I hissed, poking him sharply in the ribs. 'No talking. You'll scare them all away.'

To my relief, he obediently fell silent. Then the memory switched to the two of us riding along a bridle path as adults, with Mr Ed twitching his lips in response to Ben's voice.

'What's the matter with this horse?' Ben said after checking the bridle, whilst I sat in my saddle helpless with laughter.

'What?' Ben demanded. 'What are you laughing at?'

'It's your voice,' I gasped at last. 'He only does it when you talk.'

Ben pulled a quizzical face and turned back to Ed. 'Testing, testing, testing,' he said – to which Ed instantly began to move his lips in that ridiculous way. 'Hmm. You seem to be right,' Ben admitted, swinging up into the saddle and patting Ed's neck before picking up the reins.

'Play something for me, Jaz,' Ben pleaded as the scene switched again and we were in our old house together. When I protested that I was in the middle of a gripping chapter, he snatched the book from me and said with a grin, 'I'm your fiancé. And I'm commanding you to play for me now, not later.'

Grumbling, I got off the couch and went over to my violin case, lifting the lid as I turned around to grab a piece of sheet music.

When I looked back, I yelped in alarm at the sight of the beautiful, skeletal, blue and silver Violectra nestled in the velvet interior. It was supposed to have been a Christmas present but, after having it made in the design and colours he'd picked out, Ben was too excited about the violin to wait so long before giving it to me ...

We were engaged after two years of dating – picked out the horse-drawn carriage and the church and the honeymoon in the Caribbean together. And then ... that was when my memory got hazy. I wasn't sure how but, at some point in between getting engaged to Ben and getting married, something went horribly, horrendously, hideously wrong – and it was Liam I had married instead – whilst somehow never being aware of any difference between them, as if I had been engaged to Liam all along. But I realised now that it was Ben I had been best friends with all through school, Ben I had fallen in love with and Ben I had agreed to marry.

The daredevil stuff was all Liam. Ben had never jumped from a plane or driven a high-speed car in his life. But he had sat silently with me in the stables, watching for faeries; he had looked after me at school – been put in detention for pulling Heidi's plaits; he had gone with me to Munich to drink *Glühwein* and eat gingerbread outside in the snow; he had bought me a blue and silver Violectra and he was the one who had made me the happiest person in the world one day when he asked me to be his wife.

All the things I'd thought were different about Liam after we married made sense now. I saw us together in my mind's eye – eating at the table, watching TV on the couch, sleeping in the same bed ... And I knew that I had never loved him. But – somehow – I had married him anyway.

'Ben,' I croaked, looking across at him in the shadowy dimness of the catacombs. 'How did it happen?'

'How did *what* happen?' he asked, sounding stiff and wary.

'How did I marry Liam when I was in love with *you*?'

I had never felt two such entirely conflicting emotions. On the one hand I was so overjoyed and relieved I could have sobbed because the man I'd been mourning for months wasn't really dead and buried back home in an English graveyard but standing right here in the catacombs with me, and all I wanted was to fling my arms around him, touch his face, kiss his lips and reassure myself that he really was alive.

But, at the same time, guilt, misery and shame wracked through me because, however it had happened, I'd married his brother and been apart from Ben for over a year. And now everything was different between us and could never go back to being the same. Even the way he was looking at me was different. There was no warmth in his gaze whatsoever. In fact he looked so cold that for a brief moment I even wondered whether he remembered it all wrong too.

'You *do* remember being engaged to me, don't you?' I asked. I couldn't help glancing down at his left hand and seeing the band of white gold there on his ring finger. There was no sick fiancée called Heidi. It had been me all along.

'Yes,' he said quietly. 'I remember being engaged to you. I remember everything. You're the one who forgot.'

'I … I didn't forget,' I said, wincing at his accusatory tone. 'I just … remembered it all wrong. Who's Heidi?' I asked. I knew that there *was* a woman called Heidi, for I had spoken to her on the phone myself.

'She's my cleaner. It was the first name that came into my head.'

'How did this *happen*?' I asked, pressing the palms of my hands to my eyes, desperately trying to find some stable ground to shake the surreal feeling of unreality that had settled on me.

I knew I had done it; I remembered it clearly enough – remembered thinking that I loved Liam and wanted to spend my life with him. But all my memories of him had actually been of Ben. How could my mind have got so messed up like that? A smooth transition of love and friendship from one man to the other without my even noticing that they'd changed.

'He used the swansong to enchant you,' Ben said.

'*Why?*'

'To punish me. It was my fault he got dragged into the lake that night. I warned the swans he was coming. There was something wrong with him – there always was, right from the day he was born. I knew it and my parents knew it. He was ... unbalanced. Not right in the head. Sometimes he did things ... But he was able to disguise it almost all of the time and appear normal.'

I found I hardly cared in that moment who'd done what and why. All I cared about was that Ben was there and he was alive. I was filled with the overpowering urge to touch him and reassure myself that he was real. But when I reached out towards him, he stepped back as if by instinct. My hand dropped to my side and I was filled with hurt for a moment before anger and frustration and regret started bubbling up inside me. However it had happened, I *had* married Liam. I had married Ben's brother. Been his wife for almost a year. There could be no going back to the way things had been with Ben after that. I was Liam's *widow*. And now everything between us was ruined. I glared at him. 'Why did you let me *do* it?' I said angrily. 'Why didn't you *stop* me? Or stop *him*?'

'How should I have done that, Jasmyn?' Ben retorted, just as angrily. 'What could I *possibly* have done? You thought he was me! You would never have believed me if I'd told you otherwise! You would have thought I was a lunatic!'

'So you just stood back and let him marry me?' I raged, impatiently wiping away the tears that were streaming down my face. 'You bloody coward! How could you not even *try* to—'

'I *did* try, damn it!' Ben interrupted. 'I've done nothing *but* try since this whole nightmare began! What was I supposed to do, Jasmyn? Kidnap you?'

'You should have come to me! You should have come and told me the truth!'

'You would never have believed me, Jasmyn, *never*!' Ben said harshly, touching me for the first time by gripping my arms and almost shaking me as he went on bitterly. It was all the worse because I knew that he was right. I had loved Liam absolutely because I had thought that he was Ben. 'Don't blame me for this!' Ben hissed. '*You're* the one who left *me*! How could it have been so easy for you to forget us? How could you not even *see* me when you looked at me?'

He let me go and stood back as I put my head in my hands and wept. The pain had changed but it was just as bad. Before the enchantment lifted I'd believed the man I loved was dead. Now I knew that he was right here beside me and had been since this whole nightmare began. But what was once there was now broken, for I had married his brother and filled the space between us with a hurt and bitterness so intense that it was never going to heal no matter how much time passed.

Ben was right: I should have been able to resist the black magic. I should never have mistaken Liam for Ben no matter how strong the bewitchment. I couldn't believe I'd done it. I was disgusted with myself. How could I ever hope to have Ben touch me again now, knowing that Liam had been there before him?

You must see how hard all this is for Ben ... The phrase I had heard so many times after the funeral came back to me now and – at long last – I understood it. No wonder Ben's mother hated me. No wonder she and half his family had refused to attend the wedding. What must it have *looked* like to them when, a mere two weeks before the wedding, they learned that I was marrying Liam instead of Ben? A decision so sudden that most of the people turning up to the ceremony were still expecting to see Ben as his was the name on the invitations. He and I had planned it together, picked out our honeymoon hotel together ... And then, at the last second, I had married Liam instead. How unforgivably cruel I must have seemed to them all.

'I'm sorry,' Ben said wearily. 'Don't cry. None of this is your fault.'

'Why didn't anyone *say* anything to me?' I said.

'They did,' Ben replied. 'I know my mother spoke to you about it just before the wedding even though I asked her not to. She told me it was like you weren't even hearing her. I expect the same thing happened if anyone else commented about it.'

I had a vague memory of talking to Ben's mother around that

time but it was hazy, as if I might have imagined it or dreamt it, and I couldn't remember a word she'd said.

'I didn't realise you'd transferred your memories of me onto Liam,' Ben said. 'Until you told me in Munich that Liam had given you the Violectra, I thought you remembered being engaged to me as well. But even if I'd known that you didn't, it wouldn't have made any difference. I could have shown you photos of the two of us together and the enchantment would have made you block them out, or see Liam in my place. The same thing would have happened whenever anyone made any comment to you about our relationship, although I expect that stopped when he died.'

I thought back to the odd comments people had made to me about Ben since Liam's death – my mother, his mother, Laura ...

In my mind I could pinpoint the exact moment when the two of them had switched. I got home one day three weeks before the wedding to find Liam standing outside waiting for me because he'd supposedly lost his key. A week later we walked into the house to find Ben drunk in our kitchen, saying he'd heard from his mother that we were engaged and that he wanted to talk to Liam about a business proposal. Then they had left the house together and I didn't see Ben again until Liam's funeral.

'You just *left*!' I shouted, my voice sounding horribly loud down there in the catacombs. 'Liam waltzed in and you just *left* me there in our house with him! How could you? How *could* you? I was bewitched – you weren't! What possible excuse can you have for not even trying?'

'Stop it,' Ben said coldly. 'Blaming each other isn't going to help.'

'But you *are* to blame!' I said loudly. 'You should have come back for me!' I saw him flinch as if I'd struck him and I felt guilty for laying all the blame on him but was quite unable to stop myself from going on. If I stopped feeling angry then I'd feel a crippling sense of loss even worse than before and I didn't think I could bear it. 'You should have fought for us every day instead of rolling over for Liam and making it so easy for him to do what he did! I wouldn't have believed you at first. Maybe I never would have.

But you didn't even *try*! You just left Liam to it and moved to Germany. Oh, I could kill you for being such a coward!'

'Maybe you're right, Jasmyn,' Ben said in a voice so full of weariness that it squeezed painfully round my heart. 'Maybe I've just done everything all wrong. Perhaps the entire thing is, like you say, totally my fault—' He broke off with a wet coughing sound and clapped one hand over his mouth, his shoulders heaving with the sudden struggle to breathe as if he had just swallowed something that had gone down the wrong way. Something wasn't right. It sounded like he was choking on his own tongue. When he dropped down onto his knees, I thought at first that he was being sick. But then I realised that the only thing coming out of his mouth was feathers. They were bedraggled and covered in saliva – and they were long and black ... very much like the kind that might belong to a swan ...

'What's happened to you?' I almost whispered as he sat back on his heels, remembering the way his eyes had turned red earlier. There were at least ten large feathers strewn about the bones on the floor, looking ugly and twisted and unnatural ...

He carefully avoided my gaze as he pushed himself back to his feet, pale as a corpse with dark rings beneath his eyes. 'I had to do it,' he muttered. 'It was the only way.'

'What did you *do*, Ben?' I said, fear making my voice sharp and angry.

He turned his head to meet my eyes and said flatly, 'I turned myself into a knight.'

23

Ice Palace

'A *swan* knight?' I said, staring at him in the dim gloom.

'Yes, yes, a swan knight, what else?' Ben replied impatiently. Then he angled his head, breathed a sigh of relief and said, 'Kini's coming.'

'What?' I said, wondering what on earth he could be talking about.

But a moment later there was the sudden clattering of hooves on stone. The sound made me jump. Deep underground was the very last place I had ever expected to find a horse. When he rounded the corner and stopped before us, however, tossing his glossy head, he somehow seemed no more out of place down there than the scattered bones crunching beneath his hooves.

'What's he doing here?' I said.

'Lukas sent him,' Ben muttered. 'We need to get out of here.'

But first he knelt down again amongst the skulls and picked up the petals that had fallen from the rose. I noticed that they no longer had my name on them. When he'd gathered them all up, Ben closed his fist around them for a brief moment and, when he opened his hand, the swansong had become a plain black chain that he hung around his neck and tucked beneath his coat.

'Come on,' he said, standing up and turning back to me.

He linked his hands to give me a leg-up onto Kini's back. With no mounting block and no stirrups it wasn't easy for him to get onto the horse after me, but eventually he was seated and I held on to him for balance as the horse instantly picked up into a trot. If I hadn't wrapped my arms around Ben I would have fallen off so I really had no choice, but still I cringed to feel him stiffen at my touch.

When Kini reached the wall, he didn't slow down but went right through it, as if it was a projected image rather than a solid thing. I felt nothing as we passed through and out the other side, where we found ourselves in a castle that seemed to be made – entirely – out of ice.

Kini snorted in the sudden cold and his breath misted before him as his hooves crunched on the snowy floor of a great hallway that glittered blue in the light from the sun outside. Tall pillars made from ice bricks stretched the length of the corridor, supporting the ceiling. Even the chandeliers suspended above us were made of ice. It was something from a fairy tale. It had to be. Nothing this exquisite could possibly exist in the real world. It completely took my breath away. Kini must have brought us straight back to faeryland.

At first I thought that there was no one else nearby but then Lukas walked around to Kini's head. The horse pushed its muzzle into Lukas's palm and I heard the crunch as it took a lump of sugar from him.

'Good boy,' Lukas said softly, his breath misting in the freezing air. Then he looked up at us. 'Did you get it?'

'Yes,' Ben replied.

I loosened my grip on him so that he could slide off the horse's back. Then he turned back and helped me to dismount. His hands were off me as soon as my feet touched the floor.

'And the enchantment?' Lukas asked, glancing at me.

'Broken,' Ben grunted – not sounding at all happy about it, for all that it was something he had been trying to achieve for more than a year now.

Riderless once again, Kini turned and trotted away down the hallway, his glossy black coat even more striking against so much white. His hooves rang on the ice for a few moments, then he faded away and was gone – more like the ghost of a horse than a real one.

'Are we in faeryland?' I blurted out, quite sure that Lukas was going to say yes.

Instead he just flashed me a slightly quizzical smile and said, 'No, we're in the Ice Hotel. In Sweden. I know someone who works here.'

I knew of the Ice Hotel. Of course I did. It had been a glorious fantasy in my head ever since Ben brought photos of it into school one day after a relative had been there.

'I've seen your house, Jaz,' he said. 'Your real one, I mean.'

He showed me the photos and I was enchanted by the way the ice turned different colours depending on the sun outside, from blue to green to turquoise to white. Everything was made out of ice, from the walls to the beds to the hollowed-out glasses served in the ice bar. Everyone wore snowsuits and boots and gloves and furry hats to protect against the constant minus-five-degree temperature maintained inside. When the sun went down, hundreds of candles were tucked into ice nooks and crannies around the palace. There was no other place in the world like it. The Ice Hotel was a piece of faeryland and Ben had referred to it as my house because it looked every bit like a snow princess's castle. After we got engaged we had even said that we would go there one day when we were older and richer for one of our wedding anniversaries. We'd thought we'd probably have to wait a long time because it was so expensive. Now we were here, but not at all in the circumstances I had dreamt about.

I drew breath to demand that they tell me everything so that I could get it all straightened out in my head. But when I looked at Ben, who was lifting the black chain over his head and handing it to Lukas, I saw that his eyes were that vivid shade of red again. Lukas noticed it too and said calmly as he put the chain around his own neck, 'I think you've got something in your eye.'

It seemed that Ben hadn't been aware of it until Lukas spoke. He hurriedly blinked his eyes closed, but when he opened them they only looked normal for a bare few seconds before the red colour seeped back into them, like ink spreading through water.

'Nope,' Lukas said, shaking his head briskly. 'Not going to work this time, I'm afraid. It's a good thing I booked you a room.'

'I don't need a room!' Ben snapped. 'I can't change now. I've got to—' He was interrupted by the horrible, nauseating snap of a bone breaking in his leg. His knee buckled to the ground and he cried out in raw pain that made my skin prickle with horror.

'Try not to resist it,' Lukas said calmly as he hauled Ben up by the arm, promptly causing the bones inside that to break as well. Ben clapped a hand over his mouth to muffle the shout but it still seemed to ring loudly off the ice pillars in the hallway.

'What's happening to him?' I gasped, hurrying after them as Lukas half-dragged Ben to a door nearby.

'Oh, he's just turning into a swan, that's all,' Lukas replied, pushing the door open with his foot. 'Nothing to worry about.'

I followed them into one of the hotel's bedrooms and only vaguely took in the snow-carpeted floor, the two ice beds covered in reindeer skins with great twisted bedposts at all four corners, the window seat carved straight out of the wall and the perfect, sparkling ice sculpture of an angel in the centre of the floor.

I watched helplessly as Lukas dropped Ben down on the bed, causing his spine to snap like a stick of glass. He went white and let out what was more a breathless gurgle of pain than a scream, but Lukas looked at me and said, 'Better close the door.'

Hurriedly I did so, noting thankfully how thick the walls were. The last thing we needed right now was some other guest in the hotel coming to see what all the noise was about.

'Try not to resist it,' Lukas said quietly to Ben. 'It'll only make it even more unpleasant.'

'How pleasant can every bone in your body breaking possibly *be*?' Ben snapped. I was almost surprised to hear his usual voice for, with his scarlet eyes and sweat-soaked body, he hardly looked like Ben at all.

The act of speaking broke his jaw, quickly followed by his neck and all the small bones in his fingers as his body transformed before my eyes. Dark bruises spread out from all the broken bones before black feathers ripped through his skin, causing sprays of blood to splatter across the carpet of snow on the floor; his body shrank into his clothes, his long coat now far too big for him; his black hair crept down his neck, which lengthened with more cracking and snapping of bones; his shoulders wrenched back; his arms swept into wings and – in less than a minute – Ben was gone and there was a shivering, sweat-soaked black swan on the bed in his place.

'There,' Lukas said cheerfully. 'That wasn't so bad, was it?'

The swan hissed at him.

'Language!' Lukas said with a grin. 'You've got to learn to control that temper of yours, Ben.'

The black swan struggled out of the mass of human clothes weighing it down, promptly tripped over its pink webbed feet and fell almost drunkenly off the bed.

'Come on now,' Lukas said firmly, picking the thrashing bird up and depositing it back on the pile of clothes. 'Just stay put on the bed until ... well, until you feel more like yourself. You don't want to crack your thick skull open on the ice, do you?'

The swan shook itself angrily, dislodging the snow clinging to its feathers. Then it sprawled down on the mound of clothes in a most inelegant and un-swan-like way – like a gangly foal that didn't yet have control of its body.

'Half an hour,' Lukas said sternly. 'Don't turn back for at least half an hour, Ben. I mean it. We'll be down in the bar.'

He took me by the elbow and steered me out of the room, the huddled black swan watching sullenly from the bed until Lukas closed the door behind us.

'You're not squeamish, are you?' he said, glancing at me. 'Do you need to sit down?'

'No,' I replied.

'But you're trembling.'

'I'm not trembling. I'm shivering,' I said, through chattering teeth. 'It's bloody freezing!'

'Oh,' Lukas said. 'Yes. Of course. Sorry – I didn't realise. Knights don't feel the cold the same way, you see. Come on, we'll go downstairs and get some snowsuits. Then we'll go to the ice bar and play twenty questions. You probably have a few you'd like to ask, don't you?'

I nodded dumbly. It wasn't just the cold that was making me shake, but his voice somehow had the effect of soothing me a little. It was the light, cheerful way in which he spoke – as if nothing was as bad as it seemed and everything was going to be okay.

'I'm sorry,' I blurted.

Lukas looked at me, puzzled. 'For what?'

'For those things I said to you on the mountain road,' I said. I hadn't known who he was then, or who Ben really was, or Liam – but I remembered the hatred I had felt for him when he'd told me Liam was a bad man and I was ashamed of it.

'Oh, that.' Lukas laughed. 'Don't worry about that. I was only relieved to get you out of faeryland in one piece. Ben would have killed me if I'd lost you in there.'

We walked to the end of the hallway, the snow crunching as it compacted beneath our shoes. When we got to the end of the pillared corridor we found ourselves on a large landing at the top of a great sweeping staircase that led down to the atrium. Of course the Ice Hotel looked different every year, for it melted away in the spring and had to be rebuilt each winter – always by a new team of designers, artists and architects. But the photos I'd seen from the outside had always made it look more like a huge, sprawling igloo than a castle and I was sure there had only been one floor before. I realised that they must have tried a new approach this year by adding the stairs and wondered vaguely if some extra money had come from somewhere. I found myself focusing desperately on the hotel and the wonder of its construction, for while I was thinking about that I wasn't thinking about Ben and the pain was almost kept at bay.

The staircase itself was made of ice, but a royal-blue carpet stretched down its length to prevent guests from slipping on it. Under any other circumstances I would have been delighted with the scene. It seemed hard to believe that mere human hands had made this entirely out of ice – the staircase and the long reception desk and the great arches and the chandeliers – like a castle cut

261

straight from crystal. Elegant ice sculptures adorned the foyer: there was a perfect, flawless swan, a life-size horse rearing up on its hind legs, a majestic centaur and a vase with an entire bouquet of ice flowers inside it. They were all built around lights so that they glowed green, orange and pink in cycles.

It was every bit as perfect as I'd imagined it would be in all my time spent dreaming about it from the first moment Ben had brought photos into school to the hours we had spent talking about coming here for our anniversary one day ... Suddenly I wished to God that we could be anywhere but the Ice Hotel. Being here like this now was ruining it forever. It could never seem magical and lovely again after being the scene of such bitter heartache. Why couldn't we be in some dingy little motel that I need never see ever again?

We were provided with shiny silver snowsuits that went over the top of our normal clothes, grey furry hats that came down over our ears and thick winter gloves. Then we went into the Absolut Ice Bar – a large room with a high ceiling supported by ice pillars. The frozen bar took up almost the entire length of one side of the room and on the wall behind it was a huge ice carving of a bottle, lit up from behind. There were strategically placed tables and chairs – all made out of ice – although the chairs had reindeer skins placed on them as well. I only vaguely noticed all this as we walked up to the bar for I was too consumed with longing for things to be other than the way they were. I should have known by then that wishing didn't change anything. It wouldn't change the fact that Ben and I weren't really here in this enchanting place on holiday as we had always talked about – spending the days dog-sledding and skiing and racing on snowmobiles before returning to the Ice Hotel at night to eat from ice plates and sleep in our own little iglooed ice bedroom ...

Lukas handed me a hollowed-out ice glass full of vodka and as he did so I noticed the plain black ring on the index finger of his right hand. I recognised it because I had seen it before, but it took me a moment to remember that I'd noticed Ben wearing one just like it when we'd been on the *Queen Mary*.

'What is that?' I said, gesturing at the ring.

'That? It's something all knights are given. It protects us from the swansong and means we can't be enchanted by it. Come on, let's get a table.'

I had to carry my glass in two hands to avoid dropping it, my gloves were so thick. We went to the quietest table at the far end of the room. It was deserted back there for most people were talking and laughing around the bar. But I had to exert all my willpower to stop myself from dropping my head onto the slab of ice that was the tabletop, putting my gloved hands over my head and giving up there and then. It was so cold that I was sure any tear that fell from my eye would freeze to my cheek before it could drop away anyway. I picked up the ice glass and knocked the vodka back in one, feeling it spread warmly through my body.

'He'll be all right again in half an hour,' Lukas said.

I lowered my voice, even though there was no one near enough to hear us, and said, 'You mean he'll be human again in half an hour?'

'That's right.'

'Could he ... could he understand you when you said we'd be in the bar?'

'Yes, he could understand. There's nothing wrong with him, he's just not used to it – being a swan, that is. He can't control the body properly yet. It's like learning a new language. The one you grow up with comes on its own but any other you try to learn as an adult will never come as naturally. It takes practice.'

'Is it always like that?' I asked, remembering the horrific scene upstairs – bones cracking, skin stretching ... 'I mean, is it always that painful, changing from one to the other?'

'It is, unfortunately,' Lukas replied. 'It would be quicker usually, and so not quite as bad as that, but Ben resists it. Not deliberately, of course – it's not his fault. It's just the body's natural defence mechanism. That'll stop eventually.'

'But why does he have to change forms at all?'

'Because swan knights are both men and swans. Both bodies need to have their turn. You have to get a balance. Ben doesn't like it – he tries to suppress the swan form and ends up making himself ill. The only reason he became a knight was to find the swansong.'

'How did it happen?' I said quietly. 'How did he get like that in the first place?'

'Ludwig's princess knighted him,' Lukas replied. 'I took him to her a few months before Liam's death. He hadn't got any closer to finding the swansong on his own, so he made an agreement with the princess that she would knight him in return for his agreeing to return the song to her once he'd found it. I'll take it back to her as soon as Ben comes down.'

I swallowed hard. 'Can it be reversed?' I asked quietly.

'I'm afraid not,' Lukas replied. 'One-way ticket and all that. Knights can be exiled but they can't be unknighted. I told him all this before we went back to Neuschwanstein but it didn't change his mind.'

'What did Ben do,' I asked, barely managing to keep my voice steady, 'to make Liam hate him so badly that he would do all this to us?'

'I'm partly to blame for that, I'm afraid,' Lukas replied. 'After Liam told Ben what he'd seen at the lake, Ben went to see for himself one night and realised that it was true. When Liam told him he was going to steal one of the swans and sell it to a science lab Ben told him to leave them be. Naturally, Liam took umbrage at being ordered about. So Ben went back to the lake, found one of the swans and warned her that Liam might be coming and they should be prepared. Neither he nor Liam knew about the knights at that point. But the swan he spoke to told us what he'd said later on and we agreed they would keep their bird forms after dark for a while to be on the safe side. When Liam came that night and I dragged him into the lake, I told him before I let him go that we'd known he was coming and that if he ever came again he'd be killed. I didn't mention Ben's name, but he was the only other person who knew about it and when Liam confronted him, Ben didn't deny it. He tried to explain that he hadn't known about the knights and had only warned the swans, but as far as Liam was concerned, Ben had betrayed him, almost got him killed and was solely responsible for ruining his plan to catapult himself to fame and riches. So he swore to get him back any way he could.

'The next time Ben saw Liam was when he saw you together in your house just before the wedding. As soon as his mother phoned him saying you two had suddenly announced you were engaged, he realised that Liam had stolen a swan's song from somewhere. So he went back to Liam and told him he could name his price if he'd drop the enchantment on you but, of course, he refused. Ben left to try to find the swansong himself before the wedding but didn't get anywhere, so he went to see Liam when you were on your honeymoon and ... well ... I don't know what he thought he was going to do but they got into a fight, of course. Ben stopped it before it got out of hand because he knew you were waiting in the room thinking Liam would be back at any moment ... I know it must seem like he walked away but he was just trying to protect you. We only found out later that Liam was going to release you from the enchantment in a year or two because he'd promised Jaxon they would sell the swansong to a buyer he'd found who wouldn't ask questions. In the meantime, Ben carried on looking for the swansong on his own and when he got no closer to finding it he turned himself into a knight. It would have worked too because swan knights can sense stolen swansong from quite a distance away, but the catacombs were too good a hiding place. Even we can't see or hear it when it's that deep underground.'

'I heard it,' I said stiffly. 'I heard it all the way from the Montparnasse cemetery.'

'Well, that's because you were the one being enchanted by it,' Lukas replied with a shrug. 'So the swansong was linked more strongly to you than anyone else, with the exception of the swan princess herself. That's why Ben took you to see her. When he came to see me in the middle of the night, when you first arrived at the castle, I told him about the faery horse. You wouldn't have been able to trace the song to the catacombs if it hadn't been for Ben, because it was the horse that led you there in the first place. He didn't just sit around doing nothing, he searched for it tirelessly.'

'But he left me there with him!' I said – the words coming out louder and bitterer than I had intended.

'Yes,' Lukas said quietly with a soft sigh. 'That's true. But he knew Liam wouldn't hurt you. You weren't the one he was punishing. If Ben had thought – even for a moment – that there was any danger of that then he would have risked prison and kidnapped you. Or he would have done something to Liam. But he wouldn't have left you there if he thought you weren't safe, Jasmyn, you've got to believe that— Ah, here he is now,' Lukas said.

When Ben stopped beside our table there was no outward sign of what had happened upstairs earlier but for the one black feather sticking out of the collar of his snowsuit.

'You have a little something there,' Lukas said mildly, indicating his neck.

Ben put his hand to his collar and pulled the feather out irritably, thrusting it deep into his pocket.

'I'd better be off,' Lukas said. 'There's a princess waiting to get her voice back.'

'Make sure the others don't see you this time,' Ben said.

'Don't worry, I'll go to the castle at dusk before it gets properly dark. There won't be any problems. Stay here till I get back though, eh? After that you can borrow Kini to take you ... well, wherever you're going from here. Save you one last plane ticket.'

We left the bar and walked out to the Ice Garden at the back of the hotel – a winter wonderland of twinkling lights and ice sculptures and fine, powder-soft snow. Kini appeared from nowhere, picking his way carefully through the glass trees and wrought-iron lamp posts towards us – a glossy, living thing in the midst of so much frozen, lifeless beauty. I glanced anxiously at a couple of guests who were also walking round the Ice Garden. They couldn't help but notice Kini walking calmly through it all and I saw them point him out to each other. What must have seemed especially odd was the fact that he wore no saddle or tack of any kind. He didn't therefore obviously belong to anyone, but in such a remote wilderness he couldn't possibly be a wild horse. He seemed more like a winter mirage than a living, breathing animal.

But then he stopped before Lukas, and Ben gave him a leg-up onto his back.

'I'll be back soon,' he said, looking down at us. 'Be nice to each other while I'm gone, won't you?'

He waited until the two other guests had rounded the corner out of sight, then he urged Kini forwards and they faded away into the snow together, leaving Ben and I standing awkwardly alone.

There were so many things I wanted to say to him that I didn't even know where to begin. I needed him to understand that I'd only loved Liam because I'd believed him to be Ben. I'd never loved Liam for *himself*. I'd never even particularly liked him, not that I'd ever seen that much of him. Being two years younger than Ben and I he had never been allowed to join in our games as children. When he got older he had girls eating out of his hand, for he was handsome and charming and smooth rather than anti-social and quiet like Ben was. He tried to flirt with me a couple of times but I never responded. After we got engaged, Ben used to joke that I was the only girlfriend he'd ever had who he'd trusted completely around Liam – confident that I would never betray his trust no matter what Liam said or did ... I cringed at the memory and tried to shut it out, for it was like a newly sharpened blade sliding straight into my heart. I could never take back what had happened – it would always be there between us.

'Are you all right now?' I asked to break the silence.

'I'm fine,' Ben replied.

'Good,' I said weakly.

There was another awkward silence, during which the lights were turned on. It was not yet fully dark but the sky was a dusky grey and suddenly the Ice Hotel was lit up, sparkling with a hundred tiny golden lights, as if dressed in the gossamer cloak of a majestic queen. At the same time, the lights in the Winter Garden also came on, bringing splashes of colour to the previously pale ice so that each exquisite sculpture glowed in a bright pool of pink or blue or green or orange.

'It's so beautiful,' I breathed.

'Let's walk around it,' Ben said, already striding towards it so that I had no choice but to follow.

Despite the circumstances, I couldn't help being captivated by the Ice Hotel. Even from the small part of it that I had seen I could tell that it was every bit as magical as I had thought it would be. I'd never seen anything so lovely in my life. As someone who's been to both I can say – with authority – that the Ice Hotel is more enchanting even than faeryland itself.

'I'm sorry about your Violectra,' Ben said – the sentence coming out in a rush as soon as our feet crunched on the white-pebbled path that wound through the garden. 'I thought the swansong might have been inside it. That's why I broke it. Even though it didn't make any noise at night ... I thought perhaps Liam had found a way to stop that. The way the black roses turned up inside the case and the fact that the horse wrote the street name on the surface ... It seemed the perfect hiding place because Liam knew you loved it so much and always had it with you. I'm sorry. I hated doing it, but I really thought the swansong might have been inside.'

'It's okay,' I replied. 'I understand.'

'I left you there in Germany because I knew you would never be persuaded to trust me again after that. Then I got a phone call from Jaxon saying I should come to Paris because he was sure he'd found the swansong. I thought you would be safe in Bavaria but I asked Lukas to stay behind and keep an eye on you just in case.'

I nodded but couldn't think of anything to say. I found that I hardly cared about what had already happened – it was what was going to happen *next* that concerned me. The snowsuits, hats and gloves kept us warm enough in the frosty air and we walked for a little while in silence, keeping in step with each other but not touching. I wanted so much to take Ben's hand but I knew if I tried to touch him he would shrink away from me. Eventually we came to the most stunning ice sculpture yet. It was a life-size unicorn lying down in the snow – a proper one, not a mere horse with a horn on its head, but a magical creature from faeryland itself, almost as if whoever had sculpted it had been there too and knew what it was like. There was a bench nearby, set beneath one of the old-fashioned wrought-iron black lamp posts that reminded me forcibly of the mythical land of Narnia.

'Let's sit down for a minute,' I said. I was tired and hungry and wondered what time it was back in France. Or Germany. Or whatever country my internal clock was still wired to. When had I last slept? Or eaten, for that matter … I didn't feel like talking any more. It was too hard and too painful. And I didn't want to break the soft tranquillity that was here in the garden. But there were still things I had to know. So I drew a deep breath, summoned up my courage and, a moment later, said quietly, 'Why didn't you tell me what was going on with Liam in Germany? We spoke on the phone all the time. Why didn't you ever mention it? You must have known I would have believed anything you told me.'

Ben was silent on the bench beside me for a moment before saying, 'Partly because I was ashamed of him.' He kept his eyes fixed on the unicorn carved out of ice before us and went on in an emotionless voice, 'We said we were going to have children one day, but there was something very wrong with Liam. There always was. And I thought you might worry that it was genetic. But mostly I didn't say anything because I thought it was under control and every time I spoke to you, you were so excited about the wedding plans. I didn't want anything to spoil it.'

As if on cue, there were the sounds of clapping behind us and when we twisted around on the bench we could see a wedding party through the branches of the ice trees. They were posing for photos outside the hotel. The bride must have been cold even though she was wearing a beautiful fur-edged winter wedding dress. But if she was she didn't let it show. Instead she just looked gloriously happy. I remembered then that there was a wedding chapel in the Ice Hotel. A sudden, irresistible longing struck me and I must not have been thinking straight for I turned back to Ben and said, 'Let's get married! Let's just go and do it right now!'

He frowned at me. 'You can't possibly be serious.'

'Something went wrong – well, let's fix it! Please, Ben, let's just go and put it right!'

'Jasmyn,' Ben said quietly. 'Surely you must realise that isn't possible. We can't just pretend none of this ever happened.'

'Why not?' I said desperately. 'Why can't we do that? There's no enchantment now. We're free to be together as we should have been from the start.'

Ben turned his gaze away from me and back to the unicorn. 'For more than a year I thought of nothing but finding the swansong and breaking the enchantment,' he said in a flat voice. 'I dreamt of finding you again and putting everything back to the way it should have been. But now ... It's too late, Jaz. It took too long to find it. Too much has happened since then.'

'Ben—' I began pleadingly, but he interrupted me.

'You were his wife for a year. How can either of us pretend that didn't happen? You shared his house, his life ... his bed ... '

I cringed and felt the colour rising to my cheeks. I shuddered now at the very thought of Liam touching me. But as far as I'd been concerned at the time, we were married, he was my husband and I loved him. I only thanked God now that when he'd wanted to start trying to have children I had insisted that we needed more money saved before we could even think about it. I had thought it out of character at the time for Ben had always been the more cautious one of us when it came to money. I had assumed it was just because he was excited at the thought of having a family, not because he wasn't Ben at all.

'You can't blame me for that! I can't believe you're even bringing it up!' I hastily blinked back the tears filling my eyes for – despite my words – I felt so full of shame that it was as if it might break me apart from the inside. 'I thought he was you! I didn't know what I was doing!'

'Listen,' Ben said, turning towards me at once and taking my gloved hands, looking right into my eyes as he went on earnestly, 'Listen to me, Jaz. I never have – and never will – blame you. What happened was *not* your fault. That's not what I'm saying. But it still happened and we can't pretend that it didn't.'

I knew that he was right. After all – this was the real world now. Hurt and pain didn't dissolve into nothingness just because you wanted them to. Ben and I were not the same people we had been before all this began and the fact that neither one of us was really at fault didn't change that. But I wanted him anyway. Even after everything that had happened I wanted him back so badly that it was like a physical ache in my soul. I wanted to ask if he still loved me but couldn't summon the courage. If he said no I was afraid I might shatter on the spot, like an ice sculpture smashed by a sledgehammer into a thousand heartbroken pieces.

I couldn't help it. Tears welled up in my eyes and streamed down my face. I tried to hide them from Ben, turning my head and keeping my eyes glued to the unicorn in front of me like my life depended on it, even though I was no longer even seeing it. But he noticed at once and moved closer to me on the bench.

'Please don't cry, Jaz,' he said quietly, as he pulled me to him and put his arms around me. 'This is rock bottom. It'll get better from here. I promise.'

Sobs rose up in my throat and – although I tried – I couldn't keep them inside. All my self-control was gone; broken and stripped away, leaving me defenceless and vulnerable. I couldn't have pulled away from him even if I'd wanted to. All I could do was bury my face in his arms and weep.

'Please don't leave me, Ben!' I sobbed. 'I don't think I could bear it if you did!'

He sighed. 'We're not together any more, Jaz. We haven't been for over a year now.'

He spoke quietly without a hint of anger or blame but, even so, his words were like a kick in the stomach. I was dimly aware of the sounds of laughter and happy voices coming from the wedding party at the front of the Ice Hotel and it was like having a heart full of needles. Finally, they all went back inside and it was quiet once again. Ben rested his chin on the top of my head and waited for me to stop crying before drawing me to my feet.

'Come on,' he said. 'Let's go inside and get something to eat.'

'I don't want anything to eat,' I said, my voice hoarse from the effort of trying to retain control of it. 'I just want to go to sleep.'

I suddenly found myself wishing we were at a normal hotel. I was cold and desperately miserable. I didn't want ice and snow and cool light. I wanted warmth and brightness and a soft, comfortable bed to curl up in.

'You really should eat something, Jasmyn,' Ben began, looking upset, but I pulled away from him, shaking my head.

'No, no, I'm not hungry,' I said. 'Not at all. All I want is to go to bed. Please, Ben, don't argue with me about it. I just want to go back to the room.'

'All right,' he said softly. 'All right. I'll take you back.'

We turned away from the reclining unicorn and trudged out of the Winter Garden. A spectacular ice dragon guarded the exit but I hardly spared it a glance for all that it must have been an incredible thirty feet long and lounged in the snow with a lizard-like grace. It hardly felt any warmer inside the hotel than out and I was only dimly aware of other guests in the foyer, laughing and enjoying themselves, and the music that was coming from somewhere close by.

Ben unlocked our room upstairs and when I went in I saw that someone had lit all the candles in the little nooks and ledges carved into the ice. The room flickered with soft, soothing candlelight. Without a word I got straight into the sleeping bag on the bed in the far corner. I knew I should say something to Ben to reassure him that I was okay and to minimise the awkwardness that would be there in the morning but I simply didn't have the energy.

'I'll be right back after I get something to eat,' Ben said from the doorway. He paused, then added, 'I'll bring some food up for you in case you change your mind.'

I nodded but my face was turned away from him and I was buried in the sleeping bag, so I didn't know if he'd seen my response or not. In another moment he was gone. I'd hoped sleep would come quickly – I couldn't remember ever being this tired before in my life. But as soon as the thick door of ice was closed and I was alone in the cool, candlelit room, fresh sobs rose up in my throat so that I could hardly breathe beneath the onslaught of them.

Hunger growled in my stomach and I wished I had had

something to eat before going to bed, but I knew there was no way I could possibly have sat at a table in a restaurant with Ben, surrounded by normal, happy people enjoying themselves on holiday. I didn't want noise or people or light. I just wanted quiet and darkness and to never see another living person ever again as long as I lived.

24

Evacuation

I was woken up the next morning by one of the igloo guides putting a tray of hot cranberry juice on the ice table between the two beds. I knew this was the customary way guests at the Ice Hotel were greeted in the morning but it took me a moment to remember where I was. I had not slept at all well, for I had been plagued with a repeating dream that just went round and round in a cycle – exactly like my dreams in the weeks after Liam died. Only, this time, I kept dreaming that I was woken by Ben on his return to our room. He would gather me up in his arms, bury his face in my hair and tell me – over and over again – to forget what he had said earlier, that he still loved me, that he always would, that it was not too late for us and that now we could be together forever. Sweet relief and happiness would fill me, but then some part of me would dimly realise that I was dreaming – that this was not real. But as soon as I worked that out, the dream would start all over again ... *This* time I really *was* awake and Ben really *was* there ...

I had cried myself to sleep before Ben returned to the room last night but, when the igloo guide woke me with the hot drinks the next morning, I looked over and saw that he was in the other bed, already sitting up, still wrapped up in his snowsuit and sleeping bag like I was. He thanked the smiling igloo guide who then left, drawing the ice door closed behind her. I was cold and aware that my hair hadn't been brushed so I grabbed the hat that I had discarded the night before and rammed it back on my head, fully aware as I did so that this was a ludicrous time and place for vanity.

'Did you sleep okay?' Ben asked. He was trying to sound normal but I could hear the anxiety in his voice – as if he thought I might snap at him for talking to me.

'Yes,' I lied. 'I slept fine. Did you?'

'Yes,' Ben said, but I suspected that he was lying too.

I reached out for one of the mugs of cranberry juice and took a sip, feeling the hot, sweet liquid slide down my throat, warming me a little. We drank in silence as cool morning light filtered through the window and sparkled off the ice in the room. Although I hadn't slept well, I found I felt a lot better that morning and was annoyed with myself for falling to pieces the night before. There had just been so much to take in, in such a short amount of time, that it had been overwhelming. Now I'd had time to adjust to the initial shock, I could see things for what they truly were. And I was convinced that things were not as bad between Ben and me as I had initially thought.

He was still upset and I couldn't blame him. But he hadn't said he didn't love me any more. He'd told me it was too late to try to mend things between us but I didn't believe him. He hadn't taken off his engagement ring – it was still there on his finger. He'd spent more than a year of his life, and all the money he had, trying to find the swansong and lift the enchantment. Why do that if you weren't still in love with someone? He could have just given up and left me. Instead he turned himself into a knight even though he knew he'd have to endure those awful transformations with bones breaking and feathers ripping through his skin. He still loved me, he had to. I could not – would not – believe that it was too late.

'What happened to the blood?' I asked, looking down at the snow on the floor and remembering how blood had splattered across it during Ben's transformation the day before.

'What?' he said, looking blank.

I gestured at the floor. 'Yesterday,' I said. 'There was blood on the floor.'

'Oh. I took some clean snow from the hallway to cover it up before I went down to meet you,' he said. Then he added, 'Shall we go down and get some breakfast?'

I nodded, putting my now empty mug down on the table. Ben did the same then said after a brief hesitation, 'We're going to have to talk about … where we go from here.'

'I know,' I replied as I struggled out of the sleeping bag and swung my legs over the side of the bed. Hastily, I drew them back up as my feet trailed in the snow, the freezing air making my toes numb already. It was time to start a new day of difficult conversations and hard truths. Still, at least it couldn't possibly be any worse than yesterday … Or so I thought. As I sat at the edge of the bed and pulled on my warm, thick boots, I had not the faintest inkling of just how horrific that day was actually going to be.

Ben was a little worried that Lukas hadn't returned yet as he had expected him to be there when we went down to the restaurant but I found it difficult to feel too worried about him when I knew him to be practically indestructible, and with a magical horse to boot.

We ate breakfast from plates made of ice. I wasn't sure if Ben regretted what he'd said last night or if he merely felt guilty about upsetting me, but he seemed especially attentive that morning, bringing me coffee, insisting that I take the seat by the window and asking if there was anything else I wanted from the buffet table.

'I'm fine,' I replied. I was eager to eat my meal before anything upsetting could happen to make me lose my appetite once again so, in an attempt to keep the conversation relatively neutral, I said, 'Why are we here at the Ice Hotel anyway?'

'Lukas was able to get us a room because he knows one of the managers. Apparently the man has some werewolf blood in him or something. Anyway – the Ice Hotel is convenient because it's built on the edge of faeryland.'

'It is?'

Ben nodded. 'Every year. It doesn't matter if it's physically in a slightly different location – wherever it's built will always be on the boundary of faeryland. Lukas said it's because the magical races are all fascinated by the hotel. It's an enigma to them that it's built by humans. They think something like this should be in their realm, so they hover around it. The only thing stopping them from claiming it as their own is the concentrated human presence here.'

After we'd eaten, we took paper cups of coffee to drink outside for it was – surprisingly – actually warmer out there than inside now that the sun had come up. It was one of the peculiarities of the Ice Hotel's design that it always stayed around minus five degrees inside whether the outside temperature sank as low as minus forty or rose as high as plus five.

We walked out and saw several ornate sleighs with polished brass bells attached to the harnesses, waiting outside by the front doors. They were not pulled by horses but by reindeer. I'd never seen a real one up close before and they were not quite what I had expected. Their large antlers were velvety soft to the touch, covered in fine, smooth hair, and they had large, liquid brown eyes surrounded by thick dark lashes. When the handler said they were tame and could be stroked, I took one of my gloves off and ran a hand down the nearest reindeer's back, amazed by how soft its coat was – not at all coarse or weather-beaten as I would have expected.

'Would the two of you like a ride?' the handler asked.

I snatched my hand away despite myself and rushed to say that we did not in case Ben might think that was the reason I had gone up to them in the first place.

We left the reindeer but – by some unspoken consensus – stayed well away from the Winter Garden. After last night I found that the beautiful place now elicited only feelings of heartache. So we went around the other side of the hotel to a quieter spot a little distance away where a few ice benches covered in reindeer skins were arranged to look back at the Ice Hotel.

'You'd think they could find something more humane to cover the seats with,' I said, wrinkling my nose in distaste. Having just seen the real thing pulling sleighs at the front door, the skins left a bad taste in my mouth.

We sat down and looked back at the hotel in silence for a moment. We'd hardly spoken through breakfast and I had the horrible feeling that Ben was hesitating to speak for fear that I would make a scene and burst into tears again.

'So what now?' I asked, keeping my voice completely steady and trying to sound calm and matter-of-fact.

Ben opened his mouth to reply but then froze for a moment before jumping up, knocking his coffee cup over to stain the snow at his feet.

'Something's wrong,' he muttered.

A split second later Kini galloped out of the tree line behind us, hooves kicking up clumps of snow, mane and tail streaming out behind him. I thought he was going to fly right past us but he skidded to a stop beside the bench. Something had spooked him. His eyes were rolling, breath blasting out in agitated snorts and hooves stamping at the frozen ground. Ben reached his hands up to the horse's head, talking to him quietly and stroking his neck until he calmed down. He always had been good with horses.

'Where's Lukas?' I said uneasily, glancing back at the tree line, stupidly hoping he might walk out of it on foot.

'Something must have happened,' Ben replied, keeping his voice calm. 'Talk to him for a moment while I look him over, would you?'

I reached up to hook my fingers through Kini's bridle then talked to him soothingly, running my hand down his nose while Ben walked around him, checking for injury. I didn't like the look in the horse's eyes: a traumatised, wretched, heartbroken look as if he had seen something that had frightened him half to death.

'Here,' Ben said. 'He's been attacked by someone.'

Keeping my hands on Kini's head, I moved around and clearly saw the gash across the horse's left flank, although the blood hardly showed on his black coat.

'It's not serious,' Ben said. 'He'll be all right.' He moved back to Kini's head, stroked his nose and muttered, 'But God only knows what's happened to Lukas.'

'Maybe he can take us to him,' I said.

But Kini did not seem to want to go anywhere. He just stood, unmoving, beside us.

'Something must have happened,' Ben said. 'I just hope Lukas got away—' He broke off suddenly, eyes narrowed at the bridle Kini was wearing, and I realised that it was the first piece of tack I had ever seen the horse wear. After all, it wasn't as if he needed it – he knew what to do well enough without it.

'He wasn't wearing a bridle when he left, was he?' I asked.

'It's not a bridle,' Ben said. 'It's the swansong.'

He reached up and undid the buckles. As soon as the bridle was off, Kini was gone, dashing away as if a spring had been released, fading into thin air before he reached the tree line.

'I think we'd better go,' Ben said.

I turned back to look at him and saw that the bridle was gone and the black chain was around his neck once again.

'Go where?' I said.

'Anywhere. We can't stay here, it might not be safe. Come on. Lukas will have to catch up with us later.'

The tone of his voice stopped me from asking questions. I kept up with him as we hurried back into the hotel. To my surprise there was some sort of disturbance going on in the foyer when we walked in, with a lot of guests gathered together with their suitcases, complaining loudly and demanding refunds as staff tried to usher them all out through the front doors. I frowned, wondering what was going on, as we slipped past them and went quickly up the sweeping staircase to our room to get our bags. But when Ben opened the door, someone was already there.

Wearing the same silver snowsuit as everyone else in the ice hotel, the figure stood looking out of the window with his back to us. Ben froze in the doorway and, for a moment, I wondered if we might have the wrong room. But then the man turned around and my eyes were drawn irresistibly to the gun in his hand.

'Come in, Ben,' Jaxon said with a smile. 'No need to be shy. We're all friends here, aren't we?'

There was a moment of horrified surprise before Ben recovered himself and said coldly, 'How did you get here so quickly?'

Jaxon's face broke into a smile. 'I had a little help,' he admitted. 'Now come on, get inside, both of you.' He gestured impatiently with the gun. 'Jasmyn, my dear, would you be good enough as to shut the door?'

I pushed the big slab of ice closed with a sick feeling in my stomach. We were trapped. And no one but Lukas even knew we were here. When the door was closed I turned back; Ben's hand clamped around my wrist and he drew me closer to his side.

'Make yourselves comfortable,' Jaxon said pleasantly. 'We'll be here for a while. Half an hour or so, I should think, while they clear out the hotel.'

'What do you mean?' Ben asked warily. 'Why is the hotel being cleared out?'

'I think it's because the knights have tricked the humans into thinking there's a structural fault,' Jaxon said with a wide grin, clearly very much enjoying himself. 'It's all about to come crumbling down, you see.' With a laugh he curled his free hand into a fist and thumped it against the thick, solid wall of ice behind him. 'Oh look, the coaches are here already,' he said, glancing out of the window to the front doors below. 'Four of them. The place will be cleared out in no time.'

'How long have you been working for the knights?' Ben said stonily.

Jaxon looked at his watch. 'A few hours now,' he said. 'I'd barely broken out of the catacombs when one of them was galloping down on me in the street. I thought he was a policeman at first. Anyway, when he saw that the swansong was gone he offered me a new deal. And he gave me this.'

He held up his hand and I saw the same black ring on his finger that Ben and Lukas wore.

'So don't think about trying to enchant me because it won't work,' Jaxon said with a self-satisfied smirk. 'Someone's going to pay me for it and if not you, then the knights have offered a very handsome price. So, come on. Hand it over.'

'I don't have it any more,' Ben replied. 'Lukas left with it last night and that was the last I saw of it.'

'Oh. Perhaps I've been misinformed, but it was my understanding that he sent his horse back to you with it,' Jaxon said, an ugly glint in his eye. 'Something went wrong, didn't it?'

'I have no idea what you're talking about,' Ben said. 'I haven't seen Lukas or his horse for hours. I expect he's handed the swansong back to its rightful owner by now. We're expecting him back at any moment, in fact.'

The threat in that last sentence was only thinly veiled but Jaxon merely laughed. 'What a filthy liar you are, Ben! Lukas ran into a spot of trouble before he could get to Neuschwanstein. He's dead, I'm afraid.'

'Nice try,' Ben replied calmly. 'But swan knights are extremely difficult to kill. I doubt that little gun you've got there would do it, for example.'

I felt his grip on my wrist loosen a little and got the distinct impression that he was about to try something despite the threat of the gun. Jaxon obviously sensed it too for he took a step back and moved his hand so that the gun was aiming straight at me rather than Ben. 'I know you became a knight,' he said. 'But Snowflake over there is human – despite appearances, eh? Do you think you can get over here and disarm me before I shoot her between the eyes? Which one of us would be faster, do you think?' He glanced at me and smiled. 'It's all rather exciting, isn't it, my dear?'

Ben took a deep breath and when he spoke his voice was like ice. 'If you hurt her in any way whatsoever, Jaxon, then by Christ, I'll kill you.'

'Naturally you will, Ben!' Jaxon said sharply, his smile vanishing. 'But it would be far better all round if I didn't have to hurt her in the first place, wouldn't it? So don't give me a reason to! As for Lukas, it's no use holding out for him to come to your aid because he's already here and he doesn't seem to have been much use so far, does he?'

From outside there was the sound of the coaches pulling away, filled with all the Ice Hotel's former guests and staff.

'What do you mean, he's already here?' Ben asked suspiciously.

'On the floor down there.' Jaxon gave us his nastiest grin so far and – keeping the gun aimed at my head – bent slightly towards something that lay concealed behind the ice table.

'I never saw him without his armour and helmet on so I suppose I can't give you my personal assurances that it's him,' he said conversationally. 'But the other knights seemed quite sure this was the rogue knight formerly known as Lukas.'

He straightened up triumphantly. Sick horror rushed through me and I tried to scream but the sound stuck in my throat, coming out more like a strangled whimper. In Jaxon's left hand, held up by the hair, was Lukas's severed head. Ben's fingers dug harder into my arm but that was his only reaction. He didn't move or make a sound of any kind.

Dried blood stained the torn skin around the edge of the neck – which looked as if it had been cut through with a sword – and Lukas's brown eyes were open, which made it even worse, for they were blank and unseeing, making the head seem more like the gory prop from a play than the remnants of what had once been a very real person.

'You were right, Ben,' Jaxon laughed, 'when you said that swan knights are difficult to kill. But not immortal, eh? Decapitation will do it every time. Works for vampires, werewolves and, yes, even swan knights. The others knew Lukas was going back to Neuschwanstein and they were waiting for him there.' He dropped the head carelessly onto the ice table where it rolled onto its right side, then he glanced back up at us, blue eyes glittering malevolently. 'Nothing to say, Ben? How unlike you. I'm almost disappointed. Well, never mind. Hand the swansong over to me right now and I won't have to do anything horrible to your lovely white freak over there. I may not be fool enough to kill her and lose my advantage but you know there are plenty of other things I can do. I can certainly see to it that she never plays the violin again, which would be a great pity. Liam told me she plays it so beautifully. So come on. Hand it over.'

Ben hesitated for a long moment before slowly reaching his hand into his right pocket and drawing out a small black button. He took a step forwards but Jaxon spoke at once.

'No you don't,' he said. 'I'll keep my distance. You're a shade too quick for my liking. Just throw it over.'

Ben did so. Keeping the gun carefully aimed, Jaxon bent down, picked the useless thing up and slipped it into his own pocket. 'Now the ring,' he said calmly.

'What ring?' Ben said stonily.

'*The* ring,' Jaxon replied, rolling his eyes and holding up his own left hand to display the dark ring on his little finger. 'The one that protects you from the swansong's power.'

'It's not like that with knights,' Ben said. 'We can't take them on and off at will. Once the ring is on, it stays on.'

'Ahh!' Jaxon said with a mock wince. 'I very much hope for your sake that that isn't true because – one way or another – that ring is coming off, if you catch my drift. So I'll ask you one more time to hand it over.'

I saw Ben close his eyes briefly. 'I wasn't lying,' he said quietly. 'I can't take it off.'

'Right then!' Jaxon said brightly. 'Does anyone have an axe? How about you, Jasmyn? No? Never mind. Fortunately I never go anywhere without my penknife.' He fumbled in his pocket for it then tossed it across the room to me. I caught it automatically, but what he said next made my blood run cold. 'Do you think you can cut it off on your own or am I going to have to enchant you?'

'What?' I stared at him, horrified, hoping that I had somehow misunderstood what he wanted me to do.

Jaxon rolled his eyes again. 'Ben's finger,' he said with exaggerated patience. 'I want you to chop it off, darling. Now, we can do this the hard way or we can do this—'

He broke off then for Ben snatched the penknife from me and flipped it open, smacked his right hand down on the table beside Lukas's head and spread out his fingers before bringing the knife down hard – once, twice, three times. His finger slid across the ice and onto the snow, leaving a trail of blood in its wake. Ben tried to stifle an agonised yell of pain as he fell down onto his knees, nursing his bleeding hand. It was the most terrible sound I had ever heard in my life.

'Very chivalrous.' Jaxon sighed. 'But nowhere near as much fun. Oh well, the job's done just the same, I suppose.'

Forgetting Jaxon and the gun for the moment, I whipped off the scarf I was wearing and fell down on my knees in the snow beside Ben to wrap it around his trembling hand, which was slippery with blood ...

This can't be happening, this can't be happening ... The words ran over and over again through my head like a mantra and tears stung my eyes. All the guests and staff at the Ice Hotel were gone, Lukas was dead ... Whatever way I looked at it I couldn't see Ben and I getting out of this situation alive. Jaxon had a gun and his ring made the swansong useless. We had nothing. Nothing but ...

The knife! I saw it lying on the floor beside the table in a pool of blood and my mind raced as to how I could get my hands on it. I would have to reach right across Ben to grab it and Jaxon would surely notice. The only chance was to somehow make Ben realise it was there but I didn't see how, for he was still kneeling with his head bent over his hand, breathing shallowly, sweat glistening on his skin, seemingly quite unaware of anything beyond his own pain. I looked at the knife again and hopeless frustration bubbled up inside me for I didn't see any way of reaching it.

'Lucky thing you're not the violinist, eh, Ben?' Jaxon laughed.

Any minute now, I thought. *He's going to remember the knife any minute now and take it back and then our one chance will be gone forever ...*

'It'll be good as new in no time,' Jaxon said, a gleam of envy in his eye. 'Now that you're a knight and all that. Still hurts like hell though, I'll bet. Consider it a little payback for the beating you gave me! But even with all your new powers I'm the one who got the swansong in the end!'

'For God's sake, Jaxon!' Ben muttered and I was startled to hear how thick and clumsy his words were. 'We don't ... want ... the swansong. We never ... have—' His voice broke off mid-sentence as he suddenly crumpled over in the bloodstained snow. Jaxon made an impatient sound of annoyance but my initial dismay vanished when I realised that Ben had fallen right next to the knife, hiding it from Jaxon's view for it was directly behind him, almost touching his lower back, mere inches away from where his fingers lay curled in the snow.

'Get him back up on his feet before I come over there and do it myself with my boot!' Jaxon snarled.

I shuffled clumsily through the snow to his side, forcing myself not to grab too eagerly for the knife and thereby give myself away. Instead I put my hand down beside it as I leaned over Ben. And that was when I realised he was faking it, for although his eyes were closed, his fingers brushed mine as they reached slowly out towards the knife, dragging it through the snow to conceal it in the palm of his hand. I pretended I hadn't noticed and shook him by the shoulders as I spoke his name. He opened his eyes after a moment and gazed up at me.

'Ben,' I almost whispered. 'Are you okay?'

'I'm okay,' he said, but in a voice that sounded so far away that – even though I'd seen him take the knife with my own eyes – I almost wondered if perhaps he wasn't putting on an act after all.

'Help him up!' Jaxon snapped. 'We're going outside.'

I did as he said and felt relief flood through me. Ben was not as bad as he was making out. Although he made a good show of leaning on me, he was in fact hardly putting any of his weight on me at all. And when his face turned towards me I thought I saw – just for a moment – one corner of his mouth twitch up in the faintest possible smile when our eyes met.

'You'll stay here, Jasmyn,' Jaxon said. 'Ben and I are going out alone.'

'Why?' The question burst from my lips. Even though I knew he was armed now, I didn't want Ben going anywhere without me.

'I'm trying to be gentlemanly,' Jaxon sneered, 'and spare you from any more pain. You wouldn't want her to see anything distressing, would you, Ben? So be a man, stand up on your own two feet, please, and follow me.'

It happened very quickly. Ben gave my shoulders a brief squeeze and said quietly, 'It'll be okay, Jaz.'

'Oh, yes.' Jaxon grinned from ear to ear. 'It'll be—' But then he broke off, for when Ben released his hold on me he seemed to stumble. Jaxon was tensed for trouble and quickly stepped back, which was why the knife in Ben's hand caught his arm rather than his chest.

The ensuing shouting was drowned out by the gun going off in Jaxon's hand as he tripped over, whether by accident or design I couldn't tell, for he didn't seem to be aiming at anybody and the bullet went right through the floor, shattering an ice chandelier hanging from the ceiling below.

My eyes darted desperately around for the gun, assuming Jaxon had dropped it when he fell, but it was still in his hand and he was already propping himself up on his elbow and raising it desperately. Another shot went off as Ben ran towards me and grabbed my arm. The bullet missed him by a mile and went straight through the wall in a shower of shards and icy dust.

We sprinted from the room and down the corridor, knowing that Jaxon could only be seconds behind us.

25

The Edge of Faeryland

The Ice Hotel looked different with nobody in it. It seemed colder and larger and – of course – it was silent, so that every sound echoed unnaturally loudly beneath the high vaulted ceilings as Ben and I ran towards the staircase. I expected us to run down to the foyer and head straight for the front doors as fast as we could but, instead, Ben pulled me to the staircase leading up to the third floor.

'There's not enough cover outside,' he explained under his breath. 'It would be too easy for him to pick us off with his gun. He's a good shot.'

At the top of the stairs on the third floor we ducked down behind the banisters.

'He'll be expecting us to go down to the first floor,' Ben said quietly. Even as he spoke Jaxon raced into view and rushed down the stairs, through the sparkling turquoise foyer and out of sight. 'Help me with this,' Ben muttered, reaching out to wrap his un-injured hand around one of the banisters. I saw what he intended to do and wrapped my own hands around it at the weakest point. Together we were able to snap it off. A thick stick of ice with a sharp, jagged edge may not have been as effective a weapon as a gun but it was better than nothing.

'People will be coming soon,' Ben said, putting the ice club carefully down by his feet and then turning his head to look at me. 'Architects or owners or whoever. If they think there's a structural fault with the hotel then someone will be coming to check it out. We just have to stay hidden from Jaxon until then, that's all. He'll have to run when other people start turning up. Don't worry – we can do it. The hotel's big enough and we'll see him coming from here before he sees us.'

I nodded and tried to feel as confident as Ben sounded. But the sound of the knife coming down and the image of his finger sliding across the table kept replaying itself in my mind, making me shiver.

'What's wrong?' Ben said sharply. 'You're not hurt, are you?'

I shook my head. 'No, it's just ... Ben, your finger!'

'Oh, don't worry about that,' he said, as if it was nothing. 'The stump is probably healing up already.'

'But why did you do it when you knew he didn't have the swansong?'

'It was irrelevant, Jaz. He might not have had the swansong but he did have a gun. I couldn't trick him over the ring so, one way or another, that finger was coming off.'

In another few seconds, we saw Jaxon stride back into the foyer below, stop in the middle and shout in a voice that rang off the ice, 'I know you're in here somewhere, Ben! It's no use trying to hide! If you don't show yourself right now I'm going to use the swansong to force you out!'

Ben gave a quiet snort of disdain. 'That simpleton!' he muttered in my ear. 'He doesn't even realise he hasn't got the swansong yet. It must be incredibly difficult to go through life with such a tiny brain.'

Despite the circumstances, I felt a giggle rise up in my throat and had to hastily thrust it back down. There was nothing in our present situation that was in any way funny and – for all Ben's flippant words – I could feel how tense he was as he kept his eyes very carefully fixed on Jaxon through the ice banisters we were crouched behind.

After a few minutes of muttering over the tiny black button Ben had given him, Jaxon finally realised that he was not holding something that was in any way magical and he threw it down with a bellow of anger that made me flinch. The next moment he was stamping up the stairs and Ben said softly in my ear, 'Time to go.'

We crept away from the banisters and then got up onto our feet.

'Pray he keeps shouting like that,' Ben whispered, 'and it will be painfully easy for us to avoid him.'

Unfortunately, Jaxon obviously realised the truth of this himself and he soon shut up. His angry shouting had made my skin crawl but the sudden silence was worse. It was his long shadow falling across the wall of the corridor that gave him away rather than any sound he made and Ben and I quickly ducked into the nearest room – which happened to be the wedding chapel.

Dozens of ice doves sparkled around the altar and the rows of pews were covered in blue velvet rather than the usual reindeer skins. Strings of crystals hung about the windows making the whole room glitter with splashes of rainbow colours.

Ben pressed his back to the wall on the right-hand side of the doorway and I stood back on the left. My heart was hammering in my chest and I had to force myself to breathe quietly. It was only because it was so silent that we were able to hear the soft crunch of Jaxon's footsteps in the snow. When he got to the chapel doorway he paused in the corridor. My heart leapt up into my mouth. He must be standing just outside, looking right into the room. I glanced at Ben and he held one hand up, warning me to stay where I was. I nodded and dug my fingers into my palms as I watched him slowly raise the thick stick of ice above his head.

But, after another moment, Jaxon walked on, his footsteps becoming more muffled as he continued down the corridor. Ben slowly lowered the ice club back down to his side and then hurried past the doorway to where I stood. 'Make sure you stay behind me,' he whispered. 'It doesn't matter if I'm shot, it won't kill me.' He paused, then muttered under his breath, 'I don't think.'

I was about to ask how much protection being a knight would give him – after all, I knew that they were difficult to kill but I had also seen for myself that it wasn't impossible – but then I caught a glimpse of my reflection in the mirror hanging on the opposite wall and I stared in astonishment. For although it was me, it was also not me. It was a large mirror, set into the ice, with silver flowers encrusted all over the frame.

My reflection was wearing the same silver snowsuit that I was. But the hair trailing over her shoulders was a rich caramel colour rather than white. Her skin was pink and her eyes were a dark, chocolate brown rather than pale blue.

I stared, transfixed. It was quite clearly me – all my features were the same – only my albinism was gone. I didn't consciously realise I was walking towards the image until Ben's hand clamped down hard on my shoulder and he pulled me back to whisper sharply in my ear, 'Stay away from the mirrors!'

'What's going on?' I said, glancing at him briefly before my eyes were tugged back. 'Do you *see* that?'

'Yes,' Ben replied, meeting my gaze in the mirror. 'Something's happening to the hotel, it's—' He broke off to twist me around to face him. 'I'd rather see your real eyes,' he said, before going on, 'I told you that the Ice Hotel is always built on the boundary of faeryland? Well, it's creeping over the edge now that it's not being held back by a human presence any more. I can see the magic in the walls. This could be a real problem, Jaz. Just make sure you stay close to me and – for God's sake – keep away from the mirrors. I'm not sure that there's anything much more dangerous when it comes to faeryland than a magic mirror.'

'All right,' I said, forcing myself not to look back at the mirror and the mesmerising image of myself standing there as a normal person – ordinary like everybody else. 'But what are we going to—'

I broke off then for – at that moment – the sun disappeared from the sky, and the ice around us that had been sparkling almost turquoise in the bright midday light now gleamed silver in the soft glow of twilight.

'Shit,' Ben muttered. 'They're trying to drag the hotel into their own realm.'

Some distance away we heard Jaxon bellow, 'It won't work, Ben! You can't scare me with this Godforsaken hocus-pocus!'

'He'll be the least of our worries if things carry on like this,' Ben said darkly. 'We can't stay here now. We're going to have to try to get out. If the hotel is pulled into faeryland we could be trapped there. And the knights could be waiting outside. Christ, I wish Lukas was still with us!'

The starlight was everywhere. Tiny pinpricks of light even glowed within the ice bricks themselves, not just in the dusky indigo sky outside. I kept close to Ben's side as we slipped back out into the corridor – which suddenly seemed to have many more mirrors lining the walls than I remembered – and I quickly became aware of whispering voices, although it was impossible to tell where they were coming from. It sounded like they were inside my own head and I had to resist the urge to scratch at my scalp to try to get them out.

'Can you hear them?' I whispered to Ben as we reached the staircase.

'The voices?' Ben replied, glancing over his shoulder to check Jaxon was still nowhere in sight.

'Yes. I can't make out what they're saying, can you?'

'They want you and Jaxon out of here.'

'What about you?'

'They don't mind me. Technically I'm one of them now.' He saw my face and added quietly, 'Don't worry. I don't intend to stay.'

Still holding the stick of ice in his left hand, Ben tried to take my hand with his injured right one but I jerked out of reach instinctively, for I was afraid of hurting him. I could tell from his expression that he'd misinterpreted the action but before I had time to say anything he'd grabbed my wrist and we were hurrying down the great sweeping staircase.

The starlight and the voices were not the only things that had changed. As we came down the curve of the stairs I saw a sleek white cat with blue eyes sitting on the banister playing in what could only be described as a cloud of starflakes which fell twinkling around it. In another moment we had passed it and were on the second-floor landing, but before we could go any further there was a shout and the sharp, ringing report of a gunshot. I was already dropping instinctively to the floor, my hands over my head, when Ben crushed me to the ground, squeezing the breath from my body. But whoever Jaxon was shooting at, it wasn't us and in another moment Ben was hauling me to my feet and we were slipping and sliding down the last staircase.

When we got down to the large central foyer, I knew at once that something was different but it took me a moment to realise what it was – the ice sculptures that had stood there before had all gone. And there were some very strange-looking footprints mingled with the human ones in the snow ... We started to cross the twilit foyer when there was the sudden clip-clop of hooves on ice. I looked around, my heart swelling with hope for I was fully expecting it to be Kini.

But it was a centaur made of pale-blue ice that cantered out of the bar, hooves sparking and kicking up frosty shards as he raced past us. The floor shook and, at first, I thought it was because of the weight of the centaur. But then there was a strange low moaning sound that seemed to be coming from just outside the front doors.

'What the hell is that?' I said.

Ben shook his head. 'I don't know but we need to find another door. There's something out there. Come on – the bar leads out to the Winter Garden.'

We went into the Absolut Ice Bar where I had drunk vodka with Lukas the day before. But when we were only halfway across the room, Jaxon rushed in from the door behind the bar and instantly the gun was pointed at us once again and he was glaring at Ben with a face like thunder.

'It's going to take more than twinkly lights and a few walking ice people to scare me into leaving without the swansong!' he snapped. 'Make it stop or I'll put a bullet between your eyes and we'll see if you can survive that!'

'It's not me, you fool, it's the hotel! If you want to live you'll get out now while you still can!'

'No one's going anywhere until I say so!'

Suddenly, the whispers started up again all around us and Jaxon jerked his head around, looking for the unseen speakers.

'What the hell is going on?' he demanded, his voice rising. 'There were faces in the ice back there! I know you're doing this somehow!'

'I am not! They want the hotel! You shouldn't have sent all the people away!'

Jaxon lifted the gun. 'Give me the swansong,' he said quietly, 'or I *will* shoot you!'

He was threatening Ben directly this time rather than me. Indeed, he hardly seemed aware that I was there. This wasn't fun for him any more. I wracked my mind desperately for a way out. At any moment Jaxon might shoot Ben anyway and then search his body for the swansong himself. Whatever he had said before, he was obviously unnerved by what was happening in the Ice Palace and wanted to be out of here as soon as possible, even at the cost of his sadistic and malicious games ...

My eye was suddenly caught by a movement to my right. We were standing beside a wide pillar which – like so many other spots in the hotel – now had a mirror fixed to it. It had an embellished golden frame with silver faeries at the corners. This time, my reflection looked just like me – but she was not mimicking my movements. Instead she was beckoning me frantically. I stared at her.

Stay away from the mirrors, Ben had said ...

And yet it was Ben my reflection was pointing at. In her mirror I saw him lift the real swansong over his neck and throw the black chain to Jaxon – even though I could see, from the corner of my eye, that the real Ben hadn't moved. And then, a second later, although I could hear no sound from the mirror, I saw the bullet hit him between the eyes and pass out through the back of his head, splattering blood and bone behind him. Crumpled in the snow, Ben looked very, very dead. It seemed that shooting a swan knight in the head, whilst perhaps lacking the melodramatic flair of decapitation, still got the job done.

'All right, Jaxon,' the real Ben at my side said quietly. 'Just calm down. I'll give it to you.'

I didn't hesitate any longer but put out my hand and touched the mirror. I didn't know if what I'd just seen was a true premonition or not. But once Jaxon had the swansong he'd be free to do whatever he liked to us and I couldn't just stand there watching and hoping that Ben might find a way to get us out of it. So I touched the glass where my reflection still beckoned to me frantically. I didn't know what – if anything – would happen or whether it would make any difference but I had nothing to lose by trying.

As soon as my fingertips touched it, I was pulled inside, dimly aware of a shattering sound behind me as Jaxon fired at the mirror in panic at my sudden disappearance. A split second later I found myself stumbling out of another mirror on the wall behind the bar, a foot away from Jaxon, looking back at Ben and the broken pieces of glass on the floor at his feet.

Jaxon started to whirl around but I grabbed a nearby bottle and brought it down hard over his head before he could raise his gun. He staggered and fell back against the bar, blood running down his face, and in the next moment Ben had crossed the room, had his hands round Jaxon's throat and was dragging him over the top of the bar and onto the floor, ice glasses and bottles falling to the ground, cracking and breaking in the process.

As I scrambled over the bar after them, Jaxon lifted his elbow and caught Ben's chin, making his head jerk back and loosening his grip momentarily, allowing Jaxon to twist himself free. He began to raise the gun and I shouted a warning but Ben had already seen it and grabbed Jaxon by the wrist, slamming his hand against a nearby ice pillar so hard that he dropped the gun in the snow at their feet. I automatically started forwards to try to retrieve it but then stopped. It was too near them. If I got that close, one of them would surely hit me – by accident if not on purpose. I realised dimly that – in twenty-seven years – I had never seen a real fight before. I had only ever seen staged ones on TV where, half the time, there wasn't a drop of blood or even a hint of bruising. This was different – this was two large men trying to do real harm to each other – and I found myself shrinking back. I would never have described myself as particularly squeamish or faint-hearted

– I could enjoy a gory horror film along with everybody else – but it was different when it was happening right in front of me like this and one of the people involved was someone I cared about. It seemed more vicious, less controlled … and it made me horribly, painfully aware of how small and vulnerable I was beside them.

As I watched with my heart in my mouth, I was relieved to see that Ben had the upper hand. He was taller and broader than Jaxon. His eyes had turned that unnerving shade of scarlet once again – although I couldn't tell if he'd done it on purpose or not – and it wasn't as if Jaxon would be able to do him any real damage with his bare hands now that Ben was a knight anyway.

A couple of times I saw Jaxon try to grab the gun but Ben would always stop him and when they finally staggered away from the pillar and crashed into an ice table, I ran forwards and picked the gun up off the snow. I had no earthly idea how to use it, whether there was a safety catch or whether it was even still loaded.

I looked back up at Jaxon and Ben and saw, to my horror, that Jaxon now had a penknife in his hand – the same one he had made Ben cut his finger off with earlier. He raised the knife to slash viciously at Ben's face. Ben saw it coming and jerked his head back but not quickly enough to avoid the blade altogether and it cut into his skin a bare inch below his right eye, all the way across to his ear. He fell back into another table, one hand clamped to his bleeding face, and Jaxon turned on the spot, his eyes finding mine at once.

Panic-stricken, I realised that in picking up the gun I had effectively painted a large bull's eye right on my forehead. My finger squeezed around the trigger out of sheer panic but nothing happened – either the safety catch was on or it had run out of bullets. So I drew back my arm and threw it with all my force as far away as I could. I barely had time to wince before Jaxon crashed into me and we hit an ice pillar so hard that a great crack ran up it and frosty dust floated down from the ceiling.

I lost my balance and fell down on my back in the snow with Jaxon right on top of me, so close that I could see the blood staining his bared teeth, the vein bulging in his forehead and the pure hatred and rage glittering in his eyes, and I knew that he meant to kill me if he possibly could. My heart hammered painfully in my chest and I was so afraid for my life as I struggled to fend him off that I could hardly breathe.

But then something swung down to hit the side of Jaxon's head hard enough to practically separate it from his neck. Blood splattered across my face and chest and Jaxon's entire body spun over in the air, limbs flopping loosely like a doll's before he landed on his back on the ice with half his skull bashed in and thick streams of gore running down what was left of his right cheek.

I turned my head away and looked up to see Ben standing above me, his hand still gripped around the broken ice banister we had brought from upstairs. Then it fell from his fingers with a clatter and he dropped down onto his knees beside me.

'Tell me you're okay,' he said, blood smeared across one side of his face where Jaxon had cut him with the knife. I found myself worrying ridiculously that it would leave a scar and mar his clean-cut looks. '*Jasmyn—*' he said when I didn't speak.

'I'm okay, I'm okay,' I said, trying to smile, blink back tears and wipe Jaxon's blood off my face all at the same time.

'Thank God for that,' he replied hoarsely, helping me to my feet.

I turned my head away, unable to bear the sight of Jaxon's corpse sprawled out on the floor. My fingers wrapped round Ben's hand, gripping it like my life depended on it as I wondered whether I'd ever be able to feel safe again after all that had happened.

But then Ben said, 'What's that blood on your snowsuit?'

I glanced down at the dusky red smears on the silver fabric and said, 'Oh, that's not mine, it's Jaxon's, from when he—'

'No, it's not!' Ben said in a strangled voice, his fingers fumbling with the buttons, ripping them apart to reveal the pale-blue jumper I wore underneath, the tear in the fabric where the knife had gone through and the shockingly scarlet trails of blood making their way down from the stab wound in my upper chest.

26

Ice Dragon

I stared down at my bloody jumper in bewilderment.

'But ... but I don't feel a thing!' I said.

Ben wasn't listening, but was already hurrying me to a nearby table and chair.

'Sit down,' he ordered. 'Keep pressure on it.'

I was still stupidly thinking that there must be some kind of mistake. I couldn't *feel* anything! How could you be stabbed and not *feel* it? But no sooner had I sat down than a horrible sick feeling swept through me and – even though I was sitting on an ice chair in a room made entirely of ice in the Ice Hotel itself – I suddenly felt hot.

Ben struggled out of his snowsuit and then knelt down to tie it around my chest, under my arms and over the wound, pulling it so tight it made me wince.

'I'm sorry,' he said. 'We need to stop the bleeding. You'll be all right, Jaz. I'm going to get you to a hospital. You'll be fine.'

I said nothing. I had no idea when Jaxon had stabbed me. It could have been when we first crashed into the pillar together or it could have been during that brief struggle on the ground. But in the end it didn't matter. We were miles away from anywhere with no car, no buses, no ambulances ... I was no medical expert, but it seemed highly unlikely that someone could be stabbed in the chest and survive if they didn't get to a hospital pretty damn quick. Ben might have been a swan knight but he wasn't Superman. And already I could feel the energy draining out of me, like water running through a sieve. I felt so tired – weighed down with weariness like it was a physical weight. If I could just close my eyes and rest for a moment, I was sure I'd get some of my strength back …

I laid my head down on the ice table and it felt wonderfully soothing and cool on my skin. But I was only allowed a brief moment of bliss before Ben was firmly gripping my shoulders and forcing me to sit up.

'You mustn't go to sleep,' he said, kneeling up and putting his hands on either side of my head. 'Look at me, Jaz.' His face was only inches from my own so that I gazed right into his brown eyes – and in that world of ice and starlight that seemed to surround us, they were the only warm thing that existed. He kissed me softly on the lips – a light whisper of a kiss, and then said in a calm, level voice, 'I'm going to get you out of here. But I need you to stay awake for me, okay? Whatever you do, Jasmyn, don't close your eyes.'

'Okay,' I replied. His voice was so warm and reassuring that it took the edge off my fear.

He stood up and it dimly occurred to me that he must be freezing without his snowsuit – wearing only jeans and a dark V-neck jumper without so much as a scarf or a hat … What if he caught frostbite or pneumonia or some other terrible thing and died and I really *did* have to go to his funeral all over again?

'Ben—' I began anxiously, but he shushed me at once and leaned down over the chair.

'Don't talk any more, Jaz. Just put your arms around my neck.'

I did as he'd said, although the effort of lifting them shocked me – it was as if they were made of lead! Ben put one arm around my shoulders and slid the other under my knees to lift me from the chair. The simple action made pain blossom outwards from my chest, through my arms and down to the very tips of my fingers. I bit my tongue so hard to keep from crying out that I tasted blood. Every step Ben took towards the door jarred horribly and seemed to drive all the breath from my body.

When we were across the room at last, Ben opened the door. Somehow I had been expecting things to be normal outside. I had thought that the mere act of leaving the hotel would be to leave faeryland behind us as well. But there was no blue sky and no sun sparkling off the white snow. Instead there was star-spangled twilight, glittering like a mass of white diamonds against soft, indigo velvet. It made the snow stretching out as far as the eye could see almost purple in colour.

I could hear the rapid pulse of a heartbeat but couldn't tell if it was my own beating in my ears or the sound of Ben's where my head was pressed against his chest. He walked with quick, long strides away from the hotel and across the silver-purple landscape before coming to a stop facing the tree line of dark pines clustered together. I felt him take a deep breath, as if he was about to shout out. But then there was a noise from behind us – a low, drawn-out moaning accompanied by a strange shuddering in the ground. Ben went rigid as a board and – very slowly – turned around.

I thought at first that I must be hallucinating, it was such a startling, extraordinary sight. The Ice Hotel sparkled with all the starlight that had soaked into its bricks and there, right in front of the main doors, was the thirty-foot-long ice dragon we had seen the night before, only now it was moving, come to life like the rest of the sculptures. It looked pale purple in the twilight, its great clawed feet left deep prints in the snow, its unfurled wings glinted in the silver starlight and its lizard-like head was raised straight in our direction, gazing right at us with cold, blank eyes. A hostile, aggressive groan rumbled deep in its throat again and its long spiked tail swished this way and that through the snow.

'Shit!' Ben whispered desperately under his breath, his grip on me tightening.

Then a white shape I dimly recognised as the cat with the blue eyes I had seen playing in the starflakes earlier came bounding around the corner of the building, apparently delighted by all the snow, and completely unaware of the dragon until it was too late. The creature's massive head twisted downwards and a great stream of what looked like white fire burst from its open jaws. But rather than roasting the cat where it stood, it froze it to the spot, covering the little animal in a thick layer of ice before it had time to take a single step. A bare second later, the dragon's monstrous foot stamped down on the cat, shattering it to bits as it began to charge straight towards Ben and me, making the whole ground tremble beneath its great weight.

Ben spun around and started to sprint towards the trees, still holding me tightly to his chest. As he ran he drew a deep breath and roared so loudly that the sound almost seemed to split my head in two, '*Kini!*'

His voice echoed back across the deserted landscape, but there was no sign of any black horse, no sound of thundering hooves – although it was unlikely we would have heard it anyway above the din of the ice dragon behind us.

Ben stumbled suddenly in the snow and almost fell before managing to right himself but, this time, I didn't feel it. I couldn't feel anything – not the cold or the pain or even the fear. Just a numbness and a weariness and the certainty that we were both going to die. The only sadness I felt was for Ben, who had tried so hard to put everything right but was not going to succeed. His rapid bursts of breath seemed incredibly fast in comparison to my own slow breathing and I wished I could just find the energy to tell him how sorry I was for everything. And how much I still loved him.

Even though the dragon must be nearly on us by now, it sounded far away in my ears when it roared again and it seemed suddenly much darker than before ... a cool, soft blackness that crept right into my body. When I caught a brief, blurry image of a dark horse just ahead of us I thought I was probably dreaming it. I saw it drop to its knees in the snow so that it was only half-standing. But in another moment, Ben had swung his leg astride its back, the distinctive horsey smell I loved so much was filling my nostrils and Kini was on his feet and thundering through the surreal, dreamlike, star-studded faeryland for just a moment before there was another great roar from behind us. I could have sworn I saw a streak of white fire fly past, missing us by a bare foot, before Kini's hooves were suddenly sliding on wet tarmac instead of snow, and there was a weak, grey light and rain splashing down all around us.

The next moment, Kini seemed to be gone – if he'd ever been there to begin with – and a door was slamming open, bright light assaulting my eyes so that I closed them tight and turned my face towards Ben's chest. I wished vaguely that he would stop shouting. I couldn't even make out what he was saying above the ringing in my ears. When I opened my eyes what felt like a bare second later, Ben's arms were no longer around me and panic rose up in my chest until I saw him a few feet away, gesturing madly with his hands as he talked to another man in a long white coat. But then the thing I was lying on began to move backwards and I desperately willed my body to jump off and run to him so that they couldn't take me away. But it was all I could do to raise my head a bare inch from the pillow.

'Ben ...' The word came out hoarse and soft as a whisper but he must have heard me for he turned his head and met my eyes for a moment before a door swung shut and he was gone from view. His expression remained clear in my mind, however – vivid and startling for the fact that it was the first time I had ever seen him look truly scared in all the years I had known him.

In another moment my head dropped back onto the pillow and a great darkness crept in, pushing everything else out, including even Ben.

When I next opened my eyes, my head felt like it was stuffed full of cotton wool. I was in a strange room I didn't recognise, lit by the light of a single lamp, with rain pattering softly against the dark windows. I tried to think back to my last clear memory but my clouded mind seemed to contain only vague, half-remembered dreams and images.

I looked down and realised that there was someone in the room with me. The chair had been pulled up as close to the bed as was physically possible so that Ben's knees were wedged against it and his dark head rested face down on his folded arms on top of the sheets.

I felt the drip in my wrist pull as I slowly reached out my hand to run my fingers through his hair. He jerked awake at my touch and lifted his head. A smile spread across his face when he saw me looking at him, but I was shocked by his appearance. The wound slashed across his cheek had been stitched and cleaned but there were dark rings under his bloodshot eyes, his hair was uncombed and a layer of stubble covered his lower jaw. He looked terrible.

'You're okay,' he said at once. 'The knife pierced your lung but they operated at once and you're going to be fine.' He gripped my hand and looked at me with a tortured expression I did not like the look of one bit as he went on hurriedly, 'I should never have gone after the swansong, I'm sorry, I'm so sorry. I don't know why I didn't just leave you alone. I treated you so horribly too – Christ, you must have hated me – but I was trying so hard not to let on … how I really felt … And then I thought you were dead, Jaz. I thought I'd killed you—' He broke off as his voice caught at the back of his throat and, the next moment, his shoulders were shaking with sobs and his head dropped back down onto the bed, hiding his face as if he couldn't bear to meet my gaze any longer. He was still holding on to one of my hands but – with my free one – I stroked his hair and ran my fingers softly down the back of his neck. I couldn't remember exactly what it was that he was so upset about but he was alive and so was I, so surely nothing else really mattered.

I think some time must have passed when I became aware of Ben by the bed again – standing up this time, but leaning down to gently take one of my hands in his and press a kiss softly to the palm.

'Go back to sleep, my darling,' he said quietly when he saw me looking at him. 'I didn't mean to wake you. Everything will be okay.'

He turned away towards the door and it seemed to me that he was unsteady on his feet. I wanted to call him back to reassure myself that he was all right and to ask him where he was going and when he would be back. But everything still felt so strange and dreamlike and before I could speak his name I had slipped back into sleep.

*

The sun streaming through my window woke me the next morning. My head was much clearer than it had been before but I groaned when I pushed myself up and pain spread through my body like hot needles. I gazed around anxiously for Ben but there was no one else in the room with me and the chair that had been by the bed last night was back in its original place at the table by the window.

'Ben,' I said – or at least tried to. It came out as a sort of gasping croak for my throat was so dry.

Perhaps he was in the bathroom. I pulled back the covers, remembered the drip when it yanked painfully at my arm, pulled it out impatiently and then swung my legs around to set my bare feet down on the floor. I was shocked to find how unsteady my legs were and stumbled like a drunkard to the bathroom, knocking things over as I went.

'Ben,' I said again as I opened the door.

But this room, too, was empty. Perhaps I had merely dreamt his presence last night ... The thought filled me with panic and I was about to leave to try and find someone who might know something when the room began to lurch sickeningly around me and the crippling wave of nausea was upon me so quickly that I bent over double to throw up where I stood in the doorway, not even making it to the toilet. Pain ripped agonisingly through my chest and when I tried to straighten back up I became so dizzy that I lost my balance and fell over. Fortunately a nurse came into my room then and found me before I could do any more damage to myself.

'I'm so sorry,' I said hoarsely, 'but I've been sick all over the floor and—'

'Don't worry yourself about that, dear, it happens all the time – side effect of the anaesthetic. Some people react worse than others. Let's just get you back into bed before you rip those stitches out altogether. You're not even supposed to be walking yet.'

It was only then that I became aware of the bandages around my chest, beneath the horrible hospital nightgown.

'Where are my clothes?' I asked stupidly as she helped me back into the bed. But before she could reply I went on, 'Where's Ben? Do you know where he is?'

'You mean the man who brought you in? He left last night, dear. But he gave us the phone number for your parents and they're on their way right now.'

'Parents?' I wrinkled my nose in confusion. 'What country are we in?'

'We're in England,' the nurse replied, giving me a faintly worried look. 'I'll go and fetch the doctor. He'll want to look you over now you're awake. And when you're feeling a little better the police are going to want to have a word with you too.'

'The police? But why?'

'Because you were the victim of a horrible attack,' the nurse replied, watching me carefully. 'Don't you remember?'

Oh, I remembered. I remembered it very well. I could clearly see the murderous expression in Jaxon's eyes as I desperately tried to fight him off with my hands before Ben struck his head with the thick stick of ice and blood splattered across my face ... I shivered involuntarily at the memory. But how could I tell the nurse or the police that if we were now in England? How could I explain that I had been stabbed in the Ice Hotel in Sweden by a ruthless thief desperate to make himself rich using a stolen swansong? I didn't even know where the Ice Hotel was now – it could have been sucked right into faeryland for all I knew and I couldn't very well say that I'd been brought to England by a magic horse. I had no idea what story Ben might have told them and I didn't want to contradict his version, whatever it was, so in the end I just said, 'I don't remember anything about last night except for waking up here with Ben beside me.'

After the nurse left to fetch the doctor, my eye fell on the sealed envelope carefully propped up on the bedside table, my name written across the surface in Ben's untidy handwriting. I grabbed at it and ripped it open. A plain ring of white gold fell out onto my lap. At first I thought it was Ben's, but when I picked it up and slid it onto my finger it was a perfect fit. I didn't know what to make of the fact that he had left it there. Was he returning it to me because he didn't want it any more? Or was it because he wanted me to wear it again? Surely it had to be the latter. My memory of the night before was a little hazy but he had spoken loving words to me, I was sure of it. And he hadn't left until he'd known I was going to be all right. The chances were he had just gone to buy some clean clothes or get something to eat, or get some sleep. He would surely come back at any moment …

I looked hopefully back into the envelope and was relieved to find a note inside, but my relief quickly turned sour when I read it for it was uselessly brief:

'Jasmyn,

There are some things that I have to go and do. I'm sorry for everything.

Ben.'

I turned the piece of paper over hoping for more on the other side but there was nothing. That was the entirety of the message. I glared at it before angrily screwing it up into a ball. He'd left me. I could hardly believe it but it was true. He'd gone without so much as a goodbye. Maybe I really *had* imagined him speaking so tenderly to me the night before. Maybe it had been the effect of delirium. Perhaps there had been no one in the room holding my hand at all …

My parents arrived in a state of near hysteria that morning. But Ben did not return. Not that day or the day after. Every time I was asked, I repeated that I did not remember what had happened and – finally – the police told me that Ben had said we'd been walking back from a restaurant after having dinner when we'd been set upon by muggers who had beaten him and stabbed me before running away in a panic.

Ben had been interviewed thoroughly by the police and answered all their questions until they said they didn't need anything else from him. And then he had simply disappeared. I got my mother to phone every number I had for him, then to write and to email. But every attempt at contact was met only with silence.

27

The White Violectra

I was finally discharged from hospital three weeks later, during which time there was no word from Ben, and Christmas and New Year came and went in a miserable blur. I wasn't completely sure why but – for whatever reason – it seemed that he was gone, and was not coming back. As for the Ice Hotel, it seemed to have disappeared altogether. No one could understand it, for it had been emptied of staff and guests after concerns were raised about a structural fault, but when officials had turned up just over an hour later, the hotel wasn't there. There were no signs of collapse, melting or movement – it had simply disappeared and no one could make any sense out of it. Investors had lost money, guests had lost reservations ... but no one could offer an explanation for what might have happened to it and, already, it had its very own place in the conspiracy theory books right next to crop circles and sightings of Elvis.

A week after getting out of hospital, I went with my mother to see my grandparents. Since the attack everyone had been treating me as if I was made of glass and I was sick of it. Physically I was much recovered, but I was still struggling alone with the heartache of Ben's sudden and unexplained departure; I couldn't tell anyone about it and I had never felt so isolated in my entire life. I had put my house up for sale from my hospital bed, for I had no wish to ever again return to the place I had lived during my twisted sham of a marriage to Liam.

After lunch that day I said that I was going down to see the horses. I just had to get away from everyone for a while. I walked slowly down to the stables on my own and deeply breathed in the familiar, sweet scent when I opened the door and walked inside, hay dust dancing down the thick shafts of sunlight that shone in through the windows.

I had been running a brush down Ed's already glossy coat for about fifteen minutes when a voice behind me said quietly, 'Are you a snow princess?'

I dropped the brush in alarm for I had not heard anyone come in, but I recognised that voice as well as the question and would have known who it was even if Ed's lips hadn't twitched at the very first word. I turned around and saw Ben standing just outside the box, an uncertain smile on his face. He looked much improved from that night when he had left me at the hospital and the cut across his right cheek had healed leaving only the faintest white scar. Happiness bubbled up in me at the sight of him but I thrust it back down, annoyed with myself, and snapped, 'You've got some nerve turning up here like this after four weeks!'

The smile vanished from his face at once and he looked troubled as he said, 'I know. But there were some things that I had to go and do.'

'Things that couldn't wait?' I raged. 'Don't you realise how much I *needed* you while I was lying there in the hospital?'

'I couldn't delay leaving,' Ben said quietly. 'How are you? Are you okay?'

'I'm fine,' I replied stiffly, trying not to let too much of the hurt sound in my voice.

'You understand why I had to go though, don't you?' he said anxiously. 'I had no choice. The swan princess fled when Lukas was killed but I had to return her song so that Ludwig would be able to find her. He couldn't discharge the remaining knights until he found his way out of faeryland. They've all been exiled now and had their powers stripped away.'

'Ludwig could do that?' I asked.

'Yes. When he died he became the king of faeryland,' Ben replied, 'so he effectively rules over the swan knights now, and all the other magical creatures. I didn't think it would take as long as it did but I had to do it, Jasmyn, otherwise neither one of us would ever have been safe.'

For a moment I said nothing. I was unhappy to learn that he'd been back into faeryland but I couldn't deny the logic of his reasoning. Whilst I'd been recovering in hospital it had never occurred to me that I might not really be safe – that the knights might send someone else after us or even come themselves.

'You still should have told me,' I said, unwilling to give up my anger. 'You left without even a word!'

He frowned. 'But I left a note explaining everything.'

'Everything?' I repeated, my voice rising. '*Everything?* The note was two sentences long, Ben!'

I drew the crumpled piece of paper out of my pocket and threw it at him. He caught it in his right hand and I noticed – for the first time – the healed stump where his index finger had been before. He straightened the note out and gazed down at it for a moment before looking back up at me. 'You carry it around with you?' he said.

I felt myself blushing as I realised that I had just given the depth of my feeling away. It surely said a lot that I was still carrying the wretched, useless thing around after a whole month had passed.

'I'm sorry for this,' Ben sighed, gesturing with the note. 'I remember it being longer and making more sense. But I wasn't really thinking straight the night I left.'

'How did you know I was here today?'

'Kini's outside,' Ben said, gesturing over his shoulder. 'Since Lukas died he's sort of attached himself to me.'

I nodded. There was silence for a moment as I carefully put my left hand into the pocket of my jeans. When I asked my next question I didn't want Ben to look down and see that I was still wearing the engagement ring he had left behind. I had not quite been able to bring myself to take it off even as the weeks passed and I began to think Ben would never return. It had drawn a few raised eyebrows from my mother but when she had tried to ask me about it I had cut her off dead. I couldn't tell her what it meant because I didn't know myself.

'Why are you here, Ben?' I said. The words came out a little colder than I'd meant and he seemed to recoil slightly at my tone.

'I ... I brought you something,' he said stiffly.

I watched in surprise as he swung the box door open to reveal what had been hidden from my view before – there was a black violin case resting in the straw at his feet. When I looked up from it to meet his gaze he turned his eyes away from me quickly.

'It's ... to replace your old one,' he said.

'I thought you were broke?' I asked.

He blushed to the roots of his hair. 'I took out another loan.'

I put down the brush I was still holding and walked out of the box, closing the door behind me. Then I knelt down and unbuckled the shiny new clasps before undoing the zip and pushing back the lid to reveal the new Violectra inside. Unlike my old blue and silver one, this violin was pure white with a pale-gold chin rest and tuning pegs. My previous Violectra had been beautiful, but this was the most exquisite-looking instrument I had ever seen in my life.

'I thought ... a new violin ... for new music,' Ben muttered. 'But if you would prefer a different design then just tell me what you want and I'll have it made for you.'

Slowly I closed the lid and clipped the buckles shut before standing up. I hesitated to say anything too direct, for if Ben didn't love me any more – and I had never once heard him say that he still did since this whole thing began – if he wanted to make a clean break and try to find some happiness in a new life and a fresh start, then I didn't want to embarrass him and further wound myself by speaking too plainly. I had to think of some way of phrasing it – some subtle way of testing the water and seeing whether there was any inkling of a chance that he and I could ever be back together again, so that if he turned me down flat I would still have some small shred of dignity left intact. But after wracking my brain for appropriately delicate and ambiguous words, the ones that actually blurted from my mouth were, 'I love you so much, Ben.'

I stared at him, having just shocked myself. I could not have laid myself open to further pain if I'd tried. What if he'd just come to give me the violin? What if he turned on his heel right now and walked out of the stable without so much as a word? The image was such a vivid one in my mind that suddenly I was quite convinced that was what he was going to do and my eyes squeezed shut, unable to bear it. What had I been thinking? It was too late, he had told me so himself. I heard Ben's feet crunch on the straw and was sure that I'd embarrassed him into leaving. Tears squeezed out from under my eyelids and I willed myself to hold it together until he was gone.

But then I felt his hands on my arms and when I opened my eyes he was standing in front of me, looking right down into my face. 'Jasmyn, do you really?' he said, sounding hopeful and doubtful both at the same time. 'After all that's happened ... the way I treated you in Germany ... those things I said in the Ice Hotel and everything that happened with Jaxon. There's ... there's blood on my hands that will never come out. You almost died because of me. I thought you wouldn't ever want to see me again. That you wouldn't even be able to stand the sight of me.'

'You saved my life, Ben,' I said softly. I swallowed hard and went on, 'I know that it will be difficult for us – especially for you – to get past everything that happened with Liam. But can we ... *please* can we at least give it another try?'

I was still afraid that he would break my heart and tell me it was too late but, instead, a warm smile spread across his face and he moved his hands up to my neck and said quietly, 'You're still my snow princess, Jaz. I'll love you until the day I die and probably even after that.'

Then he bent his head and kissed me. I reached up and linked my hands at the back of his neck and for a few blissful minutes all that existed was Ben and the golden, sunny stable in which we stood – the only sounds the nearby horses munching peacefully on their hay. But then Ben jerked away from me with a sudden exclamation of pain, clapping his hand to the side of his head.

'What's the matter?' I said in alarm.

'Ed just nibbled my ear,' Ben replied.

I turned and saw that Ed did indeed have his head all the way over the top of the box door and was staring at Ben intently with large, bright eyes.

'What am I – some sort of enigma to that horse?' Ben said exasperatedly.

Helpless laughter bubbled up in my chest, for Ed was already twitching his lips back from his teeth in response to Ben's voice. I remembered suddenly back to the day I had come to visit my grandparents just before going to California and how I had stood here in this very box, my heart aching fit to burst at the thought that I would never see the delightful sight of Mr Ed talking for the only person he ever did it for ever again.

'He always was a peculiar old beast,' Ben said, putting one arm around my waist and pulling me to him whilst searching through his pockets with his free hand. 'I know I have a Polo in here somewhere ...'

Acknowledgements

Thank you to my agent, Carolyn Whitaker, and to my editor, Gillian Redfearn – as well as all the other lovely people at Gollancz – for all their hard work on *Jasmyn*. The cover artwork by Kustaa Saksi is, as always, perfect.

Jaine Fenn, Jim Anderson, Mike Lewis and Bob Dean read an early section of the book and provided some very useful feedback. Shirley Bell read the entire thing and provided encouragement, feedback *and* regular bottles of Sauvignon Blanc.

This story was inspired by various books that I would never have read had it not been for the recommendations of Shirley Bell, Joan Willrich and Christine Moffat.

My parents, Shirley and Trevor Bell, must be thanked, once again, for all the travelling, as pretty much every location in this book has been a family holiday at some point. Most importantly of all (and John Willrich deserves some credit for this, as it was his idea) thank you for the ... er ... you-know-what that we did at the you-know-where. I don't think this book would have been written without that.

Finally – Cindy, Chloe and Suki, my three utterly, *utterly* perfect cats have all continued to do a fine job of keeping me company, and keeping me sane.

ABOUT GOLLANCZ

Gollancz is the oldest SF publishing imprint in the world. Since being founded in 1927 Gollancz has continued to publish a focused selection of bestselling and award-winning authors. The front-list includes **Ben Aaronovitch**, **Joe Abercrombie**, **Charlaine Harris**, **Joanne Harris**, **Joe Hill**, **Alastair Reynolds**, **Patrick Rothfuss**, **Nalini Singh** and **Brandon Sanderson**.

As one of the largest Science Fiction and Fantasy imprints in the UK it is no surprise we have one of the most extensive backlists in the world. Find high-quality SF on Gateway written by such authors as **Philip K. Dick**, **Ursula Le Guin**, **Connie Willis**, **Sir Arthur C. Clarke**, **Pat Cadigan**, **Michael Moorcock** and **George R.R. Martin**.

We also have a strand of publishing in translation, which includes French, Polish and Russian authors. Gollancz is home to more award-winning authors than any other imprint, with names including **Aliette de Bodard**, **M. John Harrison**, **Paul McAuley**, **Sarah Pinborough**, **Pierre Pevel**, **Justina Robson** and many more.

The SF Gateway
*More than 3,000 classic, rare and previously
out-of-print SF novels at your fingertips.*
www.sfgateway.com

The Gollancz Blog
*Bringing you news from our worlds to yours. Stories,
interviews, articles and exclusive extracts just for you!*
www.gollancz.co.uk

GOLLANCZ
LONDON